BENEATH
the
Crimson Maples

BENEATH the Crimson Maples

Mark Schoedl

ISBN: 978-1-64713-533-1   (Paperback Edition)
ISBN: 978-1-64713-534-8   (Hardcover Edition)
ISBN: 978-1-64713-532-4   (E-book Edition)

Some characters and events in this book are fictitious. Any similarity to real persons, living or dead, is coincidental and not intended by the author.

Book Ordering Information

Phone Number: 347-901-4929 or 347-901-4920
Email: info@globalsummithouse.com
Global Summit House
www.globalsummithouse.com

Printed in the United States of America

Contents

Chapter One

Rooted in the Suburbs

"Shmuel, I am sorry to be so-oh preoccupied, but, I have to see my wife and newborn child. It is my firstborn. He's so mysterious, I tell you. Right now, I could just go over to St. Joseph's and dance before everyone."

"You have got to act with a little more reserved nature than that, Adlay, we do not need to draw any attention to ourselves. We've got a good thing going on here now."

"Shalom, Shmuel. We will get together tomorrow morning at the Kollel Center. Just think, I will have my own child going to Yeshiva Elementary School in a few short years where your wife teaches."

"Yes, yes, yes. All our children are gone now, Chicago and New York. All my children went to Yeshiva as it was just starting to get on its feet. Now? Yes, we have helped to make Rabbi something out of Michel and the Beth Jehudah Congregation Orthodoxy. Now, look at us. No one else in Milwaukee can compare to Beth Jehudah."

"Surely, now if you do not mind?"

"Tell Devorah we all want to see our future as soon as she is able to share with us her joy and to thank God for all his blessings."

The lithe body attired in dark gray disappears around the corner of the hospital entrance while Shmuel begins to make his way back home as the late afternoon summer heat plagues his quiet demeanor. Now approaching sixty, the gray haired gentleman crosses Burleigh Street to return to his place of residence for over 40 years. Sherman Park, nestled between rugged A.O. Smith to the east and North Sherman Boulevard to the west, has maintained its neighborly cleanliness for generations. And, Shmuel can think of no better place to rest his black fedora after returning from a long day of tailoring his client's clothing.

His wife, Gabriela, surely will have borscht and blintz awaiting him as he walks softly through the front door. The aroma of *babka* swirls in his mind as chocolate and chopped nuts stir in that leavened breaded egg cake. Life is to be enjoyed. With El beside them, how can anything overtake their simple devoted lives? He does miss his daughters, Chaya and Dinah that used to chat and kvetch about this and that, now have their own families and responsibilities to tend to. Their families are so far away in those bustling cosmopolitan cities that Milwaukee cannot match. Chaya's boys, Chaim and Daniel, always weave their way into Shmuel's psyche, never letting him rest from his quiet presence. His grandchildren always rest close to his heart. "Shalom bubbala." So, how was your day?

"Eh, we'll talk later. Dinah's on the phone. She wants us to come down to Taste of Chicago. I think she has something she wants to tell us in person."

"A child? But that's not possible. Doctor Schwartzberg told us that Micah was not able to sire any children."

"You know that modern medicine has made some sweeping changes regarding fertility over the years but there is still a deep, stirring mystery to this life, ours. Now, shush, Dinah does not need to hear any of our tireless rants. Hurry up, your borscht is getting cold."

Outside, young African American, White, and Hispanic children are busy tearing up the sidewalks on their Lite Speed Tricycles and BMX bikes, cutting across yards and yelling at the top of their lungs. Shmuel glances out the dining room window; and, is reminded of the differences between their neighbors and themselves. Darkness creeps over the eastern skyline as one more day passes by.

"So, what did Dinah have to say?"

"Like I told you, she and Micah want us to come down for the days of July 11th to the 14th when it comes to an end. Of course, I said we could make it."

"Dinah and Micah are Reformists. We're Orthodox. You know I cannot drive on the Sabbath. So, how are we going to handle this?"

"We have been through this before. Micah will drive us to an Orthodox Temple like he did two years ago when we went to their wedding. She's our child, Shmuel. I am not going to let anything interfere with that. Besides, she says she has something important to tell us. I have never heard her like this before, Shmuel." There is a levity in her voice. "I am sure it's good news."

"God gave us Dina. And, you know full well that I am a Rosh Yeshiva. I cannot just go wherever and whenever I please."

"Fine, if that's the way you want it. Great, I will get there one way or another. If you cannot ask the rebbe for a weekend off, then I will go by myself."

"How? You cannot drive."

"I'll get on a train. And, if all else fails, I will fly in to O'Hare. She's our child, my own flesh and blood. I can't just let all that go by the wayside, Shmuel. She's only ninety miles away, and I swear we see her maybe, what, two-three times a year? I need to see her, Shmuel. I know the Temple's important to you, but I find other things more important. Look, she graduated from the Torah Academy of Milwaukee, and, she had decided to go her way, Madison. And, that led her into Micah's arms. Yes, we are married for a long time, thirty-eight years."

"Gay avek, not to worry, Rebbe Twerski can count on somebody else for one weekend. Farpitzed for wild Chicago is nice. I will put together a pair of gabardine slacks for you that will leave you breathless."

"Leave your tallits home, and wear your kippah only when we attend community *beit telifah*. I know that this is important to you. But, really Shmuel, aside from my teaching position, what does it really offer us women?"

"Well you help us tremendously when we have our fundraisers."

"Only in the Orthodoxy. Everywhere else there are women rabbis and Talmudic scholars."

"Ah, I don't want to start an argument. But, really Shmuel, why can we not have some joy outside of the congregation? We have worked tirelessly for the Sherman Park Jewish Initiative; and, it has done wonders for all of us. But we live in and around goys. Oh, and don't forget all those shiksas who've lured away all our eligible men. No matter how you say it, Shmuel, we are no better or worse than anyone else."

"It is you who raised our children and we learned to revere God as one, Gabriela."

"Women do all the dirty work while the men are out 24/7 with their little businesses and Torahs strapped to their squeamish thoughts. And, here we are, still hanging on to your every word. If we don't, well, do everything, the whole world falls apart. Now really, Shmuel, could you tell me if I am straying too far from one of the positive Talmudic laws, that maybe I should repent my ways?"

"Yahweh provides shelter from the storm Gabriela. You of all people should realize that much. With it, we can reach out to others like we have with all the *baalei teshuvas* several years back. Now look. We have a thriving Orthodox Jewish community of over 22,000, of which we make up the largest portion. We are talking about serving God here, not going off on a whim about how we should eat our food before el Shabbat."

"Now that you've brought it up, yeah, there's that too."

"Like in all religions. But you and I, we both know that we are solely here as servants of God. Yes, there are things I question; but, I keep those to myself. If I really want to help my flock, I must quietly and assertively reach out. That is where I can truly help the rebbe."

"Well, don't I provide religion along with education as they enter my classroom?"

"They are just beginning life, Gabriel. We are helping adults to pursue and find their ways for themselves, to make changes for the better to help both themselves and their families as they get through their busy and trying days."

"Sometimes I think I get more out of our traditions and culture by just going to The Kosher Meat Club. There, I can get a good cut of lamb chops along with bananas, and asparagus. And, the only scary words I will hear is, that will be $13.49 Ms. Berman. Oh, and how are you on this fine June afternoon?"

"Are you talking about us?"

"What?"

"You and me. What do you think I meant?"

"Sometimes, Shmuel, sometimes I think I really could just fly away. Who wins at these pointless arguments anyway?"

"I do not know. Let God be the judge of that. I have a hard enough time just balancing the books at the end of the business day, giving favors to my best customers who are not really my best customers if you know what I mean?"

"I am going to take a long needed bath. Could you wash your dishes before you head off to bed?"

"Sure. I will be up in a bit after I talk to rebbe Twerski about something regarding Hasidic Philosophy as it relates to Talmudic Law. It all goes back to our mystical union with God through our own learned forms of meditation and reflection. I know you think that I can be a ninny sometimes with all this scholarly work I do. But I could not make it without the order and serene words that it brings into my life. Psalms and songs awaken me from my own slumber, my own troubled moments: Gabriela, there isn't one moment of the day when I am not thinking about you and the girls, our grandchildren. Everything is so interwoven, so majestic, so beautiful, yet so archaic, misunderstood. He gives me the strength and courage to face the matters that I would never ever think of addressing before."

"OK, you win my little scholar. Now, off to bed I go. I expect your dishes to be washed and put away before I leave the house tomorrow morning my little mensch."

"Shalom."

"Hey, Josie, got some weed? I've got a couple of six packs in my bag. Christina and Johnnie are gonna swing by in his GTO."

"Dale, can we just take it easy tonight. I mean, I gotta get up at the break of dawn to get to work on time."

"You're not gonna wimp out on me now, are you? We got through Milwaukee Washington didn't we? How about a little time to let off some steam? You're only young once, Josie. You could end up like my uncle Mike who's got five kids and works three jobs just to get by. He got married right out of high school, did the family thing. And, now look at him. He's never gonna get out of his mess."

"So, would you rather just run away to California, and, party 'til you puke, not knowing anyone. Meanwhile, go on acting like everything's real cool like everything's chill?"

"Whatever, there's Johnny headin' up Sherman. Are you in? OK, let's go."

"Hey Christina, hey Willie, got ourselves a twelve pack right here. How about cruisin' down to the Lake, got some dube, you got the beer. Just head down Locust till you hit Bradford Beach, then, bam, sit back and relax, let it all settle in."

"We're not gonna spend all night here, are we? I've gotta run the mail department at SMJ Advertising tomorrow morning."

"And, like you're the only one whose gotta put in a little time tomorrow? Like I gotta go out at 6:00 AM to help the old man pour cement driveways and sidewalks for houses, build basements out of mortar bricks. Try that one on for size."

"I know, but could we get home by 11:00?"

"If you say so, but Josie, you're crampin' my style. With all the shit we put up with the niggers at Washington, I thought you'd want to go out and raise a little hell before you took off for Madison this fall."

"I can't work with a hangover. No way. I'd rather die. You guys, you just can't say no."

"Well, if I did as many dumb things as you did when drinkin', I'd take it easy on the booze myself. But, Mary Jane, chronic, take a look at this. Takes your mind off everything. Wash it down with a couple beers, feelin' no pain. Know what I'm sayin'? Hey, it can't be all that bad, Josie, you'll be goin' to school and I'll be hangin' out with the old man pourin' concrete every Goddamn day. So, just count your blessings."

"Take it easy, John. Josie's just the sensitive type, that's all."

"You guys can have my beers; just get me stoned."

"That's cool mamasita, why don't you get in the back seat with Josie? Me and Johnny got some talkin' to catch up on. I mean that is if you do not mind?"

"No problem. OK, let's go."

"What's on your plans for the following weekend?"

"Oh, I don't know. Why?"

"My dad's got some tickets for the Brewers/Pirates series. He's gotta do something with ma, whatever the hell that is. Anyway, we got box seats on the first base side, steaks, like baked potatoes, chips, jalapenos & 'shrooms.

Even bringin' along some corn on the cob, beer, dube, beer, dube. What do you think?"

"What do ya mean what do I think? Sure I'll go. What else would I be doing on a summer weekend? By the way, Josie, would you want to go to see a movie sometime, your choice, you know this coming Saturday night?"

"Is this a date?"

"Ah, it doesn't have to be a date, date, that's a little strong a word. But, you know just hang out, shoot the shit. I just want to see you before you will be outta here in a couple of months."

"Oh, why not, Josie," Christina cuts in, "of course it's a date. You two lovebirds who just can't hold hands but do your best always not to step on each other's toes. It would be so evil if you would go off to Madison and never say anything beyond let's get stoned. That's so-oh crass. Come on, Josie, just say *yes*."

"Well, yeah, I mean, um, yeah. I'll pick you up since I've got wheels; and, you, well, working over at Wal-Mart won't get you anywhere. I mean, I'm just putting it out there."

"Here,"

"h-h-hh-h-h-h-p-m-m-m-hh-uh.," hold it in. Yeah, there ya go. Christina, "h-h-h-h-h-h-mha-ah-h-h-h-h-mh-h-h-hn."

"Alrighty then, Juan?"

"h-h-h- h-h-ahc-ch-ch-ch-chccch—a. Christ, what the hell happened?"

"Better stick to the beer my man. Ladies, here's the dime bag and lighter. Juan and me, we'll stick to the twelver while you girls go off to Maui."

"Juan, guess what?"

"What Christina?"

"I had a conversation with your next door neighbor, Mr. Schwartzberg. You know that Jewish dude? God, their skin's so white, you know? I mean snow fuckin' white."

"Won't see any tats on those fucks. Stick out like a sore thumb, for real. I guess bein' Hispanic's kinda hard to relate to their totally white skin. It's like, like he's whiter than white, his veins in his neck scream at you while you catch 'im walking down the street. Ya know Josie, it's like he's almost dead or something, like uncle Willie when he pulled up those lifeless zombie eyelids of his to scare the shit out of us back in the day. Their rosy cheeks really stand out. Nah, Mr. Schwartzberg can't be anything like my uncle, he's so-oh, so squeaky clean, you know. Not just because he's Jewish, I mean really Jewish, totally, big time. It's just the way he handles himself walking down the street. Besides, he's a doctor. Honkin' success story."

"What's wrong with that?"

"He's not a freak, I mean he is, but he isn't. He's, yeah I know who you're talking about. I've seen him when we were partying one day at Juan's. Kinda old, but yeah, I wanted to talk to him. So high, ya know? Baked's more like it. But it was like, like, like I couldn't, I didn't want him to see me, like he was looking right through me. *Oy.*"

"Thank God I don't smoke as much ganja as you freaks do or that guy would be drilled into my skull. I mean it's not like I'm spying on him or anything but, he's so-oh mysterious, dressed in black even in the middle of the day, walking somewhere, the Temple, St. Joseph's, anywhere. His wife, she seems more like us, older, of course. But she goes wherever she wants. That mysterious aura doesn't follow her around like him. She's more like us, totally. Him, well, I'd like to think so. But, the Fear of God stands on his shoulders. I've only been able to say hi to him a couple of times."

"Ah, you guys, he's just hooked on religion. Do you really think it is something more than that?"

"Look at some of these old homes. We've finally gotten out of the hood."

"You can say that again. Could you imagine having your car break down around here? I mean where will you get any help?"

"We've got our cell phones. Sometimes they can come in handy besides wasting all that time texting and playing video games."

"Hey, Billie, where'd you get this from?"

"Where'd you think?"

"Pinky?"

"Yep. If you wanta get some, I'll handle it for ya. When do you need it by?"

"I don't get paid until this Friday. I mean does that work?"

"I'll see what I can do. But don't hold out on me. Otherwise, it'll cost you, know what I'm sayin'?"

"Our little hang-ups up with Dr. Billie. Don't worry man, when have I not come through for you?"

"Do you think I want to be stiffed by a bunch of gimpy dudes who only hang around when things are mellow?"

"Oh, look at this, a small bookstore of all places, a couple coffee shops, pretty cool. Chrissie, maybe you and me can take a trip down here sometime this summer. Ya know, like I can pick up a couple of books before I'm out of here for good. And, Billie, Billie, Billie; if it's that big a deal, I'll pass on it."

"Nah, don't worry about it. I just don't want you flakin' out or changin' your mind at the last minute."

"Fine. Test me when it comes in, and we can meet over at Starbucks, say, Saturday at 11.00 AM?"

"No problem. It's kinda cold out. Do you wanna stay in the car or walk down to the beach?"

"Stay in the car, you kidding me Guillermo? Look at the waves splashing over the rocks at the far end of the Breakers."

"I've got some blankets in the trunk: Juan and me, we're here to keep you ladies nice and warm."

"Las aparencias enganan marron."

"Hey mujeres, I'm just sayin'. Spread the love around. Nothin' wrong with that, is there?"

"Lo que te hace tan grande," Christina cuts in, "Let's head home; or are we gonna run up on the cement rocks just to see the waves torture us?"

"After Juan and I finish our last cervecitas. Ladies, now if you will let us take care of a little business. Bottoms up. I was thinkin' maybe we'd spin over to Rickey's but, that wouldn't fit right with the ladies."

"Could we get a going guys? I mean sorry to break into all this cool, cool fun and all, but, really, I need to get home. Please guys?"

"Alright already you whiners. Let's do it."

"About time, how about it?"

"Hey, whose car is this anyway? If you could get your little friend Gracie to come along one night, then maybe we could let you take the wheel. Now Billy here knows who's in charge. What you doin' for me, girl?"

"Capitol's right up the road. Now, keep your eyes on the road and get me home in one piece, comprendeme?"

"No problema. Can't get you home fast enough."

"What about Rickie's?"

"Oh, don't you worry about that once we drop off Miss congeniality here we'll head down 27^Th. Fuck everything, right Billy?"

"I'll get out with Chrissy if you don't mind?"

"What are you so hung up about?"

"Ah, just leave me alone."

"And, what is that supposed to mean Missy, like we're not good enough for you? Sooner or later you're gonna die. So, you might as well enjoy life when you can. Look, I know we're not exactly world beaters, but every day I look across the table and see my parents. So-oh fucking old. He works at Target to help pay the rent, not even a house to show for his sorry life. When he shows up at gramma's, he turns into a know-it-all, like everything he does is so businesslike, like he has no pulse, so poised. Hell, he can't even tromp on the gas pedal. Like he's become this lifeless, silent, kiss ass Joe. So, before Madison makes you a stranger, remember this queen bitch. What comes around goes around. Gotta do what you gotta do, right?"

"Oh, right, and pay back's a bitch. When haven't I heard that big boy. Take it any way you want it. You shit. Like the whole world revolves around you. And, you're right about one thing. Your parents are pretty much bottom feeders."

"Like I said, ya gotta do what ya gotta do. Hey, I didn't make the rules."

"Oh, don't you worry. I ain't gonna follow yours or anyone's. Keep up that hole of a life you call fun. You'll find yourself in your own vomit."

"Retch!"

"Alright already. Juan, if you could. Let these girls out so we can get down to business. God, Josie, you don't buy everything Chrissie says about us, do you?"

"Look, I'm kinda tired. See ya round, alright guys?"

"Those chicks think they're gonna find something better than us."

"Guilly, what isn't bullshit? Now could we get a goin'. My happy lappy awaits."

"How about it, big guy, let's do it."

Chapter Two

Old Friends Reflect on Old Times

The incessant piercing sound of cicadas breaks the sultry silence of the hot late June afternoon as young Jerome walks home from mass. A copse of crimson maples huddled around an empty lot sway lightly beneath the heavy skies. Jerry wipes away sweat from his eyes as he makes his way home.

"How's your mother doing, son?"

"Huh? Oh, she's fine Mrs. Jefferson."

"You know we're very proud of her. And, we hear your sister has been accepted to sing at a university."

"Yep, she starts at Viterbo University pretty soon."

"Viterbo University? Hmn. I must admit that I have never heard of that place before. We will sure miss her beautiful voice in the church choir."

"Oh, you don't have to worry. She's only going to La Crosse. Mom worried that she wouldn't fit in with the Catholic school, but Jackie says that everything's OK. She walked around the school and really likes it. Mom says that she really wants to become a professional singer. Mom wants her to take voice lessons to become an opera singer. Jackie wants to become a diva she says. I sure hope she makes it."

"Oh, you can be sure that your sister will be just fine," Mr. Jefferson cuts in, "no one has belted out sounds like that since Nancy Wilson. Something wonderful happens when she sings in front the choir. It's a thrill so heavenly that no words can describe it."

"OK, Kenny, I'm sure we do not want to bother our poor neighbor with flowers in the midst of love."

"I'm sure one day I will learn how wonderful love is, but now I just worry about finishing my homework so I can play basketball at the YMCA. You know I can really shoot it from the top of the key."

"God bless you, son. How about a glass of lemonade? You know my wife has made some wonderful brownies to go along with that luscious lemonade. Alright, shoot. Got something more important on your mind?"

"Na, nothing that can't wait. I can clean the bathroom later on. It's too hot to do anything else anyway."

"Wonderful, here's your lemonade and the Mrs. is goin' to get you a couple of those heavenly concoctions of hers. So, how are you doing these days, son? I mean I don't see you around too much anymore and was wonderin' if everything's goin' alright with your mother and yourself?"

"Mom's always at work."

"She has two jobs as you well know. I don't think it's ever been easy to make it. I worked at A.O. Smith for over 40 years. It used to be hoppin', like it had a life of its own. I mean there were people from every lifestyle: white, black, you name it. My children are all grown now. They have their children and their own lives to manage. Education helped two of my daughters to get a start. "

"Don't get me wrong now, none of it has been easy. But with our strong faith, and love, we have never forgotten where we came from. Anita lives in Minneapolis and Cherry chose Atlanta to raise her family. Thank God, my boys have stuck around and brought some wonderful lasting memories with 'em. My grandson Derron is your age. He is so fascinated about those computer games. I hope one day you'll be able to meet him. I don't want to impose but life's so short; oh, and here's some of those brownies my better half's been telling you all about."

"Thank you Mrs. Jefferson."

"You're welcome. Tell your mother to stop by. I really would like to see her. I mean if that is alright with you. We have a lot o' catchin' up to do. It sure would be nice to chat 'bout things goin' on since her promotion at work."

"You know that she has quit her job over at Popeye's?"

"Praise the Lord. We were always praying for her safety."

"A-men: lotta bad things goin' down there all the time.

Now, would you let this precious little man enjoy his little treat Eugene?"

"You know Charity, I was thinkin' that maybe we could have Jerome and Derron get together sometime, you know, at something goin' on in the neighborhood, over at the Boys and Girls Club. Derron's no slouch on the court either Jerome. He's grown a couple inches over the last school year. He's just a bit taller than you, but I'm sure that you got the moves to keep him out of your face. How's your fade away jumper?"

"I'm working at it, but mom wants me to keep hitting the books. She says that I can't count on basketball to pay the bills, but she comes to every game we play at the YMCA. Coach says that my defense and boxin' out is coming around. I can't wait to get onto the junior high team next year. It's just that, well, the game is easier for me. I mean I still have to work at it, but it's a lot easier than figuring out probabilities and understanding how rain and erosion affect how we live. I mean I am sure that it makes sense, that it can help me out in the future. But really Mr. Jefferson, everybody around me talks about street smarts is what really counts."

"You hear that enough and you will be joining them on the bench over at bum-park. My youngest found out the hard way. Now he's, he's, well let's just say that Jesus is helping him recover from the scrapes he's put himself through over the last twenty years. I don't want to scare you, son; but, that is no way to end up I tell you. You've always gotta fight those temptations. Those things that can bring you to your knees. I know you don't want to hear this my little man, but we're all on our last legs if we don't stay the course."

"Well, I had better get going. I'm sure mom's worried about me."

"Do you want us to call her and let her know where you are?"

"Na, that's alright. Thanks for everything Mrs. Jefferson."

"Have a wonderful afternoon; and, don't forget to say 'hi' to your mother for me."

"Oh, I won't. I'll tell her to call you when she has some time."

"Well, thank you Jerome. Thanks for remembering."

"Bye."

"Children, they're so precious."

"Yes, then when they grow up they see things go on like those two abandoned babies in the park that the kids who found them were mere babes themselves. And, of all places, they were found beneath the basketball hoops last fall. That's what goes on, Charity. It gets no easier the older I get. Look at De Marco. We've lost nearly everything we owned to help him get back on his feet. And, to think of it Charity, he talks about all our past pettiness when he's been swimming in a cesspool of madness. I swear to sweet baby Jesus that if I had to hear one more of his rants against the way we raised him all those years ago, I swear on my mother's grave that I would have to take him out."

"Oh, could you quit it with all the theatrics, Eugene. We never said we're perfect. If we were, we would have nothing left of this house now would we?"

"Right, since these are the cards we're dealt, we will just have to play along."

"Plod along in quicksand is more like it. "

"We all have our faults sweetheart. Heaven help us to bring distress to anyone much less our poor, poor baby. He's trying Gene. He's been driving truck for a couple years now for Gosh Sakes."

"He always talks about putting together some new R&B record. I mean, ain't he old enough to dump his stupid pipe dreams that I'm tired of hearing about. He was a journeyman at the Paper Machinery Company and the fool couldn't hang wid the pressure. What kind of man does that? Throws it all away, says he's gonna be the next R. Kelly. My God, who in this world is gonna to listen to him? That son of yours thinks I don't have a brain in my head, that I lack sensitivity."

"He's your child too, Mister. You think you're the only one who has to put up with his antics?"

"Remember when mother moved back in?"

"Don't remind me."

"Dementia was her serum to tell everyone how dad treated her."

"If she was half right about your father, I can see why she lost it."

"Lost it? Please. She suffered from a disease that left her unable to cope with the world, to forget vital parts of her life. It's a disease."

"Well, now she has since passed on, and now we have to pick up the pieces of our own lives, God-willing."

"Amen to that. De Marco needs to find a woman to settle down, to cure his own ills."

"I sure hope so because he will not get one more dime from me for another of his countless schemes. You know where every dime ends up? His boozed up talk, "just one more time dad," I can feel it churnin' in my bones—ya know I got it, babe. Please. I won't ever bring any of it up again if it all falls to pieces. Nah, the child just rolls another snake eyes. He can't see the light Charity, down and out's all he knows. Like he'll spend his last dime on a 40 before it all clicks. He's on his own Charity. I'm tellin' ya. No more secret handouts from our nest egg. You hear me? Of course, let him go out and conquer the world. And, like every wasted day, the haze returns. A man his age, for the life of me, I just can't understand why he won't settle down. Tell me Charity, what more else can we do for him?"

"Hold his hand, give it up to the grace of God. Why are you always so hard-nosed when it comes to De Marco, Edward?"

"Oh, I wholeheartedly agree. He has to let Jesus in. That much I do know. Now how about if you and me make some magic again. You know that recipe of yours', sweet potato pie?"

"You know I have peach cobbler thawing from a week ago.

Just gotta heat it up. Why don't we go with that?"

"Oh, that sounds heavenly for tomorrow morning. Coffee and scrambled eggs to go with those biscuits your sister brought over. How 'bout it?"

"That's fine. Why don't you start on the crust while I get some cleaning done?"

"I thought we'd do it together."

"I will join you after you get the crust in the pan. When you're done with that, just give me a holler."

"OK, see you in a bit."

As Charity is dusting the living room, she spots an elderly gentleman strolling slowly past the house.

"Is that you, Paul?"

"Why, yes. So what's going on at the Jefferson household these days?"

"Not a whole lot. As they say, no news is good news. Care to join my husband an' me for a cup of tea and some of my very own peach cobbler?"

"How can I pass on such an offer on a stifling day as this?"

"Say Edward, we have company."

"Oh, yeah? Now who would be coming by at this time of the day? Paul Bogdanov, really? So how long has it been, what?"

"Oh, I think it was last year at Halloween when you brought your grandkids by my place. Actually, they're my great-grandkids. But, yes, that's right."

"Don't be such a stranger old man, right Charity (she goes to the kitchen to pick up the iced tea and to quick microwave the peach cobbler)?"

"Hey, just getting out of bed and facing the world every day is a chore that I sometimes do not manage very well."

"You can say that again. So, Paul, what has been going on with your life lately?"

"Aside from putting in a few days of meal delivery over at Hart Park, I may wander over to see my grandson. Well, I never was good at anything, no hobbies. But, hey, I sure enjoy good company with a little iced tea and that wonderful cobbler of yours Charity."

"Why thank you, Paul. Do you know that I am getting Edward here to become quite the baker?"

"It gives me an excuse to be with the woman that I have loved for over fifty years. I don't want to pry, but, have you been able to find someone to spend some time with?"

"No I haven't. After Janine passed away and all that lost time that followed, well, you know."

"Well, we all have been there done that. Church has been my redeeming quality. Anita and I spend a lot of time over at Unity Missionary Baptist to help people in need."

"That's right. Women with children, the homeless, drug addiction, you name it. We have all kinds of people from every walk of like coming through the Church's doors. Without being able to help our youth, I do not know what would keep us going. After our children've left the nest. And, by just becoming part of the Parish, we have found that we can still make a difference."

"I tell you after I dragged myself out of my mess several years back, I thought I could breathe some life into my lonely existence. But that hasn't seemed to work out."

"May I ask you how old you are?"

"Eighty-three, why?"

"Oh, I just was wondering," Charity muses, "Edward has just turned 73. I'll be 72 this fall. My health, God willing, is excellent. I've got nothing to complain about."

Edward enters and adds, "One thing I don't miss is getting up for work every day. How would I have a job at Smith after all the shake up there with the dwindling revenues from working on the Lines with the truck frames for thirty years? Ya know that transitioning over into water systems couldn't have been that easy."

"You can say that again. I took my daughter over to the new Evinrude plant in Sturtevant, and I could not believe what I was seeing. All that technology, the workers seemed to take in everything what was going on around them. I sure didn't. God, ever since the sixties that company was laying people off for months at a time. Then the eighties came along, and many of those people never returned. Smaller numbers were the norm."

"You can say that again. Nothing was done by management to turn things around. They wanted us to offer any advice on how we could make some changes to improve manufacturing results and employee morale if that was ever a concern. Any advice offered was overlooked, I can tell you that much."

"If it translates into money, management would listen, well, at least most of the time at OMC. Unless of course a lot of effort was called for on their part."

"You guys seem to have such wonderful insights into your plants. Why did things fall apart so long ago?"

"We all had our hands in the cookie jar," Edward laughs, "like that old football line goes, if you ain't cheatin' you ain't tryin.'"

"I'll second that. I spent fifty years in that plant; and, all I wanted to do was stay out of the way of the big wigs. God, that place was depressing."

"That's why they call it work my man. Want a refill?"

"Nah, that's OK. I've got my fill. Great cobbler Charity. You have a real gift. My mother-in-law, God rest her soul, could not have done better. Spending a Sunday afternoon at my in-laws was not all that bad. The only thing I detested was to try learning how to play bridge. When that didn't work, they tried to get me to learn sheep's head. I guess you could call me a simpleton. Just bringing home the bacon was enough for me. Quiet conversation and a martini or two was all I ever wanted. Once I walked in the door, the last thing I wanted to do was to play some game to keep my wits about me."

"Well, as you know Paul, the Lord has brought peace to Edward and me. God knows we have had our days. See those two copper plaques on each side of the wall?"

"Yes I do."

"Edward, could you read the plaque above us?"

"Surely, the bodies of the unjust shall, by the power of Christ, be raised to dishonor."

"Now across the way:"

"The bodies of the just shall by His Spirit be raised to honor, and made comfortable to His own glorious body."

"Wonderful. You see, Paul, the older we get the more in tune we have to pay attention to our next life. Salvation, devotion to our Creator is all we have to look forward to. This world is not ours anymore. Let us hope that Jesus has something in store for our children's children. I have worked at our Church as secretary for over twenty years. I can't say that things worked out for everyone. And, Lord knows some of us have had more than our share to cope with."

"And, let's not forget, Charity, that others can make things impossible for any of us."

"Yes, yes, Edward. But I know that what I did made a difference for others in need."

"I'm sure you did Charity. But you must understand that factory work is a different animal. It's about survival. If you let up, someone's gonna walk all over you. It's like we're all criminals but we desperately try keep a straight face at all costs. Otherwise nobody's gonna be eatin' tonight, right Paul?"

"Yeah, that's the underbelly of it. We all know that you gotta go along to stay in the game."

"But this is not a game, gentlemen. We are talking about the house of our Lord Savior, Jesus Christ."

"Then you have to face your own death, and be alright with it sweetie. Even great-great grampa Julius couldn't disagree with that. You know he worked with his team of Negroes putting together pontoon bridges for Burnside's push into Virginia at the War's end. The horrors we still endure to this day, Paul. Slavery still lurks in the hearts of most of us. Jim Crow's just a small part of it."

"My grandfather brought over my dad when he was just two years old. White Russia was becoming Godless Red. Nothing's changed, Ed. Sometimes I just feel like I just want to hide from everything by falling asleep behind the sports page every night, and let the ghosts still fly around in my head. I'd doubt that it was any different for you."

"Who has to live in all Milwaukee's dirt that has blown around this town for over a century? It wasn't you Whites, I can tell you that much. As the inner city keeps growing, how many of your kind are hangin' around my man?"

"Well, you're right. But we all did what we had to, didn't we? It's almost six o'clock. My daughter's asked me over to her house for dinner. You guys, I really enjoyed spending some time with you. Maybe we can do this some other time."

"Don't be a stranger, Paul."

"Maybe you can swing by my place sometime, have a cup of coffee. Please, stop by any evening. I don't have much going on. So, whenever you're out, please stop in. It would be nice to have someone over and talk about old times."

Briskly walking past him in dark outfits, two heavily bearded gentlemen briskly step by him as he tips his Brewers cap to them, and he slowly makes his way home beneath the auburn twilight. Before heading home, he stops over at a nearby park and sits beneath a huge elm tree as starlings and crows fret about, children frolic higgledy-piggledy, and mothers make sure their dear, sweet children have *played it safe*. The amber skies swim into view, framing his presence, as Paul tucks his white hairs into his worn out Brewers cap, thinking about what he will have for dinner.

Chapter Three

Winning Isn't Everything

"Lo que to hace tan grande, Dewan? Hey, English, know what I'm sayin? This ain't Mexico."

"Now what did you just say?"

"Nothin."

"Nothin', huh? Not trying to pull one on me, are you, Jose?"

"Nah, I'm just letting you know that you aren't the king of this diamond. Desi, me, and Johnny kick ass around here. Better stick to basketball. So, chill bro'."

"Fuck if you're gonna tell me what I can or can't do, pappy."

"I'm just passin' along what I see. You're out of your league Dewan. I know Jasmine and Shirley plays softball—hey, they can take a lot of guys. I'll tell you one thing. I would pick them before I'll pick you homey, 'cause you ain't got it, comprendeme?"

"Keep it up, Josie; and, I swear I'll take your sorry ass out. Besides, your little love-bird tomboy squeeze Shirley Johnson's the ugliest thing ever. You know, she always tosses you those sweet little rose pedals when you're up."

"I'm so-oh touched by your concern for a sister. Yeah, but I can't stop her if that's her thang. Ain't that right, Stump?"

"What, oh, yeah, they're angels, aren't they, Terence?"

"Ah, alright, shit face, c'mon now give it to me."

"Bases loaded, we're up one, two outs in the bottom of the ninth. Can our track star here hit the ball out of the infield?"

"It's goin' right down your throat."

"OK, big boy, let's see what you got."

"Alright Josie, let the girl do her thing." (chorus of voices) "Last out. C'mon Julie, let's get 'm out."

"Hey, what was wrong with that one?"

"Hey, that was at my ankles."

"Yeah, right, next one of those will be called a strike. I thought you had some cajones bro'."

(Pitch is fouled off down the right field line). "Desi, come on dude, ah why didn't you chase that down?"

"Johnny, I'd like to see you frame that one down into the strike zone. We ain't sitting out here to give 'em a bunch of chances to beat us."

"Hey, I've chased down some sure home runs today, saved your ass last inning as a matter of a fact."

"You ain't all that."

"OK, so I'm not as good as you; but, there's no way you're gonna run that one down by the fence."

"Hey, one hit takes care of your super team, Jose."

"You just worry about yourself. So, Dewan, how many hits do you have in this game? Ah, would you look at that, whiff, strike two. Looks like Dewey's gonna finish it off for his team coming back from five runs down..."

"C'mon, shit face, you can do better than that."

"Take it easy Julie. Dewan would stand in front of one of your inside pitches to tie up the game."

"Shut up, Jeff."

"Hey she's just lobbing in the ball, dude. You ain't exactly the best hitter in the world Dew."

"Bring it, shit face."

"Aw, great pick, Jose."

"Safe! Georgie's up."

"Julie, you gotta move toward me when he hits at deep short like that."

"He was safe by a mile, Jose."

"Alright, let's get George. We'll do alright in our next at bat, but let's not give George one right down the plate."

"Ducks on the pond, George. One base hit ends it for 'em."

"That's right T.P."

"OK guys, don't let anything get through. Back up a bit, Shirley. George likes to get around on the ball—it could be coming your way."

"Alright Julie, let's go."

(Swings) "Do ya got it, Timmy? Pick it up. Out! Great pick Jeff. Shirley, Johnny, and Jimmy are comin' up. Let's go guys. These guys haven't got a chance against us."

"Why did you swing at the first pitch? At least make Rochow work at it a bit."

"Hitting a softball's different than hitting a hard ball, Jose."

"I've seen how they bring it in fast pitch softball Shirley."

"I know, but it's getting late—I wanna go home."

"Popping it up to the pitcher is about as bad as it gets: OK, Johnny, drive one to the fence like the couple you did earlier in the game."

Ball one. Strike! "Hey, John that was right in there. What were you looking at?" Crack! "It's rolling to the fence. Go! Go! They're not gonna get ya Slide! Safe!"

Jimmy steps up and hits a slow rolling ground ball to Johnny Huerta; and, gets Jimmy out but the speedy Johnny Heuer makes it in as Jasmine hits a chopper back to the pitcher, and the team's at bat comes to an end. "Alright everybody, we only need one run to get back in the game. Let's bat around. Jimmy, "Anil, and Flo: yeah, only swing at what you can get hold of. Ball two (instead, he swings and misses). That's OK, hang in there. Good ride, straighten it out. Ah, hit right at John. Wait, he overran it!

C'mon, put on the gas, around the horn, yeah, do it. Stand up Jimmy jogs over home plate). Tied up, how 'about it? Now, let's get in the winning run and end this game right now."

Anil lines out to Shirley at third; and, Flo steps in.

"Alright everyone, move in. We're not going to let her beat us with her feet."

Flo swings and misses on the first two pitches: Jose and company feel a sigh of relief—Julie throws a pitch high and outside, and Flo watches the pitch connect with the bat. "Down the line: Do it. G-Go, Go, Go!"

Flo stands on second as Manley steps up. Manley, an overgrown thirteen year-old with Left Tackle written all over him, swings for the fence, fouling off two pitches. "You gotta keep it in play Manley. One out. Let's get Flo in and end this bullshit."

Next pitch Manley drives the ball to right center, but sure-handed Johnny camps under the ball as the astute speed demon Flo tags up and takes third. Down to the last out, the least baseball minded player, Beth, steps up. Although a gymnast and tennis enthusiast, playing with neighborhood kids gives her some time to hang out with her friends to get away from her overbearing mother. Besides boys are all over the field. So, why hide out from her newfound presence as a smart and beautiful young lass?

Strike one! "OK, Julie. Just let her hit the ball if she can even get around on it."

"Ball one, Strike two!" Julie releases the ball, comin' down the third base line, let it go foul … g-go get it, Julie!" Julie tears down to get the ball as Flo hurdles over her, mustering up every ounce of effort to reach home…

"Safe!" Yeah, ooh-hoo, Game Over! Beth beat out the pitcher's hands rule as Julie's indecisive move to the ball trickling down the third base line finally put Dewan's crew in the win column. Baseball is a game won in moments, nanoseconds slowed down by the mind ordering it into a filmstrip reality that even a player of limited means can turn out to be the hero. Such realities only pop up infrequently. However, when they do, they will remain with the youth for all her years.

"Yeah, yeah Yeah!!! We beat you with our secret speed. So, what do you have to say about that, huh, Josie?"

"That was close. Beth just beat it out."

"Flo comin' down on shit face, jumps clean over her and struts into home."

"If Julie would've moved on that ball right away we'd be talking a different tune."

"You told her it was going foul, and it just hugged the line."

"That was the closest game we've played all summer. But next week will be a different story. The same ole' story. Comprendeme, Moreno?"

"Got nothin' to say bro'? C'mon now, spit it out."

"Why bother? You think that you can just push your weight around—I ain't scared of you."

"OK tough guy, what you holding back? Just say it."

"Why don't you just lighten up, Dew. God, every time someone doesn't go along with you, you like to make a big deal out of it."

"Why don't you get lost, Flo. This is between Joey and me, Right pappy?"

"I'm alright guys really. Me and Dewan have some things to settle on our own. We'll see you next week."

"Take it easy Jimmy."

"You're just doing what he wants, dude."

"Nah, I need to deal with this crap that's been goin' on for a long time."

"The loser's gonna run away and hide. Now just get lost. Like Joe says, we got some things to work out. Now, take off, all of ya."

"Jose, could you give me my bat?"

"Sure."

"Thanks."

"Alright Anil, see ya. So, Joe, now that you're on your own, what are you gonna do when I get hold of your sorry ass?"

Quickly, Dewan grabs hold of Jose's shoulders, violently trying to thrust him to the hardened infield dirt but the latter pushes back. They tussle about for a bit. And, finally Dewan wrestles him to the ground. Dried dirt flies wildly about as the amber sunset reflects over their youthful presence while Jose pushes the determined aggressor off of him.

Now both stand up, walking back and forth in semi circles, as panting, eyes stiffly lock in upon one another.

"Your mother sucks donkey dick."

"Ooh, that hurts. Like the only thing yours can do is make babies."

"True, but at least she doesn't get busted with a crack pipe walking by her lonesome down Bradford Beach getting stoned like the goat that she is. I mean right in front of the cops: Had to be the easiest bust of all time. What a winner."

"What?"

"Oh, like your best friend Jesse crapped that out, like you didn't know about that? Everybody knows black boy."

"Brownie thinks he don't have shit in his own little back yard. I'll just have to beat it out of you. A couple of my cousins were in in 2-7."

"That was my aunt bright boy. My mom's never touched dope in her life."

"Same thing, Dewey. Dad says the apple never falls far from the tree. We're Latin Kings bro', South Siders."

A flurry of jabs and a roundhouse left lands off center of Jose's neck. Hatred fills his eyes as he bull-rushes Dewan, pushing him into a nearby chain link fence. The two scurry around, trying to attain any advantage they can muster.

A sudden force lands on both youth's necks. "Now are you two satisfied with yourselves?"

"What? Hey old man, why don't you just get out of here."

"You won't get rid of me that easily (he tightens his grasp upon their shoulders). Let's go gentlemen. Now!"

"OK, OK, could you get your hands off me that hurts."

"See those bleachers over there? If you guys promise to be good little boys and make your ways without any hassle, yeah, I can loosen up a little bit. And, don't even think about trying to run away or this old man will have to put the hammer down. Yes, that's better: After you."

"What the hell do you want with us? Can't you mind your own business?"

"So I should just ignore you two slamming each other into the fence, you know, maybe some cracked teeth, a broken jaw— no big deal, right? And such language: I'd have had my mouth washed out with soap if my parents ever caught me cussing up the world like that."

"Like, whah-what do you care about us, like since when do we need some old dude comin' 'round here tellin' us what to do?"

"Eighty-nine years old, oh, and by the bye, no more cuss words or I'm going to have sic Marshal Law on your unruly souls. Understand? Yeah, that's why I still have that little hold on your necks if you haven't noticed."

"What do you want from us?"

"I have great grandchildren that are older than you. And, do you think I would put up with any of the behavior you two displayed this evening?"

"Yeah, when they get away from you, I bet they do a whole lot of shi-yit. Ah-I mean crap you have that no idea what's comin' down."

"Yeah, right, nobody's an angel 24/7. But it's all been done before boys. And, let me introduce myself, I'm Frank, Frank Cardini—I live right across the street over there with my wife Eva—been married for over 70 years. She's why I still get up every morning, kiss the sky. And, you're?"

"Dewan."

"Great, how about you?"

"Jose."

"Pleased to meet you. Now I bet you two are wondering why an old fart like me is interested in what two mad at the world young thugs are doing with their summer vacation time?"

"Not really."

"Well, at least we can say Dewan is honest. I mean who cares, right?"

"I don't need a lecture old man. My parents play that game with me every day. That's why I'm hanging out here and not going home until super late."

"So, we've got two tough guys who are gonna fight their way to fame, right?"

"Maybe we are. So?"

"Look, I don't want to pontificate. I done my share of bonehead play's myself, running, hiding, striking, struttin' my stuff. Hey, but 1939 might as well be 2013. You boys ain't doin' anything different that hasn't been done before. Cool is up one day and becomes passé the next. Why do I say this to such young world-beaters like yourselves? I'll tell you why, because once you hurt someone else or yourself, it will stay with you, you can no longer run from it. It will eat at you, and it will be hard to rid yourself of the mess you took part in. And, I know that old story that the young are always feeling so invulnerable and tough is simply a fairy tale. When I was your age I was trying to fit in, hung out with the cool guys, and later on, tried to get a date with Miriam. Boy she was somthin', a real looker. But as time went by, all those fears I had about what my friends might find out about me wasn't about them. It was about me. No, really. You guys and your little struggles are really all about yourselves. Always fighting for number one, right?"

"Hey, my mom just texted me. I gotta go. I don't know about you Dewan; but, it's getting late, supper's waiting."

"And just a minute ago you said that you could stay up all night tough guy."

"Alright, so what's your point? I'm thirteen years old. I've got the rest of my life to work and have kids."

"I'm talking about life, Jose. Whether you're two or forty, it doesn't matter. You need to think for yourself. There's plenty of people your parent's age who can relate to and freely address things. But, when it comes right down to it, they just buckle under the pressure and go along with their friends and loved ones. It's easier, ya know? I mean look at you two, such enemies. You've made your choices. Now, you've gotta follow through, and grab the bull by the horn, right? Don't want to show you're a weakling, that you can't take it. Or am I wrong? You know, I'm too old and feeble-minded to have any clue as to what's going on with you kids and all the pressure put on you by your parents and everyone else.

OK, I can see you guys have things to do. And, I can't stop you from throwing punches—the minute I leave, you two will go right back at it.

Now, before you guys tear outta here, I got a quick story about yours' truly and World War II. In late' 43 we started the Italian campaign, and made our way into this town, Acerno. As we pushed forward into the town, dead bodies were laying everywhere, and that smell, nothing like it. That's something you'll never ever forget. I don't care who you are. Anyway there was all this cement and brick mortar strewn about, you could tell it must have been a church. Everything collapsed inward, the arches, the ceiling, but the altar was in perfect condition. Now, I'm not trying to tell you about God or miracles or anything, but it sure was strange that the entire inner structure was left intact, pristine. And, about going over to fight Fascism, the Nazis? No. I only went there because I didn't want to be put behind the eight ball by my parents and friends. War solves nothing. Took a long time for that to sink in.

That's not even what I'm getting at. What I mean is that once I saw that people made the difference in society, making political decisions, running the school board were people just like you and me. You know I saw that they were only there to find work, no great shakes, to support their family just like poor, poor pitiful me. But people are the real reason funny things go on in this world. Yeah, it's always been wrong, this world. We've just gone along with it. Fight it? Oh, yeah, like if you can't beat 'em, join 'em.

I came back to work at Allis-Chalmers; and, when they folded, I moved onto Bucyrus-Erie. I realized that work fed and clothed my family, that I learned to keep my opinions to myself and got along with others as best as I could to keep the ball rolling. But those were not relationships really. Putting food on the table. That's all. I couldn't play games at home or with friends. Instead, I learned how to keep my distance. That's all I have to say. Like me, you're on your own. Selfish, isn't it? Just realize that everybody sees what you see. That your piece of the pie will eventually sour. It always does. That includes you, me, everybody.

Oh, and one more thing, you see this field? Every Thursday evening girls' softball takes to the field under the lights. Something to see gentlemen. Some of these girls can put you boys to shame. Some can chase down deep drives in the gaps and make spectacular catches. It wouldn't hurt either of you to see what talent some of these girls possess. Finally, see the green peace frog on the black top near the pool? Let's all three of us make our way peaceably over there."

"What for?"

"What do you think? Cm- on, take a stab at it. No? Not interested? Let's go guys. Now that we're here, walk beneath the green circle of love hand-in-hand. Oh, now that wasn't so hard now was it? It's kind of nice to be part of Milwaukee's golden public parks, isn't it? I mean the quaint green frog and all. Friends, beats being enemies: Now I'm not telling you boys something you boys don't already know. But, if you choose to make your way in this world by going with the flow, remember, someone has taken the time to tell each of you that it starts and ends with you. Nah, I'm not talking out of the side of my mouth. Or do you want to live in fear every moment of your life? In my day, it was Sugar Ray Robinson. He could throw a punch and move around the ring with such confidence, like he'd forgotten himself. His quest usually was intense; but, he too took his share of punches. When you hunt, you are also hunted. You can't rationalize this stuff. You'll have fooled yourself if you think any of this fluff will make your life any better. Your very weakness is yours, mine own sanctuary. OK, maybe I'm harping a bit too much, boring you two. Sneak around, see where it gets you. Once that pain upstairs kicks in, it's time to see what's goin' on. This stuff is more important than any punch you'll ever land. OK boys, ciao."

Both kids looked at each other a bit shaken by the whole thing, and ramble their own way home as darkness blankets Dineen Park. Out the corner of his eye, Dewan spots his neighbor, an old man quietly minding his own business reading the Journal/Sentinel beneath the patio light, shooing away some loose neighborhood cat that just won't leave him alone.

"Oh, God, what was that dream about? For Christ's sake, for the first time that distant dream felt so real and so awfully important." Another day has begun, and old man Bogdanov brews a pot of coffee, bowls up a couple poached eggs while pouring a glass of freshly squeezed orange juice. Why those important dreams void into the great unknown bothers him. Why, a man with all his faculties cannot connect with something as important as, "Ah, there's the paper. Boy those Brewers," he mutters to himself, "with no pitching, what are they gonna do? How could Attanasio think this team would ever be competitive with that starting lineup? Ah, it's all about the money. Can't fill the seats forever with that starting rotation."

"Right, somehow they'll turn it around. I don't know about that. This season's over, that's for sure." Slowly he eats breakfast and finishes the paper as these two quietly curious cats focus wide eyed at his last piece of strawberry toast. "Here ya go, now share it you two. Oh God, gotta shower up before I get out to that garden. He puts on a CD of Samuel Barber's Adagio for Strings, Opus 11. "God, I can never get tired of this. So beautiful and peaceful for a dirge, melancholic yet uplifting, fearless." The raven's claws retract, the soul opens to something whole, anew, native in spirit. Eighteenth century Venetian composer Tomaso Albinoni stirs the sea and sand with effortless grace: the dead flows into life, the *pierrot* takes off his makeup and touches the burdens of a lost child. Everything moves with slow precision, the tick-toc of his baroque grandfather clock breaks the silence of the living room's barren silence.

Paul heads out to the garage to pick up his shovel to plant some junipers he is replacing in the front yard that have not recuperated from the drought of 2011. Paul also has a patch of blueberries and grape vines that he watches with the utmost care. His deceased wife, Janine, taught him long ago to revere nature's many splendid things such as the smell of freshly dug up dirt, slugs motionlessly lying in the pile, the ants flooding the yard. Nature calls only if you are there in her presence to listen to her open secrets, that you too, are hers no matter how much you may want to hide from her pathless chant.

He shakes off the dirt from the roots of the dead shrubs, planting and replacing them with the new junipers that blend in beautifully with the line of statuesque arborvitaes standing erect against the shaded property line of his yard. Cucumbers and zucchini are already popping up in the soft June sun. Midday approaches, the sun awakened, Paul beaten by its tireless wrath, steps back into the house to take a break from its virile prowess. Barnard waits for him in patient silence as he steps into his office to take a breather.

Barnard can sit upon his master's lap for hours as both look outside, the cars methodically make their way down Roosevelt Road, Porgy and Bess pour out through the Bose speakers, as the majestic sugar and crimson maples along the street flutter about in ominous unity. Little Jalen scoots about on his old Big Wheels while his mother looks on, taking down her wash. To beat the busy time of children getting out of school, Paul grabs his backpack to pick up some Coconut milk, walnuts, and pasta to make some lasagna for later on. For a man his age, Paul still can get around. Many of his friends do not keep in touch with him anymore. He used to think that it was something he may have said or imposed upon them in some way or other, but has realized over the years that he was going to say or do what he needed to. If the other took offense that was alright.

There is aloneness in life no matter how one needs to be consoled. To stand on one's feet to let his feeling be heard is not some idle game or an attempt to avoid getting hurt. It really is about taking responsibility for one's own matters and showing a presence that caters to the moment without deceiving or allowing the other to go on with his ebullient front. Pick 'n' Save is always busy but is it not very near to his home. The long walk does him good, especially with summer approaching. He's still got his International Harvester Scout to get him through the rainy days and dire cold weather when the winter roars in.

"All those craft beers," he muses as he wanders about the store, "ah, look at that, Widmer 'Killer Devil Brown Ale. Cool, gotta try that out. Hmm, from Oregon of all places. Bunch of hippies. Looks good. Good Lord if I could go for that Mescal/ Tequila combo again. Na, hands off. I've had my fill of that crap." He pops the six pack into his cart and looks for the ricotta and mozzarella cheese. Now off to the Swiss Chard, and onions, great. "The noodles are in aisle 13 as I remember. Yeah, yeah, there they are."

He goes to the fast lane, pays for the beverages and food, and makes his way out the front door. As he arrives at home, he runs into youths getting off the bus as school is out. It is amazing to see that the students are so tied up in their own worlds, that the old people like him are essentially non-existent, transparent. Old age has become a time for contemplation and becoming more of someone who spends his time away from the public. It is not that he has to be upbeat and happy like he was as a young man, but the ghosts have not left, spurring on his inescapable loneliness, a bugbear he cannot ignore. Not that he cannot handle dealing with that worrisome cocoon every now and again; however, its lugubrious presence simply will not leave him alone.

After Paul puts away all the groceries, he goes out to check on the shrubs. The water has soaked through. So he carefully pours in the dirt and packs it in with his feet.

"Hey, quick come over here son. Let me put some pressure on that. Come quick over here to the sink."

"I can't be here, sir."

"Look, tell your father you've gotta see a doctor. I think stitches are needed. Now hold still."

"What's that?"

"Neosporin, it's a disinfectant. Now just wait (he closes the wound up with a butterfly bandage). What happened?"

"Never-mind?"

"Oh, so now we're gonna play that game?"

"Hey, what are you doing with Isaac?"

"He took care of a cut on my finger, father."

"Yeah, I think you should have it looked at it. It's a pretty deep cut."

"Sir, if you don't mind, we will take care of it from here on out."

"Your neighbor, that bully George pushed me to the ground where I cut myself on a piece of glass."

"What is wrong with you people? We just want to live in the presence of God. And, all you people do is push us around."

"When was the last time you have spoken to anyone who didn't go along with your Orthodox beliefs?"

"You mean Chassidim?"

"OK, Chasidim."

"Start by learning something about us. Do you like to read?"

"My eyes willing."

"Sholem Aleichem wrote some stories that *Fiddler on the Roof* was based on. Isaac Bashevis Singer was a Nobel laureate: *Crown of Feathers* is a starting point. And, if I were you, don't expect us to socialize with you. Now if you'll excuse us."

"I've lived here for almost forty years. You think I don't know that? Yeah, I know you guys have your reasons for your reclusive nature. But don't tell me it's all about racial hatred. Look at your child, Isaac. He's what? Seven, eight years old? No kid knows your people's plight. Sure, they're gonna pick on him, because look at him, he's different: like he's wearing a sign on his back that says, kick me."

"Alright that's enough Sir. Look, all we ask is that you leave him alone."

"I think you and I should get our flag football teams together to show our true colors."

"What are you talking about? We don't have time for all that nonsense. We are followers of God, pure and simple."

"Well, if we wear the flags of our little groups at least we will know what team we are on, what we stand for."

"Come on Isaac, let this old fool rot in his bitter mind."

"*Shalom.*"

Before Paul walks back in the house to prepare his supper, he takes a walk back to the garden and quickly weeds it. Upon opening the door, Barnard and Sheba stretch out into the yard, prancing around it without making a sound. Perhaps this precise silent movement is the mystery that has drawn Paul towards his new roommates.

Chapter Four

A Little Rain Never Hurt Anybody

"Jasmine, I was wondering if you could get out of the house for the day. I've got clients coming over to talk about their insurance options, the whole shebang—I know, boring stuff, right? Your mother's gotta make a living. Your father's been out of the picture for a long time. Without this money coming in we wouldn't be living in this slice of heaven, Now Shoo! Now Jazz. I mean it: I don't have any time for your petty rants."

"It might rain today."

"I know. "

"So-oh, why don't you go over to the Mid-Town Center. Surely you can find one of your friends to tag along—I mean, what else are you gonna do on a day like this?"

"Sleep."

"More like clean that mess of a place you call your bedroom."

"Alright, just let me get dressed; and I'll be out of here before you know it."

"Bring an umbrella. I don't want you coming down with a cold or anything like that missy." Young and dispirited Jasmine has found that with all the time she has on her hands she can feel those deep, deep thoughts creep in. With all the methods she and her mother have worked on to keep her life busy, it has not necessarily been able to keep her mind at ease.

"Grandma always says that life will get better—just do what you need to do now in school is to make sure that you will have positive opportunities that you will cherish when you graduate from college."

"College?"

Jasmine has not yet gotten to high school; and, she was held back in kindergarten. Her mother has been told that poor little Jazz did not quite actively participate with her teacher and classmates: she became withdrawn from everyone around her. Funny, even all these years later, she still has that shy stream of indiscriminate emotions rushing through her, that things really haven't changed except her awareness as a child growing into her mother's secret adult world.

Her father, a genuinely nice man, wandered from one job to the next; and, without courting alcohol or drugs, Manny simply drifted north off the beaten track to Cadott, Wisconsin, leaving the family life behind without really opening up to his wife about it: "Look, I know all you think I am a bum; but, hey, I can't even seem to find anything to get hooked on much less sex." Lifeless and meandering into the north woods has allowed him to get a job at a local diner that serves low-end cuisine that everyone can agree is not worth the four dollars and 97 cents hamburger plate combo, (along with fries, and a coke) will fetch. Yet, an assembly line job it is, providing him with the meager earnings to get out into the wild world of northwestern Wisconsin, a wild that is quietly drifting away as more everyday people picnic in Cadott's parks and woodlands.

During the night, he moonlights as a bartender at the same establishment. Her mother believes that living up north gives *lazy Manny* the chance to eventually drift away into oblivion when everything falls apart. Not that Manny being Manny is completely wrong. There have been those eerie moments late in the evening when Jasmine would glance over at her mother as that lost look would reveal itself. It seems that even though her mother has become a successful insurance sales agent, something hidden lingers very close to the surface.

A once aspiring flutist championing the greatness of the late Jeanne-Pierre Rampal, Jasmine has tried desperately to make a go of it; but, with each day of band practice for the upcoming football season, the youth has her doubts. She practices her mother's favorite, Bouree, working some life into it, that can at times bring smiles to her number one fan. After a quick shower, Jasmine quickly dresses in her black tights and her copper colored Uggs, grabbing an orange juice and a piece of toast, and tries to remember what she forgot.

"Oh yeah, that's right.," Jazz grabs her iPOD, a silver windbreaker and umbrella as she heads out the door. Quickly she texts her friend Danelle to meet her over at J-Bees, popping her umbrella as the cool June sprinkles turn into a steady flow of rain. The dampness can be sometimes overwhelming as she determinedly pushes forward making sure her prized rustic Uggs steer clear of the water puddles. Mid-Town is nearly a two mile walk; and, Jasmine has learned to enjoy the exercise after her bike was stolen at school a year ago. "No worries:" even her mother admires the fact that Jasmine has not been so tied to the car culture that many of her friends have learned to use to their advantage. "Hey, the bus is running. So why sweat it?" (She steps onto the oncoming bus).

Several years' back Mrs. Padilla has become committed to not being tied down to a car that ultimately ruins the environment in multiple ways, and somehow young Jasmine has quietly stepped in tune with her mother: the bus is not a degrading thing. It may take a longer time to get to the mall; but, the teen-ager does get there safely and quite comfortably. She has always known that no matter how much she wants to, her tireless quest to fit in, to become an integral part of her friend's lives, she is ultimately alone. No matter how cool it is to become part of her friends' worlds, she has to come home, weigh those experiences, and decide if she should become a part of their popular or even less-than-popular decisions.

She keeps these things to herself because the young adolescent feels these ranges of emotions away from the school and her outings to school events. They are purely of the time she spends away from everyone, including her mother, at the library or in her bedroom. Competitiveness has never been her central mantra mainly because she only practices the flute to join the marching band upon entering high school at Milwaukee Washington. Her mother has reminded her that a very small percentage of athletes ever go on to use athletics as a stepping stone to pay for their tuition, that possibly a musician with solid academics can acquire both a scholarship and financial aid package. The house payments and expenses are all she is able to cover. So, a complete free ride through college will never be an option at the Padilla residence.

Since she is under-aged to work, Jasmine spends a lot of time with her friends at the Mall. However, with limited cash, she spends most of her time on the cell phone or playing video games. Her mother feels that those video games are the same time consuming activities that pop music was in her day. Any way you slice it, the array of games and their cultures provide an escape from an all-too-often cruel reminder of the world as it is for persons of any age.

Traffic is light as the midday rain continues with the sounds of water rushing off the cars with a measured evenness. Perhaps high school will be better than junior high: the dire realties pointed at Jasmine by certain girl cliques have made life at times unbearable. Just getting up for school at times has been a major task. Of course, Jasmine, dares not to let anyone know about how she feels about it. Why would she want to hear some other pragmatic response to cure her ills? After all, the whole process of making friends has been a hard pill to swallow. Ah, but one must push on if one is to succeed. Jasmine, a soft and articulate soul knows this. But, so far, not much has worked for her. To a fourteen year -old, Rampal classics are a hard sell: boys, Chris Brown, and a late night out at the Mall are more to her liking.

As her mother has said many a time, "nothing comes easy. You have to work at school to eventually make something of yourself. Where are your friends gonna be when all the fun times are gone and nobody's around to pick up the pieces?"

Everything's so regimented, so tied into some payday of sorts. Maybe she will find a man with a beautiful smile that will come into her life and; bam, a world of possibilities will open her worlds to new heights. All these disjointed thoughts spin in her head as she passes the Albright United Methodist Church at 56Th and Capitol Drive. Just a bit northwest of here lies Mid-Town Mall: First Starbucks then Pick 'n Save. Ahead is the outdoor Mall where Jasmine spends much of her free time. What makes this a bit different is that she has taken the initiative to head over to Mid-Town without anyone else.

Things come into focus much clearer when she walks to the Mall. Everything seems to move in slow motion as she steps off the bus. No wonder why a driver's license is such a big thing to a teen. Not only is it an entitlement into adulthood, it also broadens a person's perspective of the world. In just over an hour, she could attend a Badger football game. To the south, Chicago's big shoulders reside on the Great Lake's southwestern shores. Lord only knows what the youth has considered doing by carrying the Windy City squarely upon her shoulders.

"Danelle, what's up?"

"Hah? Jasmine, yeah, I, well I—yeah, I got your message but I'm sorry. But, but, like ye-ah, Tom's comin' over. Can't keep 'm off me. We got the house to ourselves, besides it's raining out and all. Sorry babe."

"Oh, that's alright. There's not much going on over here anyway. It's like I got the whole place to myself."

"See ya around girl."

"You too, Danelle. Tell Tommy I can't wait to hear about his baseball—that league stuff and all."

"Gotta go, girl, m'bye."

She wanders into Game Shop, peaks into Nails Today, nothing … Just down the way is Rainbow. "Oh, there it is! 'No Way'! In all its big blue colors—with my bleached jeans, it would be so-oh cool. $21.99 H-m-n. I'd have to clean up the whole house three times to buy that." Jazz's birthday's right around the corner. "I've gotta get mom over here." What is this empty feeling that has quietly pursued her hollow being since she could remember? Her mother always tells Jasmine how difficult it was to be an adult: that she could never relive her years of youth once they have disappeared, "so you must enjoy them while you can."

"Lord, Jesus, could you take me from this God Forsaken place"—that message that comes and goes with eerie frequency—you know, all those statements of the unfortunates, the crazies: the bipolar's, schizo's, and all those *weirdo soft poets* that nobody wants anything to do with—the everyday order of things. Does anything make sense? Ah, the angst of a budding teenage intellectual: surely, everything will click eventually. She caresses a short cut black and white dress with long, snug ashen chiffon sleeves all for $19.99. She has been drawn to the dress now that many of her friends are spending more time with their beaus while she is setting herself up to tackle geometry and physics.

Even though the prices are reasonable she cannot quite grasp how she will ever convince her mom to buy something as risqué and free -spirited as the inexpensive clothing this store offers to the public. With nothing

to do she wanders down 57Th Street over to Culver's to get an ice cream.
"Hey! Watch out where you're going!"

"I'm sorry, I didn't see you. I was—thinking about something I'm currently working on

Here, I'll get the door for you—my name is Damon; and, you're?"

"Jasmine."

"Jasmine? Pretty name, yeah, like some sort of aroma from a beautiful flower."

"Thanks."

"Hey, where are you going?"

"To get some custard: Now if you don't mind."

"You know, I know this sounds stupid, but-but, ah, I was wondering if you would want to go out with me."

"How old are you, sir?"

"Sir? Well, I've never been called that before."

"You haven't answered my question."

"What? I yeah, right, I'm seventeen."

"I think you're a little too old for me."

"Well, if that's how you feel about it; or, maybe you're just plain scared."

"Scared? It's not like you can't hurt me seriously, ruin my life, you know?"

"Well, if that's what you want."

"Hey, where are you going?"

"Where do you think?"

"Home?"

"Where else?"

"Come on, have some custard with me. I mean, that's if you'd want to?"

"You know that you have the most beautiful smile, beautiful white teeth—green eyes like the green, grass." A real poet: that is the beautifully present Damon.

"Would you like to take a walk with me after we get done here?"

"Nah, I've got a car—just got out of work from J-Bees."

"So, what do you like to do?"

"Anything but play the flute. It's not as easy as it looks."

"Yeah, like a basketball Jones leaping up to steal the ball in mid-air from a fast-break pass."

"I guess."

"Not much into B-ball, I'm an artist. I mean, I'll play with the guys, but graphic design, that's where I really got it together."

"Really?"

"Yeah, really. What, do think I'm lyin'?"

"No, it's just that—I don't know. I think you just want me to, to go along with you, ya know?"

"What, like steal your soul?"

"Yeah, like kinda have your way with me, then leave."

"You think every guy's like that?"

"I'm not saying that. It's just that, that I really don't know who you are; and, out of the blue you wanna take me out, fourteen-year-old Jazz."

"Look I don't know why I am attracted to you; but, boom, like that you stole the show: you can just say 'no' if that's what you want."

"I'm not saying that; but, yeah, I'm kinda afraid. Hell yeah, ya know?"

"Look, I'll just go—I mean ice cream is no big deal … OK, I'll have a custard sundae."

"Now don't you—I'll go along with that too … Two vanilla custard sundaes … Thanks. Could we sit over there?"

"I thought you were just afraid of me because—you know— I'm black."

"No. You're quite attractive. Not even my mother could deny that. It's just that, well, nothing ever seems right—everything, I mean all my thoughts just spin around in my head like a top at a million miles an hour—never stops. I know it's me; but, Damon nothing's ever right no matter how hard I try to make things better."

"A philosopher?"

"No. I think you know what I'm trying to say."

"Just say it."

"Nothing's gonna work out. It hasn't when I was just a child; and, it isn't now—like my mom tries to keep me on this path because dad was such a mess."

"It's like I'm trying to get away from everyone, my cousins and friends—they don't care about me—all they want is for me to go along with them. The more time I spend with them, the less I want anything to do with them. I know it's me; but, what can ya do?"

"That's pretty heavy shit."

"You can leave right now—not even you can keep my mouth shut. Like, like, here I am and the floodgate's open."

"Hey, would you take it easy? We just met. It's not like we're getting married tomorrow. Relax, like. Need a ride home?"

"That's cool, but don't tell me what I can talk to you about. I'm so-oh tired of that."

"I can always take off and leave you alone."

"Why do you guys always gotta be on top of everything—I mean at school, it's your football, your basketball—girls' sports are not as important."

"You think I don't know that? I was a geek graphic designer that wanted to paint Malcolm X on canvass. I mean expressing the softness in the hardened man. You can't do that in writing. That's what I'm about. Besides, do you really think all us dudes are on top of everything? Shit, we go along a lot like you probably do. Pretend, pretend—to make it through another day. I don't want no trouble with some of dem dudes who can really make my life hell. I just go along with the stuff to get on wid my own life on my own time. For real. See this t-shirt? One of my instructors designed it—it's about Black Power startin' from the streets and workin' their way up. You can't tell me your folks had it tougher than us. And, this goes back to slave dayz. Know what I'm sayin'? A long, long fuck of a time."

"I can't tell you what it's been like for you; but, I don't think too many people are really happy. Yeah, my mother's done alright, she went to get her Master's Degree right over there goin' to night school at Concordia. I feel like it's all about bein' quiet about things and getting things done: kind a like school. *Don't make any waves.* My dad's tryin' to take pictures of black bears up north. Never partied or caused trouble. He just, like my mom says, isn't goin' for everything everybody else is doin'."

"Kind of his own person?"

"Yeah, but not really. Dad never wanted this. He's college educated, worked at Target as some kind of manager when I was little; but, it just didn't work out. Two years ago, he moved up north—we've seen where he works—he doesn't care about us Damon. It's like I've never been born— he's started a new life for himself; so, it's sort like I'm on my own."

"Me too: My mom works two crappy jobs and I take care of everything around the house. My older brother ran drugs— became a snitch to stay out of jail as much as he could. Now, he could be dead for all I know.

Haven't heard from him in a couple years. Ma of course says nothing. But, I know it's gotta hurt her a whole lot. Jimmy was pretty cool. He never hurt nobody. Ah, you know—there ain't no good paying factory jobs for people like me who just want to work to start a family—everything's a game. I even see it in the eyes of the important people on the news: The President, people like that. You're right, we're all just tryin' to stay out of trouble. Not even that can save us. Just hopin' to be left alone ain't gonna cut it either."

"Could we get going? It's so windy that my umbrella will be torn to shreds if we stand out here much longer. So, where is your car?"

"See that dark brown Civic over there? Let's do it."

"Pretty cool."

"Yeah, I've been workin' here for almost two years. The manager says I could become the receiving manager after ole' Bill retires next year. Hey, for now there's not a whole lot else goin' on 'round here. I'll probably take her up on it. After you."

"Why, thank you Damon."

"No problem. Oh, and art school—the staff over at True Skool—hip hop, the fine arts, events, you name it. And, the staff—like they got real skills—for real."

"I never heard about this place. Where is it?"

"It's over at 48[Th] and Fon du Lac. Mostly black and Hispanic— but, yeah, there's some whites and Asian dudes, lotta girls. You'd really like it. Whenever you wanna go, you just say the word."

"Let's just get used to each other first before we do everything together."

"Shy's cool. But you gotta get out there."

"Like my ma always say"—"It's a lot easier doin' these things when you're young. When you're old, ya got too much goin' on to chill wid the crew."

"Responsibilities fall in your lap, ya know, whether you like it or not."

"My mom says school is more challenging than work. It's just that deadlines must be met with good results; and, you need to be as positive and courteous to everyone even if others do not deserve it."

"Yeah, that's sort of the thing that bothers me. But, hey, I don't want to walk over people to get my way. I want to bring solid skills to a company that will pay me by what I can offer 'em, not have to kiss up to get what I want."

"I live over at 57[Th] and Burleigh, right on the corner."

"Alright, let's hit it." Quietly they make their two mile ride without saying another word. Jasmine puts her cell phone number on Damon's iPhone. Hesitantly, she reaches over to give Damon a soft kiss; and, waves good-bye. "Call me tomorrow afternoon if you have any time."

"Sure, after work I'll give a call, say 5 o'clock?"

"Wonderful. I'll be waiting for your call. Love you." Those last two words strained off her tepid lips as she scoots up to the front door. Rarely would she have to ever use those words even with her mother around. "Love You" sort of brings a connectedness to her bubbled world where everyone always seems to be at arm's length. Jazz does not know what to make of her first love interest, Damon. She does not even know what his last name is or where he lives. The inner city does not frighten her because it has brought some of its graying qualities within blocks of her neighborhood. Whatever it was about him, Jasmine feels that light optimism only two yearning hearts can wield. Maybe, just maybe she can be truly happy. She pays heed to one of her mother's many mantras, "just wait and see."

"Oh hi, Mrs. Bartusek."

"Well, look. If it isn't our little queen of academia. Kinda crappy out there isn't it, walking home through the drizzle and all."

"Nah, I got a ride home from a friend I met up at the mall."

"Was that Danelle?"

"Yeah, we met up there 'cause her mom let her use the car." "Well that's good. Genie and I were talking over old times. I'm sure it would bore you to no end. We're having some pinot noire Genie here brought back with her from California. Would you like to have some Sprite—Coke?"

"Sure, but I want to take it with me to the room while I practice my flute."

"I didn't know you had the zeal to take on such a task girl. Although I like your enthusiasm. Mrs. Bartusek and I will try to keep things quiet down here as you practice."

"OK. What are we having to eat tonight mom?"

"Tofu and eggplant lasagna along with salad and garlic bread—I've already eaten but there are leftovers in the 'fridge. Grab some and take it with you."

"I will. Nice to see you Mrs. Bartusek. I haven't seen you in a while, not since, since—."

"Yes, it has been over a year now. With my kids and Ray at home, there's never a dull moment. So, as I was saying, Ray's mind is on work 24/7; and, this chick is not sitting around waiting for her man to see the light."

"Look, I know a beautiful woman such as you needs to be comforted by her husband. Why don't you go to him to talk about it?"

"I have on many occasions. He just puts things off, like he's in his own little world and nothing will pull him out of it. So, Genie here takes her long raven hair to the bars for a little love and devotion even if it comes from some stranger."

"You're an adult, Genie. You don't have to drag me into your seething little trysts. Just do what you have to do."

"Really? All this gossip bores an old girl like me. Tom brings me comfort. I've been secretly dating him for almost a year now. Jasmine knows nothing about him; but this weekend I've decided to invite him over for dinner. He has two children a little younger than her; but he's agreed that this is a good way to break the ice. Have an informal barbeque out back on Sunday afternoon; and, just talk—see how things go."

"Well, that all sounds wonderful. But seriously, Alice, if I hear one more *keep it to yourself* ' blurt out of your mouth, I swear you won't be seeing me for a long, long time."

"The whole world doesn't revolve around you either missy. Besides, if I don't want to hear about your affairs, I don't have to."

"Right, it's your house, I understand."

"No, that's not it. I try to get rid of my own little problems so I don't feel so anxiety-ridden and listless all the time. I'm tired of going through the motions and having to listen to how sexy and smitten you are with all those hard bodies that snake their way into your life."

"Well, I'm sorry you feel that way. Just when I thought, we were going to patch things up. Ta-ta, and all that sort of thing. By the by, if you hear from your ex-, tell him I'm available, that is if he wants—."

"Go! Take your petite little ass elsewhere you, you h-m-ah-h-m-n, you loathsome cunt."

"That's not nice. I'm gonna freshen up a bit after I go to the bathroom. Then we'll sit down and talk like civilized adults."

"Alright deary (*I love to hear what she's gonna dump in my lap after she gets off the pot*)."

Moments later Jasmine finds her mother quietly eating a bowl of ice cream for dessert as Double Jeopardy wraps its evening show.

"So, how was your practice session?"

"It was OK. It's just that it's so hard to play well with passion all the time. That's what I tried to work on in junior high: consistency and to play with emotion. I learned that last semester. Now I want to play more difficult material, to hit the highs and lows with precision while I mix the middle range with those extremes. It's not so easy mom."

"I never played an instrument; however, I cleaned homes and attended night school to hold onto this house. Yeah, I was scared alright. God, I had no idea what was going to work from one day to the next. But I stuck with it. Jazz, I didn't start out with a steady clientele base. I thought of quitting thousands of times; but what were my options? Not many, right? I hate what grampa said to you when things were going wrong, *you gotta do what you gotta do.* At some point I had to put the cleaning operation behind me and start selling car insurance; and, when that clicked, then home owner's insurance came along. It's not like I'm a natural at this stuff. Just because I passed the tests did not mean I was going to make it as an insurance agent. I had to accept the fact that I was starting over and would be competing against agents who've had many years of experience—it's a scary proposition. But you too have your own road to follow. Your friends will all pull you from many different directions, some you'll not be comfortable with—you have to make the decisions that work best for you. Now I know that many of your friends have begun dating. When the time comes for you to go out with a guy, you are going to have to decide if he's right for you. Now as much as I'd like to think that I know what is best for you. I don't."

"But mom, do we have to talk about this again?"

"Now just hear me out: intimacy is not just about sex. It also is about what is going on in your life from one moment to the next. You will have to decide whether your boyfriend makes you happy. I can tell you one thing. The pangs of hurt are telling you to evaluate the relationship."

"It's not like you have been dating anyone since dad left."

"I know, I know. But I have gone to lunch with dates: none of 'em have worked out. I keep all that stuff to myself until I feel good and ready to talk to you about it. If the relationship dies hard, at least I didn't bring that stuff into your life."

"OK, can I have some ice cream now?"

"Under one condition, if you wash the dishes after you finish up. Now, I've cleaned all the pots and pans; so, there shouldn't be much left for you to do. I've gotta get over to the downtown office to drop off some important client information at the break of dawn; so, I need to get some quality sleep; and, tomorrow, I've got to run something by you if you don't mind. I would like to talk to you around seven if that is OK with you; like, you don't have anything planned for tomorrow evening, do you?"

"Nah, I'll be here."

"Great, good night little princess." Alice gives her a quick peck on the cheek and gets ready for bed.

"Try to make it home a little earlier—your mother wants to talk to you here at the dinner table. I know it's just leftovers, but you know how your mother and lasagna just sort of hit it off."

"Yeah, I know. But it's summer; and—you know, I'm finally getting to see people from the city besides just my school friends."

"I know, I know. But you must realize that when things get tough your old mother here will be the only person around for you… the world's not like school dear. People, well, many of us just want things our way and don't really care who it affects."

"Whatever."

"No, I mean it Jazz."

"School is just a part of your life—you still have to live with people who may not necessarily march to the tune of your own drum, Understand?"

"I guess; but ma, I just met this guy, yeah he's a senior, I know all that—but look what happened to you and dad."

"You waited all this time to tell me about your new beau, a Senior? You're gonna run him by me real soon. Don't need some mistake to mess with my child."

"And, about your father: believe me, I know. There was a time when your father really meant well; then, something just went blank—he, well you know, I think he lost his will to go on. I mean we all want things to go our way right? Well dad lost all hope in his ability to freely and openly love me and you."

"Mom, like this guy at school has this tattoo on his arm, like it says "Respect before loyalty." Is that what you are trying to say?"

"Girl, one day you will be with the man of your dreams … there are some things that he needs to face about himself that has nothing to do with you. What I am trying to say is that life is little less clear than anyone can explain to you or me for that matter, especially when you bring somebody new into your life. There will be things about you that you will have to bear all by yourself because, because many times people—your friends— may not want to hear about your plight—they got their own issues."

"Sounds like a broken record mom. We just talked about this. You think I don't know what's going on around me, like, like who does anyone really know?"

"I can't disagree with you there my brilliant tragedian. But honey, I can't wish away all the bad things you will encounter. Whatever cross you will have to bear you can talk to me about. I know, it's your boring, controlling mother. Really Jasmine, I am here for you. Some things are not kosher for you to talk about openly with your friends. Look, I wish I could tell you that I am crazy and I just don't know what I am talking about. It's not as simple as all that. Believe me, I wish to God it was.

Your father and I have already been divorced for years. Now I'm not going to say it was a mistake that we ever got married. We had you, we had plans to build a house out in south Waukesha. But it all just fell apart. God, he is such a beautiful man; but his heart was just not in it. I think he still is trying to make some sense out of his life. You can't have the answers for other people. Manuel just shut down from everyone—a-a-and he really bottomed out. I don't know what to tellya."

"Mom, dad could speak his mind."

"That's what I'm talking about. It's not a perfect world. No matter where you go, some have it easier than others, or so it seems. Not everything's black and white."

"So, why bother?"

"What's that supposed to mean?"

"Like, like no matter what I try to do somebody can come along and take it all away from me no matter how hard I try."

"Your mother didn't raise you to be a defeatist."

"Why not? It's all bullshit anyway."

"I will not hear any of it—it all depends on how you look at things."

"Whatever."

"I love you—you know your mother wants to see you happy— I'm here for you no matter what."

"I know. See ya tomorrow."

"Say, where did Mrs. Bartusek go?"

"Mrs. Bartuzek's gone, Jazz. Her husband called her and she had to leave. No, that's not it. Mrs. Bartusek and your mother had a war of words. She's been in there a goodly amount of time. We'll try to patch thing up when she pulls her rear out of there."

"But mom; you were such good friends."

"Yeah, well, this wasn't an isolated incident. Mrs. Bartusek wanted me to become more of a friend than I was willing to be there for her. What I am trying to say is that I enjoyed her company but she was asking me to take her side on something of which I honestly didn't want to talk to her about. Ultimately, I don't think we are all that unique. I just don't want to get involved with her ideas of right and wrong when it comes to her family and her own concept of having a solid relationship with her husband. That ball does not belong in my court, Jazz; and, she wanted to draw me into her inner circle. Besides, her father doesn't even call her anymore. It's hard to be everything for her, Jasmine. Ah, that's enough. Now, let's just drop it."

"I'm sorry I've taken so long Alice; but, really I've got to get a going. My boyfriend and I have something important to talk about; and perhaps I'll get hold of you sometime soon and we can have lunch together." ...

"M-bye, Jasmine."

"Not so fast woman. Couldn't you just hang around a bit longer so we could catch up on each other's lives a bit. It's been a long time since I've seen you—I've got some wine from a vintner up the road: your fave, Pinot Noire."

"Alright, but just for a few minutes. I really want to talk to Paul about some things."

"I won't keep you lovebirds away too long. I just want see what's going on with you: no telling when our paths will cross, with my busy life and all; oh, and, let's not forget your jaded love life."

"Oh yeah, where do I start?"

Chapter Five

Reminiscing about the Good Ole' Days

"Oh, don't give me that look. I've gotta hit the sack soon enough anyway. A little talk with a glass of wine'll help me with my little beddy bye."

"Could you pour me some of that pinot noir?"

"Grab a cup on the counter. There you go. Anyhow, you know I found some Absinthe down at the liquor store, with some opened Iron Horse perched behind some burgundies. Just like the old days."

"I'll stick to my pinot noir. Want to know what the beach is like?"

"I've been to San Francisco and Carmel."

"No, like Santa Monica, the haze hanging over the ocean, sort of like a hazy fog."

"Nobody's ever stopped you before."

"Well, I can tell you the water's cold—the Pacific isn't all that peaceful. But that's not the main deal. Here we are walking past some British pub on Third Street, heading toward the Pier with our kids; and, like you cannot help but feel in tune with that Blue, Blue Sky. Anyway, here's LA's seedy populous hanging out below the clouds, makes you just want to turn around and head back to Sea World; but, something churns inside—so we go forward. Ah, but right there to our left alongside the building in the shade sits a woman; God, she really isn't that bad looking but the sun has done a number on her—motioning to her open wrinkled up brown bag which has few coins in it—and, no, don't even bother asking. Yeah, that's right, the hubby wouldn't give her anything. So, we just mosey on like nothing's happened. God, I find that so white; so-oh pretentious you know?"

"Anyway, two blocks down we get to the corner of Third Street and Ocean Drive, so swank, California's elite must hang out at that hotel/restaurant. That vast blue skyline cannot elude you—with that California sun cutting right through your sun block like, like you've never put any on. Anyway, we wander into the sight of this tall, lean Black dude, wearing girl's slippers half the size of his humungous feet, dragging his sullen temperament across Ocean Drive—the light's green, everyone's giving him the horn, but like some zombie, he shuffles one lethargic foot in front of the other—hey, he's got all day, right? So, what are all these people in such a hurry for? Can't they see the majestic resonance in those statuesque Palm trees across the way ready to shower him with their shaded alms after he crosses? So those busied drivers will have to sit through one more stop light? Don't they know that this is California, the land of possibilities? Just kidding honey."

"You always have been theatrical in the way you talk about things."

"I was just trying to tie in what you and your daughter were talking about. Your little one's growing up fast."

"Yeah well, I just don't want her to get the idea that she can take the oeuvre of becoming a waif and can take advantage of my simpler nature."

"Your eldest daughter, she's not doin' so bad, now, is she? Hey now, smile, you should be happy she's got a beau. "My son Jeffrey won't even leave the house. After school gets out, he's at home in his room doing his homework. I should be thankful right, can't pry him out of that room—he's not running with the gangs and getting high on meth, but his shyness pangs me.

It's like he can't shed it. It just follows him from one day to the next. But, I really don't see any difference between his popular younger sister, J anie prancing around acting like the world shines solely on her and that preppy little jock boyfriend of hers. That will all come crashing when he leaves."

"You know how horrible those years were for us, Genie? What makes your kids any different? There comes a time when all that veiled secrecy comes pouring out, and try as you might, there's nothing you can do or say to stop it, or to ease the pain."

"I know. It's not that I will even try to stop it after all those years of therapy and marriage counseling. Everything falls apart."

"By the way that reminds me: a friend of mine told me that Norm caught you and her friend in your own bed together a while back."

"Yeah, so?"

"So? Norm's not the kind of guy that swings that way. He's not one who's gonna put up with a roll in the hay, especially one he's walked in on. Besides, ya did it in your own home with your kids around and everything."

"Would you ease off the gas? The kids were at school and Norm lied about going on a business trip to Houston. Besides, our whole relationship has been sort of non-existent for years."

"How could you do that to him—I mean I know you two were having your problems; but, Genie you two have been married for what, has it been fifteen, yes, fifteen years?"

"Makes you feel a bit better when someone else has fallen off the horse, doesn't it?"

"Now what made you think that?"

"Oh, I don't know. Maybe it's the fact that you still think I bedded your dear sweet first love David Cardinal."

"You think I am so vain as to carry that crap around for all these years?"

"Yep."

"Genie Bartusek, you know we all called you the queen of crabs."

"I can't deny I passed it around a bit; but, did your boyfriend ever come to you with that problem because of me?"

"No."

"Well alrighty then, there you have it."

"What?"

"I never touched David. Can't say I've never thought about it. Yeah, smokin' hot. It's just sex, Alice."

"God, is that all can you think of ? What about Norman and his feelings? That it's just sex; and, whatever you do can be explained away with a simple 'yeah you know, it's just sex'. Like Norm is some mindless piece of meat that needs to be kept at a distance so you can take care of your own seedy needs."

"The relationship's been dead for a long time now, Alice."

"You serious?"

"Christ, Alice, I have moved out of the house over three months ago. And, yeah, you got it. He's filed for separation several weeks prior to my leaving him: divorce is right around the corner."

"You're not seeing that guy anymore?"

"Jack, Trudy's brother, no; but I have met this wonderfully sweet man from the Falls. We've moved in together last month although I still keep my apartment. Gotta have my independence Alice."

"What about the kids?"

"After over two years of marriage counseling and our silent weekends they had a pretty good idea things were not going to work out."

"Have you talked with the children?"

"They know I'm not coming back if that's what you mean. Our lawyers are talking about divorce papers—irreconcilable differences. Me and Jack, you know that changed everything, allegedly anyway. Yeah, Norm wants to raise the kids, like he's done any of that since we've been married."

"I've never knew love until I held Jasmine's young hand. How can you just walk away from all that?"

"I'll tell you how. We slept in the same beds but we couldn't even hold each other. Forget the sex even though it's been a "no-no" forever … I love my kids but it's been over for a long, long time. The, how can I say this, no this is how it is—like I was able to quit my Assistant Manager job that I hated with a passion, like this straight-laced young man walked into the store; and, yeah love bloomed. He built us a home and we welcomed three beautiful children into the neighborhood over the past fifteen years. Beautiful, charming little Allyson I will watch over closely. Yes, all three are getting used to not having their 'old lady' around anymore but I will continue to help Allyson with her spelling and reading"—

"That little literary thing in you: yeah, I can see little Allyson becoming the next Genie Bartusek."

"Nah, she's just getting her feet wet. Let's face it, Alice, we all must scratch and kick every inch of the way"—

"At least until Norman Bartusek walked through the front door."

"I cheated every inch of my being by walking down the aisle with him; but, are you gonna sit there and tell me that you wouldn't have taken that calling card if you were presented it?

Alice, we've slept in separate beds for years. That's something this woman's not gonna put up with as long as I have my say."

"You think I just threw in the towel with Manny? No. But, he couldn't get from point A to point B. So, I had to hold onto the house. You know he only makes a two hundred-dollar monthly alimony payment for his own flesh and blood."

"Who says the way we do things creates a better world for anyone, much less our own families?"

"I don't want to end up on the streets like those poor souls that stare at me as I cut through the park. You think I want to end up like that zig-zagging around everyone just to make sure that Jasmine and I are safe for at least the time being?"

"In counseling I brought up the issue of Norm's employment situation at Johnson Controls. He never gave me a straight answer: always stating that everything in the Engineering Department is fine; besides, this is his concern, why should I worry about it? Right. If he believes that there is anything I need to know, he'll let me know. I can't change him, Alice. He's his own person. He's ruled by his Fears: I swear to God I can't do this anymore—just dragging along, wishing I could just drift into my next life."

"Nobody wants to hear all that, Genie. Some things you're just gonna have to settle on your own. And, don't tell me I have no idea what you're talking about. I mean, who brought all this on miss priss?"

"Oh, thank you for sharing sweetheart. Why not just get lost?"

"I swear Michel Leiris' Autobiography had awoken me from my somber beginnings but it was just a foreshadowing of what I would face after I met Norm. Survival's not gonna do it for me anymore. My therapist thought it would be a good starting point, delving into the Male Thing and all. Fuck, the Rape of the Sabine's and other horrors, men—Norm, how does he fit into all this? A recurrent world of hopelessness, destitution: Couldn't you just fly away from all this *best of all possible worlds*? Talk about nothing? Man, what more can I say? Not even Colette could save me from my withered self. I'm tired of soft lies and distance. This new guy Paul of mine—he's just a hack at Cutler Hammer shipping out product Online. He's never gonna own a house; but, he talks, listens. A schlep he may be, but he brings home the bacon without building his own walls along the way."

"Well, I sure hope you know what you're doing. I mean you've only known this guy for a short time. Really, Genie, you're not a kid anymore. Who knows what you're gonna find out about this new guy down the road?"

"You can say that about anyone. Besides, I just know I couldn't sit there and drown in my suffering anymore. Oh, God, death couldn't come any sooner: every day to know that if therapy and counseling were my only outlets, I might as well just end it right now. The melancholy of the 'burbs: It's all yours, Alice."

"Silly petty little suicide thoughts: really Genie, my heart bleeds for you. So what if the world is not to your liking? You think you're the only one who has reservations about the way things are? At some point you gotta get up and get on with things anyway."

"You're afraid. I don't want this, this contrived silence, like someone's pounding on the bell-jar, and its non-stop echoes reverberate, take hold of me, ha-huh, they just don't stop, can't, draining, killing me bit by bit."

"Speak for yourself. You sure are one for dramatics. Maybe you've missed your calling, my little Nina Simone. God, it's like I have to deal with petty clients every day, spelling everything out for them twice, thrice: lose several because they've found someone cheaper, then I come home and hear these rants from Jasmine—yeah she's a kid, then you come along—same old shit."

"I didn't bring up the messy little rumor girl. That was all you; and, once you get me going there's no stopping me."

"Oh, and look the moon's full. Your poetry was always lousy. Your heart even less so. Well, I guess you still have your face."

"And, that ass. Watch it Dave wherever you are. The Damsel still has a thing for you. Only if I pulled it off would she be so right about me. You don't want to know me. I'm just a casual face that makes her one and only annual appearance only you continue to hide away from your own little problems. Like you don't have your own little drama?"

"OK, Sappho, there's the door. Don't let it hit you in the a-ass on the way out sweetie."

"Like her, this man crossed my path and I'm crippled with pain that he would not acknowledge me, this Aphrodite, veiled in wanton secrecy: Now I sachet through the pillars without a care as to what others may see. Now it's me and my man, Paul. The pangs of life were telling me something.

Yeah, I took advantage of Norman; but, he can't even dance. Socrates as an old man learned the vicissitudes of music and dancing. It's not too late for him; but, if he thinks that holding things together at the home front, raising three incredible children is going to fulfill his life? Well, he can always talk about that bad, bad vampy little vixen ex-of his that destroyed all his hopes and dreams."

"God-willing he won't cross paths with another wench like you."

"The rest of the pinot noire is yours. Oh, and if that guy doesn't work out, maybe you could give Norm a call. Could be worse right? On the golf course with Norm at St. Thomas while the kids are being taken care of by their nanny back in freezing Milwaukee. Got a ring to it, doesn't it? You'd have quite a financial portfolio though; wouldn't you guys?"

"Good night *by-itch*."

"The siren must go." Genie leads herself out of the house, masking her hatred for an old, old friend with that stoic expression imprinted upon her face. She scampers away from the home with an indifference that only the great ancients could accomplish. What to do, where to go? It's 7:30 and all the bustling about of the day's events have come to a crawl. The moon's rotund fullness consumes her very being as those youthful thoughts of Sartre's "if you are lonely when you are alone, you certainly are bad company" confront her—she pulls out her iPod and cannot decide who to call, with the neighborhood hidden from her, Genie finally calls her beau.

A reckless friendship can no longer cut into her own matters: now if only Alice can put that ugly situation out of her mind and get some beauty sleep.

"I wonder if Paul's home."

"Hello?"

"Hi."

"What's up?"

"Oh, nothing. I was just wondering if you were doing anything."

"Well, actually, I'm over at Café la Boulangerie in 'Tosa waiting to get a salad and a sandwich."

"I'm only a couple miles away, perhaps, I could join you."

"I don't see why not. Do you have a way of getting here—you know, without a car from your place, it's a good several miles."

"Ah, I'll just hop on the 62 and walk the rest of the way down 76th Street."

"Are you sure you're up to it?"

"You go ahead and eat. I'll meet you and take you over to the Sherbrooke."

"Or do you have to get home to get some sleep?"

"To box up and mail out cartons On-line after twenty years of that shit? You kiddin' me? A couple of Cosmopolitan martinis and I'm set … Hey, is there any chance I can spend the night over at your place, I mean if that's all right with you, being closer to work and all?"

"That's fine. I could use some company after being shut out by an old friend of mine. A glass of Chateau d'Yquem with some of their duck will restore my spirits. And, don't tell me it's no big deal. I swear that everything's crashing down. I can't even see my kids until next weekend."

"Give me a couple of Miller Fortunes; and, whew, I'm set. No, really, Genie, we've been over this ad nausea; and, don't lay that crap I've never had any kids, how should I know? No, this is how it is. You had kids. You've played that game of being one up on people like me when in reality you're just lonely and want to connect. So forget putting on airs just to have someone to talk to. Wrap with me darlin'. I'm all ears. Ain't goin' anywhere. The Dude's got it goin' on if you know what I mean."

"Don't give me that shit. Fuck yeah, I'm lonely. Who isn't? OK, OK, so, who, yeah, I mean, I love you, I mean, fuck dude, every day waking up, wanting desperately to connect with Norm and my three kids and knowing that it's just a pipe dream.

I'm not trying to one up you, straight up, I need you—just want to talk to you, touch you, make love … God, I'm so-oh tired of keeping everything to myself, trying to solve my problems on my own—nobody gives a damn about me. So, I want to know what's going on with you— fuck the government, everything looks right, but it's not, never been. Nothing's changed. Don't give up on me. Everyone's left me because they want to hide from what I might find out about them. Swear to God."

"You little sleuth you: Nobody cares sweetie. My parents just raised me. All that mattered to them was whether I was gonna get a job where I wouldn't be a burden to them; and, if all goes well, just maybe I'll drag along some grandkids to bounce around on their knees. Then, when that didn't work out as they would have liked, why was I not finding a mate; and, not having children like they did? God, there' got to be something wrong with that child of ours. What did we do wrong? And, if I would add my two cents, well World War III would be peanuts to what they'd want done to me for ruining their lives."

"My children are whole new worlds. Paulie, I don't want them to become emotionless kids who just go along with conventional wisdom; and, say, what else was I supposed to do?"

"Look, Norm, can he really be that bad? Or is he really afraid to open up to you. Do you use your looks to work to your advantage?"

"Oh, God, man. I've spent two years in marriage counseling; and, all I've learned from that is does my old man want to get on with things—like he's gonna have his own things he keeps to himself but he can't even say what's off limits to me. Everything's a mystery that's been so vital in saving our marriage, Paul."

"What is it that really matters to you?"

"That he will never divulge anything to me about his work problems— like, 'I'm in a bad way. I just might get laid off '. You know the way Milwaukee's labor market has been crashing for a long time."

"Before you were in kindergarten. Christ, when I was young, inner city kids were running drugs—the factory jobs were already getting swallowed up. The only reason I got a job at Cutler Hammer was because my uncle who'd just retired from Eaton, put in a call for me after I filled out an application. Driving for Crescent Electric was a job for kids just graduating from high school—try keeping a straight face doin' that job with a college degree. Anyhow, soon thereafter, I'd received a returned call—I spent my day in the warehouse, boxing up orders, palletizing shipments; and, for five years that's the way it went. Then the idea of On-line order got set up; and, voila, the rest is history. My uncle got the ball rolling for me; but, I put forth the effort, kissed ass; and, yes, got off my soap box that I'm gonna change the world: you know your little 'Blows Against the Empire' crap. You think the upper class is gonna let you just change things with a few choice words and a wave of your magic wand? Hell, Genie, disorder has been King before India became a people. You're just like everyone else, including me. We see what's going on. Yeah, but, I wanta get paid. You won't even go to work, but as long as Paulie's around, *I'll get by.*"

"Like everybody else, you just give up."

"What did you ask me for the other day before you left my flat?"

"What?"

"You know, money, money for some pricey shoes over at where was that place in Mayfair?"

"Oh, Viktor, Victoria. Well, isn't it alright to want to have nice things, to show off for her old man?"

"You're going to have to get a job. Why not put an application for some place like Viktor Victoria?"

"The only job I had was 15 years ago until I had my Jeffrey. Then, it was Norm who took over everything that had to do with money. Sure, I paid the bills and put money away; but, I surely wasn't going anywhere at Target—hated everything about that place. I mean I love shopping there— so organized you know— everything's neat—in its place."

"Genie, somebody's gotta put up with the bullshit: you can't just preach your great ideas without seeing first-hand what is going on. Yeah, there's a lot of bad things about work—the corporate disorder, everyone's on pins and needles—that sick silence. I don't care where you apply at or where you end up getting a job—but you're not getting any more money from me. I've been with Hammer for a long time—yeah, I haven't received a lot of promotions, don't want to really; but, hey, I still get up every morning and put in my two cents. It's not easy for anyone Genie. You're right. Take care of your own demons 'cause people don't want to hear about it'. Keep pluggin' along."

"Yeah, it's the old I got my own troubles, you talk about your own crap with someone else."

"It's like that for me too—always the same. You've been all over the world missy. Really, they roll with what keeps them afloat no less than we do over here. God, it's all bullshit—I don't have any answers, but I love you. Ah, here comes my salad and sandwich. Ta-ta."

"Wa-wah-wait a minute!"

"Now what?"

"There's something I've been waiting to ask about last week, about Jeffrey, you know, when he spent the day with us as the Park."

"Yeah, what about it'? 'Remember when you told Jeff his shyness was a sort of lie"

"Yeah, so?"

He's my son, Paul. Some things are off limits: he's at a tender age when everything means so much."

"Oh yeah, so impressionable—tell me Genie, what makes his fears any different than that bully of a kid that screws around with every child in the apartment building across the street? You know who I'm talking about."

"Oh, he's just obnoxious."

"Right, cross his line and he might just lose it—what's the difference? I mean, like you said earlier, you just lost a friend because she didn't want to hear about your stuff especially in her own house."

"How did this all come back to me? I was talking about how you had no right to tell him how you think his shyness keeps him from seeing others for who they are."

"Couldn't have said it any better. Look, we've been dating for just over two months—maybe we should back off the gas pedal a bit—take a break."

"Ooh, you little chicken shit—not you now."

"Like what? I'm asking you what you want out of this relationship, 'cause let me tell you, your threats don't work with me."

"Like you'd really want to see me end it like that (she snaps her fingers)?"

"I love you; but, there's no way you or Jeff, Norm, your long lost brother, my parents, nobody is going to have your ultimatums pushed down my throat."

"What are you talking about?"

"You're not going to tell me what I can say or not say to Jeff—it wasn't offensive—I was just not going to let him blame everyone else for his own fears, plain and simple. He's fifteen Genie—not a child anymore: far from it. Innocence lost is more like it. He's gotta know that he needs to take the bull by the horns when the chips are down because nobody's gonna do it for him. It's his life Genie, not yours, like it or not."

"Grown up, huh? My brother just disappeared—walked out of college—didn't let anyone know what was up with him. Not yet twenty: vanished. Left dad with the college bills—Marquette, Paul, not some state school. He was a bright kid trapped inside himself like Jeff. The creep just took off without saying a word, leaving a note. That silence cuts through me every time I walk into my parents' home."

"Who's pain is it Genie, his ghost or your own?"

"Ooh, you'd better meet me at Burleigh and 76Th Street by ten fifteen or I'll tear your lungs out. You shrew."

"On the dot or else, right?"

"Don't push it or you might just be sleeping on my doorstep."

"Nah, I'd just sleep in the car—I've got a hatchback you know."

"Ah, that's so special—Burleigh's comin' up—remember, 10:15 at Burleigh and 76Th. 'Bye, love ya'."

Norm would never stand up to her; but with Paul, it comes natural. He sees Genie as a beautiful person that is no less fragile and soft-hearted as he himself is. His mirrored image remains before her without all the queries and hidden realities Norman presented her with. Sex is solely a part of life but the caressing and soft eyes make all the difference:

Marcus Aurelius' statesman stone eyes are but some lost myth she built through a sophist's gaze, its mold the consensus of a rationalist's compromise. Even though he's degreed in civic cartography, Paul could never find a job that required such skills; and, the need to compete with Genie with her European odyssey into Descartes, Spinoza, Pascal, and Schopenhauer is her own journey ("wholeness of truth" quietly simmering beneath the wall of Popular/unpopular acceptance of *your own lot in life*). Like the chameleon, Genie has blended in.

She realizes she was just trying to get away with what she could with Norm. Paul as his own man, is no less needy than she; however, he will not take her orders to keep him in line that she believes will make her own life more comfortable. After all, no matter how much more passive the violence unravels behind the white picket fences, its hidden sword eventually thrusts out from its shadows.

"Hey, hey, hey, look who we have here, little Ms. Joan of Arc come ridin' down on her white horse."

"Only problem was da by-itch burned at the stake. Ain' dat right Joe?"

"Yeah, well, she sure is a hot one, ain't she?"

"M-m, I've seen better. So, what you doin' out here all by your lonesome; 'cause ya see, the night is our time—Niggaz, understand? Hey Joe, wouldn't you like a pretty little piece of white ass like that?"

"Put you' keys away sweetie. We ain't gonna do nothin' to ya—just havin' a little fun is all."

"Cracker cain't talk like all the rest. Put 'em in front of a camera; and, dey's whole world lights up. But a couple jigga's like us wander into their little heads, and not a word comes outta your mouth. Like you got some kinda disease or somethin'. Fuckin' us to no end. Like I'd like to see some of 'em live where we do? Ain't that right Whitey?"

"Ah, sorry for not introducin' ourselves. Of course I'm Joe and this here my girl, Shajuana; so, who are you?"

"What you doin' around here at this time of the night? Ain't too many Whites hangin' around here at this time, huh, Joe?"

"No, can't say there is."

"We ain't got all night. What's your name?"

"Eugenia."

"Eugenia: Is that Jewish or somehin'?"

"I don't know. I guess."

"Biblical, ain't it Joe? See? It ain't too hard to talk. I know that's what you think all us black folks is good for: lazy, good-for-nothin' junkies who can hold a tune, you know."

"Look, I don't mean any trouble. I just want to catch the bus—should be here any minute."

"Well, it ain't here yet. Got your .45? God almighty, I could just pistol whip dis bitch, let her know what it is to live in their hell they all gave us—like how'd you like to know what it is to get up every morning knowing the only way my boys get out of this shithole is to get into the army. There's a War on, Eugenia. Now, how would you like dem choices. Hell maybe there's a Burger King or McDonald's dat they can work thei' ways up. Where are Dejuan and Tony anyway? Show up when they need some money. Me? I clean toilets and deliver pizzas in my beat up Elektra. Something my old man left me when he up and died. I do like that furry white heart that hangs on the back window though. Joe here's a security guard for the public libraries in the area. Neither of us make enough money to get out of here. "

"We're stuck. Beats most other places this big world has to offer I guess. But, you ball and chain types could front five of our families. Cat's still got your tongue? Ever hear of a black some years back called James Cameron?"

"No."

"Well, old James, he started a black holocaust museum a while back some, thirty years ago, I think, at 4^{Th} and North, somewhere no white folks gonna be hangin' around."

"It's all On-line now honey at abhmuseum.org: so, really, I mean dis. You got kids, right (she nods)? Shit still goes down. Schools can't show lifetimes of sufferin'. The schools would cut that out anyway. Eugenia, tell me, do we have to keep doin' this same ole' song and dance and fall into our worst nightmares? James himself got out of Marion, Indiana by the skin of his teeth. A crowd of whites hung around to celebrate a lynching of two young black men."

"Hours of two bodies blowin' in the wind, hangin' from the trees. Young James was cut down before he joined his two hell-bound nigga's. Yeah, I know. 1930, long time ago, right? Here comes your bus. Remember: abhmuseum.org. Now, get out of my sight you piece o' shit before I take you out o' dis world myself."

"One more look at that whore; and, you ain't sleepin' in my bed; always got your dick doin' the talkin' for ya. I swear, sometimes I wished I'd never been born at all. God Help me: You, you miscreant."

"Sure ma."

"Keep it up 'n' you can take your sorry black ass to Cali-a little sooner than you thought, you, you shit!"

"Ain't it somethin'?"

"What?"

"Like, all my life I've tried to get along with someone like you, but the only thing you worry about is being on top."

"Taken from some scum bag like you, well, nobody's perfect."

"Yeah, I'll sleep outside. Figure I got 'til September to get my ass movin'."

"You sure are some piece of work. Let's go."

"You need to get off your own soap box and see what's eatin' at you."

"Who says?"

"H-m-m, does it really need to be said?"

"Let's go nigga, let's quit wastin' our time on this bench and really get down to some business. Hey, what's Tara doin' tonight? Yeah, said somethin' like she was gettin' the gang together for some ribs and potato salad."

"Yeah: Let's stop by the liquor store on our way and pick us up some Cobras."

"Don't forget to pick me up a couple of St. Des for yours truly."

"How could I forget? Let's do it?"

Chapter Six

Let's Do this for Pops

"Ooh yeah, baby—n- no, no, no, no—keep going, don't let up—we got our whole next life to sleep. H-mm-m-m-h- wh-a-ahh, yeah, yeah, le-et's go, hm-m- ah"—smitten with her beau, Diane Bogdanov muses as she softly strokes his long salty raven hair."

"I always aim to please my Mrs."

"Don't get too complacent in your own deluded security blanket."

"I could say the same thing."

"Quick, to the showers—we need to get going to dad's house."

"How could I forget—Christ, please tell me I sent off my last political articles, yeah sent all of 'em out last night—I'll finish up my blog when we get to Milwaukee."

The early morning winds swirl about the quaint McHenry, Illinois neighborhood. The South Pool Street homes quietly maintain their mid-twentieth century A-frame gentility as everyone has left for their day's responsibilities. The sun peaks into the kitchen window as the two lovebirds begin to contemplate a long weekend spent at her father's home.

"Why do we have to go to your father's house anyway? I didn't invest in his life—I only want you."

"Kurt, my dad and I pulled through some tough times. Hell, you should know more than anyone how hard it is just to get someone to listen to after you went off the deep end."

"I can tell you about people I used to know who just went out with consumption. Look at their soft side, resting in their coffins with that otherworldly presence they assume—yeah, it was them; but take a look around you. Who gets along?"

"Oh, the poor ole' Rodney King soul who walks away after he says to everyone on live TV, *Can't we all get along*? Then years later, after taking out a couple houses along the way in his own SUV's, the man's pretty wife-to-be dials up 911, like three hours after the pill popping giant Rodney had fallen to the bottom of their pool in the middle of the night … I care about you Kurt, but I also am committed to my father. We both pulled through our own crap, how? I don't know. But don't tell me that I have to sit in this pin cushion -sized house because you couldn't find anything worth talking about with others in your own life."

"Maybe I'll spend some time on the Fox River and bring in some Walleye while you can go and shoot the shit with your old man."

"Look, we've been dating for two years, right?"

"Yeah, so?"

"Well, in that time, have we gone up to visit my dad—even for Christmas?"

"No."

"I'm not going to let you drive a wedge between my family and us. He was such a loathsome old coot; but you know he came around—could've sunk from despair but he didn't. He's still here; and, I won't let his spirit die because my lover who's basically gone down the same road can't have his way."

"Sorry that you feel that way—just kidding. My work— everything I do lets me be a hermit: kind of anyway. He's an outdoorsman you say?"

"Well, he fishes, doesn't hunt anymore. But he'll lug you around the state to tell you stories he told my sister and I growing up. Wisconsin's a little different than the prairie states you're accustomed to—a little marshier. You've been to the Kickapoo River—those bluffs overlooking the waters below. I guess that's what makes my childhood life a little different from my adult world—aside from your love, of course. C'mon, let's go—coffees' on the counter in your favorite touring cup. See, here's our breakfast, voila—a couple of peaches, pears, and a whole baguette to go."

"Cream cheese?"

"Land-o'-Lakes: we'll use my car so we don't waste any of your precious native petro."

"Like I have a going interest in any of it: alright—the old man's gotta relieve himself before he hits the road."

"I think I should get you a catheter. My God, you go more often than when I spent a drunken night out with my college friend's way back when."

"Great sex'll do it to you. I'm still your man, aren't I?"

"But c'mon Kurt, you're going two three times every afternoon we have things to take care of. Like, maybe you should go see a specialist."

"You know I've seen my physician late last year about this time: he checked my prostate and gave me a clean bill of health. He offered me some over-the counter antidotes to my active glands, but you know I feel about pills."

"Can't be your diet—how about a little exercise? Maybe you can join my group over at Curves for a little aerobics to drain that insipid lethargy out of both your mid-section and your urethra."

"Ooh, I love it when you use words like that. It makes you so authoritative."

"C-mon, let's get going. It's not like we haven't talked about this before. Get the suitcase while I pull the car around front."

Kurt enjoys the ride up Route 31 to Johnsburg. He has spent a lot of time there as he wrapped up his environmental studies for one of his clients.

"Oh, so we're not taking I-94?"

"Nah, I'm gonna take the 12 up to the I-90. For some reason Madison's been on my mind—just wanted to try something different."

Up State Highway 12 Kurt sees a lot of the creeks and shallow lakes he gathers his water samples. He mixes with a lot of Illinois DNR folks that have much more extensive educational backgrounds and work-related experience; however, with an On-line course here and there, paying some attention-to-detail, and a little elbow grease, Kurt Toyekah considers himself their equal.

As Interstate Ninety approaches, he reflects upon what these rolling hills of southeastern Wisconsin mean to an almost entirely flat Illinois. Has the Wisconsin Ice Age made that much of a difference in how those glaciers have pushed and receded to form such glorious bodies of water as Lake Geneva or those magnificent bluffs overlooking the northern shores of Lake Winnebago? All these towns are named after Indian words and not a native soul is to be seen. That is fine with Kurt: he enjoys wearing his Polo blue denim jean shirts with those stylish alligator leather boots of his.

Those teachings of Margaret Meade all those years back at Oklahoma Central allowed him to see that cooperation was non-existent. Even today, media personnel still twist Meade's message to fit their own plans: perhaps this is why one of the most important Americans for change of the early twentieth century became apprehensive of relating anything to the press.

Cleverness is always fashionable: the once powerful Kiowa and Comanche Tribes would end up surrendering to the inexhaustible numbers of the White Man. Even though they could outride any soldier setting foot in their backyards, the westward push with its trains and annihilation of the buffalo (their food source and kindred spirit), along with the millions homesteading behind the Expansion Wars, the nomadic idea of a timeless life had completely dried up in less than a couple of generations. News could not outride the tribes in their perilous scrapes against the US Army: for some reason, no one seemed to care or question America's inherent need for the Native's annihilation before it was too late.

He can look out the rolled down car window; and, for miles in any direction all Kurt sees are old two story homes resting atop rolling fields of corn and alfalfa. The only humans seen or heard are moving about the highways in their polished metal horses: sort of like his peoples on their reservations in southern Oklahoma—hidden away from the American public. Lake Okauchee, a spacious body of water surrounded by an abundance of maples, pines, and oaks flows with the free rolling hills down to the choppy lake waters, shimmers radiantly beneath the ever-present sun.

"Look at all the cottages tucked away in all those trees."

"I know, and look over there, a bar. Can't go anywhere in this state without running into one of them every so often."

"So, how far are we from Milwaukee?"

"Waukesha's just a couple minutes away—we should be at dad's place in about thirty minutes."

"OK, I'm gonna nod off a bit. Wake me up when we get there."

"You go ahead. We'll be there before you know it."

Her Honda Accord purrs along as thoughts of their childhood trips to Madison and Wisconsin Dells, the vibrant green trees and free flowing rivers and moraine formed lakes spin around in her head. Mother would take care of the hotels and restaurants side of the ledger while dad would always take the time to learn about Devil's Lake and climb the rocks with the girls. Of course, mom would join them when they went swimming at the lake. One time they even had a picnic where dad took care of everything, from cooking the green beans and cut- up potatoes to grilling the hamburgers and hot dogs. And, yes, mom would make sure that the paper plates and napkins were put out while she made sure they would not spend the whole 30 minutes filling themselves up on Shasta cherry soda and Geiser's potato chips. After all, mom brought some of her own German potato salad for the *young ones* not to get too crazy on that junk food.

She pulls off the I-94 exit at Hawley Road and heads north. Within 10 minutes, Diane nudges Kurt: "we're here."

"Wow, look at that. Red and pink rose bushes all around his home."

"Cytherea's to be precise. Yeah, he's picked that up when I helped him get off the booze. Keeps him connected. To be truthful, I thought he would have given it up after that one season of planting. But the man's got the green thumb. I can't wait to see his garden after we get settled in."

"Could you bring in my jacket while I grab the suit case?"

"Sure."

"Lead the way. Don't wanna scare the old man."

"Really? Like my dad's Archie Bunker and you're, well you walk on clouds."

"Couldn't have said it better myself. The spirit of the golden eagle is always within me."

"Here, all the golden eagle means is if you're a Marquette fan. Unless of course if you can tone down the fact that you are an American Indian. And, not many people around here are gonna know a whole lot about the Kiowa Indians."

"Well, maybe we're gonna enlighten our little White friends a bit."

"Yeah, several black families, whites; and, oh, I am sure our Chasidic Jewish neighbors will really want to hear about your plight. The Holocaust trumps everything here, Kurt like it or not. So, just ease off the gas pedal and take things a bit slower. This is dad's domain; and, we are his guests."

"Like they say, When in Rome…"

"Alright, alright, just watch your tongue, Kurt. It's not like we've made ourselves regulars around here."

"Lord, how long has it been since I've last seen you?"

"I've spoken to you by phone over the past couple of years. Diane needed to take care of Diane."

"Two years too long. And, you must be?"— "Kurt, Kurt Toyekah."

"Welcome to the Bogdanov residence."

"Come on Diane. Let's show your better half around the place before you guys settle in. By the way, I've put together some pictures in the back room. I'll join you after you get your bags put away in Diane's old bedroom."

"Everything's the same since I left it a few years back?"

"You betchya … So, you guys'll meet me back over through that door when you get settled in?"

Diane does not know what to make of her father's little secret to show them: he is usually quite up front about how he handles things. Usually it involves bad news when he used to bring things up out of the blue. Yet Kurt likes the queen-sized quilted bed and the pastel-colored wallpaper adorned with traditional white curtains and a beautifully refinished walnut armoire. After a brief jaunt to the men's room, Kurt joins Diane in the hallway as they make their way to the backroom.

"Oh, dad, there's Hals. Where'd you get it?"

"I just went On-line at the Senior Center and ordered it: *Boy with a Lute*. What do you think of it, my Maestro?"

"Not bad. Vibrant colors, gay mood. How can you go wrong with that?"

"Diane here feels Hals' gay and festive moods are covering up something more dark in nature. Isn't that right sweetheart?"

"Whatever you say dad?"

"He's learning, isn't he dear?"

"OK, dad, what's behind the curtain?"

"Just two of the most precious creatures you've ever laid your eyes upon: Sheba and Barnard." From behind a curtain covering an old desk scampers two perky little felines.

"Oh, just look at them, so full of life they are … Dad, you don't mind if I pick up this brown ball of fur?"

"No, not at all. I thought the biggest clue would be all the litter box smell coming from the basement. You mean to tell me you two kids didn't pick up on that?"

"Well, no. If there's one thing I know about my dad is that he can be quite the finicky type when it comes to cleaning."

"I owe it all to my mother. She couldn't stand a messy room. By the time I'd gotten my own apartment after I started at Evinrude, I was all set for the domestic world: cooking took some time to get the hang of; but, the cleaning part of it was a piece of cake."

"Kurt, grab the gray one: Sheba. Yeah, Sheba. Ah-h, look how she takes to you. Don't they make a cute couple, dad?"

"You know, Mr.Bogdanov, I'm not much of a cat person, any animal for that matter. I like the great outdoors: you can't take the free spirit out of the hard winds of central Wyoming. That's my deal. I can still hear the call of the great Golden Eagle from my ancestor's doorsteps in Hobart, Oklahoma… the red clay dances around me as the fierce winds pay no heed to my timid nature."

"A true poet: couldn't have said it better myself. Too bad about my furry little friends though. Ah, I thought you were gonna spend some time getting unpacked."

"What's to unpack? Oh dad, you two have just met. Spend a little time with him, and you will see that those deerskin moccasins of his wear out just like your leather work boots."

"OK, OK, so I can be a little full of myself sometimes."

"Like us pale faces SAY my boy: We became too big. We just didn't destroy your land and people; we couldn't find our way out of our own hell."

"Don't let that turquoise necklace and silver bracelet fool you, dad. Good ole' Kurt here can fall prey to his own little whims as well."

"We're people just like you are, Diane. We can fall off the trodden path; but your people, you gave us the horse, the Comanche's and we ended up becoming the marauders of the southwest. The nomads that we were, we still had our reverence for others, even you until we were made to have southwest Oklahoma as our last resort. Oh, there you go Sheba. Kurt's got his own hair to manage. God, do those things shed."

"I know. But they're so cuddly and full of energy: gives me a shot in the arm. An old man like me sometimes has it hard enough to get off the pot in the morning—an adrenaline rush can snap ya out of it quite quickly. So Kurt, what superpower was ever fair and soft-spoken? I can still hear old Teddy shouting from the pulpit, *walk softly but carry a big stick.*"

"Whatever works, right?"

"I'm just joking. For whatever reason, we've all just decided to get lazy and follow along with our leaders no matter how insane their talks became. With two former passing time champs, I'm sure Kurt and I will get along just fine, thank you."

"Mr. Bogdanov, you can't excuse your inactions. I mean, you were part of the sixties when things exploded! Bringing into the world two beautiful girls—things were never quite the same again."

"Kurt: all I did was keep my job, go to Kiwanis meetings, and try to smile even when I knew things were not quite up to snuff … To me history is just a mirror I've used as an excuse not to get off my recliner. Then of course, after my wife passed on, I learned how to become a full-fledged alcoholic. And, if it wasn't for my dear sweet little girl here, I don't know if I would ever have snapped out of it. God help me, there are still days when just escaping from everything remains fixed in my brain and there's just no way of getting round it."

"At least you recognize it."

"No, I've said it."

"Dad, you don't know how refreshing it is for you to admit it. I mean, you know me, Miss big shot's gotta tell everybody what's going on with me even if I can sense all the consequences will drag me back to square one the minute I leave the discussion."

"I never knew how to explain it to you. It's like all I knew was how to get through another day without stepping on anyone's feet too much; and, then Kurt, here is this petite creature that could have stared down Reggie White and just given him the most righteous tongue-lashing about fair play and honor that even Martin Luther King, Jr. would not dare touch on even his most life-affirming days."

"Ah, dad, I just knew the bullshit that was comin' down from others; and, don't you dare tell me how and when to stop—fuck it! After a certain point everything falls to pieces, smashing into broken shards of glass, and yeah, maybe I will not be able to pick up the pieces; but, ya know, I took the bull by the horn when shit hit the fan—all those people hanging around for a little drama, a few laughs—then everyone split. No one stuck by me." Softly, Diane releases Barnard to go run around the house with his sister.

"Don was cool."

"Yes, but dad, I was not suited for him. According to him, my only interests were clothes and crashing Pearl Jam concerts. Everything he bought came from Harley's on the East Side of town. It was like the free spirit and some ultra conservative businessman trying to make sense of a relationship that just wouldn't hold up for very long."

"I think you saw your big sister have her way with it; and, once you found such an opportunity, you seized it. They say the apple doesn't fall too far from the tree."

"C'mon dad, you've gotta give me more credit than that. Look at me now, Kurt and I are still going strong after over two years of living together—and, really dad, I consider this more of a marriage than the entire six years I spent as Mrs. McGowan."

"Perhaps: But you got to admit, that guy had class. That house of yours up in Mequon; hell, you could fit two homes this size into that, that..."

"Tudor, Dad. I swear sometimes you and Kurt should get together—all you'd need would be a TV, fridge, couch, and toilet—throw in a shower and you're good to go."

"Don't forget the clicker and my own king-sized bed; otherwise, it's a no-go."

"Ah, poor baby."

"I gotta say, Don was right about one thing: Pearl Jam. She's carted me to three of their concerts. I mean don't get me wrong, they're considered the world's best; but, couldn't we just take in a Chaquico or a Vidovic recital at Chicago's Sherwood Conservatory Hall once in a while?"

"Say no more: Eddie Vedder. God, everybody tells me how Sinatra's voice can flatten out to no end; and, then you got that grueling monotone of a Vedder. I don't know if she told you, but when she made this her home for several years, that's all I heard was his stuff—over and over like a broken record. No matter what I may think of Frank, he's got more talent than our little save the world Eddie does."

"Mr. Bogdanov, I didn't know you had such a pessimistic view of our dear Eddie."

"You don't understand Kurt. I had to live all their ceaseless accomplishments over and over during those years. This song, and I grant you, a beautiful one at that, how could even an old duffer like me forget it, *Immortality*, now, yeah, even someone I can't stand can occasionally hit on all cylinders. But the rest is for the birds. Besides, those guitar riffs I'll never understand any of it. It's all yours' sweetie."

"Dad, you can't be so old that that you're not moved by *Not for You* or *Corduroy?*"

"Only the words interest me now dear, like when Deborah kept playing *Imagine* on her little 45 record player we'd gotten for her 11th birthday. Now, you wouldn't remember that—you were just three; but, those words I could never forget, *no hell below us, above us only skies.* I would have to remove myself from the room whenever she played that because it was like the first time I ever went to church in my life. Like I was converted or something: but, hey, why get sentimental about something, right? Look, I know you and your sister aren't on the best of terms, but she tries. Maybe she doesn't know how to show it, but I grant you, Deborah can surprise you if you just would give her half a chance…"

"Do you know I've just received a text from Deb—she wants me to come over right away that she has something she wants to talk to me about."

"Really? The last time she asked me to come over to her place was when she needed a baby sitter to take care of her grandkids when Tommy and Jonathan joined them for a night out at the Fox and Hounds. Let me tell you, little kids can be a handful when you want to get them to go to bed after they've just made a mess of the whole house. My great grandchildren can already spot me as an easy mark. My yelling days have been put to rest a long time ago."

"She says it's urgent, that you'd understand."

"Understand? Right, like since my drinking days everyone thinks I'm the biggest loser who's ever walked on the face of this earth. Not you of course, Diane; but, I don't think Deborah will ever forgive me for how I've handled things since your mother's death."

"Mom's been dead twenty years, dad."

"That doesn't mean your sister has not given up her need to remind me that I was a drunk who couldn't kick the habit 'til I got through the DT's and was forced into rehab. God, then there was all those physical problems alcohol abuse brought along with it that might have even been worse than my drinking days: although Debbie won't say anything about it, I'm sure there are things about my drinking she will not discuss with anyone including myself."

"Well, I'd better get a move on. Do you have anything to eat?"

"Yes, I have a leftover roast and some corn on the cob to go with a couple of baked potatoes unless Kurt has something better on his mind."

"Nah, that's fine. Besides, later on I have to finish some work that's due by tomorrow."

"Some beer's in the fridge if you want one. Yes, I still have a beer or two every now and then; and, no, I don't fall apart like the Scarecrow in the Wizard of Oz. For now, I'll get the corn and potatoes on the grill with a little bell pepper and mushrooms— we're good to go."

"Does Diane know you still drink on occasion?"

"She's already looked in my ice box; and, front and center is my Sprecher Belgian Dubbel. It's not the drink, Kurt. It's me. There'd be something else to wander off into if alcohol couldn't do the trick. Who knows? Maybe a ghost would enter my life. I don't know. I'm not physically addicted to it if that's what you mean. God, I don't know what to say. Anyway, if you want one, just go ahead and grab one. How about this for the amateur in me, *Let Go and Let God.*"

"Look, no drugs are on my list as me, a once faithful twelve-stepper can attest. I was always stuck on taking my inventory, stumbling all over the place without anyone to see what a mess I really was—ghost rider is more like it. Chasing windmills where the well's run dry. Man, I'm just gettin' started—want any more? Ah chucks. Where was I yeah, well, after I got off heroin, I spent another four years on methadone. Some of my compatriots would pick up their monthly state-allotted amounts at the hospital and be flying off the handle in uproarious laughter on their way back on the bus.

I thought once I cleaned up from heroin everything would work out. Once again, the haze set in; and all I can think of is scoring some Oxycodone, to escape from the world somehow, like nothing could change how I felt: I'd be gone before I hit the floor, swear to God. This was way before I met Diane. Before I was forty, I got off methadone and left therapy for good. The NA meetings even ended. No more secrets to conceal.

Lay off the beer man. Do you really want to walk down that road again? I mean, toward the end of my heroin use, I could see through my eyelids. The lid's skin became transparent; I even became aware of it, didn't really care either. Hell, I just don't look in the mirror anymore—not too hard to do if you know what I am sayin'? The score was the goal—now don't get me wrong, I was shocked by it at first; but, after continuing to shove the needle into my skin, I'd soon forgot all about it. Only the mug shot I'd seen years later revealed how fucked up I really was.

Attempt to deal, theft: suicide was right around the corner. Look, I don't want to bother you with all this, but mom didn't really care about me; and, dad, he died of consumption: didn't have anything to say to me after he moved to Gallup to work in the mines. You know he walked into the mine corridors every day; and, one day, he, his body just gave out: spent, done."

"Yeah, I would go on to college; but I was just doing what was expected of me. Ole' Kurt ain't goin' down into the mines to make a living, oh no. Like a waif, I just wandered from one day to the next, plodding along, just lying to everyone to get by. You know, just getting up in the morning is hard enough; but, then to fill all the time in between, connect the dots: the pain, well, that became so burdensome that heroin became my fast slow way out—you know? Passion: like a comfort food."

"Look, you don't have to tell me your life story. I think we've put survival as the carrot before the horse. My last therapist years ago told me that I have a wealth of experiences to draw upon, that I know my own problems and the ways of the world. From this, I will know what to do: to not worry about everybody else and to just do my own thing. I mean really; whatever they thought, so what? Good for them. There's real freedom in that; and, I didn't have to learn anything to understand this. It's naturally me. Believe me. I know how to screw it up. The ghost got my ass tied up in so many knots. Not to bore you, but, as an old man, I realize that I have no reason to do that anymore, feeling sorry for myself, you know? That has always stayed with me, but, you know, this problem, me, it's not rational or irrational for that matter. It's this nasty void crawling inside of me that I just can't shake off. "

"Let me put it this way. What I do know of me is pure illusion. That I can easily admit. But everyone around me still plays the same old games, soft lies here and hidden problems there. And, and, somehow everyone comes out of this madness unscathed for the most part, right? Or maybe I should just go along with all this pooh-pooh and just enjoy the last few years of my life. I mean what other choices do I really have?"

"You think we Indians have our natural worlds to connect with? When I was a boy, we were drilled with the Kiowa warrior as a brave and virtuous man with fortitude and generosity. And, of course with the poverty we experienced growing up, we really felt to be separate from everyone else. Like, like we were the chosen losers whose only aim was to eventually go back to the reservation."

"But you got your degree."

"Yeah, and I got out of Hobart. I took Diane back last year to Carnegie. She wanted so badly to see a real-life Powwow. When we passed Shiprock on the open road she almost lost it. God, is it something to see. Makes anyone wanna crap their pants. Out in the middle of nowhere; and, of course, Four Corners whistles in the tireless winds. Jack rabbits, road runners, and this stoic rock essentially salutes you while the tumble weeds float over the open highway: "Navajo, Indians of sheep and rancid coal mines are just fucking everything up. Pay the miners good; and, hell, they can't give up that death trip. What's changed? Eat shit and live, right? So anyway, getting back to Diane, yeah, I had told her there were many powwows nearby in Illinois and Wisconsin. But she was set on making the July journey. So we went. It's funny when you show up when you are almost forgotten. It's like I was almost White if that makes sense? We got hundreds of photos and memories. One day I went by myself to Quo Pah Ko where my mother is buried along with so many former American Indian soldiers. It's a testament to our warrior spirit. I lost myself man. It's not about the Indians or White America for that matter. It's about me, about you."

"My cross to bear."

"Yeah, also to see how our Leaders such as Lone Wolf who kept to his word, and expected the Supreme court to follow suit regarding the taking of our lands the US Government originally had given to us years before. Didn't happen. Child's play. Those soldiers, warriors of spilt blood over the generations in a land which we were literally pushed onto, were dying for what America stands for. In World History we read about the Hmong hill people originally from central China that would be pushed 2,000 miles over 2,000 years into what is now Laos. Within a hundred years we would be manhandled by the Ojibwa from our Wyoming home to eastern Wyoming where the Lakota would send us packing to our final home in southwestern Oklahoma.

In Texas, the marines really tattooed us after we showed no quarter to civilians for years and years. A thousand miles in less than 100 years Mr. Bogdanov. I looked around the room and everyone was shocked at what happened to these proud people. Everyone was being pushed, and we ended up with our Apache and Comanche brethren in this arid part of Oklahoma. I'll never get over all that red soil blowing in the silent sun. Things moved lightning fast with trains and guns in this country. We Kiowa's hardly had any time to catch our breath.

Within the tapestry of the fearless Wolf and the Bison's horns, our people could not stand against the White Man. We were helpless. I don't want you to think I am dumping all my problems on your shoulder, Sir, but I want you to know where I'm coming from."

"Look, son, I certainly have reservations about what we've done in the past, and all the romanticized crap that tends to put salt on all the open wounds of its crippled victims. It's the same. You know when I watched a TV show some years back about wolves in the wilderness, Some Indian Leader stated that ideas have to be accepted by a tribe or America for that matter until those ideas come to bear fruit. It's a popularity contest. What does it matter what side of the coin it comes from? If I cannot accept the wholeness of truth, then what's the point of going on?"

"Power and money, yeah, no wonder I could not develop a good lasting relationship. Putting out hardcopy for the Examiner-Enterprise was everything my life was about for years until heroin consumed everything about me lock, stock, and barrel. I think our souls are consumed by the fact that we have no real connection to life. How's that for summing things up? After Diane walked into my life, everything has changed. Not saying that everything's smooth sailing, but Mr. Bogdanov, we want to talk to you about something before we leave."

"Well, you've got the remainder of the weekend. Look, I'm gonna flip the corn and potatoes. Could you pull the roast out of the oven with those red oven gloves over there? Be right back. By the way, my name's Paul. Here, put out their food dishes. Barnard and Sheba always eat right before I do."

Kurt smiles as he honors Paul's wishes, then meticulously pulls out the meat from the oven and sets it on the front stove burner and sits down at the kitchen table. As Paul enters the kitchen door, Kurt reaches in the refrigerator and pulls out a beer. "You know Mr. Bogdanov, we've become so short-winded just like you guys living off that crap food they feed us."

"No son, we've just become lazy and went along with the program. I can go to Sendik's and get a good cut of rump roast for just over four bucks a pound. See, things ain't quite that bad."

"It's all about relationship, connecting to someone else. That's what I've been trying to say."

"You think I don't know? Like the only thing I have to bitch about is my failing health, doctors telling me what to do? That I'm hidden in my own mask of deceit? You think I do half of what they want me to? Hell no, I do a lot of walking and drink a lot of water though. By the way, could you grab me a beer from the fridge, pretty please?"

"I don't know. What would Diane say?"

"I don't know. I'll leave that up to you."

"Got any snacks?"

"Some peanuts and Doritos are in the dry cabinet next to the oven. You like sports? The Brewers are on. You know. Bob Uecker and company."

"Football's all that I watch."

"I should think so. Sooner country and all that hullaballoo. Wilkinson, Fairbanks, Switzer; and, now Stoops is trying to bring them back to what they were when old Barry ruled the roost."

"Suicide's the word for football. But, no, go ahead and turn on the game. I'm all right. And, no, I'm not going to get you that beer, bud."

"Ah, I'll get it myself. Now, if you'll excuse me. For the rest of the evening, could we please put down the sloppy drunk topic (he turns on the TV and gets a hot plate to place the roast on). The plates are in the cupboard aside from the oven on the second shelf. I'll get the knives and forks in just a minute. If you want to toss a salad, the lettuce and tomatoes are in the crisper below the beer."

"Ah, baguette. May I?"

"Go ahead. You might as well pull it out. God, it's almost nine o'clock. Where's your fiancée? Fuck, can you believe that?

Lohse's the only one doing something, and bam, he gives up a three run homer. I can assure you one thing. This ain't goin' to be the Brewers year, that's for sure."

"Even spring football makes the news in Oklahoma."

"The Badgers and Packers are big here too. Even Hartland-Arrowhead high school football has caught everyone's attention. Look, sports aren't just about winning and losing where all the cheating comes into play to make sure that the coach hangs around for a couple more years. It's also the pure athleticism, breaking into the seam for a long gainer, the tackle pulls to set a tailback on his way for a first down."

"I know, I know, you've gotta take the good with the bad."

"Would you forget about society and its rules? If you want to play that game, give me a couple days at the Library. I guarantee you I will find as much dirt on your ancestors as well as mine. It's us, Kurt. You about you, and me about me. The rest of it? Who cares?"

Chapter Seven

When I Was Your Age

"Aw, would you look at that, Kaisha: what are you doing with that ignoramus Jose—I mean did you have to come around here and steal pears from an old man. Dude, what's your deal anyway?"

"Dewan: why don't you just leave me alone, Fuck off! Kaisha, don't take off. Please, please. We don't have to stay here."

"Kaisha, you mean to tell me that you find this guy good enough for you? Lots of guys would give their lives for you; but, not, you—this spic is your own choice. I don't buy it."

"Just leave me alone Dew. We ain't doin' nothin' to you. I can't tell you why. But don't you try to mess with us. We've been together for a while now; so, so get lost."

"Look man, just leave us alone: Three's a crowd."

"Dewan, look, Jose and I are going to see a movie. We want to spend some time alone."

"My posse would be diggin' this little tidbit. Yeah, you go on. But leave Bogdanov's pears alone. He shares his fruit with everyone. He doesn't need your shit thrown in. Nah, what the fuck? You guys go do what you do. I ain' gonna crash your party." Slowly he walks away from the two, and cuts through Bogdanov's back yard. Dewan Jackson has had a difficult time fitting in with the neighborhood kids because his parents have closely disciplined him. He was not going to be their last ray of sunshine to fall from the clouds. Too many siblings and cousins have fallen prey to the great game of escapism: drugs and malt liquor, the cobra of their ashen remains, lives never lived. Dewan's interest in math and computers will allow him to grow and prosper within the world and to bring beautiful new children into a world that his parents can spoil rotten. At the same time, he will not have to shoulder the sordid lives of others that have fallen into the pit of Black inner city Milwaukee.

He ran an 11.75-second, 100-meter dash time. This is where his father feels that Dewan could attract himself to powerhouse colleges nationwide.

Of course, his mother will have nothing of Dewan playing any football if she could have it her way: her brother, once an aspiring outside linebacker for the Milwaukee Washington Purgolders, had destroyed his knees a long, long time ago. However, Jay Green is a gentle man He's embraced the life of a truck driver and never imparted to others any broken dreams or fleeting hopelessness that so many from the 20th and North Avenue neighborhood have accepted without batting an eye. Nonetheless, by twenty-one, Jay's legs became a major issue for him. Recently, he has moved into the office because getting in and out of trucks has become burdensome.

Dewan would become the happy-go-lucky family intellectual where everything is possible. Just because his family has stepped away from the impersonal horrors of the everyday inner city, life does not mean that the Jackson's will stop here. "We will not fritter away our time and let Dewan to fall through the cracks. He will make something of himself."

Nevertheless, Dew's parents do not know what it is like for an intelligent yet impressionable African American youth in today's world not to become part of the pack that parties and secretly sneaks around Roosevelt Park. Video games and social obligations do not enable him to become part of his school friends' social lives. Peer pressure is not the issue. Dewan too is looking to tame a girl, to shine his light; and, cannabis? Nah, that does not interest him. After all, his older siblings were part of that game, and now young Dewan must find other ways to pass his down time.

"Dewan, you mean to tell me you don't have anything to do on a Saturday night? You know when I was your age; I was already having my way with the ladies."

"Dad, could we talk in private."

"You mean you can't say what you need to say in front of your mother?"

"I'm serious dad: could we talk in the back room for a bit."

"I'll be back in a minute Shirelle. Dewan has something personal he needs to get off his chest."

"Could you shut the door dad?"

"No problem: now what is it you have to say?"

"I just saw Jose with Kaisha—you know he's dating her?"

"I hate to tell you this but us old folks have our own concerns."

"Like work?"

"At times, but not really. We have our interests outside of the office. Your mother finds solace in the church. I myself have read all of Zora Neale Hurston. Behind all the voodoo and ritualistic mysteries of the Deep South, I've found a sense of what mystical, magical Haiti must have been like beyond the plantation hook Napoleon heaped upon her. Work son, hoisting case upon case of Miller from one bar to the next is something I hardly spend a lot of time thinking about."

"So, why do you do it?"

"To put food on the table: what do you think? You know, I've put together several plays before I graduated from Stout, but son, the world isn't kind to someone who wants to live a life of solitude. That quietness can leave you claustrophobic: so much so that a nuclear blast would be more preferable."

"Dad, I don't have any friends."

"I think it's about a girl, isn't it? Could it be that girl you mentioned earlier?"

"Nah, she's Jose's girl."

"Look, just because someone else is dating that girl does not mean that you might be tangled up in her heart."

"How would you know?"

"Have a seat … Now, I know you may think that everything you are doing is the first time in the history of the world. And, don't get me wrong, you are unique. NO, no, no … now just hear me out. I know that you think we at times are getting in your way—that that no matter how you measure it, we're here just to keep you in line. I've dabbled in religion: Christianity, the Muslim Faith—Buddhism, it is all thought. None of it is entirely true. Everybody's trying to sell you something even if they know it is not all true. All have their own images just like your school mates and teachers. They give you a path to follow, but ultimately you have to open your own eyes.

"I cannot delude myself. When I met your mother back in the Stone Age, I thought everything would fall in place. And, it did for the most part. But Mark won't even contact us, tell us how he is doing. Jenna only shows up when her children need clothing, or when she needs spending money. Now you've seen her come in many times asking for a few extra dollars here and there. It's not that she's not gonna pay us back, son. She never talks to us. We're like a burden to her. But it's about her. I'm gonna tell you this son. Don't you ever think you're going to blame us for your broken dreams. I love you no matter what; but I will not feel sorry for you. OK? I've had my fill. Hell, we all have. If I am wrong about that sweet young girl, tell me about it."

"Mr. Johnson's her dad. There's nothing I can do, right?"

"Not unless you respect her wishes."

"Even if she flirts with me?"

"I can't answer that for you; but you must remember that Jose's involved. Secondly, whatever answer the girl gives you, you must honor. Otherwise, you've got a mess on your hands; and, since you're in the middle of it, you'll pay the price. Reading between the lines does not get you a *get out of jail free card*. Everyone sizes up what's going on around them; and, the truth has little room for its ways. You know this. You've adjusted to situations all your life. Find someone who lets you in otherwise you'll catch a whole lotta heat."

"What if I can't get over her?"

(Darren Jackson softly places his hand on his son's shoulder). "If you go that way, there is nothing your mother or I can do for you. You will have to face the music. Mostly, all I know is that it won't be pretty."

"I know, but she's so beautiful dad."

"What can I say? Anyway, one more thing. Now, I know that there are times when you want to throw it all way, the way we push you in school. Life's tough. I'm not gonna lie to you about that. Even all the great education you come up with cannot steer you clean of scrapes thrown in your lap. Trust what is right."

"Who do you trust?"

"I trust people who tell me how they really feel about something even if I disagree with them: I could care less what a person believes. What matters to me is does the person have the gumption to see things as they are or is he gonna fall back in line and be like everybody else?"

"You can't trust yourself if you'll be just spinnin' up there in that little ole' head of yours and wonderin' when it will all come to an end."

"No matter what I tell you, son, it's all up to you."

"Well, I know that already."

"It's also what you feel in your gut. Ain't nothin' all rational about us, son. If you're walking around and that pain's just wantin' to eat you alive, ya'd better take a moment to sit down and let things settle to straighten things out. Take some time to think 'em through."

"Dad, will I ever find a girl, you know, for me?"

"We're all connected. You may get knocked down a few times, but you'll get right back up. Nothin's easy. If you look at how many times you've failed in what you set your mind to eventually you'll bat a 1,000."

"Really?"

"Guaranteed. Look, there are some things you are just going to have to resolve on your own. Right now, your sole job is to maintain your grades and move up on the track team of course."

"But dad, running takes a lot of work: all the training and running when I don't feel so good, to feel like I can't take one more step—my shins."

"There are things in life you are not going to like; but, by following through, you are preparing yourself for whatever may come your way after that."

"But dad, most of this stuff doesn't make sense."

"Well, you've got a point there. But we've all got to put our problems behind us to face whatever comes our way."

"Hey, look. Aisha's just arrived with mom and her two kids."

"Yes, it's Jeremy's birthday: we're going to have some cake.

Your mother wants you to be here for them. That is if you don't have a hot date."

"So funny: might as well. I don't have anything else to do."

"You guys already ate?"

"Your mother made some biscuits and catfish along with sweet corn an' yams—son, you can't just wander home whenever you feel like it—it's nine o' clock already. Ah, there's leftover's in the fridge. But save that for later. Cake and ice cream waits. 'Hi you two'. Darren and I have been waiting for you all day."

"Hi grampa. I thank you for my new bike. Mom wants you to put it together because she says she doesn't know how to."

"No problem. I'll stop by tomorrow after church and get you off and running as soon as before the sun sets. Dewan, could you get the door for Chad and Jeremy? Great: After you all."

"Darren, could you get the candles while I get the plates," Shirelle cuts in, "we don't want to make this too late. Aisha has to open up at the Mall tomorrow."

"What time is that?"

"Eleven," Aisha muses, "the boss won't make it in until after two—says she's got something she has to take care of before she swings by."

"Maybe she will give you more hours now that you've been there a while."

"Four months now dad. Macy's actually helped me earn a few more bucks. You know I'm even meeting my numbers—beating them some days. I have been given off hours up until recently. Ah, what am I saying anyway? Who am I kidding? I'm twenty-six, dad, and all I've got to show for it is barely $300.00 a week."

"How many hours are you getting a week?"

"Just over twenty, why?"

"That's right around 15 bucks an hour, right?"

"Yeah, but dad. I'm never going to get full-time hours. They'll have to pay me benefits then. I can't see that happening. Most of my counterparts are teen-agers. Their only concern is to show off their booties and collect their pay. But yeah, I've become more comfortable with myself. The funny thing is that I don't have to be pushy or sneaky about getting my sales leads and using those phony approaches management harps on. I just go out there and try to sell the customers what they want, and not try to heap other purchases upon them unless I really can see how to better match up an outfit with them—know what I'm sayin'? It beats living entirely off AFDC and food stamps."

"We'll talk about that later after I drop off you and the kids. It's Jeremy's day today: how old are you?"

"Seven."

"Seven? My little man is growing up right before my eyes. It seems like just yesterday that you were going into pre-school. Chad, could you stand in front of Dewan and me as grandma gets a few snapshots."

"Wait dad. Could I get the candles lit before you get the pictures taken?"

"Sure. Now, Aisha, why don't you stand between Dewan and me—alright everyone, SMILE!"

"Once more. SAY CHEESE! Still now! OK, that's it."

"Boom, OK, boys and girls, let's sit down and get some of that wonderful cake grandmother has taken all day to prepare for Jeremy's big day."

"Dad, could you turn off the air conditioning? It's getting a bit chilly in here."

"Anything for you my dear."

"Now my little man, come over here and cut the first piece for your mother Aisha … Now don't be shy, pretty little cake ain't gonna jump up and bite you. There you are, exquisite."

"But gramma, I don't wanna do this anymore. Here."

"Now Jeremy, grandma can't do everything for you. Take the knife in your hand, don't worry, I'll guide you (Shirelle gently guides Jeremy's hand back and forth across the German chocolate cake as Darren makes the rounds pouring milk into everyone's Styrofoam cups)."

"OK let's all take a seat as Gramama passes around everyone their cake. Oh, I forgot the ice cream and whipped cream … now how could I have forgotten the most important part? C'mon Chad, let's go to the kitchen and get the goods."

"So-oh, Jeremy, where are you gonna take your new BMX bike after grampa puts it together?"

"I'm going to the Park with Jimmy and David to go to the swimming pool. You know Dewan I can streamline now. I passed it on Friday."

"Oh yeah, what's that?"

"Ah, I just hold my hands out straight and kick my legs until I swim from one side to the other."

"Really, well I never took any swimming lessons myself; so, what's next big guy?"

"The freestyle," Aisha cuts in, "I want these two boys to handle the water 'cause I want them both to go to Madison; and, the campus is almost surrounded by Lake Mendota."

"Cool, dad wants me to go there—he thinks I can get a scholarship for the track team."

"Your times have blown mine away; but, track really wasn't my thing."

"You know Aisha. Dewan will be running for Washington next year. We've talked to the coach and he believes if Dewan progresses along like he is doing now, there is no reason that he'll be leading the JV in the 100 and 200 meters. By the way everyone, I've got the ice cream and Chad here brought in the spoons—bottom's up."

"Yeah, he even said that I could run in a couple of Varsity relay teams if everything works out with my times on the JV team."

"But dad, you know that Wisconsin gets some totally big-time athletes? I mean, I'm sorry that you were the one and only thing at UW-Stout."

"You got that right. Black magic running right and left through the backfield; and, put up record times on the track team. Didn't crash the party, but hey, I sure showed all them white folks that the handful of blacks on campus weren't gonna lay down. After all, that's where I met my book worm of a wife. And, the rest is history."

"That's right Chad and Jeremy. It's never too early. Soon you two will have to go away to school—your mother's right, Madison is the place for you two. So, how's the cake?"

"Great gramma, could I have some more ice cream?"

"Go for it. Here you go."

"You know Aisha, I was wondering if sometime me and the boys could take in a Brewers game later this summer?"

"Hey, I want to see my blue crew—haven't seen a game since my senior year. Soda, hot dogs and brats in the parking lot, we're on, right boys, with Rickie Weeks by my side, of course."

"Yeah!"

"OK everyone, take your forks and plates into the kitchen while Dewan here throws out the cups and paper table cloth. Come here you two, and give gramma a big hug. Ooh, love you, now you be good to your mother, she has a lot going on now."

"OK dad could we get going? It's past ten; and, I've gotta get some rest before I open up tomorrow."

"We're taking the Suburban everyone. See you in a bit Shirelle. You don't need anything from the store? No? Great, let's go now guys. Gramps isn't getting any younger. He needs his beauty rest too."

"Mom?"

"What Chad?"

"I gotta pee."

"Hurry up! Your mom needs to get to bed."

"Do you gotta go, Jeremy?"

"I already went."

"Good boy. Now go with your mother while I wait for Chad. See you in a bit honey."

"Darren?"

"Yes, honey?"

"Make sure that you get home right away. I have something to talk to you about."

"About what?"

"We'll talk about it later."

"I get the message. Are we ready, Chad?"

"Yes, grampa—bye gramma Jackson."

"Bye precious. You keep cool, ya hear? Love ya."

"OK, Chad, Jeremy and your mother are waiting. Shall we?" Darren opens the back door for Chad and straps him into his car seat, and they head out toward Aisha's apartment. On the way, there is little chat as he slowly makes his way to Teutonia and Burleigh, an old flat that abuts an old A -frame bar named Midnighter's. He really does not know what to make of it: for the past four years, Aisha and her two boys have lived with her parents. And, now Darren is conflicted as to what to do to alleviate her troublesome situation. That ugly old boorish brown façade with that white front entrance looks like some hangover dating back before Milwaukee tipped its stein to old world Germany.

Neither of her love interests has contributed any money to help her move into a life devoid of such grinding realities. In fact, she does not know how to get hold of either anymore. Her dad told her that "those dudes couldn't even get arrested if they tried: both always on the run from commitments." And, work? Forget that. They have worked hard to maintain anonymity in a world where only the fortunate would pay the bills that truly mattered. Nothing's changed. One rises up from obscurity as another falls.

All the fighting for alimony payments has led her nowhere. After years of struggling to make a life for herself and her two children, she's turned to Buddhism meditation to lighten her load. She's grounded herself in Freedom from the Known, relinquishing those anxieties and ghosts of yore, quieting her anxiety-ridden psyche from its inherent strife.

She has accepted that she is the problem, that life and all the talk of everything being a wondrous joy ride is but some line to keep people from getting too close. After all, who does she really know? Everything is some storied illusion that is supposed to entertain her acquaintances, to hide all the secrets and lies that have piled up all through her youthful years. And, now that thirty peaks over the shadowed horizon, Aisha feels ready for something new, vibrant, and yet everything remains as it has always been: distant, elusive.

She wants to make her sons' transition into their teen-age years less than the extreme hell she has put herself. Of course, with friends whose only interest was getting high or falling head over heels into rough foreplay after some local hip-hop affair, all she could sense was the innate loneliness she would feel the next day after all the party's haze has drifted away. Aisha desperately hopes that there is something more to life than being tangled up in mired relationships that ultimately die in confusion like all the rest, being left to piece together a wobbly jigsaw puzzle that never quite fits.

Her children, god's gifts, tend to avoid her sullen moments and turn their own on when the day's stillness overtakes their controlled quietness. Darren has supported her through her travails for years, and wants her to make it. After all, those two young faces stare back at him from the rearview mirror. Clutching the steering wheel, he turns south onto Teutonia and makes a quick left as he turns into the empty driveway.

"Thanks for the ride dad. Why don't you just swing by tomorrow and put the bike together while you're taking care of the kids. Turn on Sponge Bob and share some orange juice and French toast with them—works like a charm. I'm telling you dad. What do you think?"

"You know what I think about this area."

"Here are the keys kids—mom will be up in a minute. Now dad, we've been through this before. You know that for right now, this is all I can afford. And, no, I don't want to try my hand at something I don't like. Real estate sales is high turnover, and school's out of the question. You know I've never liked school."

"Yeah, but did you try? You know, it's a new day."

"Maybe for you or mom, but it's just not me."

"Doors will remain closed for you."

"Good, I'll just have to find a way to open my own doors."

"Dad's not gonna bail your little butt out anymore, understand? Your mother and I have given you money time and time again. Those days are long gone. Like do you really care or is it just another stopgap to tie you over and it happens all over again and again? It's time for you to figure out what you're going to do with yourself or just maybe we will have to take those children from you."

"You're not their legal guardians anymore dad."

"What?"

"Oh, don't be so shocked. We never really got along. Everything was a show not to let mom get stuck in the middle of our little spats. Bye the bye, I don't know why mom didn't tell you about this earlier—I had your lawyer forward my decision well over a month ago … Oh, I get it. So, mom didn't' tell you about it, huh?"

"I, hmm-n, who have you decided to take care of the children should something happen to you, you shit."

"Harsh words coming from an angry, bitter man. Maybe it's time you took a look in the mirror."

"You think you know it all. Hell, I was shoveling shit before you were born Missy. That's right, why look so shocked? It's either everybody's against poor little Aisha or what she's learned from sitting on a couch doing nothing year after year. I don't wanna hear about your therapy and just what the therapist theorized about. Her opinions hold about as much water as mine or anyone else's. You and your spite: haven't you had enough of that crap?"

"You're just trying to lead me around your game of fear."

"Jesus Christ, God, if I gotta listen to all this shit from you again my little Zen girl, please. I've heard all your hysterics a million times before.

Hell, even the guys that knocked you up disappeared off the face of the earth. Can't get anyone's attention, can you, girl?"

"There's nothing I can do about them. Wait, there is one thing I could do. I could try to lure them back to my little love shack and make sweet love to them. That is of course if I could ever find 'em."

"You and your bullshit—follows you around like a buzzard waiting for an animal to perish: Save it for some drunk that spills his sorry ass out of that corner bar. Or better yet, wallow your little black ass across the street and drown your sorrows in that ornate little graveyard across the street."

"Yeah, if I do what you want me to, and then everything will work its way out, right?"

"Like that Buddhist crap you've followed hook, line, and sinker? You've started your little Yoga venture, haven't you?"

"Yeah, so?"

"So, life isn't about what we've been taught has it? Why all this samsara laden with karma, that dharma embracing into nothingness yet everything, everything yet nothing: Godless god! It's about me, Chad, Jeremy, you, the guy crossing the street over there … We're all gifts. You can't find it through me. It's all in your head dad. Work pays the bills, and yet is such meaningless garbage that I've stopped trying to make sense out of it. Like it's some held fantasy that will save me and my boys. But it won't dad, no matter how much me or you try to rationalize it. You even told me that a while back, remember?"

"Tell it to your mother, maybe she'll listen to all your worn out excuses. I'm outta here."

"Aisz you' nigga."

"I don't have time for this shit. Some people just don't get it, do they, sweetheart? Get someone else to wipe your ass, because honey I'm tired of always having to pick up the pieces—what would grampa and gramma have said if I carried on like you have? Starved to death long time ago, how about it? You're twenty-six Kaisha. You ain't getting any younger."

"Well, gramps is dead; and, gramma? She's good for a sweater and purse at Christmas time. Otherwise, well, you know, say nice things and everything goes along peachy, right pops?"

"Yoga helps me deal with the people who ain't gonna turn around, who'd rather throw everything away and sink into their own puke rather than admit they need help. Yes, it's a spiritual journey: thought I'd never say that, that edge in me disappears, cain't waste energy on all those foolish thoughts swimming around in my head."

"You New-Ager You—oh, by the way, that reminds me. Dwayne, remember him? Your own flesh and blood just took off without saying a word to you or anyone. It's been a long ass time hasn't it? Well, he done told me that you did something that he found out about."

"More crap coming from my little spinner of darker tales. OK, just what was it that he told you?"

"You'd deny it anyway even if it was completely true."

"I'm your father. What do you think I am, some kind of lying lost soul?"

"You tell me. Oh, and about Dwayne, I ain't playin' you if you know what I'm sayin?"

"I'm just sayin' I gotta go. Until you can come clean."

"Oh, and about Buddhism, all these opposing forces, they're just someone carrying out the crap while we desperately try to hide. When it's heaped upon us we fight back in our own way, karma, you bet. What else can you expect from us? School's out, dad. I'm not your little baby anymore. And, I don't want to be part of your mess especially when I know next to nothing about you or mom."

"Wait 'til your mother hears this."

"Maybe I should take everything back, right? Games, gotta love 'em. Better off dead, that's what."

"I don't know what's gotten into you, why you're so angry all the time? Or do you want to end up one day with an empty whiskey bottle dangling from your pouty little lips and all you have left is the stale, empty room you've ended up in. And, the only way out for you is some heart attack or stroke."

"Very poetic dad; but, really the compromising really fits your personality, don't you think?"

"Ooh, God help you."

"Nobody has any answers daddy-o. Now, if you don't mind, I have two beautiful boys waiting for me upstairs. Listen. I'm tired of all this drama that plays out all too often. The only thing I really learned from you and mom was to carry myself with some dignity while going about my business. But what does that have to do with me—when things, things just fall apart?"

"There's some things you're just gonna have to solve on your own girl; and, don't give me this about 'I've got Shirelle'. Well I admit that I would be hard put if something ever happened to her. But there's things that we don't tell each other, that I accept as my own; and, just deal with it as best I can girl. I ain't perfect. Come to think of it, neither are you."

"That's a cop out dad; and, you know it."

"What?"

"I've heard that crap all my life. It don't mean nothin'."

"Enough of this. I gotta get going."

"Yeah, that's right, leave. You think about what I said if you have the balls."

"Hey, no daughter of mine's gonna get away talkin' to me like that."

"Your tough stuff's gonna put me in my place, right?"

"Hear that mocking bird carrying on? Well one time he's gonna meet his match, that ole' hawk's gonna swoop down on him and finish off his showboating once and for all. Get me?"

"Is that a threat?"

"Take it any way you want, sweetie. Now, don't go hangin' around with all that white trash that piles into that redneck joint."

"Good night."

"Take care … See ya tomorrow around nine for breakfast?"

"If you show up at all."

"You always gotta get the last word in don't you? You must've picked that up from your mother. Oh, and one last thing. Why on God's green earth do you always have to wear those hooker shoes?"

"Hooker shoes? I paid good money for these."

"Yeah right, five inch heels."

"Oh, I know, actually six inch heels, lime with transparent soles. Dad, if you haven't noticed, I'm a beautiful woman that's bringing her call to the world."

"We'll talk about it after you get back from work tomorrow, OK?"

The stillness of the summer night rests beneath the transparent new moon as cars pass by. Saturday night has awakened, as the regulars make their way into Midnighter's seasoned ride. Behind the lithe steps of young Aisha the screen door shuts.

Chapter Eight

History's Lessons in the Third World

"Ucc-ch, virotay verabotay, this wondrous onslaught of rain calls to mind our great ancestor Methuselah who upon his last breath, just days later the magisterial waters fell from the heavens. And today, Today of all days we have a man from distant lands to spend some time with us to talk about of all things scientific and God-like wrapped in an enigma. Just kidding folks; I ask everyone to stay afterwards because, well, we have today's featured guest who will remind us that we are all part of this wonderful and strange planet we call home. Anyway, he is a supervisor of one our very own—Moshe Tambor, son of Marvin and Ruth, our future chemical engineer Let us give them all a hand."

"Today, we will put aside the Talmud and its precise laws to delve into the mysteries of this wondrous land we call earth, our home. And, without further ado, let us welcome Mr. Ha Chen who resides just minutes from the temple."

"Hi everyone. We sure picked a bad day to do this. Ah, but anyway, a little bit of rain can open up the sinuses, can't it? As you can see, my trusted servant, Moshe is quite the taskmaster. He will handle the computer images while I talk about something that America has walked away from: that something is hydroelectric power in this country. China is by far its number one producer in today's world. And, now the trend has worked its way into southeast Asia, you know, where Vietnam and her neighbors have taken from us and snaked their way into Laos, its beautiful waterfalls, rice patties and dozens of native species which includes that huge catfish that terrifies most Westerners. Even that freshwater peace turtle slowly splashes about in Vietnam's prehistoric lakes and ponds."

OK, alright, yes I scripted that first paragraph. However, from now on, I am on my own. Well not completely anyway— here are a few facts and figures I have on hand—so, you will have to excuse this scared follower of Christ, from the WELS in Wauwatosa—no, I am not asking you to come join the WELS. But, if you do, I have the pastor's telephone number: just kidding. Anyway, Moshe, rebbe, could you dim the lights a bit? July is the Plum Rain season in Shanghai, and the sticky, sun consuming weather worsens as you head south down the Mekong River. Why do you think we are so skinny? Yes, rice and mangoes, catfish, coconut drink, and herbal tea are our favorites. But in summer weather like this, we have no choice but to stay thin.

Look at the Lower Mekong, wide rivers like wild, restless tree branches wind their way through green grass fields, the monsoon runs for days, humidity follows, and bugs thrive everywhere. It is not some travel destination. The Lower Mekong is a food source for over 50 million people. So business people and politicians take their time to build these things. Even stinky Europeans have sided with the peasants. A lot of money to be made in the first couple of decades following their construction. For example, Laos dams sell hydro-power to Thailand; and, Thailand turns right around to pawn it off to Cambodia. It's sort of like the rich giving the really poor electricity at high prices because they have nothing to barter to become competitive partners. So the world learns to do what is best for itself while its poor neighbors just hold on to not falling too far down. OK, so we all want to hear more positive things, shall we?

Many of these dams are built like many in China. The difference is that, with warring roundtable discussions Europeans and my fellow Chinese compatriots have made it clear that danger/evil can sprout at any time. Here is a picture of Xayaburi Dam in Laos. It is about 30% complete. By 2015 the Xayaburi Dam will completely block the Mekong River. In addition, the people of Thailand fought the Decision to start construction on the Dam—you know with start-up money and possible environmental problems, Thailand's own EGAT signed an agreement with the Developers to purchase 95% of the dam's total output of hydroelectric power.

Does anyone know what Mekong means? Anyone? It means 'Mother of the Water'. This 2,700-mile river starts in the southeastern mountains of China here on the Smart Board, flows along Myanmar's and Thailand's border, continues on through Laos and divides Cambodia, and here in southern Vietnam branches into a prong of streams, a, a, what do you call it? C'mon, somebody's got to know, right? 'A delta?' That's it, a big, huge delta fed by the rains, breaking apart and flowing separately into the Pacific Ocean—four different places—one, two three four.

Dams will change the flow of the river; and, with new computer program projections as this brief video illustrates, the dam developers can assess where and how the waters will run after each step of the dam is completed along the River.

By the way, after this presentation, you can meet with Moshe and me beneath a tent set outside for—don't worry I can't screw this up, Moshe gave me the list: apple tea and Turkish coffee with blueberry scones, carrot muffins, and zucchini blossoms. Maybe some other time, if you would wish me to return, my wife and I can stop by and bring some of our very own Chinese creations.

You know, we gave the world its first Restaurant and Italy would not be the same without Pasta: Where else but China?

Oh, and where do you think the first Dam to collect electric power was founded? Appleton on the Fox River, I think in 1882. So, Wisconsin is not all bad news, now is it? Oh, this slide shows some vital statistics: Outside China, 30,000 megawatts of power potential dams are being built. Now, what are megawatts, you say? Megawatt is simply a measurement form of hydroelectric power. Here's an example: 1,900 megawatts generates enough energy to supply 1.9 million homes; and, if you want to bring that into a more local number, 2.4 megawatts can supply electric power for 420 homes. I think that will take care of all of Sherman Park and then some, don't you think?

China is the number one source of power created by Hydro -electric Power. This picture of Three Gorges Dam which produces up to 35,000 megawatts of Hydroelectric Power was recently completed: water pollution, landslides, and a resettlement of over a million people are part of it. The

Yangtze is surrounded by mountains, and corn farmers have had to move up into them as the rising waters have pushed them further into the clouds. The Grand Coulee Dam in Washington, not the Hoover Dam, is America's most powerful dam producing just under 7,000 megawatts hydro-electric. The dam that was completed during World War II just does not compare with China's big boys. In fact, there are two more roughly 12,500 Megawatt dams appearing on the Jinsha River, a Yangtze River tributary that runs in the valley of huge mountains as the photos show. Look at those mountains; and, within these two sources of energy, more will be produced than America's big three: The Grand Coulee, the Sacramento River, and Hoover Dams.

I guess America does not trust hydroelectric power, at least what it can potentially do to our environment. Here shows Indian Tribes in Oregon fighting to reclaim their river fishing rights by taking down some of the dams of Columbia River tributaries to let nature take its course.

Obviously dams, even when they allow the waters to flow beneath, its deep and dense cement and iron-fortified walls, enables the fish to go about their business, yet can still disrupt the secrets of nature that we have yet to understand or have ever even thought of. Along with European architects and engineers, 1995's Mekong River Commission that includes Cambodia, Thailand, Vietnam, and Laos consult with each other before beginning any project that poses any major changes on the Mekong.

To Cambodia's far north Lies Khone Falls: an $800 million dollar dam is proposed—its access roads and a bridge are the only things put in place. Look at the Falls. Look at that. No words can describe its beauty. Passion simply fills my heart. The 400 megawatt Lower Sesan 2 Dam must await careful studies before any dam work will take place. Yes, food supplies can be affected, but like these native creatures, we too are only a part of nature. When we hurt it, we hurt ourselves.

Look at the Laotian worker, committed to his work: the once poor farmer worrying about feeding his family now has a model constructed for his children's children and their own futures. You think America's slow down affects only Europe? Think again. Our modeled dependency has all fallen. So too will it in China, Vietnam… Remember the Laotians forced to move are placed in worse living conditions than they were accustomed to. Besides, we can destroy fish migration patterns if dam planners are not careful.

Even our own DNR could not save the matter even with their best fish hatchery schemes. Oh, look here at all the naturalists from Myanmar to the Delta. Like us, they too are committed. This is our home, the fresh water dolphins of a remaining 70 to 90 individual population along the Myanmar, Cambodian, and Laotian borders, share the Mekong's gifts. And, Laos, that sea of green nestled within the mighty Mekong, looks on in ominous silence. Look at them frolic about in a vast sea of green, and not having to worry about us meddling in their affairs. Just makes you want to cry doesn't it.

No matter how much effort the twelve planned dam construction conglomerates put in does not mean that anything will work to save the second most vital river sanctuary in southeastern Asia. We must understand that we are no less fallible than we are victorious. Our minds balance out the positives and negatives. My years as a controlled man of physics and calculus can never say I am the law. I guess it's just the kid in me—the dolphin meanders around the great Khone Falls. Nothing we can do or say matches the soft truths that evade our most heralded ideas.

Now, before we unleash our five star generals to erase some other madness that starts within us, maybe we should stand up and say something, do something that shakes us from our very core. OK, OK, so I read the whole thing. My broken English is not pretty, but that's who I am. Sound good, doesn't it? Marshall and Eisenhower aren't the answer. Neither is all the madness taking place in Afghanistan. And, forget the same old rants of just going along to get along. War never creates peace. Can we not all agree on this?"

"Let us give Mr. Chen a round of applause. I can assure you he is just as considerate of others at work as he has been here."

"Wait, wait everyone. Let us take a few minutes to answer any questions any of you may have regarding the Southeast Asia hydroelectric push?"

"Well put, my brother Moshe."

"Yes, I would like to know how this affects ours and my family's lives."

"Good point. Moshe, please."

"Are you sure?"

"Yes."

"Well Mr. Kramer, I think you can agree that we are all part of the world right? No matter how small our clan becomes, we still must peek out into the world around us, no matter our beliefs or thoughts on how things should be done.

I mean, isn't it kind of nice that even the leading minds of Europe, and China admit that no matter how well we go into a new dam project on the Mekong, we could fumble the ball all the way to Jericho and never be able to have the opportunity to rectify anything? The porpoise swims at our mercy, so, now does our ability to care for it because we have taken the huge risk that threatens its very existence. That includes our brethren the tortoise. How is he any less vital than we are? We have imposed our newfound energy source upon them. Now, the once poverty-stricken Laotian farmer, counts less on the river's meandering merits and more upon the construct that no native could have ever conceived of. We have chosen to become tenants of the Mekong, plain and simple. WE ARE RESPONSIBLE.

I guess what I am trying to say is that we cannot afford to run away anymore. Vietnam is just a line in the sand—we could also say the same thing about Milwaukee or Wisconsin for that matter. "Go Bucky! Madison, how about it? As an aspiring engineer, I feel that a good job is not everything, nor is giving back to my community: A devoted world citizen, I want to share this place we call mother earth; and, not just about survival issues. That green, green world cannot go on as a crimson dynamo without all our efforts to support these people and their homeland. History taught me about the Vietnam War—fumbling the ball doesn't do it justice. Saving face cost the lives of untold millions. We still have not taken responsibility for Agent Orange. Babies are still born unto their parents with birth defects. I'm no martyr; but, really, if our leaders will not take responsibility for their own miscues, why should any of us?"

"Son, when I was your age the draft was on and the War was coming to a head. I agree, the killing on the nightly news was brutal, but if this, these dam projects can prove successful while they monitor the effects to the river and the fish; well, why not let them give it a shot?"

"Oh, I agree wholeheartedly. However, when something goes wrong, they must act on correcting the problems immediately. Otherwise, a river perishes its peoples, and the diversity of life is once again ruined because we waited for the professionals to tell us what to do while they sat on the sideline. And, once again here we sit as we watch everything unravel before our eyes saying, *well, they did the best they could; but, really what could I do?* I'm tired of being stymied by the resilient mediocrity of an Anna Karenina? I mean, why aren't there people helping others in a time of crisis? "

"Instead we go about doing things in our own way saying we're imperfect, only Yah-Weh can come to my rescue, my consolation? Is not it, simply our own fears, something we can't face about ourselves? How can we atone if we just go along?"

"The clock stops, Moshe: time passes on."

"Well, then, that's it. Always expect the same results" Pain and anguish—power and control are physical properties—our thoughts. The mind is just a tool like the monkey that uses a stick to itch its back. Call it god, call it what you will. There is precision in uniformity but it has gone to extremes. My dad told me about a tornado wiping out Barneveld, Wisconsin a while back; but just travel by that sewage behemoth near Stickney on the Stevenson south of Chicago?

"You've become cynic young man. Perhaps you should spend more time at the temple and help out at the school."

"Oh, I agree; but yeah, I'm still part of Temple Beth El, always make sure I attend all the trips to the Arboretum. Yom Kippur for me is every day, to wrap myself within God's grace— to let go of the masks I've chosen to wear to be accepted. Who gets along? I mean really."

"OK, that was an interesting way to end the session. Now, we hope you will join us just outside beneath our tent. Yes, it is raining quite heavily. Strange for such a temperate July: Mr. Chen and Moshe have brought some great refreshments and bakery to keep you all warm while we share our thoughts and concerns of those electrical giants moving into the third world. No matter how little we think our voices are, we must not forget to speak our minds. This is our world; and, as Moshe made clear, the authorities, their only concerns are to take care of themselves and their families. Our country, no matter how much better, whether it is the first or fifth amendment, we destroy ourselves and our loved ones by just worrying about getting what we want. Shalom. Come, Mr. Chen."

"Beautiful day, Rebbe Tverski."

"Isn't it though? If only a rainbow will shine a light on this damp, gray day. Shalom. Now, please, Moshe, really: I see your car is parked across the street. What would your poor father and mother say to you about this? Bringing all this on yourself, you know? Perhaps you should just leave. Sorry Mr. Chen, it seems our ingrate Moshe can't take his foot off the gas pedal."

"Moshe, Can I just talk to Mr. Tverski in private for a moment?"

"Could you hurry it up a bit? My girlfriend wants to go to an art exhibit on the East Side."

"On a day like this? I just want to go home—take warm bath—Shanghai in July never this cold."

"What can I do for you Mr. Chen?"

"What's that those men over there wearing?"

"Oh, that's a prayer shawl, a *tallit*."

"What kind of hat?"

"A huckel black hat. Look I know you are passionate about dams and their problems; but, we, we, you see, have our own concerns. Even some in our little worlds, like Moshe, they, shun everything we are about. It's not like we mean him any harm; but he's, he's, ha-aaah, how can I say this, his own cracked world has reared its ugly head."

"He's young, yeah?"

"Feel out of place, Mr. Chen? How do you think my husband feels when he goes to school to pick up my precious Nathaniel? All those people around here look at both of them like they are from a different planet. We just want to go about our own lives; and, whatever you think about us, that's fine, I guess. Tolerance has its place. I think we can all agree on that one. I mean with Mao and all, I am sure you have gone through back to your homeland. But Sir, you must realize that family and *challah board* means more to us than you can imagine. I know you think we are strange fellows walking around in these woolen clothes, hiding from you. But I think everyone does in some way. The Temple brings us together, drags us out of our isolation, with school and Torah readings to open our spirit. Understand mister?"

"Yes, I am a foreigner too. My English OK. When I read it, I am better. But you need to see what is happening. Those dams wake up a lot of people, millions of people, the river and land too is disturbed from its nature. Rebbe Tverski talked with Moshe and me about it. I need to improve my speaking, so he looked at the speech, and thought that it was good, yeah, rebbe?"

"Certainly: we want to reach out to the community, but we don't feel welcome. So, we go to our work and celebrate here tucked away from the world around us."

"China and southeast Asia no different. The same. Lot more people live in land of my childhood, Mr. Tverski, more problems. We too have the *Book of the Dead*. Life is illusion. To reveal oneself is religion. We rather have problems, hide. Everything same."

"For some reason, the worlds of people want nothing to do with us: pariahs. Mr. Chen can you understand that? Pogroms still exist in Russia, constant threats in the Middle East and Europe. We are not allowed to become a part of the community, so we just want our own small world to enjoy one another's company. The only thing the world can relate to is that inane *dreidel*: Americans are so taken by gambling that maybe they possess some sort of childish fancy to the joy it can bring from a limited world of winning and losing. I don't know; but, Sir Chen, we are happy with our lives. Whatever you and others think about us, we can accept. After all, tolerance is a beginning."

"Or maybe you think I need a *menorah* for my fireplace, you, you— nobody's smarter. I bested everyone at Marquette—physics, third level calc—where I worked at Johnson Controls, many starting out make nearly as much as me. China is impossible. America so beautiful; but work there, see how you like it?"

"That is your choice, is it not?"

"Hey, he stole my hat! Grab 'm!"

"Step on it Moshe."

"What'd you do?"

"I took one of their black hats, that's what. 'Go'! Doggerel, you, you holy men. Millions more died in China under Mao— nobody was there to help us either."

"And, you thought I was the live wire. Took balls, though."

"Relax, Chen, they don't drive in their cars on the Sabbath. You're good to go. No one's gonna catch us."

"Everything's wrong, Moshe. Who cares about any of this?"

"Touché. Hang on."

"Look at all those Orthodox Jews chasing the car down the street."

"Well, they're not going to catch them without reinforcements," Genie Bartusek rubs Paul's shoulder, "they'll head back to the synagogue and get their umbrellas. It's really coming down now, Paulie. Let's say we go to Goldi's. And, from there catch a couple of drinks at Von Trier."

"Not so fast: didn't we come this way so you could talk things out with your friend, Alice?"

"Ah, she's, she hates me and there's nothing I can do about it. I told her about what I thought. I told you this last week. She claims I'm too egotistical to get over my good looks."

"Nah, you can't help it you're so hot. You know you remind me of that woman from a Femmes' video long raven hair and ruby lips, pouty no less, straddling a little kiddy merry-go-round horse, up and down, you, you sweat thing you, yeah."

"What's the name of it?"

"Promise, why?"

"I'll pull it up in my cell phone. No biggy, Paul. I just want to see what kind of pervert I'm hangin' out with, that's all."

"I could ask the same thing about you, ya know."

"Sometimes Paul, I don't know about you, like I can't figure what's going on in that pointed little head of yours. But I can say that it's probably quite nasty."

"Like a crowning of thorns?"

"You could say that."

"Christ, Paul, it's not like you have a lot of friends. So, Onan, aside from your lazy hobby, what kept your juices flowing?"

"You know, maybe-um-following in my father's footsteps like becoming a Jaycees member, how about something like a Free Mason?"

"Paulie, a Free Mason: simple redneck lost in thought like some Proustian figure who never really knows where he's coming from, just hooked on how he fits into his surroundings. Really, who wants to hear your sordid story of lost, so-oh lost?"

"Who's Proustian? You mean Proust?"

"OK, Proust? A comedy of lazy characters cloaked in their thoughts they keep to themselves. In early twentieth century France, their petty hatreds and positive self-assuredness they employ to social climb at those readings/soirees, whatever you call them, well, let's just say you would fit right in with their soulless witticisms, you lout."

"Well, at least you can say I have some cache."

"Panache."

"Yeah, couldn't have said it better myself."

"Don't push it."

"You brought it up, I didn't."

"Hopelessly tragic perfumed with comical pretense is more apt. Oh, would you look at this woman? Yes, I can see how you would confuse her insatiable fire with my own cat-like presence."

"Whatever that means? Hopelessly tragic, yeah, I'll give you that."

"We're all kinda lazy, can't really get going."

"Haven't your ever thought about being a writer?"

"That's for the birds, but seriously Paul, I am tired of trying to figure everything out. I just want to know you, to talk things out without fighting about the same old shit. I never had that with Norm. You know I want to have a child with you. I can't go back Paul. That's been played out a long time ago. Just let me know when you're ready. Just don't take forever or heaven help me."

"Hey, if I'm not ready now, I'll never be. Like I said, I've made an appointment to see Doc next week. Anyway, I'm tired of sitting in front of your friend's house. I don't want to deal with the cops."

"Cops? Do you think I'm some kind of thug?"

"You know darn well that anyone on edge, including your friend, could easily make things ugly for you if she felt threatened by your snoopin' around."

"For Christ's sakes, she doesn't even know you nor has she ever seen this old Honda come around her house before. Besides, she probably thinks that I've become homeless."

"Well, she's got a point there. I mean, it's not like you're the most hands-on person I've ever laid eyes on. Nah, you'll always land on your feet with the way you can work things."

"I don't know if I should take that as a compliment or not. You're so the provider. But, yeah, let's do like you said you were gonna do with me last weekend."

"What was that?"

"Head east to Goldi's."

"Right; and, spend every dime in my pocket on 'girlie' things."

"Couldn't have said it better."

"Alright; but, do not get me involved with your spats with your friend anymore. You can get on the bus to talk things out. Man, it's coming down even harder. We're gonna get a couple inches before this is all over."

"Cool. So we're on?"

"Yes, but no eating out. I've got some leftovers and some bakery I picked up a few nights ago, Oh, that Greek lamb stew?"

"Yep. That's alright. See these flats?"

"Yeah, so?"

"They're the only things you've gotten me so far."

"Genie, I told you until you get some kind of job that splurges are off limits. Who's paying for all your toiletries and beauty salon treks?"

"You're no fun."

"I'm taking you to Goldi's, aren't I?"

"Right, just to look around."

"You can get something; but, I'll decide whether or not you can walk out with 'em."

"How much?"

"Do we gotta go through with this again?"

"Let's go home?"

"Alright, two hundred's your limit: unless, of course, your ex-Norm can scrape together some pacifying cash to please that smitten pretty little smile of yours."

"You know I've applied at several temp agencies and have come up with nothing—you know I haven't worked in a long time."

"And you know that I don't bring home a whole lot either, Genie. Without you, I struggled. And, now I've got you living with me. Ally's been over to spend the night several times. It all adds up, sweetheart. You know I love you, but this can't go on forever. Hell, why don't you get a job selling shoes so you don't have to drag your precious little feet all over town with those little Arab shoes you've got on."

"Two tone flats you mean."

"OK, two tone flats. I'm giving you a two hundred-dollar window. Isn't that enough to get you through for the next couple of months before your children start school? Like, I can just see this little Ms. PTA taking care of all her children's educational needs, helping others. Hey, you've got a college degree, right? Why don't you try to get some work at one of the schools in the area?"

"I've thought about it, but I've been out of school for a long time. And, really what can I do?"

"I don't know, but it's not like I knew a lot about circuit breakers before I started at Eaton. It wasn't like that was the only place I applied at either. Babe, I needed a job. Yeah, it's just a job. I ain't never gonna rule Main Street. But, hey maybe I don't want all the crap that goes with it. Those silent looks on management's face: they talk like they're so sure of themselves. It's all a put on. And, of course, my deal is to act like everything's peachy. We're all just trying to get by, only the stake s for them are much greater. But the grind trickles down. How many times have I told you this? It ain't no TV show. It is what it is."

"I'm still your crimson dynamo."

"Five star. When McCartney comes around Chicago, we'll get tickets. God, if we could see him at the Soldier Field. Saw Pink Floyd there a life time ago. I Didn't expect much. But, God, I've never seen anything like it. McCartney would be nirvana: Wings Over America, yeah."

"A new pair of stilettos and a crocheted top would blend right in now, wouldn't it?"

"I love you as long as the whole deal falls under $200.00."

"You saw those prices at the sidewalk sale a couple months back."

"Yeah, you know what I like best about you?"

"Tell me."

"Like when I feel ripped up inside—I can tell you what's on my mind, that all the measuring up crap falls away, can tell you what I need to say without worrying about some big rock falling in my lap, like I can really say what I need to say."

"I keep telling you, Paul, that just because I was married with three beautiful kids, that didn't mean everything was hunky dory. I'm still wondering how I ever went through with the life I had with Norm. I mean he's a decent enough guy and everything. I mean he's a good provider, but he does nothing for me. My friends, hah, where have they all gone? They used to tell me that opposites in the bedroom attract. My fetishes just overpower him, and his meager attentiveness dares not touch my weaker side."

"I don't know. Sex is great, no problem there. Just don't start ordering me around because that is a definite turn off."

"I think theories are just make-believe. We've got to find our own selves."

"And hope to God that special someone won't use it against us."

"We women have always known that in weakness lies strength. We've hadn't had much choice with you guys ordering us around like we were your slaves."

"Anything can change at any time. I only know about right now. Oh look. There's a parking spot just past Goldi's. There's a couple of umbrellas in the trunk. Wait here."

The rains break the pavement with an eerie presence, the gray skies consume the buildings as the lovers inch their way through the tumult. With no one in sight, they make their way into the store with only one salesperson there to cater to Ms. Bartusek. In from the rain, she talks openly with the women as if they have known each other for years. Meanwhile, Paulie, his thighs soaked, closes the parasols, shakes them and sits down as Genie selects a couple of shoes to try on.

"Oh, would you look at that Cavalli top, Chrysanthemums, purple, red, yellow—114 bucks. Hey Paul, c'mon, what do you think?"

"It's so you. Keep the taxes in mind. Nothing over 200. Remember?"

"I'm going to try it on; oh, and could you get those beige stilettos in a size 9?"

"I'll have a look. Anything else before I get back from the back room?"

"For now. I'll keep my eyes open while you look for my size." Paul enjoys watching her childlike excitement as she moves into the fitting room. Weather like this in July is rare. And, really all Paul wants to do is to rent a couple of movies and brew some Columbian Coffee he's recently picked up from the corner store. Really, all this dilly-dallying about would be fine if skies would clear up. Even being in from the rain cannot shelter him from the cold. The dampness cuts through his clothing. His mind focuses upon just getting home. If only she would make up her mind soon.

The Honda Civic sits just outside to shuttle him back where his own lamb stew and a cozy bottle of Cabernet Sauvignon silently awaits.

"I don't have them in your size; but with a similar look and your gorgeous lithe legs, I just thought you might want to try these on."

"You're right; and, I was wondering if you might have these in the back'. Sure, tries these on while I take a look."

"Paul, would you look."

"How much are they?"

"Seventy-five—fifty per cent off."

"I don't want to go to my credit card, Genie. Two hundred's all I got."

"Chic fashion never goes out of style."

"And, when September comes, I'll be hearing the same thing again. How many times do I have to say this, Genie? If you want this stuff you're going to have to try much harder to get a job. You know how much I make. When habits cost money, you can bet I'll put my foot down."

"I did find these in your size. Oh, would you listen to that rain? For the last two hours it's been just been coming down in buckets. Look at her, Sir. Beautiful, no? Would you care to look at anything else?"

"No, but I'll take the top and the two pairs of shoes."

"Honey, could you take these to the register while I go to the bathroom?"

"See you in a bit."

"Here, put the remainder on the credit card. Sure thing. Paul, you sure have a beautiful wife."

"Girlfriend; but, yes she's great. So, how are you?"

"Fine, but this weather is starting to get on my nerves. It's so-oh cold! It's like October weather, you know?"

"Oh, I sure do. All I want to do is to go home and get a bite to eat before I call it a day. A warm bath sounds out of this world right now."

"I have kids to take care of once I get home. You know: once I show up, everything falls on my shoulders."

"I wouldn't know what that's like. I don't have any."

"You don't?"

"Nope. Genie does. She's got three."

"Divorced?"

"Separated. She's quite firm that it's not going to work out with her husband. They're not compatible."

"Who ever said we're compatible?"

"I don't know. I think you have to be who you are with your loved one."

"Sometimes that's even debatable."

"It's only my own fears that everything will fall apart— nobody else's."

"Been there, done that. Are we all done here?"

"Sure are Ms."

"My name is Susan; and, if you ever need anything in the future, please do not hesitate to give me a call."

"My name is Genie Bartusek. Here, I'll write it down on your business card with Paul's cell phone number, and our address … There."

"Great, I'll get a flyer out to you on our summer sale a few months down the road."

"Wonderful, Susan, you've brought a little sunshine into this bleak afternoon. See ya."

"Now, didn't I tell you to keep you purchases under two hundred dollars?"

"Twenty-five dollars over. Be happy it wasn't a hundred plus. Ah, Paul, could you carry these bags while I get the umbrellas."

"Anything else?"

"Nah, let's go."

"After you."

Chapter Nine

Things Could be a Whole Lot Worse

"Hello?"

"Hi dad. I was wondering if we could talk about our little excursion into your neck of the woods a couple months ago."

"Sure, why not? It's not something I said, was it?"

"No, no, no, no. It's just that, well, like why didn't you tell me about the two cats you have in your possession. Kurt's allergies were out of control for a couple of weeks after we got back. And, Tommy, well, that was a disaster. I thought you were going to spend some time with him?"

"So, this is how you get things done? Figure out how to shove it down your old man's throat, you know, but do it in such a way that I have nothing to go on, kind of hang me out to dry. Oh, and about the cats: how was I to know about Kurt's allergy problems with cats? Next time you come, I'll just take them over to the neighborhood vet."

"Well, at least you can understand what I have to say. That's a first. Doc likes the money I put out for your hearing aide."

"That old thing? Hell no. I've picked up a new one which doesn't make those sharp ringing noises in the middle of dinner or playing bocce ball after I finish up my twice weekly 'Meals on Wheels' delivery routes. Best investment I've ever made."

"Did you ever activate that cell phone I got you for Christmas a while back?"

"No, why?"

"You could have let me know, and I would have gotten you something you would like better."

"At my age, really Diane, things really don't mean much to me."

"Right: since mother died all those years back, you haven't done a whole lot with yourself."

"No, and you spent what was it, seven, eight years here nursing your own wounds while you told me what to do with my sorry life."

"You're starting to be overly critical again papa. You need to tone yourself down a bit. I'm just trying to help you, that's all. You know we care about you; but, sometimes it seems like you're on your own island if you get my drift."

"Trying to escape my boring life since your mother's passed on, please save it. You couldn't even say those words—they'd be too, too harsh. Cause too much tension. Maybe even cause some fists to fly. But that wouldn't do. My ticker's solid babe: scout's honor.

"You smug old cuss. I swear to God. If it wasn't for Debra and mom, I'd have left your sorry ass out all by your lonesome. Chill out. Don't you know that if I wasn't there to help you through your bouts with alcohol and depression, you'd no be longer a part of this world?

No really dad, you've gotta hear this, like, like everyone would gladly tune you out. You understand what I'm saying, don't you? I mean, you have a way of shutting everyone out; a-nd, one day, papa, no one will have the time of day for your cantankerous outbursts. Like you're the only one who's got problems on this planet? For God's sake, we all do, DAD."

"If you think I am at war with myself, yeah, sure, there are those moments; but, for the most part my dear, we just don't talk—never have. Now just hear me out. I've listened to you about psychotherapy, and, it's all so cold—like not even you little Ms. Sunshine's got answers for everything! And, these cats, yes they're warm and dreamy, but when I go outside to weed the garden, they tear around the yard ever so quietly and look at the world in wonder, something I enjoy to no end. Better than all the silent treatments I've had to put up with you guys."

"Ooh, why do I even bother with you? For heaven's sake, Debra just wanted you to spend some quality time with Tommy; and, what did you do? Took him to dinner, and he split to go out drinking with his buddies—but, hey, he's just following in your own footsteps."

"You're living with your own as well, need I remind you. Now, I'm gonna cut to the chase if you don't mind—all the time you spent the last decade laughing at this old bag o' bones—and, yeah, at times I literally rattled in complete paranoia, like, like everyone's out to get me. And, yes, sure I bottomed out too many times to count, but let me tell you, who the hell are you? I've seen you, what, twice in the past five years? After you split with your writing gigs, you have made yourself pretty scarce. Only an occasional phone call, but that's it, Diane. I'm sure you've had your reasons, but I think you have a problem seeing your own little part in all this."

"Some teen-age analysis, like the only thing I base my thoughts on are that victorious Adlerian power prowess? There are consequences to your rude behavior, dad. All we're asking is that you have some respect for others. It's not like we're asking you to save the world or anything. How about realizing that we also have feelings?"

"Right, shut me up in a corner so that I can, we can all get along. Diane, you don't even show up for Christmas, Thanks-

Giving for that matter. We're not that close, Diane. Heaven knows, I let your mother run the show for years. And, yeah, I showed you two the beauty of Wisconsin on the bluffs of the Kickapoo or sitting atop those sheer cliffs looking out over the Lodi farm fields. Life is not knowledge or religion: those are two things I have gladly failed at. Ah, maybe there's religion that's not like going to church anyway. *Anyhoo* , I'll tell you one thing. I know there is something about me that frightens you, a certain openness I can't really explain. You're not the expert at that, not me, nobody. I'm tired of this stupid game. Doesn't really matter from what I can see. If you want social graces, find someone else. It's all lose, lose babe. That much I do know."

"You know mother died sixty feet from the slot machines up at Oneida. I had no idea she was there. Where do you think some of our IRA's ended up? She took care of the investments. Mom was the banker in the family. Everything fell apart quite quickly because I never saw any indication of this on our tax returns. So, there you have it sweetheart. Take it for what it's worth. My lost life of beers and hard stuff mirrors hers, doesn't it?"

"You can't blame her for your DT's, dad. I had to haul you in a couple of times when you relapsed, that is, if you haven't forgotten—dearie? Secondly, how do I not know that you are making all this up just to irk me?"

"I may be old but I haven't lost my way, Diane. And, I'm tired of hearing nobody's perfect. It wasn't a mistake that led your mother to unload thousands on the casinos. A couple mature IRA's just whisked away by her game of chance if you know what I mean? I'll leave it at that. Money is something that I don't have to worry about anyway. I'm set. Besides, I don't crave alcohol anymore. Hell, I can even enjoy a Leine' every now and then. Just ask your beau. Look, if you want me out of your life, just say so."

"Ooh, you vile cruel, lonely old man. All I ask is that you take the time to think of others before you go running your mouth. You'll take care of your sorry ass. Yeah, that's right: Don't drag me into your little pity party. Now I know what it means when they say old folks revert to their childhood ways. We've already passed that point of no return with you, haven't we?"

"You're making mountains out of mole hills. If you want to control what I have to say, that won't fly here, sweetheart. I may have been standoffish in the past, but now, by God when I see something I don't like, I will say it come hell or high-water. Otherwise, oh God, someone's at the door. I've gotta go."

"Aren't you gonna go and see who it is?"

"It's Kendra with little Joey. Do you want me to call back or not? I will understand if you don't want me to."

"Call me Sunday evening around eight, I mean, if you don't have anything going on?"

"Then eight it is. Talk to you soon. M'bye."

Taking a deep breath, he walks toward his cats and closes them into the visitor's bedroom. Ok, it is time to see what is going on. Looking straight into Kendra's eyes, he briskly opens the front door.

"Fancy meeting you here. Joey, my little big man why come on in. Kendra, what can I do for you on this sweltering afternoon?"

"Grampa, I need to speak with you about something important. Do you have some time to speak with me for a bit?"

"I've got all day. Hey Joey, here's a couple of watermelon candies. Want some? It's alright, isn't it?"

"Sure, what do you say Joey?"

"Oh, that's quite all right. His smile's more than enough."

"Grampa, I really need to talk with you, right now if you don't mind."

"Let me get out a couple of your nephew's toys. I have a feeling this is gonna take a while."

"What's he pointing at?"

"Joey, what do you want?"

"Drink, there."

"Could he have a little Pepsi?"

"Why, yes, my dear little world beater. A little ice, and, voila there you have it. Here you go. Come, let's go into the kitchen so we don't get the rug too sticky." The old man softly kisses his future as he turns, "do you want anything to drink, eat?"

"Nah, can we have a seat?"

"What's the matter?"

"Go ahead, grampa."

"You sure you don't want a cup of coffee?"

"No gramps, I'm fine, really."

"Alrighty then."

They sit adjacent from one another; and, for a moment, silence consumes their presence. "Gramps, I-I-I don't know how to say this, but, but—But, but—Oh God, you're—you, I, I mean you have no clue."

"I don't even know why you came here. I mean, Joey's never stepped foot in this house if that's what you're getting at? I know you all think I'm just a sick old lout with one foot in the grave, ready to cash in when I pass on. You all know what my will entails, so what do you have to tell me that's so vitally important?"

"Please, grampa, don't make this any harder than it is for me."

"Well?"

"H-m-m-ah-h-m-n. I…ah-um… I blew 50 Grand at the tables."

"What?"

"I didn't mean to; I, I—"

"Now, now then. Come here. I don't bite, Please?"

Softly, Kendra puts down her purse, looks down, nervously falling into his arms.

"Whatever it was, you'll get through this—But 50,000 bucks, Kendra? That's some heavy loot."

"I know gramps. I blew it. What else can I say?"

He strokes her long blond hair as she uncontrollably weeps onto his soft shoulder. Kendra, a Dean's Honor Student and patroness of Easter Seals, falls limp into his arms, wearied by her alms, her mind too distraught to face anyone much less her husband or task master father.

"Sit down, princess. Why are you telling me this? What about Kevin, your dad for that matter?"

"Because they're too busy climbing the ladder while I, I rot in my skin—fuck, why even live anymore?"

"Kevin and your old man have done pretty well for themselves. They could probably buy up this entire block if they wanted to. I mean Hales Corners or here? I want you to tell me what's this really about."

"But, but"—.

"Kendra, you have not come here ever with your mother. That's really no big deal. I've never spent a whole lot of time with my parents after I started a family, but I gotta tellya, this sounds a lot like you want me to give you the 50,000 to take care of business. It's not about the money. Nah, that's not right, it is about the money. Yeah, I've got a whole lot more where that came from, but you can't just shove it under the rug like the two little friends I've got hidden in the back room."

"Friends?"

"Feline friends. Since old Rudy passed on a while back, I picked up these two furry creatures stirring about in their own room. They're the only friends I have in this world: never had anyone I could call a friend, unless I went along with their whims. Don't, won't do that anymore. I know that I am alone, who isn't? You have to make your own decisions. Here is the grown up thing, Kendra. You've got to make up your own mind, understand?"

"I want the fifty-thousand-dollar loan."

"Like how are you going to pay me back? Last time I checked, you don't have a job. Besides, how did all that money evaporate from gambling so quickly without your husband finding out about it? I know, don't tell me, you've done some creative accounting to take the edge off the big chill."

"Kevin would kill me. I—he's nice enough, but you have no idea what kind of temper he has when he loses it. And, don't you tell me it's alright, somehow things will work out. The fuck if you know old man." She quickly wrestles her hands from his clutches, grabbing little Joey as he grabs her purse.

"I will do it, but you will have to make a visit to my attorney's office next week sometime. What day is good for you?"

"What do you think?"

"OK, let's make it Monday afternoon at 3:00 P.M. If things change, I'll call you."

"Alright, I'll swing by around 2 to pick you up. I don't want anyone in the neighborhood to stick their nose where it doesn't belong."

"Somehow or another we all wanted it this way, precious. I say come out in the bright of day with guns blazing. If they want to martyr you, let 'em. They know what they're doing; the big sleep will be them. That devil they, we have all made up in our own way. Are you gonna get any help?"

"Help? What do you mean by that?"

"Seek out a psychiatrist—open up—step out of your shell; or, do you want to stay hidden, say to youself everything will work its way out? Or you could subscribe to the old just get by from one day to the next?"

"I'll tell you what. If you don't pay me pay back before I pass on, that $50,000 will come out of your mother's inheritance: like she really needs it. But yeah, that's the angle. I hate to say nothing's free, but if the shoe fits."

"Just be ready at 2 when I swing by. Come on, Joey."

"Oh, and one more thing. I too need love. Kevin and you were so idyllic. Look at you, so attractive, so young. But really you're all just a bundle of nerves, just had to do it to get off. I know, I'm just a drunk who still warms up to his cognac and amaretto on a cold winter night. I am not dead yet. How many times do you think I heard people behind my back telling others, once a drunk always a drunk? Now, look at you. Maybe your craving has sent you packing for good if you're not careful. You've fallen apart sweetheart. Not even the money can change that scenario. Still broken. All I can say is you'd better do something quick or some other monster's gonna rear its ugly head."

"Like I don't know that?"

"Champ, have another piece of candy for the road. May I?" Softly, he strokes Joey's chestnut brown locks, and hugs him spiritedly.

"So long prince charming, the Queen has her affairs to tend to."

"Remember to be ready here Monday to see your lawyer at 2."

"You be here on time or it's all off."

"Say 'bye' Joey."

"Bye-bye."

The poplars and lindens sway in the sweltering heat of the mid-afternoon sun as hundreds of black folks listen to the words of Ajamou Butler, a young and respectable poet, bringing inspiration, music, and soul food to his guests as "Heal the Hood" enters its third year at North 24th Street and West Keefe.

"Hey, everybody da food is wicked, like I said, let us celebrate this life the only one we know of. Student Minister Abel Muhammad, do you have anything to add before we wrap up this annual community festival?"

"Yes brotha'; Even though others have caused our problems, it is up to us to carry on, to take the responsibility for change. Brother Farrakhan wishes us to refocus, ta heal the hood. Remain Proud, Afro-Centric!"

"Last but not least, everyone as I said earlier, I will not die young. Without job creation, our peoples will continue to fall into desperation. We don't want another bang-bang Detroit or St. Louis, but it does not look good for us."

12.8% of our black brothers remain in the system's jails right now while 47% do not have a registered Wisconsin Driver's License. How can they get to jobs when many of them are not even anywhere near the Metro bus line? Take a ride out to the suburbs. Look around, and just remember that 77% of all homicide victims are African Americans. Makes you think, does it not?" Keep working at it people. Without us, Milwaukee will cease to exist. We make this town go, not Mr. and Mrs. Smith from Whitefish Bay or Glendale.

"We are its culture, its pulse. But, hey, everybody's a little broken in some way, right? That's why we need to find what we can do best and work that into helping rebuild our community one person, one home at a time. Heal the Hood! Let's not cash out. Spend our money in our neighborhood businesses, create jobs for our youth, and spread our seeds should we hope to have our DREAMS to Grow. Like I said a thousand times before, WE NEED JOBS NOW!"

"Brother Ajamou, hello."

"Hello, Damon."

"This is my girlfriend, Jasmine."

"So, Jasmine, what do you think of our little piece of heaven?"

"Well, hm-n, I, ah, it's kinda neat, I mean those African bongos, you know I play the flute, classical baroque really, but, yeah, they're really good."

"Really good, yeah, the first time I heard them come 'round, I had to get 'em for this event. Damon here's doing really well over at True Skool. He's even entered some of his creations into several contests."

"I haven't won anything yet, but I am learning how to handle questions from people judging my work. Not everyone gets what I'm putting out there either. You know, sometimes it seems like they don't want to see what it is I'm showing them."

"What do you think about Damon's work, Jasmine."

"He's good with colors. I don't know why he doesn't paint."

"It's all about the jobs. Jasmine, you don't know what it's like to not know when you're gonna eat again or when the dimes can't pay the rent anymore. And, you know there's not a whole lot you can do about it?"

"My dad kind of lives like that."

"Oh, yeah? What does he do?"

"He works at a diner and works the bar at night."

"That's steady work, right?"

"He told me that things don't work out like they do in books. Everybody knows their part; and, when you're in trouble, you take care of it to survive. If you don't, ah, you're on your own."

"What do you think about all this Heal the Hood stuff?"

"I know things are not good. I didn't need to come here to know this. Sherman Park's a little better off than around here."

"A little better?"

"OK, a lot better; but, something is not right about this, about everything."

"What do you mean?"

"I, I think it's all about us. Mom says 'she thinks everyone knows that everything is wrong but nobody has done anything about it'. Don't you think so, Mr. Butler?"

"You can call me Ajamou. But you need to understand that we need to resolve some issues which have never been taken care of. Just stay in school, and you will see that some things need to be pushed forward."

"I can guarantee you the 3 rd Street Riots a lifetime ago will be buried by something a whole lot worse to come along if things don't change quick. Every major pitfall has this same issue, the black community with this dirt blowing around for a hundred years, and then some. We're equals, EQUALS. Now, if you don't mind, brother Damon, Ms. Jasmine. I need some things to tend for before I leave. Good evening."

"Could we go now, Damon?"

"Why?"

"I wanna go home. That's why."

"Chuck, hey bro', what you doin' Sunday? Wanna go over to the Park, you know, fuck around with Jackie and JaJuana?"

"Sounds cool. Not a whole lot goin' on right now. Yeah, you bet. Nothin' else doin' right now. You drivin'?"

"Pick you up around noon?"

"Cool. Hey, there's my ride. See you then."

"Be cool."

"Could we go now?"

"What's up with you?"

"It's not like I wanted to come here or anything."

"So, what's that supposed to mean, like this wasn't vanilla enough for your taste?"

"I'm half Hispanic if you'd like to know. It's not like blacks are the only minorities in Milwaukee."

"We are the majority. Have been for a long time. So what if we want to blow off a little steam, let people know we's fine, but enough's enough. And, if that don't work, hey, you're gonna hear about it, brick by brick. Hear what I'm sayin'?"

"Loud and clear. Now, can we go?"

"Lead the way."

"H-m-n-h-mmm-ph-don't ever put me through that again."

"What? Like, you can only be locked in da game if everything goes your way or what?"

"Or what? Yeah, right."

"All right, well, if that's the way you want it, fine."

"Aw, you kidding me? Why can't you put on something like Rita Ora or Pixie Lott instead of this, this"—

"C'mon Jazz, li'l R&B, Jazz, feelin' me? SPEAKeasy, partyin' in style, drink flowing, listen. 'Strobe a la mode', always somethin' right? Comes on like he's on fire. Know what? Another hoodie killed before his time and we gotta take the sick words of the toady police chief, the media layin' it on again like never before— just another, hoe', two-bit dealer, who cares, right?"

"Oh yeah, and Jank or whatever, wasn't it what we listened on the way down, that photographer you can't stop talkin' about?"

"I've been to a couple of his shows, cool cool, cool, gotta tellya. He even talks about doin' stand up—doesn't go along with the world's buzz, really, do you? C'mon now, like you're not running' around in your little way to avoid the kidney punches, who ain't doin' that? Everything settles in sooner or later. The real question is, is it them or you that's doin' you in?"

"OK, OK, I get it. But next time I might just say no."

"Don't give me that bleedin' cracker shit. Man, if you want out, say so. Don't come around cryin' and shit, den sayin' like the rug's gonna get pulled right from under ya pretty little feet. What do you think it is like to be reminded you're black every day? Not when you feel like it, I mean every fuckin' day. Yeah, we ain't perfect. We've done some nasty shit ourselves. But you guys, yeah, right, hey, don't ever admit you did nothin' wrong. Look at where we live, Jazz? You think there's any chance most of us gonna get outta this?"

"You can sit over and talk with you' mama like you like to do, joke with her. I know her, she's, she seems nice and' everythang."

"No, this is how it is with mom. I have to keep improving my flute play or she will find a way to get rid of me."

"Ah, my heart bleeds for you. For Christ's sake Jasmine, you saw that black lady wanderin' around the parking lot when we first got here. What do you think she's gonna sell those turkey necks for?"

"I'm not that stupid. But Damon, you even told me that a lot of Whites buy drugs from around here, right?"

"Hey, it's free enterprise. You got the money, I got the goods."

"You cross my mother, you're gonna find out that things will not go your way for a long time. It's not just grounding, Damon.

Mom can get her way for a long time if she wants to."

"You can leave the hood and head for Whitefish Bay without being questioned why you're there. Me do that? C'mon."

"Yeah, you're right. But Damon, I'm not gonna get a word across to any of your friends here."

"You're learnin'. Hey, when I was a kid, some rich bitch made the news for bein' kidnapped. Elizabeth Smart's face was all over the news forever— took a long time to find her, but they did. At the same time, seven-year old Alexis Patterson disappeared. To this day, they haven't found her. You gonna tell me they really care what happened to her? Christ, Jazz, open your eyes. We're fightin' all these wars, and we can't even get along right here in our own backyards."

"I want you Damon. You're so-oh nice. But people do what they do. Heaven knows, even Jesus hasn't been able to change our ways. God do I hate church. They talk about all wonderful things; and, nothing ever changes."

"I don't know where that came from. But, yeah, we's some gnarly dudes—dudettes too. But really, Jazz, how do you think anything'll change if we cain't get beyond just getting' along?"

"God, can't we just drop it and get home. My mom's gonna have a million and one questions; And, no Damon. You have no idea who your dealin' with. My mom, I swear, she'll fight to the bitter end."

"No holds barred, huh? Look, I don't want to dwell on this 24/7. But I cain't just sweep it under da rug, and act like everything's OK."

"I haven't even seen your mother yet."

"Well, I can tell you one thing—you'll never have to worry about seein' dad anytime soon."

"There's no way he and my mom could spend ten minutes together without World War III comin' down. You're right about one thing."

"What?"

"It ain't all about money. There's something about us, I mean all of us that's just not real … Lost, ya know?"

"My mom's had all the therapy and meetings she goes to. And, to go with her alone anywhere scares me to death. Now, Damon, I know you think I'm naïve. But I know that our secrets keep us apart. Like last month when dad drove me back from Cadott just to talk to mom about things.

She couldn't even look him in the eyes. Mom always told me dad was a no-good bum. That's not it. I don't know what it is, but dad was calm. Mom got really tense, like she was starting to shake."

"How was it up there with your dad anyway?"

"Pretty cool. Got to go out with Rosalyn's Husky while dad brought his cameras along."

"Did you get to see any bears?"

"Plenty of them. He took me twice out there when he had a whole day. I mean dad talks to the DNR and shares what he finds with them. I just wish mom could see how cool dad is. Rosalyn loves him. I can see it. She doesn't ask him for much 'cause he's always there for her. Even though they don't live together, I don't feel like I'm walking on egg shells around them."

"Your ma's not that bad. So she's a little mean. My mother can be quite tough when she has to."

"I don't know why you would think that just because mom's got a nice house and car that we have a better life than you do. I mean, I can't compare my life to yours because I have no idea about your family. We talk about my mom, but that's it. I haven't even seen your mother yet. You know what? I bet you that she doesn't even know that I'm going with you."

"Would that surprise you?"

"Whatdya mean?"

"That you're white."

"No kidding: you and mom talk like you're having the time of your' lives while I just sit there and wait for her to give up so I can touch your hair, kiss you all over in my secret little hiding place."

"Babe, let me tell you. Nobody can tell you that you are one ugly chick. I see the way my friends looked at you today. I mean you could have anybody you want. Chose me, I get that. I love to be with you, yeah, I gotta say it freaks me out to be in public with a white girl. But, you, you are worth every dime I put into the chrome wheels."

"Just don't let it go to your head. I've seen some of your friends. They can get a little wild sometimes."

"I can handle 'em. What about you?"

"You mean why can't I get any friends? I won't play their game."

"That's a tough one."

"My mom can bring it on just like yours can. It's all about keeping me in line. Ms. Clavadatcher told me about all the money involved in getting into a stringed quartet she knows about—you know the traveling and practice time. She even asked me why didn't I stick to basketball. At least I could get a scholarship and do both. Maybe even come up with a little extra cash by getting some scholarship money."

"Your mom told me what you said to your coach. Good luck trying to get onto the J.V. team."

"JV? I could make varsity if I put my mind to it."

"Whatever?"

"I beat you in one-on-one a couple of times."

"Like I didn't let you win?"

"OK, let's go over to the Park; and, this time bring you're A-Game—no excuses."

"You know you white folk are only good at your outside game, can't slash it inside to take it home."

"Can you jam it?"

"Hah?"

"I said can you stuff the basketball? You know I can touch the rim."

"Yeah, I'd like to see that. You never took the ball inside on me once."

"What you talkin' about anyway?"

"Like my dad said, don't show your hand on the first date."

"OK. Sister, you're on; and, while we're at it how about ten bucks says I take you by five up to fifteen."

"Oh, is that so?"

"M-h-m."

"Alrighty then, you name the time, and I'll be there. Oh, and if someone doesn't show up on time, that person has to pay up, fair enough?"

"Yeah, you're on."

"Win by five, please. Don't be surprised if I double that little number on your bony little ass."

They pull in front of the Padilla residence as the evening shade creeps over the white ranch home, signaling another day has wound down, that a once hectic Saturday afternoon rests, secluded beneath two enormous evergreens, as dogs bark from across the street. Slowly Jasmine climbs out of the passenger seat, and Damon coming up behind her, strokes her left shoulder upon heading to the front door.

"So, how was your day you two, back so early on a Saturday afternoon, no less?"

"Do we have any soda around?"

"Now, Jasmine, you know how I feel about soft drinks. No we don't, but I have some freshly squeezed lemonade; A-a-nd, if you two lovebirds don't mind, you can grab two plates and silverware from the kitchen—lemon chicken and potato salad with green beans and sweet corn."

"Who did you make all this food for?"

"For you two, who else? We have apple pie and vanilla ice cream for dessert. Oh, by the way darling, Tom's coming over at about 9, we're going out for drinks with some friends. Now, I expect you to not only clean all the dishes, but I also expect you to practice your flute sessions"—

"The Flutes of San Souci, yes mom."

"Never get our little Frederick wrong sweetie. Damon, our pristine prodigy here could get a nice chunk of money for college if she stays the course. What do you think of that my dear little Damon?"

"Great."

"Great? Is that all you can say? Jasmine here has a chance to play next summer at the PAC with both string instruments accompanied with a pianist. Mozart anyone?"

"Mom, I'm sure that Damon doesn't want to talk about classical music. He's, you should get a look at some of his games he put together. He's even made some cartoons for children."

"Have you made any money at it yet?"

"No, but my mentors have told me that I always need to focus on speed and accuracy. With a little understanding of the programming part of it, I'll be fine, especially in the gaming end of things. That's where the money is, of course. But I'm also working on editing film; you know not just rap videos, accentuating their moods and all that. The more confident I become, the better things will be. Interviews and all that stuff are right around the corner—I'm gonna make it, Mrs. Padilla."

"Did I ever say you weren't?"

"No, but, if you must know, True Skool takes both creativity and the business side of things and shows you what you need to work on to get there. These people have all been there, most are still working out there in the field in one way or another. We are looking for work, Mrs. Padilla, not asking to be charity cases."

"Damon, do you think I really care that you are black and all that? No, no, no, no—hear me out, please, I am not trying to get in your cool aid. My daughter here, Jasmine has not had a whole lot of friends. The only advice I had for her was simply to give and take when she makes new friends. Jasmine, I know your mother seems to get hard on you sometimes' but Ms. Clavadatcher says you have promise—you've been with her for a while now. And, she says you're ready to take the next step."

"You know I can get a scholarship to play basketball mom. I still don't have any idea what I am going to do yet. College is a long way off."

"Honey, we've been over this a million times before. There's some things in this life you can't take back."

"But you even said yourself everyone needs a second chance."

"And, I also remember telling you right after I talked with the coach that there are some things that you can't take back.

She'll never let up on your remarks."

"Oh, yeah like talking to the coach in her office that I thought I wasn't getting enough playing time?"

"Like gramps told me a long time ago. Honey, sometimes you just gotta eat crow."

"Could I have that apple pie right now, Mrs. Padilla?"

"Sure, help yourself Damon. The pie's on top of the stove and the ice cream's in the ice box, go figure. But really, Jasmine, if you want to try out for the high school team I will understand, but you're on your own. I'm not going to bat for you."

"But, but"—

"But nothing. You want to be an adult, well, here's a chance for you to step up to the plate. People sometimes will not give in even when they're totally wrong—it's like they—I'll put my myself in the hat as well—like we, how can I say this, we are at the end of our tether. And, so help me God, they're not going to get the best of me."

"Like the little tussle we had when I was a kid and you were trying to convince me that dad hid my doll away when it was you?"

"Are you sure you got that right? I don't remember any of that. When was this?"

"We found the doll in your winter chest mom; and, then you said you didn't know how it got there."

"Yeah, well, I think you have tricked yourself into remembering it just how you wanted it. You know, just that dad and you are such good friends. Dear ole' dad who sees you for a whole month. The only things he does is pay for your clothes and tennis shoes while I bought you that little silver specimen I'm sure you will practice tonight and daily from here on out. No excuses, right Jasmine?"

"Yeah, I guess so."

"Why don't you clear the dishes and clean up the kitchen. Your mother's gotta take a shower and get ready. Tom will be here in less than an hour. Damon, it's been a pleasure. Have a safe trip back home."

"We'll see you around, Mrs. Padilla."

"Your mother's not that bad. Sure she's gonna put the foot down a little bit. Hell, my ma can do that whenever she feels like it."

"You're getting the nice mother game. Things get a lot worse when I am facing her by myself."

"Ditto: do you think my mom doesn't play that game? That's the way it is. Nobody said life's fair. Here's my plates. I gotta get going. I told mom I be home before dark. Gonna have to come up with an excuse for not being hungry."

"Why don't you tell her you're dating a White girl like for the whole summer?"

"You're so funny. Well you were gone all June. I'll get 'round to it. Ya just gotta cut me some slack. Damon'll come through. I always do. Here, give me a kiss. Great, I'll call you tomorrow after I get off of work. Maybe we can get something to eat at the Mall—kill some time; whatchya think?"

"Sounds like a plan. Love you."

Methodically, Jasmine washes and rinses the dishes before she fills the dishwasher. The thought of cleaning up the dirtied pots and pans is overpowered by the listless feeling she gets when thinking about playing the flute for a solid hour plus before bedtime. Perhaps her mother means well.

Jasmine cannot quite put her finger on the entire motive behind her mother's brazen spirit regarding that flute. Whatever it is, she really doesn't care. Ultimately where is the joy in her young life? The pangs of her own existence have played with her for fifteen years, and have not relinquished its sullen grip. Her mother has told her repeatedly that "everyone has their own little thing to work through." But what exactly is it?

No matter how hard she tries to improve her life and relationships with her boyfriend and schoolmates, she can never seem to piece it together. At least her mother has enabled her to stay out of attending the all girls' Sisters of Divine Savior Catholic High School in Wauwatosa where her grandmother works as a secretary. Free rides are not her thing; but she will have to remain on the Deans' List if she plans to attend Milwaukee Washington. Will she always somehow manage to reside on the periphery or will she break through and let the past crumble beneath her footsteps? Big question to a world devoted to avoiding such simplicity at all costs, right or wrong.

Like clockwork, she finishes up her last colander, and heads into her bedroom to practice The Flutes of San Souci. Poor old Fredrick is probably turning over in his grave as this pristine youth tries to bring to life a baroque arrangement only he could imagine in his mind's eye.

He, a warrior of European greatness, was once a youth as a jailed victim left to witness his beau's head severed by some behemoth, as its gray existence wobbles about on the barren floor's lifeless expanse. Then being thrust into livestock and economics courses to appease his hardheaded father as the gentle marshland of the Oder River quietly remains pushed to the periphery of his wounded psyche. His stern father smiled as young Fredrick's agrarian lessons bloom for Prussia's spring planting as War would be the only mark he would leave in a World that spares no quarter, his flutist triumphs now having fallen to the wayside, remain but a distant memory of a childhood that he would never be able to piece together ever again.

"Hey Jazz, Sammy has just pulled into the driveway, we won't be back until late. If you need me for anything, it better be important: better to tell me now if there's anything you need, tell me now or forever hold your peace."

"No, I'm fine: I'll probably pop in a Netflix and make some popcorn. This music is so new. I don't know. There's so much passion and dreamy qualities of this arrangement that I, I can't quite figure it out."

"Remember when you were so hooked on Grieg when you were knee high?"

"Well, yeah, mom. That's when you brought home The Grinch Who Stole Christmas. God, it was so weird, so out there, still so normal, you know?"

"Yes, sweetheart. Take care. Love you."

Chapter Ten

Why Does Everything Have to be so Difficult?

"Oh, God there she is, 'Queen Kaisha'. Ph-ah—with that dick, Jose. Fuck, why don't I just go hang myself. All this grief she's put me through?"

Dewan senses her attraction toward him, not because he is black; but she too seems to be entangled in her feelings toward him. She, so devilishly careful; and he, a bundle of raw desire just waits to implode upon her eminence.

Shadows lurk in the recesses of his mind like some Medieval Gothic horror story, like Count Dracula rubbing shoulders with a modern day Zombie. Ceaseless pain that eats at Dewan's castrate heart, his dispirited sense, a civil war of unrest plagues, implodes within the throes of his hidden sorrows. He, walled up by his oppressive unrest, cannot let go of her presence. Kaisha's gift, his torment, walks beyond his reach. That dimwit Jose, his antagonist, walks so confidently, almost as if he knows that Dewan is his crippled nemesis that cannot relinquish his constant suffering, his unrelenting martyred conscience. Jose feeds off his loss, a loss he can no longer shelter.

He waves to Jose as they now walk past him, catching a glimpse of her glorious face, raven hair, every soft step a coronation for his own kingdom, a kingdom only his delicate nature can surmise. Unrequited love! How can he go on? Why would he really want to? Even his father cannot alter his thoughts. How can a person who rarely partakes in libations rationalize his own career of regularly schlepping beer to taverns, Seven Elevens, and restaurants?

Like, how can Darren, dear old dad, really expect such a sensitive miscreant as Dewan to go along with all his altruistic mumbo jumbo just because "HE PAYS THE BILLS?" There they go toward the Mall as Dewan does not know what to do with his time as the dog days of summer begin to set in. Gone are moments of a fresh early summer where the flowers and trees speak to the soul as birds would ceaselessly chirp with such eloquent ferocity as now brown grass and drier heat emotionlessly takes over the City, as death has reclaimed the living. Its presence quietly consumes the once spirited appearance of a once frolicsome youth as Dewan. His plague, robust as it may be, is rolled up beneath his brown eyes and his explosive smile as he slowly makes his way back home, thinking that school is a "good thing" to rid himself of the endless doldrums. Dewan's floating within a Sargasso Sea that, no matter how still its nature may be, has taken on a life of its own that he cannot rid himself of. Its grip never really lets go, feeding the hollowed frenzy that wallows from his solipsistic recesses.

Christ his sole companion is his only true friend, the Second Coming, his only Savior. How did he really come into this world? Really, where is the earth, Wisconsin, in a World Map's spiritual terms? Is there such a thing? Why must he have to run, compete in his Junior Olympian masquerade that literally tears him apart every time he prepares for the spring's City Conference Track Meets? What is winning? Losing? Right, just do your best and everything will take care of itself. How can everybody be so sure of himself?

Inside, Dewan dawdles about, directionless, like a dirtied sock he cannot get rid of. Why he hangs on, he cannot really answer: always the same. It is just that, well, those comparisons to other parts of the world, how good we've got it, who died for us and why, are those truly meritorious witnesses? Surely not. No, he will not go along for the ride; but really, what ride is there? Those binding thoughts muddle his every step.

Dewan knows that no matter how wonderful things have been explained to him, darkness seeps beneath every kernel of truth, demystifying life, segregating death, death he so desperately cherishes to take him from these bitter realities. Somehow, all that he has been taught has failed him. Has he failed him? To be brutally honest is to be somehow negative: nobody will stand by him, not even his parents. Shirelle seems well meaning, but if push comes to shove, Jay, his uncle always manages to be the referee when things get out of hand. Why do all this 'going along'? How does the cancer fester without anyone just walking away from this show? Church is so uplifting but once he leaves everything returns to normal. Everybody plays his part. Excelling in school is a piece of cake for the family's future scholar. He also recalls the moments a zealot Serbian classmate has spoken in front of his eighth grade world history class about how the impact of Jesus Christ and the Studenica Monestary in central Serbia has made upon speaker Zifko and his family. That thick Serbian accent and Cirillic language still honoring his fatherland, speaks of naïve art and strange architecture so vibrant yet distant, that is tucked away in a foreign land, where those pristine voices of the chanteuse he has played from his laptop demonstrates that it cannot be all for show.

Dewan's search is new: he is young but American and the Eastern Orthodoxy nestle beneath the same bloodied leaves of his neighbors towering crimson maples. "The body and blood of our lord Jesus Christ" reside noiselessly in Dewan's alms. Still, why can he not receive the hand of Kaisha while that sick, debonair Jose struts his magnetic persona into her heart, tearing his into a maelstrom of madness, a storm no matter how soft, will only harden? Yes, the rocky road is his; and, his alone. His true nature unknown changes without his awareness.

Without the smile of his beloved Kaisha, how will he be able to go on? Like his father had told him, he will not feel sorry for him if she says "NO" to his wishes, he must find a way to go on—there are some things only Dewan will be able to feel and work through. This harsh truth bothers him to no end because he has found no reason to continue in a world requiring all its masks. And, even at his young age, he's wandered into a world whose secrets reveal little good will and a silent world where hornet's nests fester beneath all his quiet moments. In other words, can he lead a loving and fulfilling life or take the hand that is dealt him?

"Mom, could I have a salad? It's too hot out to eat anything else."

"Sure, the lettuce and cucumbers are in the crisper, and the tomatoes and mushrooms are just below it. Your favorite dressing's just inside the refrigerator door."

"Couldn't you make it for me?"

"Your mother's got to pick up her grand kids. Aisha's gotta work. She also has a date tonight so they will be staying overnight. Now, Dewan, you're not a child now. So please, help yourself. Now I've got to get going. If you don't mind, momma's gotta go."

"Mom, I love you."

"You're not going to get all sappy on me now young man. I love you too. Tomorrow night your father and I are going out with some clients of his. You won't have to take care of them. Aisha will stop by tomorrow afternoon to take pick 'em up. Now, if you want, I can ask Aisha if you can babysit her kids if she goes out another occasion at her place on Teutonia. You're my man now, Dewan. You don't have to give me an answer right now. Just think it over and let me know after you've thought about it, OK Dewan?"

"Sure. I sure could use the money. And, I have taken care of them over here; and, well, I think I did pretty good. Don't you?"

"Dewan, those are my grandchildren, do you think I would ask your sister if you could babysit her children if you weren't able to take care of her babies?"

"No, Aisha's kinda cool. She can tell me what's up without being hung on how everybody around her is gonna take it. Like the way dad can't boss her around no way no how. Now ma, don't you sit there and tell me you don't know what I'm talking about. Dad ain't know more about what's doin' for him than anybody else. He's, he's just more important. At least that's what he's told me many times—you know this. He's said this thing over and over—now you know Aisha will back me up on that."

"Look, I'm not gonna get into this with you right now. Although I would wish your father was here to hear this. It's like you're ganging up on him behind his back."

"Right, and like you guys don't say crap about us when we're not around or so you think."

"And, just what do you mean by that?"

"Like you don't think I haven't heard some stuff you guys said about me when you thought like, hey, Dewan's not around, I'm just gonna dump a lot of crap about him. He's just not getting any better. Don't you know mom? I'm fine. I may not be the best Joe around; but, hey, I don't stick my nose where it doesn't belong. But these games"—

"Games? A kid your age? What do you know about life? Damn. Sometimes I could just send your puny little soul off to Siberia young man. Like the whole world revolves around you. Like you're the whole world? Really Dewan, you see everyone's little blemishes but you can't see your own."

"All I want is to be seen for who I am. Sometimes mom, I know you're not gonna like this but you guys got your own. You just ain't got the guts to admit it. Like, 'cause you put food on the table, it rules everything. It's a lie, and you can't deny it. I don't care what you say."

"Ooh, you little, I gotta get going. Between you and Aisha, I don't know who are the obscenest little brats? Like you can shut down and act invisible all day long. And, then show your hurt little feelings and feel sorry for yourself, dumping on everyone just to show that you've been hurt. The problem with that preposterous assumption is that you take yourself out of the equation."

"Why Dew, because you think us old folks owe you something? Yeah, right. Now I gotta go. Your father and I will talk to you about this little man tonight. Now, don't think you're gonna bug out on us. If you aren't here when I get back, you won't be doin' a whole lot until school starts. And, that will be just you going to school, coming straight home, and doing your homework. Got it? Hey, you can stay in your room 'til your heart's content, Mister. Ah, that'll do wonders to get you into Northwestern or Cornell though, won't it? We'll make a journalist of you yet. Now, you just sit right here, and daddy and I will be sittin' down to iron things out. It's about time, Dewan."

Dewan goes off to his bedroom and shuts his door, reflecting on the moment his eyes fell upon the presence of Aisha. Until now, her very being has been the only thing that has made sense to him. Everybody else, for the most part, has settled for their dominance over him from past foibles: they have felt he would never openly talk about unless of course he wanted to tarnish his reputation even further. Little does he realize that they too are a reflective mirror, that their pettiness and ribald behaviors are tucked away deep within them, they too are playing a game where there are only losers."

"Looks like you've heard everything me and Dewan said, didn't you?"

"What are you talking about?"

"Big ears Darren's gotta get all his angles covered."

"My little missy seems to be getting a little paranoid."

"Oh, cut it out—it ain't gonna be all right by playing this out anymore."

"Whatdya mean by that?"

"Can't you just love me, hold me and let me—all of us come in? Why must you make everything so difficult?"

"You got your own sweetie … you want me to dig a little deeper?"

"Oh, could you?"

"Like last week, you went on ranting in front of Dewan about that time I hit you with a shoe in the head, not meaning to, mind you. But hey, hey, hey, it hit you flatly in the head, no blood or bruise, but, you cradled in the fetal position, I swear to God, you'd go into a coma just to get your digs."

"Let your white birds smile up."

"The sixties are over honey."

"Like she said, we've all caught the same disease. I could sing this into your hollow ear all night long."

"Right, right, right—let's have one better cry for the road."

"Sometimes Darren, can't you see?"

"No I can't. Enlighten me."

"Maybe I oughtta put that CD on again."

"And I'll find that song and play it over and over until you get so tired of it you'll have to raise the White Flag."

"Oh, so now we're back in the ring with Dewan. You always wanted me to cover up your little doobie-do with the kids. And, now after all these years you want to be our little peace maker. NO! Your gonna listen to me. You who puts a few hours a month with, with, ah, the United Way. Great, to save the children. Wonderful. All those do-gooder programs are necessary for the messy businesses like the one I work at—that includes ME and YOU by the by."

"I could starve right now, yes, guilty as charged. Is that what you want to hear?"

"About time."

"Enough of this: the game is death. There's no life to this— catch twenty-two and all that rot."

"And everyone plays, strokes, hustles."

"And rots in our own puny little brains."

"Yeah, and put on the best Jim Brown stiff arm."

"You mean King Kong."

"Cool."

"You know lowland gorillas have smaller penises than you guys?"

"Is that right my little amateur anthropologist? But their testicles, insanely honkin'. Nah, but really, is that what Mandingo is to you?"

"What are you talking about?"

"I caught you pulling up our Big little man hosin' some cracker ass from those wack mags I found in Dewan's the room a while back."

"So what if I was watching my man take care of business?"

"In the Airport waiting area with all those people all over the place?"

"Well, excuse me for not living up to your standards. You're no more a world beater than me or anyone else. I'll tell you one thing. You ain't getting anything from me until you get your junk out of the trunk."

"I ain't gonna change any more than you are. Now, if you don't mind, could you shut off the lights. Mandingo needs his beauty rest."

"You wish."

Darren is a great score keeper, but little does his wife know that he is an incessant closet porn monger, pulling up a peek here and there on his lunch hour. The horn that drives porn has clouded his world: *Skin Diamond* and *Sinnamon Love* guide him home in a secret world of play that can turn on a dime when he can no longer hold back. Brush away that tepid shell: Heaven help him when those stars' pop out of his distant eyes.

Chapter Eleven

You Gotta Take the Good with the Bad

"Hello?"

"Hi Paul, it's Jerry—Jerry Coleman. How are you?"

"Jerry? I thought you have died some time back. Where've you been all these years?"

"Oh, a little bit of this, a little bit of that. Yeah, well, I met up with old man Cardini a couple weeks back, and he told me you were still around."

"Right, I know, hangin' in there for who knows what?"

"Ah, it's not that bad, champ. I mean, yeah, just getting' out of bed some days seems almost futile; but hey, I still head out for the Columbia Marsh, got a million pictures of red-winged black birds and Sandhill cranes and never get tired of it."

"Done any fishing lately?"

"You kiddin' me? Plenty of bluegill and perch to go around. Landed a large mouth bass, can you believe it? Just got back from there on Sunday, and spent the entire weekend with 'Tosa's seniors—little bit of golfing too, not that my game's ever improved any. But got in an evening round of golf before the sun went down. Then after that, took in a little walleye at Norton's and danced the night away with my compadres into the wee hours of early Sunday morning. Think I had any gas left in the tank? Hell, all I can say is life hasn't been better for this old guy."

"But, guy: I haven't heard anything from you in years. And, now, out of the blue, I hear from you all these years later?"

"You were still getting off the sauce chum. What did you think I was going to do with you?"

"That's not all true, Jerry. Yeah, I was still nursing my wounds with my meetings, trying to patch up with my mishaps. But Jerry, booze or not, you're gonna sit there and tell me, armchair boy, everything's gone smoothly for you?"

"Whatdya mean?"

"OK, c'mon Jer', I'll spell it out for you. No matter how you play the game with people you too, I trust, know that somehow some hairy poo stuff flies out of your mouth no matter how hard ya try to keep things mum. You know, like saving face. I gotta tellya champ, it's not like I'm ashamed of what bomb I dropped, but the people around me, well, let me tellya, their looks scared me a helluva lot more than those tight-assed Nazis did with my kinfolk back in the day."

"You just don't get it, chum. We all have to bottom out about ourselves. I did back in high school. Get on with things, buddy. C'mon, man. I just don't want to drop dead without doing anything but stewing in my shit. It's not like I've had an epiphany or anything. Besides, this crap's all old hat. Life's what you make of it. Really Paulie, who wants to hang around some malcontent and listen to all his baggage anyway? Aren't you fed up with all that? I mean you of all people should know that it's a waste of time sitting in your own pity party."

"Let me tell you something, Jer'. I'm not saying you're all wrong on everything—yeah, I've seen how my mood swings have put me in the dog house, sure. But, I'll be damned if I'm gonna let you or anyone tell me what's going on with me especially someone I haven't seen in what: eight, ten years? Oh, and by the by, tell me, what is there to get about all this part of the play? All this God Father analogy crap bores me to tears."

"I just wanted to touch base with you, maybe spend some time sometime soon. My God, Paul, we don't have a lot of time on this earth. If I wanted to fight anymore, it would have to be with someone of the opposite sex."

"Right, sit around, have a cup of coffee, m-m, ha-mmn-n, say nothing. Whew, get in the fetal position while everybody's away. And once again, here I am licking my wounds. But when company comes, put on a happy face. Hey everybody's got their thing, right buddy—keep the ghost to myself and paste on my best smile even though I'm tired of this same old routine over and over? High school's never went away, Jer'; and, your cattle call is no different than anyone else's. Yeah, you could say I'm calling you out."

"You son-of-a-bitch. I've never heard so much whining from anyone. No wonder why I've never done anything with you in so long."

"Take your two- bit show on the road Jerry. I'm not going to live in your shadow anymore. If you think I'm full of it, great. Find your greener pastures. Say what you mean and drop your fences. There's a whole world out there who'll go along with your little structured life; you know, as long as you go along with theirs'. Look, you can tell all your friends how that much of a loser old Paulie is. But, man, like your gonna sit there and tell me you're simply not killin' time. You know, holding the bag 'til your number's up? You just don't get it, Jer', do ya?"

"Right, like I haven't heard that before? I will pick and pick at your sorry ass before you wake up and see that maybe sometimes all I want to do is spend some time together and shoot the breeze."

"That's not it, Jer'. When you pull a quick one on me, I'm going to ask you what you meant by what you said."

"You've gotta stop thinking that we're all out to get you. Believe it or not, Paul the world does not revolve around you. Save your drama for someone else."

"We could say the same thing about you. Just not gonna let you or anyone get away with something so vile because that's your own cover."

"Let's drop it. OK, OK, you win. I agree that the whole game's about keeping the shoe on the other's foot. We're all guilty of that. But, really Paul, 'can't we all just get along?'"

"No Rodney, we can't. But, I'll tellya there's something to be said about clearing the air."

"Like what?"

"Like, letting our little minds fall away and find out all lot more about each other, about ourselves."

"Let's not get into religion or politics."

"Ah, c'mon Jer'. Both are made up by us fools. Sort of like football, just passes the time. I'm just sayin' that there's something better than king of the hill. Nobody wins, Jer'. I think we can all agree on that. If you want to thrill someone else with your brash talk, why, have at it. It's just not gonna happen with me anymore. Give and take, compromise, screw all that crap. If that's what you're tellin' me. And, that stuff, well, c'mon Green Bay, football couldn't come any sooner."

"Alright already, I feel your pain, hah-aah, do you want to hook up any time soon, you know shoot the shit?"

"Right, catch up on things. Are you free next Thursday, say around noon down in your neck of the woods, say, Café la Boulangerie over on Underwood and Harwood: you know a little lunch and a cup of Joe?"

"Great. Hey, not to rush you or anything but I've got a date over at Balistreri's. Tell you all about it next week."

"OK, big guy. My two little mavens and I've got a date with my beautiful flowers. Don't have to leave the house. Everything's right here in my own backyard."

"You've got to be kidding me? Your seeds have been dried up for years now. You are putting me on, right?"

"Nah, I got two furry little friends who have made my life bearable. Mind you, they're cats. They even spend their time roaming my little kingdom and keeping all those squirrels out of my garden—no rabbits either. Best thing since ole' Rudy."

"That German Short Hair came in handy for pheasant hunting."

"Oh, you got that right. Best bird dog I've ever had, hands down. And, in the water? Nothing could compare to him. He sure was something."

"You could say that again. That one time when that winged pheasant was running through the cornfields comin' right at me; and, wham! Old Rudy's jaws tear that wild bird from running up my leg."

"Those are the reasons I've given up hunting. The grocery store's a lot easier to deal with. But, hey, I'll let you get a goin' on that hot date of yours. See you next Thursday at eleven, right?"

"You got it. And, if you have to make any changes, you don't have a cell phone do you?"

"Nah, wouldn't know what to do with it if I had one."

"They're not that tricky, I guarantee you. Anyway, my telephone number is 414-741-8255."

"Got it. We'll see you then. Bye."

Paul has felt the pangs of the strings throughout his entire life upon addressing fearful things with those he truly cared about, but the strings have lessened in their incessant tingling. His illusory demons wreaking havoc upon his every moment, heightened by his sordid thoughts, his anxiety-ridden torrents taking hold of him, just as he would be trying to improve his lot. And, yet always falling short, he became cloaked in his conundrums chasing felicity, listlessly falling to despair's depths.

Now he spends less time analyzing his surroundings, freely engaging with the peoples and creatures who come into his everyday existence.

The illusory notion of security has fallen from his brow. The teachings of existence are solely of the past. Today he struts about his Cytherea's with his two furry feline friends as they maneuver about the plants with stoic precision, while the midday August sun scorches the parched grass, he turns on the front yard sprinkler. In the back, the second crop of zucchini and russet potatoes, having just ripened, he makes his way to the garage to pull out a spading fork and bushel basket.

Noiselessly they rub up against him as he gets on his knees to pick the zucchini squash. From the front yard, a man's voice break's the silence. "Hey, Paul are you back there? It's Eddie, Eddie Jefferson."

"Well, hello, Mr. Jefferson, and you must be the son he's always talked about."

"Yes, Mr. Bogdanov."

"So, what brings you two over here in the middle of the day?"

"We're gonna get right down to the Nitti gritty if you don't mind?"

"Well, I would expect that since we rarely spend a lot of time together."

"Well then: Fire away."

"My son here, De Marco, would like to ask you something."

"Shoot."

"Mr. Bogdanov, I, I, well, I was wondering if, if you know, you could help me get a shot at a job at your Evinrude plant?"

"Edward, De Marco—I haven't worked at OMC for about eighteen years. Now, yes, I still have ties there. I don't mean to be rude but why do you think I have any pull at that place?"

"C-mon Paul, De Marco is just asking if you might know someone who, you know, maybe can help him find a job at Evinrude?"

"You drive truck, right, son?"

"Yeah, but I don't know what that has to do with finding work at Evinrude. For starters, the plant is in Sturtevant, near Racine."

"Yeah, I know. So?"

"That's an hour's drive from here: you're gonna put a lot of miles on your car that way, with gas prices and all."

"I can take care of myself, sir. And, yeah, Racine's not that bad, kind of a smaller Milwaukee when you get right down to it. It's not like I'm leaving a lot behind here if you really must know."

"Are those your furry friends?"

"Yep."

"We're heading over to Dale's, wanna come along? I mean I know you're not too cool with the booze scene and everything?"

"N-n-n-a, that's alright. All that biz was because of my own pity party, really. Everything is hunky dory, seriously. Be right back."

Paul leads his treasured felines into the back door; and, before he places them in the back room, he feeds them some leftovers and pours them each some milk. Softly he pets them for a brief moment as De Marco fidgets about going to some old codger's tavern just to get a free meal and a couple of drinks from his gregarious father.

"Ready, gentlemen, after you—now, De Marco, right? I spent my whole working life there—have only been back there once since I've retired—high tech, the place is now. Sturtevant's no Milwaukee, but Racine's kind o' funky. I'm sure you've been there a time or two?"

"That's not a big deal Mr. Bogdanov. First things first—I have to get the job before any of this matters."

"But it does give you an opportunity to become a top-line machinist. We may not catch Mercury but we put out a helluv an outboard. Watching a tandem 225-horse 6 cylinder rev up against anything, Yamaha included, bam! The real thing; and, with R&D up in Ontario, Canada, we don't fool around my good man. Put all of that eleven hundred-pound beast on the back of your Bayliner, and you're gonna do some serious deep sea fishing—little pricey with the gas and uptake; but, hey, what are you doing out there anyway? Forget about life for a while and go after that tarpon you always feared landing. But, hey now you've got the balls to land that monster."

"Easy my man—don't you scare away my son before he's even got his feet wet."

"It's gotta be more than just showing up for work day in and day out, Jefferson, or he won't make it. Punching in is for wimps. You've gotta have heart, son. I lost it somewhere along the way trying to be the goody-two-shoes. You can't make it on desire alone. The money? Yeah it comes down the road once you get your feet wet. But even that couldn't save me. Retirement did though, in a strange way. I'm sure you don't wanna hear about my sorry ass story. So, tell me, son, what can you bring to the table?"

"What?"

"You know, what can you offer Evinrude if you could get that interview?"

"I can run a lathe if that's what you mean, can even make my own cutting tools. Yeah, I've gotta a way to go to get the CNC machined parts aspect of it down, but I have monitored my work with computerized technology. Haven't done it in a while, not since I lost my job at Paper Machinery company—man that killed me—I was this close to becoming a Machinist. No lie."

"You know Paul, DeMarco here was already a Mold Maker with them, pulling in a lot of money with no layoffs."

"I don't mean to brag Mr. Bogdanov, but I was pulling in over twenty-six bucks an hour, then stone-faced Baumgartner, had different ideas about my abilities—the guy who's a little long in the tooth—he's older than you Mr. Bogdanov, for Christ Sakes."

"Last time I checked, I was still breathing. And, no, you couldn't give me one more day on that gray lifeless cement floor where the only emotion I felt was when I was being pressured."

"The higher ups?"

"Anyone: work's like everybody's doin' they're best to put out a great product. But that ain't the half of it. The grays just take over. And, the only thing I could do was to smile and act like everything's OK."

"Ah, you just gotta deal with it. Water off a duck's back, right Paul?"

"If you say so."

"Let's go up to the bar dad, not too many people are here yet. It's almost five o' clock. You'd think the place would be hoppin', bein' Friday and all."

"I don't know about you guys, but I'd like to get hold of those two Heileman signs, and plant them down in my basement bar."

"Yeah, that would just be like you Jefferson."

"You got a problem old man?"

"Yeah you. Your son here has been a perfect gentleman."

"Oh, hi, Dale, I'll have a pineapple juice and a large bowl of vegetable beef soup. Nope, no sandwich but could you get me a side of those devilishly exquisite waffle fries, throw in a pickle, and we're set."

"How about you two? Or might you need a few more minutes to decide?"

"Nah, I'll get this dad. My father will have a Miller Genuine Draft, a bowl of minestrone soup and a turkey sandwich while I'll have a Pina Colada, a house salad with Ranch Dressing and a Reuben Sandwich on Rye with sauerkraut with a bag of Potato chips to top it off."

"Another hot one today, hasn't it been, boys?"

"You can say that again. My tomatoes are starting to wilt a bit from the sun. I'll tellya, September cannot can come soon enough."

"Your Miller and Pineapple Juice—and, here's your Pina Colada, you've got that life on the beach feel about things don't you?"

"Ah, I was just thinking about Jamaican port-reggae. You know there's some women I'd heard about done some wild stuff down Jamaica Way. I'm sure you don't wanna hear about it anyway."

"Nah, that's OK, it's good to get out of my comfort zone once in a while."

"That's cool. Yeah, well, you know people like Lady G and Timbalee. You know she needs her 'Supaman back in da bed, all this slang teng, beat that chest, yell out, your world's like a cartoon, bright colors, blue skies, the ocean's never too far off, I might be bedroom ridden wid my love thang, but it's all cool, Up and Live! You know how it is."

"If you say so?"

"And, no tests, man, live, do your own thing—otherwise life drags on forever, it becomes your noose, man."

"We've got our little slacker poet/philosopher, Cheers!"

"So, what's you drinkin' anyway?"

"Ginger Ale, why?"

"Oh, nothin', I just thought that you were here so much that, maybe you'd get a snort in every now and then."

"After more than thirty years behind the wheel, alcohol can get kinda stale. I'd rather rap with you guys than partake in a Tanqueray and Seven: not that there's anything wrong with that. It's just that I've had a lot of practice and you guys seem so absorbed in yourselves that my curiosity's been piqued a bit."

"Ah, old Paul here is gonna go to bat for my son to see if he can get out of a dead-end job and into something that shows some promise."

"A future, ya mean?"

"Yeah, I don't know what's happened to this country, but something doesn't add up."

"A lot of things ya mean. The financial markets, War, hyper-inflation, poor wages, a boat load of unskilled jobs. And, all we can do is wait for all our politicians to get us out of this mess."

"One thing I can say is that even if Obama doesn't seem to connect on resolving anything with Congress or the Senate, he has this calmness about him like addressing an audience regarding White on Black crimes. I've never heard any other leader just simply state matter-of-factly, this has gone on too long. His interest is to put these base actions to rest by legislating criminal and civil statutes designed to prosecute effectively so we can finally get on with things. Obama seems to be a saddened man. But, I gotta tellya, which president hasn't gone down that road? Son, you weren't around when President Kennedy strutted his stuff; but, he seemed to be onto something great, even more prolific than anything his predecessor, Eisenhower did. "

"The Machine cannot be dismantled by any one person: to me, politics is a business, perhaps calculatingly more-so, like make you believe that everyone can be prosecuted who steps out of line."

"Oh, I'll go along with you there, Dale. Somehow we've all become silenced at a certain point; and, things just fall downhill from there."

"Like you guys know what suffering's all about? My uncle was stationed at Port Chicago in Frisco back in the Big War."

"Dad, could we just lay off the heavy stuff for once?"

"No, we can't. If you haven't forgotten, Paul, you basically ran out the door a few months back because you couldn't handle all this racist crap in your neck of the woods, like you can't take a look in the mirror."

"Look, man, nobody wants to dwell on all this crap all day long."

"No, no, no, it's alright Dale, really. Jefferson."

"What?"

"You're right. Us Whites did a number on you, but, tell me where were all you guys were when the lynching's went down, when whole towns burned to the ground?"

"What are you getting at?"

"You know the old cliché that an American couple enjoys a good laugh at people's strange behavior whereas a Russian couple can only tap into the dark soul of human existence?"

"Yeah, so?"

"So, you're not the only one sent on a slow, slow death march. Men cut off their arms and legs in the far north Solovetsky death camps because they couldn't do it anymore. Not because they were Russian but because they were all too human, the harshness of life simply did not crush them physically but psychologically, that was a different story. They had enough, just done themselves in. Who wouldn't have done it any differently?"

"Like Masters throwing you in the fire, raping our babies, silencing our futures. To this day, I have no idea why not a million more Nat Turners didn't break their way right into the Plantation's front door."

"If I recall, Nat only killed one person, a woman if I'm not mistaken. He was like an Alfa male who had all his beta friends do all the work. He just pointed his sword and watched all the mayhem, the blood and guts unfold before his very eyes: another so-called tough guy who would've been killed off by the mob in a heartbeat."

"And, of the over 300 who died at Port Chicago, two hundred were black. They were told by their CO's to do all sorts of things that would blow the whole place up. A-and guess what? Of the fifty crackers arrested 47 would be out in less than a year after the War ended. East St. Louis and Tulsa weren't the only insane bones thrown our way."

"And, what would you have done Eddie if you were safe from harm's way?"

"I don't follow."

"Would you have stuck your neck out or would you be more like everyone else who just followed orders and went home like any law-abiding family man?"

"Hey, all I want is to feel my own blackness, express it when I feel like it. And, no, not like all that Black Power shit, Hell No! To just be myself, thank you."

"No shit Sherlock. Like daddy always told me about this Ukrainian kid who got his kicks by telling on all his so-called *kulak* enemies of the people, even his parents' friends, you know just to get them killed by the Reds while everyone was starving to death. We're human beings Ed. That's all. 1934 in the Ukraine, six million already dead, hell we'll pump up the merits of Pavlik Morozov, even make a hero out of him. He, this man boy killed at the hands of his own flesh and blood, as the Communists rally behind his notoriety to assure them they've got everybody's back side. Even those who knew the rascal's real deal. Keeps you alive, right? There's gotta be a new "Obey" Propaganda t-shirt my grandson would buy in a heartbeat. Make him proud of his heritage. It's just entertainment Jefferson, no more, no less."

"Now, how does any of that make sense?"

"It's not supposed to. We're talkin' reality here. C'mon Jefferson. Who are you gonna stand up for when everything's pointed at you?"

"Guys, guys, could you quiet it down a bit? For a couple of old coots, you sure know how to get under everyone's skin."

"Terry, you take over here. These guys don't know when to let up."

"Sure thing. Tell you what Theresa, could you tell Raul and Jaime to pick up some roma tomatoes for the weekend—we're gonna need them for the softball tourney down the street."

"What if I go and get them myself?"

"Cause you're so cognizant of burning fuel that I thought I'd let the boys get some time out of here before all hell breaks loose a couple hours from now."

"Be back in a bit."

"Au revoir."

"Boys, boys, I think the time is right for a little I'll have a Blue Christmas without you, I'll be so blue just thinking about you…"

"Elvis and Christmas, 'c'mon everybody knows that that fat fuck stole everythin' from us brotha-asz. Don't you have any Al Green or James Brown'?"

"Careful or I'll ram some Albert Johnson down your throat."

"Wait a minute, you got Coltrane, don't you?"

"Yeah, but he's retired for the evening—just listen Ooh, ooh, ooh, ooh. Ouuh, You'll be doin' all right, with your Christmas of white, But I'll have a blue, blue, blue, Blue Christmas."

"Tis the season and all that good stuff. Cheers! So, Bogdanov, what do you think of that?"

"Let it snow, let it snow, let it snow."

"I like your thinkin' old man. How about a beer?"

"Nah."

"Why not?"

"I gave her up a while back. Haven't been in a bar since."

"So, why now?"

"De Marco and me have been tryin' to get something goin' And, ah, well, now's as good a time as any to get my feet wet again."

"Could you guys excuse my father and me for a moment:

Dad, could I talk to you for a moment?"

"Yeah, shoot."

"I mean out in the parking lot. Please?"

"After you—see you guys in a bit. Keep the seats warm." Out of the shadowed tavern, they step into the bright sun. "See that clown up there, son? I don't want you to blow this.

Paul's givin' you a chance to get on your feet. I still don't buy what you told me what happened over at Paper Machinery. I know it's been years since that went down; but, why couldn't you have got set up with one of their vendors—anything—word of mouth, I mean drivin' a box truck route at your age? Christ De Marco, really, what did go down?"

"You think that crap hasn't spun around in my head a million times dad? Man, the lady at Wisconsin Job Service told me maybe I should consider relocating to another part of the country. This is my home; and, this recession? You've never been through this. Yeah, the unemployment numbers have dropped for what? Retail and McDonalds? Maybe I can use my own car and do a little merchandising for eight bucks an hour."

"You gotta get goin' with the times. Nothing's changed. There are no free lunches."

"Nah, this is all about you makin' sure ole' De Marco here doesn't end up movin' back in with you and ma."

"What?"

"Oh, please. If you haven't noticed little ole' me can figure things out. You're right. Things haven't changed, dad. Everything's wrong—hey maybe I can kiss up to the Man. And, who knows? The sky's the limit, right?"

"Don't push it with me, son. I know thing's ain't exactly cool. You go anywhere, anywhere else in the world, thing's only get worse, that I can assure you."

"Put it this way, dad, who picks our tomatoes, makes our clothes? Third world bro'—there's no way out of it."

"Like that Mexican play I just saw, *nadie sabe nada* as all the perverse shit from The Priests' gets smoothed over because nobody cares. We'd like to think we do—Nah, fuck everything, right?"

"Where are you coming from? I mean, what does any of that have to do with me? So it's all one big mess yeah. And, you're part of it, ain't You?"

"Actually Vicente Lenero did the play. Milwaukee's not all what is in the news. Nobody knows anything, dad. It's all about overlooking things to get paid. And, no, I'm tired of this, this compromise. There's no beauty in it, it's just—survival, and without being able to express myself to what I really need, what's the point to any of this?"

"That's what a woman's for, son. Now, don't get me wrong, your mother and I have had our moments—she's the ship— without her, don't know what I'd do. Yeah, we all can die in a heartbeat. But just by looking at her makes everything OK. I don't want you to crawl into your shell and never come out. I'm just tellin' ya that coming home would be a horrible idea. Nightmare's more like it. We'd be at each other's throats day and night. You know how your mother can get sometimes."

"You can't skirt around things with me, dad. Your boy's a grown man. And, if I want to check out of this world, ain't a single one of you who's gonna stop me."

"Sometimes, son, I swear, I wish you would have moved far away so I wouldn't have to listen to all this rot over and over with you. Ask a girl out for Christ's sake. Is it really that complicated? No, no, no, no, just hear me out. You're so right. Going to work doesn't do a whole lot of good if you have no one to share it with. But don't drop your shit in my lap because you don't have anyone else to talk to. Your dad's an old man—it's all about myself, yourself. I'm just as lost as the next guy. But, I'll tell you this, when that hardness wears off, man, the sun never stops shinin'. See, your old man's not so mean-spirited and racist as you think. I just don't know Bogdanov or Terry. They're like aliens from a different planet."

"It's not about color dad. It's what lies beneath the stink. I will not dare pick up that schlock I thought was real for so -oh long, ya know? Now, the Old Man's gonna come through for me. I don't want you to blow it for me. He wants to help. That's obvious."

"Just as long as you know what you're going to say to them if Bogdanov can set you up with an interview."

"I've been ready for this before you asked me about joining you to talk with him."

"See, I just knew I could get the clown to smile for you."

"Come on, let's wrap this up. I don't want to spend my whole Friday evening at some old folk's tap."

"So, welcome back. Everything A-OK? Great."

"De Marco, I'm gonna get a-going, but I was wondering if you could give me your telephone number—there's one thing though, I would like to see your resume before I put the call through for you. We've just got to be on the same page when I get hold of the operations manager. Look, I'm sure you're thinkin' that this old fool is just blowing smoke up your ass? No, you were quiet in there, just listening to the rest of us jabber about somethin' totally off the track. If only Ryan Braun would have taken a page from your presence. You're a true gentleman. If there's a way I can get you in there, I just know that everything's gonna work out. If you can get that interview, maybe it will be for shipping receiving or working in the paint department—at least you've got your foot in the door—at first, you might have to take what you can get. But you let them know where your skills lie, be open to more schooling. And, if I were you, I'd know where and how long it would take for you to get the skills necessary to become a Machinist: Be Ready for Anything."

"Now, Paul, you oughtta know that us folk know how to be transparent, spent all our lives doin' it. Now, De Marco here, he may not have lived through the Daniel Bells' and Everett Tills' crap swept under the rug but there's been more since, like Ernest Lacy—you know Milwaukee has the highest percentage of black men in prison—almost 13 per cent. Tell me we haven't learned how to handle ourselves."

"If that's a 'Yes' De Marco, here's my telephone number."

"And, your E-mail address is?"

"paul.bogdanov@gmail.com."

"Willie Mays all the way baby. Ryan Braun couldn't even hold his jock."

"I'd take Paul Blair before he was beaned as my all-time Center Fielder. He could play a shallow center field and catch everything hit over him."

"Yeah, but Willie made that catch in '54 that changed everything about playing the outfield. Even Blair benefitted from the Man who had no weaknesses."

"The '73 Mets fans would have something to say about that."

"Ah, he already was well into his forties. How long did Blair last? Besides, nobody's catchin' a line shot sent deep into the gap, not even Paul Blair."

"Seventeen years. No one put him out of the line up even after he made a comeback. He was traded to the Yankees in '77; and, after Reggie Jackson misplayed a fly ball, Billy Martin replaced him with the newly signed Blair. Jackson and Martin came to blows while Blair continued his magic now from right field instead of center field."

"But Willie could do everything. He hit for power while maintaining a solid batting average, steal bases, you name it. Greatest ever."

"Mays isn't the only great player out there. Blair got hit in the noggin— life flashed before his eyes. Mortality sets in a bit. I'm sure you can relate to that now that you've joined the senior citizens club."

"Speak for yourself. You know that thirty to fifty per cent of us inner city folk are not only unemployed, but even before everything tanked we were more than twice as likely to be receiving government handouts than all you White Folks. So, don't sit there and tell me that just go out there and do the best you can 'cause, boys, ain't nothin' even close to bein' fair about this game."

"Didn't we agree that we all look the other way—hey, everybody's doin' it—you ain't gonna see me holdin' the bag?"

"Like lemmings headin' for the cliff. No one's gonna stop us now."

"Ya know Terry, we should sign you up for Comedy Central— ha, ha, ha, you's just a barrel of laughs, monkeys more like it."

"Oh, Edward, Edward, Edward. Just what am I going to do with you?"

"Throw on Blue Christmas once more, he'll get a kick out of that one I'm sure."

"Oh, I know."

> *A candy colored man they call the Sandman*
> *Tiptoes to my room every night…*
> *Go to sleep everything is all right.*
> *I close my eyes they I drift away*
> *Into the magic night I softly say*
> *A silent prayer like dreamers do…*

"Yes, yessz, el maestro, Paulie, do as Dreamers do, only as lovers can ride…"

"Give it up man."

"Who the fuck do you think you are? Some pasty, wrinkled old used colostomy bag that my old man forgot to throw out?"

"Dude, hey, would you ease up just for once. Look at him such style, panache. M-ppha-ppf-ew. Look at you, oh so-oh heavenly, glide, schmooze, with that passionate kiss. Oh, yes all the time, spin, strut, those hips move with the sun and moon. Only in dreams. My man's still got it."

"Don't tell me you know this cat?"

"Our own little candy-colored clown, Paulie, you kidding me, da mae-an's still got it—*into the magic night I softly say … my dreams of You.* I can't help it. Remember all those years ago when our little twinkle toes here was loaded to the gills on those luscious dry Martinis, dancing to those ghosts of some long lost vision, his unanswerable void just out of reach, twirling, pirouetting in unison with your own tortured existence."

"Yeah, yeah like in Lost Highway where that blond chick just gets lost in that shadowless power fucking, thrusting: emotionless prowess, queen of cunts, the dude's just blown away, swallowed whole, uncouth wad held on by gravity's last gasp, can't it figure out, doesn't really want to, what to do, where to go. She's just a lost soul cavorted in the rapture of the scream of some timeless wanderer, some ne'er-do-well sated by life's countless sorrows, aroused by his tireless shadow. The poor chick cannot evade his pain languishing just beneath the surface even if she wanted to."

"OK, alright already. Here's twenty keep the change. Oh, and De Marco, there's enough in there for you to get another drink."

"So, you've spent a lot of time here before?"

"Yeah, I was known to close down the place every now and then. Even drank young lads and lasses under the table when I got the chance. It all comes to an end sooner or later."

"Shameful man, Bogdanov. I knew you had a drinking problem for a while there. But, putting the stranglehold on our very future. Damn-man, that's all I gotta say."

"I don't know if I should take that for a compliment or not. You know Jefferson, it took me a long time to get off the booze and look at every wrinkle in the mirror. Now hell, I can't even face myself in the mirror. I can't even recognize my crater face with only a few traces of white hair left on my noggin. Have a drink on me, boys. The bathroom calls. Remember De Marco to forward me your resume. If everything checks out, I'll get you your contact."

"Ready any time you are Mr. Bodganov, my little philosopher king."

"Paul that is. I may be headin' for the scrap heap but I'm still kickin'."

"No really, Paul. Thanks for everything. If this works out, maybe we can get a bite to eat. Whatdya say?"

"One step at a time Eddie. Ciao Terry. In your dreams you'll dream of ME."

"Say, talk about strange, I was down in West LA, on Wilshire, and around the corner this '69 candy apple red Coupe De Ville convertible cruises up, engine purring, and this middle-aged chanteuse, hot babushka blond wench shakes her head, the warm summer night takes over. *We want the World Now, now? NOW!!!* Breaks the silence. Wow. God, Morrison couldn't have choreographed it any better. All that shambled reality hidden by all that hallowed prowess. Makes you think. Twenty seconds and that elusive woman disappears into the dreams of yesteryear. Story of my life."

"Can I ask you a question?"

"Shoot."

"How can a guy with all that flair end up owning a bar of broken dreams?"

"Dale is sort of the clown that, like you, he shuffles about through the nightmare as quietly as possible but his life can't be defined by the roll of the dice. That shit's for those chasing that elusive stairway to heaven. What I mean is that the financial investment world dragged my heart into the dregs of death. Not that this was a way out of it, but yeah my theatrics are all played out to the fullest. Candy-colored Clown, Edward, just can't help but gettin' off in my own way. You know, I don't even drink. My wife and I play small ball. We've been to Italy thrice. Campania, watched the mountains flow into the Mediterranean Sea, Vesuvius hovering over us with its sordid, evil intentions, the *camorra* offing your ass even if you're minding your own business, Sicily and Aetna, hot damn. I feel so on right now, and I don't even need to rhyme or make sense of anything: it all just comes to me."

"I guess you're your own party."

"Tell me something Bird Man."

"What?"

"You mean to tell me that you've never heard of the man, Eddie Jefferson, upbeat jazz, cruising by in a limousine can take you out of that long, dark, and dreary alley, hoppin' to the saxophones and double base blendin' in, the piano backin' everything up, she may be gone for good. But, hey, a new neighborhood's right around the corner."

"I think you should take your music and mold it into a play of words, some farce where you don't know whether you should laugh or cry."

"You are the soul where I lose all my control, crazy you know:

I'm your slave, De Marco. How I worry about you hangin' around your tight-assed father. Just kiddin' man. But hey, could it not rain to take away all this brutish humidity, sticky and odorous. For God's sake y'all, could you catch us a break. The azure Amalfi Coast just rolls in and out with noiseless indifference."

"Here's your dough. I'll drop my act if you'll drop yours."

"Eddie, Eddie, Eddie, it's all about you, champ."

"Oh, we'll never cross paths ever again, that I can assure you. After all, who's friends?"

"Don't you know my man, it's all about you, capiche? Cross my heart."

"By the way, what does *omerta* mean?"

"So you spotted that on my old God Father t-shirt, the code of silence. Everybody lives by it. Nobody wins at this game Sir. But we keep tryin', hopin' and prayin' somethiing'll come my way. So why do you think your strings will bring *las flores* out even in the middle of the frozen tundra? Serious now. The party's over."

"Why bother? Let's go son. This nut case doesn't know when to clam up."

"Bogdanov walks listlessly through the searing heat. Is this Baton Rouge or Milwaukee? Hell's more like it. The windless cumulonimbus clouds peer down upon him in stoic silence. From the reaches of the majestic oaks as, above, a sole egret pulls in its pristine neck, flapping its towering wings through the sticky skies.

The air slows its crystal clear motion, its day no less enigmatic than his—he spins from his sweating brow as the sun tears through his withering presence Could his house be any further down? All that bullshit that poured out of Terry's and Edward's mouths is now etched in his strained thoughts. Just hold it in for another couple of blocks. God, I gotta piss again, never leave the house without my Scout. Fuck all this walking. God, why don't I get a wheel chair? Everybody else has one nowadays. Yeah, no shit. Maybe I oughtta get one. Beats all this walkin'."

Back to good ole' neurasthenia. His daughter with all her know-it-all "self-help books," yeah, she's the one who's claimed she too climbed onto the couch—lies, lies, all lies. She's rotting under all that nonsense about being so intense, so more well-rounded than everyone else. She's just a frightened child that's scared to death that someone might hear her frail silent scream. Who isn't? "She ain't comin' around anymore, she's spread her wings, so she says. Right, just don't ask me for any more money. The skeleton wanders in to help me then she comes in with all that bravura like Deborah. For two to have seemed to be so different are so-oh alike. Fuck, if I ever told those two what I thought of them they'd shut me out for good."

Maybe Deborah's right, all I have to offer someone is my pity party. Right. Who is she? So distant and self-assured. Round-and-round it goes. "Why do you take me to all those stupid movies? Like you think I can't see through all this shit—going through the motions. Can't even spend one minute with me after the movie ends. Nope, gotta get home to her hubby and make sure that all his cultured whims are taken care of."

The fact is Paul does not feel whole around his daughters. They are so much more educated and well-traveled than him. Yes, he has provided for their education and was there for them if they needed a shoulder to cry on. But, even if his wife would be nasty to them, ultimately they would lean to her because he was so aloof, so inattentive to their frail needs. Some people take a lifetime to turn around. Others, well, trip right off of mother earth, so utterly befuddled by the innate quietude of everything that they seal their fates. Paul stands within her essence, his experiences left in the past. It is not that he is harboring a lifetime of crosses to bear; he is just in need of the love from another, the distance taken away.

Janine's elusive tears fill his presence as Paul steps into his front yard, and moving to open the front door, he sees her face, tears pouring down her masked prowess. Nobody's schisms are any more pristine than another's. Janine, an old, old woman before her time leaned upon her affectionate nature and responsibilities to make her the center of attention. Lifeless Paul shielded from the amber sun ducks inside the front door and stares into his living room.

Janine left herself behind, she her own ghost. Neither is capable of toppling the monster they have created over the years. Yes, he always knew. She too, the household's dominatrix, couldn't fend off the welts of the silenced years that consumed her spirit like body punches taken from a boxer just waiting for his damsel to open up.

"Come on kitties," Paul muses. He leads them into the kitchen for some bite-sized nougat of sirloin tip leftovers.

"Oh, a couple of phone messages—I'll get 'em in the morning." One thing retirement offers is a life bereft of schedules. A few bites of sirloin tip and rice, and it's off to bed before the traditional weekend comes in focus.

Chapter Twelve

Coffee Klatch in Hales Corners

"Now, I wonder who that could be. Girls, I'll be right back. I hope the men didn't forget something. I don't know what I'd do without Bobby. But, hey, it's nice to have the house all to myself with all you sweet souls to get me out of the rat race for a while. Be right back."

Deborah Bierman briskly makes her way to the front door as her close friends' chatter on about anything and everything in her spacious kitchen.

"Samantha thanks for stopping by. I thought you'd be busy with your kids and that new profession of yours."

"Stefaniak Realty can wait. I've finally gotten an opportunity to get some subcontractors out to a couple of homes in and around Muskego to get them ready for sale. The owners finally realized you've gotta spend money to make money."

"Come on in."

"Why, thank you."

"Hey everybody, this is Janice Marion, my neighbor. There's a chair right over there. Claudette could you skootch over a bit and let our young friend have a little room."

"Claudette Parsons. Darlin', I think I could be your grandmother."

"You, no, really, I'm not that young."

"I'm sixty-seven; and, be-lieve you me, I feel every bit that number—lollygaggin' around's all the more I can muster most days. My husband vanished into thin air. That's why I make sure to meet up with the girls as much as I can. Don't feel sorry for me. I've had some time to lick my wounds. Wouldn't, no couldn't live through that ever again. Once is more than enough. But, honey, you sure are a breath of fresh air—what has kept your sweet little boom-boom in suburbia?"

"Hales Corners has always been my home. I coach girls' softball over at Whitnall."

"I'm Muriel, Muriel Janoz. Girls, would you look at her. My God, you are drop dead gorgeous. And, girl, I'm not the kinda person just to hand out compliments. Mrs. Marion, should your husband ever stray from you; he'd be a fool and then some."

"You should see my daughter, Christina; she's heaven on earth, really. Marvin spends more time with her on the diamond than most fathers do with their sons. She's really, really good. I plan to be right there when she enters Whitnall High. That's if I'm still coach. Ah, enough on that. I'm sure you're all bored to tears on all this sports stuff."

"No, silly: at least you've got somethin' going on with your kid. Anyway, we'll start with Tara Schwartz here; a divorcee who I am sure could use a man about now."

"Oh, really I'm not that pathetic, am I? Or does it show? Just kidding. Anyway, I am an English Literature professor over at Carroll College, those kids, and I do mean kids are a handful even at a small private college like Carroll. But, I wouldn't have it any other way. I can utter Chaucer's *Miller's Tale* over and over. And, Shakespeare? Oh honey, if I had my druthers, I'd spend my whole day teaching just what the man tried to convey. Like, like is anyone listening? Do we have to act like the characters in MacBeth or Othello that are not real?"

"Hi, Janice I'm Regina Heberling, you don't have to worry about me sweetie. There's no depth to me, really. I pour everything into my desserts: you've just got to try my homemade key lime pie— if that doesn't suit you, little ole' Samantha here can fix you up with a wonderful slice of my lemon meringue pie. Life's wonderful when you never had had to step foot in an office. Although I must say that, I have two kids in Whitnall right now, along with my baby Aiden who's just turned six. He's got a mind of his own, like he has his own off and on switch. Well, I guess you know what I mean with your little girl?"

"Yes I do. Could you please get me a piece of lemon meringue pie along with a just sliver of your key lime? Funny, only Snickers and Pepperidge Farms Pies have filled my sweet tooth because I can't even get spaghetti or chicken soup right, unless of course if Ragu or Campbell's Soup is at my disposal."

"Aw, that's all right dear. I didn't find love until I was forty. And, no, I don't have any kids. I leave all that up to you guys to worry about because my beau, Nathan, Nate, he's so smooth. He brings me some of the Financial information he puts together for companies all over Milwaukee and Waukesha County, even Madison. With computers and financial experts working alongside him, my little *artiste* can breathe life into the most boorish bottom line. Me? I can spend hours in the back yard watching that shy oriole and cardinal peak their vibrant little beaks out from the shadows. Oh, and if you like egg whites, I know sham tort can show up every holiday; but maybe you could take some home with you. Don't worry about the Corning pan. Just return it to Debbie after you're through. No, really, dear, we're the ones who need to lose the weight. That petite outfit you're wearing. My, my, my, I don't know the last time I could have worn that. Oh, I almost forgot. I'm Yvonne Scarborough an artist at heart.

But right ladies, doesn't she just inspire you to go to the gym like yesterday?"

"Not really, just partake in these luscious éclairs and some devilish Old Soul Ethiopia. No, no, no, that's right Claudette, you can park your plump little booty over at Starbucks and nurse those hot café mocha's all day long."

"Café mocha's? You'd better pour me a pitcher of Long Island iced teas and garnish that with some delightfully home baked glazed peanut butter cookies. This boorish trap I call my life."

"Booze? The only drink I could ever master was those childish minty-green grasshoppers we had as kids at Christmas time. Ha-hah-the first taste of beer sent me right to the pits. Never drank again. That was a lifetime ago. I'm Shelly Jundt. My husband's a developer who built this cream-brick house over twenty years ago. Now he's building homes out in the Kettle Moraine sticks for filthy rich people even older than us—well actually I'm thirty-seven, they're well, let's just say they're a few years my senior, but they're all like the friends I've never had in high school."

"Yeah, like that forlorn lost little child who couldn't get out of her own way?"

"Speak for yourself, Sammy. I'll just wrap that sexy little ruby boa around my fuchsia t-dress and sachet to my twentieth year high school reunion and show all those hapless snow cows just who in this world really rocks."

"Oh, my heart bleeds for you. I have two sons that are about ten years your junior. Hey, fifty is the new thirty, right. Ah, sounds wonderful but Ponce de Leon ain't got nothin' on me. Diana Ross and Catherine Deneuve can still bring it. So, I'll never see thirty ever again. That long blond hair of yours. Catherine could never define you, you precious thing you."

"Wild at heart. Enough already, got any brandy? Just kidding. I've got a long way to go with getting my real estate career kick started. My husband's pharmaceutical sales business is going great now but he has to pay for his own health benefits. He's been a private contractor for a while now. John says the company wanted to weed out all the dried up seeds as quickly as possible. Like, who are not the dried up seeds? I've been there. But he's talking less and less about work. I think he might get let go. After all, he's only under contract. I think I've got the bug for selling homes. Girls, it's in our DNA to make a go of it even if my hubby has one good idea to my thirty. We're both 1099's— little scary if you know what I mean. I've asked him how things are going but he's always so evasive."

"Honey, you're probably right. That's why I'd teach Shakespeare all day long. He shows us the stage, and it seems that's the only place we thrive. Turn out the lights, and, well everything remains hidden behind the scenes."

"Shakespeare was also comedic."

"I know Muriel. That's why I'm here. To get away from all that stuff. I know a couple of cops from the inner city. It's not just guns and drugs. Babies are stolen to be adopted illegally, some end up dead, left behind in the malaise between darkness and light. Sure, it's a rarity, but it happens. Shakespeare is only relevant because we just hang on to what we got. You don't need to be a genius to know that."

"OK, Yvonne, have a drink on me."

"Come on Debbie, you go girl."

"Angus, the old by-itch still's got it, *the girl's got rhythm, she's got the back seat rhythm, the girl's got rhythm.* Me in my sveltely pressed burnt umber and white glen plaid skirt scampering forth with my trusted Union Jack top. If only Bon Scot didn't have a romance for getting out of this funk."

"No, no, no, no, no, no, no. More like George Clinton telling everyone what funk is really about."

"Can't touch this?"

"Wrong."

"So, what do you think about all of this, Janice?"

"Whacked: not boring mind you, yeah, kinda cool, cute in a way like at a dress rehearsal. But really, do you girls have any type of music you listen to while we talk our pedicured little lives away?"

"Techno pop, house music, you know, An American in Paris, unkempt chanteuse Marianne Faithful, pretty much everything except artists that are so full of themselves that they seem to be real. I don't wanna say Pink. Maybe you might think she's it. But, yeah is anyone really that good? Amp up her lyrics and you know. How can she not have your attention?"

"There's still Usher and Nikki Minaj, sure. It's hard to put a finger on. But, yeah, Janice, we'll amp on some of our medleys in just a bit."

"Right, Samantha. I'll go pull out some of my fave's."

"You should hear what some of my young athletes pull out of their iPhones. Makes me want to go right back into the womb. F-this, f-that. That's not even the half of it. Like the boisterous dude just wants his girl as one of his conquests, too frightened to see and touch her as a beautiful young creature without all those ridiculous ideas of what love is really all about. Like us creatures are all their little conquests, you know? Like I'm some kind of tool of that worn out bed-ridden trade we can't seem to get rid of no matter how hard we try."

"Misogynists one and all, right girls? Men can't live with 'em, can't live without 'em."

"Right, the same old bouncing ball. Can't wait to get off that train."

"Ah, might as well get on the train 'cause what are you gonna do if you can't get on?"

"Ah, we're all just babes when it comes to that sweetie," Claudette coos, "My old man ran away, left me with a mortgage. I'm not kidding. He's sort of like Leo F. Burt of my Bascom Hill days. Like he exploded onto the scene then ran, heading for the hills. Ain't no one gonna find 'm.

He's probably up in Canada doin' the free wheelin' devil-may care thing. One shelter to the next: rumors flyin' around that his brittle old bones are still as shifty as ever. He's not worth enough to be chased unless of course I wanted to find his sorry ass. For what, more headaches that will never end. By the way, I'd love to meet your distant old man, what's his name anyway, yeah, that's you Debbie, your father."

"My father? You kidding? Now why would you bring him up? You know I set up this little gathering today because dear old dad called off our visit to the movies. He's distant, don't know why because he could care less about anything. Doesn't even want to spend any time with his great grand-children."

"He probably knows more than you're letting on about your kids, Deborah."

"Says who?"

"Come on, we're all whipping up our little just deserts. Like when you make it over to my place: this chick from way back, you can get some of my vibes, *happy, sad, crazy wonder against the fog, walkin' my cat named dog.* Norma Talega was right there with Neil Diamond with such simple overtones, perpetual dreamin' without all our sappy ideals like just leave me be unless you wanna come along with me as I softly reach out to you, holdin' me, holdin' you. It's all so clear to me like it was just yesterday. That was when music was still quaint, not so vitally important to all us pop star wannabees."

"Look at the Dutchess go."

"T'aint no part-time thing, but even my sweet imagination cannot do it justice."

"Love, girl."

"What else is there?"

"My lonely shack's just a mile from here."

"Claudette, if you want to get hold of my old man you're going to have to find him yourself."

"Are you serious? I don't even know his name."

"That's your problem. I've tried to set him up with a few women from my church. Some were quite striking if I must say so myself. A couple he even took out but nothing ever materialized. I talked to the last one and she said he just took her out to eat like it was some business partnership, not even acknowledging he enjoyed her company much less letting her know how everything went."

"He's just scared."

"Yeah, whatever. If you want to find him, you can get it done. You're old enough to make it happen if you want it bad enough."

"My life's like a one-hit wonder Norma—don't you ever tell me everything's the same—I'll find that out for myself."

"Ooh, feisty little Claudette."

"You got that right, ain't nobody going to push me around."

"You're still not going to get dad's vital information. Besides, he's eighty-three, isn't there someone on the beat to your own drum who's more into someone up your alley like Joplin or Hendrix?"

"Those piqued days of torturous youthful compliance are long gone. Even the straight ones I admired before I retired hanged themselves, like Mayor Norquist—with his little secret love-in with the help."

"Yeah, but at least his wife stood by him."

"Well, Ms. Figueroa got a nice settlement for sexual harassment: can't say I blame her though."

"Ah, she climbed back on the horse and is riding again today. Can't say the same for Norquist though, taking his wife down to Chicago and never looking back."

"You know she's accused somebody else of sexual harassment before ever meeting Norquist. I mean, cannot men have any regard for decency?"

"Ah, money's just the standard by which we all run around in circles for. We're like children who can't let go of our little blankets dear mom handed us way back when."

"So, you're saying, Mistress Marilyn's got her thing going' on?"

"Another pay day takes her one step closer to South Beach."

"She's no spring chicken anymore."

"Right, without love, there's no telling what she might be capable of."

"I'll drink to that. Now how about some sensuous, soothing music that can tame the vile beast?"

"By the way, do you have internet capability with speakers?"

"Of course, my hubby has his office in the room right around the corner."

"Would it be alright if I put on some music to take some edge off this stifling heat?"

"Everyone OK with that?"

"Sure, what kind of music."

"You'll see."

Janice finds her selection on You Tube, and Medieval Italy comes alive.

"Kind of goes with your cathedral ceilings."

"They'd only be better if Robert would let me rip out that cheap looking pine and put in choice ceiling beams made of, say, cherry wood or maple."

"That would cost a pretty penny," Shelly interjects, "My husband will do it for you if ever you decided to go that way."

"I know a couple of subcontractors who could do it for cost," Janice smiles, "I could even help you get rid of that traditional rose wallpaper and bring in a little lighter with a meringue or a soft sand paint job myself."

"You mean in exchange for all that Jungle Jim and see-saw garb we've given to you after you moved in?"

"Yeah, and I really enjoy painting. If you wanted, you could even roll up your sleeves and help me."

"Ah, that's alright, Robert and I dance to the tune of the same drum on that one. No matter what needs to be done in the house, we always rely on the rolodex to take care of it."

"Right, let your fingers do the walking," Regina chimes in, "if you've got the money, flaunt it."

"You've got that right. With all our tax accountants and financial advisors on the payroll, the last thing I want to be caught dead with is a paintbrush in my hand. No offense, Janice."

"None taken. It just gets my creative juices flowing with my interior design background, I like to visualize the whole experience and see how everything turns out when I've completed the job."

"You know, Deb, pretty soon that little child of mine is going to leave the mud and slides behind. She'll become the next Linda Evangelista."

"If she is any resemblance to you, my dear, that is an understatement," Yvonne nods as she sips ever so contently on her third cup of coffee.

"My Juliska salad plates, they blend in with the vibrant blues, you know; that soft azure that grabs hold of you as if you're just coming out of a deep, deep sleep."

"Are you sure you're not a poetess?" Tara asks. "Communications major who's only used the talents to lure my hubby into her black widow's existence. He steps out of line, rest assured, he'll know which way to turn or else."

"You got a flare for the dramatic as well: maybe you should stop by next semester and see a play we will put on; and, not some old worn out Strindberg or mainstream play. We are actually delving deeper into Harold Pinter's repertoire—dragging one's feet never felt so good."

"That's alright, my dear. I've got enough problems in my life to be shown them onstage. I wish I could say things were alright at the Bierman household. It just seems that as I aged, I've become more distant from my children … Like they've got their own lives and keep their distance from Bob and me."

"Emotional distance."

"Yes, Claudette, you're right. But how do you take away all that space?"

"You can start by letting them know that you are a person who is fragile and lost in this world no less than them."

"And, let them take everything we've worked for all these years?"

"Deborah, this is all illusion no matter how you look at things."

"Right, that coming from a woman who's trying to get my dad's telephone number from me."

"You're just avoiding what lies right in front of you."

"And, what's that Dr. Brothers?"

"Yourself. Now, I may not have a wonderful lover in my life or all the trappings you have gathered throughout the years, but I can honestly say that I haven't fooled myself—it's getting late. I really ought to be going."

"You're not running out on us, Claudette?"

"No, Muriel, but I am tired of thinking that this beautiful music and coiffed closeness can lead to anything precious."

"This Girl from Ipa Nima knows that she needs to be seen."

"There strolls out the door our veteran damsel."

"So in distress that her quivering lips can no longer hide her wind-swept pouting presence."

"Oh, come on now, Debbie, Claudette deserves better than that now."

"There's some things Claudia's going to have to address on her own my dearest. Sometimes my own loneliness tears at me even when everyone's home for Thanks-Giving where not even Robert, bless his soul can even rescue me from the blues."

"Could we talk about something else now? Like my youngest Anthony following in the footsteps of my soul mate. He may not be the muscle bound jock my Tommy was but at least he will not be stuck schlepping around doors and trim around for a bunch of small-time carpenters."

"Doesn't your son have a college degree?"

"Yes, in Philosophy. My husband tried to talk him out of it, but it was no use. Tommy wouldn't let his old man win that battle. He's really good at philosophy. Tommy would talk your ears off about European Philosophers or the Ancients and openly point out their strengths and weaknesses. He's been at that gigantic breeding ground for dummies in Wauwatosa for over three years, and is losing his patience with trying to get a decent job."

"It's not that good out there, Deb. If you haven't noticed, a lot of people are struggling, people even older than us," Tara chimes in.

"Lots are out on the streets. Who knows? Maybe to get their fifteen minutes of fame on the Nightly News is all they can hope for."

"I know, I know. It's just that he's falling into his grandfather's old ways. You think I want him to end up digging in garbage cans for survival, being transparent to everyone else trying to make a decent living. My son-in-law, Jerry has offered to help him but to no avail. I even talked to my father about intervening. He knows Tom is a whole lot more than he can handle. Jerry's got his own concerns to deal with. Dad even said that the Twelve Steps would have no idea what hit them when Tom would enter into the room. God help him, I just hope he doesn't kill somebody coming back from one of from his blackout nights on the town. He's my baby, ya know. I can't help it but, what can I do?"

Samantha grabs her napkin and hands it to Deborah to wipe her tears from her soft cheeks.

"I can't tell you that I know what you're going through, dearest, but I can see my James starting to pick up those antsy characteristics."

"Right, like what am I supposed to do now? Life's not some polished movie or well-written newspaper clipping. It's raw with a lot of down time. And, woe unto all that downtime. Hollywood's got no corner on the market as far as being alone from all that topsy-turvy stuff that is smoothed over with all its bells and whistles."

"Sammy, it's not keeping him busy. He's lost in his own mixed up reality, like Claudia, it's something your son can't escape."

"I paint those very emotions on my landscapes which are actually portraits. You guys have seen some of my work. You'll see more of it this fall when we meet at my house in November."

"What do you call that, that artist you like so much?"

"Oh, yeah, Kees Von Dongen: A radiant light, a breath of fresh air in this mundane game we call life. That's only part of it though. My work evolves on its own ride with colors and shapes of the moods and feelings that surround it. Deborah, art expresses life. It can never define or be more than my, your own life. I mean how do you quantify or qualify life for that matter. But when I stand before some of my best work, I become quiet, like all the agonies and ecstasies fall to the wayside. No more Xanax for my anxieties. Calm takes hold of me, like I really should be here without all the hang-ups I keep finding myself rooted in."

"So deep, Yvonne. I know what you mean, my little Zen master. We've just got used to all the trappings of our favorite expressions. Whatever turns you on can't be all that bad, now, can it? Or am I just barking up the wrong side of a tree?"

"You know, all that the game playing crap that means absolutely nothing. Well, thank you for your candid revelation, Yvonne. And, Daniel was surrounded by lions in the Old Testament; and, they welcomed him into their war-torn pride. I sure hope my son turns things around or I don't know what I would do. He's my son, Yvonne. I could care less if he would embarrass me. I don't want him to hamper his life or to scare off some poor little creature that wanders into his presence. I may be a lot of things, girls, but—how can I say this? I know all this clever talk is just a crutch. I just don't want my own poison to help him slide further down the wrong path."

"We all have our drama, Deborah." Janice strokes her curly red hair.

"You have to let Tommy reach out."

"My grandmother was an alcoholic. God, she was a mean, bitter old cur. My mother told me she didn't want any of us to touch the bottle. I drank but was so scared that I didn't ever drink beyond my limits, a beer to or two and that was it. I shut out gramma. If you want Tommy to come around, you might have to open up with him just a little. I know that sounds so easy, but I find myself lying with my daughter all the time. Sooner or later that's gonna catch up with me."

"Right, I agree. The caramel banana pudding I am nursing might as well be castor oil. I am sorry that I haven't been much of a hostess this afternoon, but I am going to have to ask you gals to leave. Please, my festive spirits have crashed. No, it's me. I-I-hah-ah-h-h, let's just say I've seen better days. Oh, and Janice, I might just take you up on remodeling my living room and kitchen. That tiresome wallpaper has got to go. Who knows? Maybe we can get Robert to think about replacing that cheesy pine wood ceiling with some quality wood."

"That would be a great investment for when you want to sell the house."

"Hah-ah-h, well, as my dear husband would say is that a home is sort of a dead investment. It creeps along in net worth as you're paying all the bills, heating and electricity goes right through the roof, then the central air breaks down. Besides you've gotta cut the grass and trim the trees, it's like beating a dead horse. I can't break out of this funk that's fallen over me. Oh, it's just that Claudia, well, she opened up a can of worms about me that, quite frankly, I've kinda decided to ignore. And, now I just can't get rid of it."

"I understand completely. Just try to do yourself a favor by arranging your thoughts. My own petty little mind wants to turn everything negative into something less painful. I can't do that anymore."

"Well, when we want to sell the house, we're gonna ask for the Jungle Jim set back."

"That's fine, but, you can dismantle it and drag it back to your yard, that is if you want it bad enough."

"Touché. God, you're so beautiful Janice: So mature for your years."

"Not really. I'm just as phony as anyone else when I'm at work or on the field. Bliss comes from touching my husband's soft shoulders. What I am trying to say is that my life is never about becoming. It's about right now. Potential is about a work, art. What do I need a path for? Money in the bank? Am I, are we really being fair with others when we take it to the bank? Deborah, I truly enjoy seeing you. That's my bliss. If they're not gonna take it to the bank, it might as well be me, right girls?

Besides, is this world really pathless? I mean why do I really need to follow what anyone says?"

"Cause I wanna eat?"

"But seriously girls, am I really subjected to their views. Is what they telling me, are those their true thoughts anyway?"

"Girl, every day is Halloween."

"Oh, so precious, Shelly."

"Until the run-around changes."

"I don't know."

"Who does?"

"Nothing new under the sun girls."

"So, why not change?"

"We could go round in circles all night long on this Missy."

"C'mon, I've meditated, stood in the position of a tree and its branches, frightfully painful stuff—it's still just exercise. You're right about that one. Anyhow, about the house, I'll get hold of you once I talk to Bobbie about it. I gotta clean up before they get back from their golf outing."

"Ta-ta, just give me a holler whenever you're ready."

"Sure will. Maybe we can get together for a couple of drinks sometime soon."

"Why not? You sure you don't want any help cleaning up. No, you'll get your chance next year if you stick around, that is, with a bunch of middle-aged hens."

"Don't sell yourself short. What do you think it's like trying to build the confidence of a strike out queen into just making contact with the opponent's hard stuff? It's kind of cool to see all you guys as you are— not who you want me to think you are. I mean I just tremble with fear whenever I come across such plastic people. And that's every day of my life."

"I really gotta go Janice."

"Bye."

As she closes the front door behind her, Deborah turns around and glances into the foyer mirror. Perhaps a little more rouge to brighten up her face and lipstick to go with her ruby red coiffure.

Three o' clock, her two golf enthusiasts will be home soon; so, quickly Debbie fills the sink with dishwater and Joy, clearing the table of its dishes, silverware, and coffee cups as those heavenly soprano voices disturb her intents to push on. "Off with that shit," she howls as she returns to complete her tasks. She places the cotton napkins in a pile to be carted off to the washer, the ornamental doilies to be placed back in their usual hidden place.

Within an hour, Deborah cleaned and swept up the entire kitchen as she peers out the bay window; and, yet there is no sign of the guys.

"Existential thoughts of the end tear at my brain, hah, like I'm supposed to have outgrown all this shit. Screw how things should be. Fuck me! I'm tired of cleaning up this house without any help. Maybe we should move into a pin box house out in the country somewhere in the sticks like Fredonia, buy a plot of land for under 30 grand and build our own little utopia. Fredonia's a long way from Robert's office but, hey, he can manage with his old Camry while she shuttles about the countryside in her brand new burgundy Acura MDX. Not a fair trade off, but with the sale of their home here they can pay for their new abode in cash and bank the rest. And, if Bobbie wants to get the full effect of tax breaks, well, by all means they will make those payments."

Downsizing all the time from 4,000 square feet to just under a 1,000 just could do the trick. However, is the odor of cow manure and pigs oinking in the middle of the day going to make her life whole? Or is she still running from herself like her father hints at from time to time? Maybe buying the farm makes more sense than it has ever before. What does this middle-aged couple have to do with yuppie Hales Corners anymore? Been there done that.

The sound of their SUV pulls into the driveway with Jonathan studiously playing his video games. Robert walks into the house while his son pockets his cell phone to put away the clubs in the garage.

"So-oh how was your day?"

"Great. We went up to Brown Deere Park and I shot a 98. Jonathan finished with a 91 but he retracted several shots."

"What do you mean?"

"He cheated. You know, dubbing a shot and hitting another without taking a penalty shot."

"He'll grow out of it—he hasn't even turned 18 yet."

"Honey, every day I go to work there are those who stretch the truth to hide their own mistakes while people such as myself look the other way so we don't get into a massive argument."

"Why are you always so intense about your problems at work?"

"Because that is the way it is, sweetheart. There's no getting around that."

"I am the best Cad Cam designer they got. Not to brag but they want to bring on 3D Imaging."

"Jonathan's picking up on Maya Imaging quite quickly. Maybe in your twilight years you two could become a consultant team like the Bischoff 's up in Port Washington."

"I think Jonathan first needs to settle down at River Falls before we bounce all these highfalutin ideas off one another. Besides, it's hard to walk away from a full benefits package and over 150-grand a year salary just to prove to myself that I can make it on my own."

"But you've told me you have helped others work the bugs out of their programs."

"Yeah, I'm no less involved in software programming than I am aiding in designing new electrical components in order to decide which computer hardware works best to monitor the entire network within a manufacturing environment. This is worldwide. Everybody's looking to do things cheaper and faster with little room for error. This isn't some crapshoot that we can just play around with from day to day. Everybody's on board, but some are more in sync than others. I've been doing this for over thirty years, the last twenty-five with Allen-Bradley. I've priced myself out of the market. Milwaukee's far from what it once was when it opened its new plant in the eighties."

"Now, I don't have to tell you that manufacturing in Milwaukee or Chicago for that matter has become kind of a joke. But you're right. I do have excellent consulting skills; and, I won't do any more *pro bono* work for anyone if I can help it. Or, oh, I don't know, maybe take up painting classes and become the next Jackson Pollock. Leave my print on tomorrow's movers and shakers. What do ya think?"

"Oh, Jonathan do you have to play that stupid Grand Theft Auto game all the time. Is that how we raised you?"

"Ma, it's just a game."

"Right, with whores and street gangsters, how comforting. My son the addicted gamer ... I could think of more constructive things to do with your time."

"Get any better at this, and maybe you'll see me at the Pokémon championships of us geeks taking the world by storm. But, hey, I'm already packed and ready to go up to River Falls next week. What more do you want from me?"

"Maybe when you get up there, you should get a job to pay for all those girls you're going to meet up there."

"If I can find one that is more than enough mom. I'm not some kind of pervert."

"I know sweetheart, but you've got to ask a girl out even if you think she's going to ignore your advance. Honey, it's not easy for anybody. Just think about like it's that video game of yours, like you're in the moment and nothing can stop you."

"Oh, mom, do we have to go on about this anymore? What's to eat?"

"There's a leftover rib roast and Greek Salad in the fridge. Your father and I are going out for dinner. By the way, dad told me you beat him."

"Well, I pretty much got his number every time I go out there with him."

"Maybe you should have taken out golf in high school."

"Mom, they shoot like four, five over par. I'm like, um, way worse than that. They like got me by about fifteen strokes. Whitnall's got it goin' on when it comes to golf. I'd rather focus on school and bring my clubs up to River Falls to get out of the dorms, give me something to do on the weekends."

"Well, first you're going to have to find a way to get there."

"Ah, give and take. It's all good. Jonathan can take care of himself."

"That's good. I've gotta talk to your father for a bit. There are also some desserts left from my little get together this afternoon. Help yourself."

"Robert, I was wondering if you would want to go out this evening, say, go out for dinner."

"Yeah, I'm game but not those fancy schmantsy bistros you always drag me into."

"Would you just listen? I'm talking about the Brew Town Tap near Brookfield Square—low key yet elegant."

"I've found their meat and fish to be lacking in quantity."

"The presentation and food is second to none; however, the beef seems a little on the cheesy side—you know enough to feed a homeless robin."

"Really, I've always found their serving more than enough to fill me up."

"Darling Brew Town, c'mon now, they rap with you—after a drink or two, maybe a Sauvignon Blanc before I sit down for a luscious New York strip with a baked potato and asparagus. Now that sounds tremendous. Whatdya think?"

"It's a hotel restaurant."

"Yeah, but I get enough food to fill me up. You can't tell me it's a Howard Johnsons. They really put their all into making it a place for everyone to roll up their sleeves and relax to a quality meal that's not too pricey. You know. I haven't eaten since breakfast. I famished."

"I assure you sweetheart; we will make sure old man Bierman gets his fill tonight."

"By the bye, what took you so long to get home?"

"We didn't have reservations. So we didn't get to tee off until after ten o'clock. OK, OK, so we had coffee and a bag of chips. Not exactly your greatest lunch."

"I'm sure they sell apples and oranges at the pro shop."

"Bananas actually, but, nah, really those Lay's potato chips hit the spot. It looks like you're ready to go."

"Yes sir."

"How was your little wing ding?"

"Fine. Yeah, we got all our inner voices chattering away at a mile a minute."

"Well, great. I'll be back in a flash."

"Now, after you shower, could you wear that navy blue sport coat I got you for your birthday?"

"I know, and those grey cuffed woolen slacks to go with that incredible paisley red and royal blue tie that you're constantly harping to me about. By the way, my manufacturing VP digs it to no end. Where did you get it?"

"Macy's at Mayfair."

"I'll let her know on Monday."

"Like when was the last article of clothing you have ever purchased?"

"My shoes sweetheart; that's one thing I will never let anyone get for me. What's more important than keeping my feet free of pain?"

"Alrighty then, I'll be waiting for you in the kitchen. Our little man-child is watching the house for the evening."

"Why don't you get their number on the Internet and make a reservation. It is a Saturday night. After today, I don't feel like hangin' out in the lobby for an hour until a table opens up."

"Love you."

"Jonathan, I don't want to see the house torn up by all your friends when we step out for the evening. Just to let you know, we'll be back before eleven; so, if you do sneak some of your buddies in, we're going to get home sooner than you think."

"Like I've ever had a lot of people over here?"

"We have our ways, son."

"Nah, I'm not doing anything tonight, but watching a little ESPN and catching some Z's."

Chapter Thirteen

A Sunday Afternoon Spent in the Sticks

"Fancy meeting you out here Christina on such a fine Sunday morning."

"I'm waiting for my ride to stop by and pick me up. He says he wants to take me to some place special before I take off next week for Madison."

"I don't want to cause any unease with you, but if I may, ah-hah, my son, Jacob—he's not comfortable with our ways. I don't want to make his life any more difficult than it is—mathematics he excels in; and, Chasidim will interfere with his schooling and desire to experience life with less dedication than ours allows."

"Sure, I'll help however I can—I don't know what I can do. But yeah, I can tell you something what is he can expect to find. I know that may seem a bit vague, but I don't know if it's really that different."

"Us? We're a modest bunch, trying to make ends meet like everyone else but it seems so wasteful, your world you cavort in."

"I don't want you to think I'm showing you in a bad light, Mr. Schwartzberg. I mean I don't ever go to church. Don't really want to either. Just 'cause we don't want to shack up in our house. Who do you know that's out of your backyard, Mr. Schwartzberg?"

"Probably about as much as you Ms."

"What's the supposed to mean?"

"I really don't know a whole lot. You're probably just as scared as I am. You're, how can I say this, you seem so assured, but behind that beautiful face of yours, you're probably scared to death that someone might point you out before all your friends, everyone. I'd like to think I'm sure in my own way but not really. Behind my spectacles and black Borsalino, I have some comfort in realizing that there is something that works no matter what anyone else says or does about me."

"Personally Sir, I don't really care. I mean if that's what gets you through the night, hey, great, cool, ya know?"

"Wonderful, I know we've not spent any time together. I go my way. You go yours. Why are you so taken aback that someone such as myself may not want to join you people who are so intrigued by us but really don't want to have anything to do with us?"

"Taken from Darwin, I think I can pinpoint it. The bigger the group gets, the more powerful is its club. Therefore, no matter how positive our intentions, they fall no less hard. And, like you guys, if you'd compete for the big stick, you'd be no less evil as you are great. It's inevitable, you know?"

"Let me tell you something about my Faith: Baal Shem Tov, you shorten it to Besht means Master of the Good Name. The Don Cossacks whipped us, broke our will to run a business. So he started the ball rolling by letting the Rabbinic Soul fall in order to open our hearts and minds to mysticism, the Cabal. You've heard of Madonna, haven't you?"

"Of course."

"Well, she's studied its merits and freshness for years. You can't say it's not just some schmaltzy garbage that lone kvetching Yiddish freaks embrace."

"Infinity, yeah. I don't know about you, Mr. Schwartzberg, how do you even try to define it?"

"Humility, live modestly. Why waste any of god's gifts to feed us? Tell me, Christina, haven't you felt that being truthful, leaving out feeding or protecting all your fears and desires, I mean not shutting them out but just to be selfless, living in *mitzvoth*: to observe God's commandments in complete quietude."

"How do you know what's in your books are not the whims of your leaders, you know? Keeping people in line? That's what I've gathered from being bombarded with the bible. It comes out in all angles of everyday life, Mr. Schwartzberg. You know. Your son will be picked on like the rest of us."

"You're such a pessimist, you know that don't you? *Chesed*, loving-kindness. From that God walks through the door."

"Poetic, I'll give you that."

"We don't have TV's or radios. Forget video games, and computers are used to look up things, not to waste your lives on video games. Look, we started out being taught the Cabbala in Yiddish all those years ago because many of our ancestors couldn't read and write. It's not about being right or wrong: We're Jews, plain and simple. Take it or leave it. Now about my son, Jacob."

"What do you want to know?"

"I'm driving him up into the North Woods to attend summer camp at Ramah with a bunch of great mensch before school starts: He's going to meet a lot of kids, some even from Israel. So, yes, I am really excited for him."

"What? Like a coming out party?"

"I guess. It's a start. Public high school—he's going to be a junior at Milwaukee Washington."

"Well, he's gonna be afraid. What do you want me to tell you? It's tough for everybody." "That's not very encouraging."

"If you can't face the truth about everything he's gonna deal with, then why have you become a dad?"

"Softly he strokes his *peyots* with his nimble fingers. None of us is right in this world. Satisfied?"

"Right, some live off the dole and recite psalms all day or cater to your kind at the butcher shop down the street. What happens when some dude walks into your tailor shop and wants to have his suit altered for the homecoming dance?"

"What? Like we're going to throw them out, asking them never to show their faces in Kosher Land ever again? Jacob, this is Christina."

"Hi Jacob."

"Father, could we go?"

"Surely, we've got a long drive ahead of us. You've got everything packed I presume. Tooth brush and tooth paste? Swimming suit, towels? Wonderful. Well, Christina, I will talk to you after I get back."

"Christina, dad is well meaning. He just wants to be honest, but that doesn't always go over very well."

"*Tzadikim* is all I aspire to young girl."

"A righteous bloke is more like it."

"Where did you get that from?"

"Harry Potter. Where do you think?"

"You're such a whiner. Get in the car."

"Wow, a brand spanking new Subaru, cool."

"See, Christina we're not always out of touch with the world around us. Perhaps we can pick up on this conversation where we left off tomorrow afternoon sometime."

"Shalom Mr. Schwartzberg. Nice to meet you Jacob."

As usual, Guillermo is late. She texts him and sits down on the curb. Chrissie seems aloof from her surroundings, mulling over the conversation that just transpired, Mr. Schwartzberg usually so distant and emotionless, sort of like most people she meets, dropped his chameleon act and put his heart in her hand. Well, somewhat anyway.

Maybe that is really what she has missed through those rancid school years of becoming like everyone else to fit in: to somehow let go, to not worry about where she may end up, that intellectual ego dumped for her real self to spring forth.

A ten year-old Mitsubishi Lancer breaks the silence, thrusting to a halt just yards from her. "Where have you been, Guillermo? It's already past noon."

"Want to get something to eat?"

"No. I'm saving every dime for when I go to Madison."

"Wow, so I bet you'll never guess where I'm taking you?"

"Don't have a clue. Come on Guillermo; please tell me, please. I don't want to find out that we're going somewhere that I really rather would hang around with my parents."

"You gotta give me more credit than that girlie. I bet you've never heard anything about this place. But you'll be blown by away this, I'm telling' ya."

"OK, Billie. What's up? Give it to me straight."

"You know, back when my dad graduated from high school way back in the Stone Age, somebody knew about this place near Eagle that is so cool—Paradise Natural Springs. He took me here right after I graduated, so calm, serene like. Makes you think, you know. Like, how does this make sense? You seen The Shining, didn't you?"

"Nah."

"OK, well, it's like when you go somewhere; and, you can see the people way back in the day, in the late eighteen hundreds, like these rich folks from the past like you can see them right when you get near the Old Spring."

"Pappy told me that there were beer cans and cigarette butts all over the place. However, now it's clean and cool, like you're gonna freak when you see this place. I'm tellin' ya."

"Waukesha? I've never been here before. Kinda nice? Lot different than where we come from, ain't it?"

"Big trees, roads are even wider: God, look at the houses. They're a lot bigger than ours."

"I know we talked about this before, Chris. But yeah, I know we probably party too much. School's not my bag. When we get to lay foundations for houses, who do you think is moving the blocks into the basement area?"

"Well, Billy, you're the new kid on the block."

"Oh, so funny. Yeah, that's true, but some of these guys have been doing it for a long time. All can carry two blocks at a time with one hand. I'm workin' at it but, God; there are times when I wish I would o' tried goin' to school, like you. The money's good but my body's sore all day long. Rain's good, got the day off unless we got some inside work lined up just in case."

"Dude, I have no idea what I want to do. Ya know I talked with that weird guy Mr. Schwartzberg."

"Oh, you gotta be kiddin' me. I don't know what their deal is."

"We talked for the first time. In fact, he approached me."

"You didn't go off on 'm like you do with us."

"Guillermo, he just wanted to talk to me about his son, the poor guy's goin' to Milwaukee Washington because he ain't gonna be anyone of them—he's a math whiz. The man just wants to see his son have an easier time getting along with other students by going to a high school like Washington."

"A Jewish dude around Blacks and Hispanics: now that's a trip. He better realize that it's a war in high school. He's gonna have to learn the ropes on his own. I mean every day I went to school I wasn't aware of the all the mind games goin' on. And, yeah, sometimes it came my way, and they just had to fuck with me. So I just learned to face them, you know, just stare 'em down, give 'em my best. Point blank, right in their face, tell 'em, I'll tear your lungs out bro."

"You got that right. You think us girls are any different? I mean, we're scared to death just like you. You know, cat fights can start anywhere."

"Yeah, you're right; I've seen some pretty nasty fights between chicks."

"Yeah, some of those black girls could go at it forever."

"Anyhow, Mr. Schwartzberg flat out told me that he's just as wrong as you or me. Not that he's trying to right that wrong. But this is what bothers me."

"Woe, woe, woe, woe, woe—hold up there. What's that supposed to mean?"

"Simple—I can't just go along with everything or dodge the real shit. That shit eats at me. I mean just to avoid things makes it worse. I mean Guillermo, all those ideas I have of everyone, you, me included. They're just 'cause I'm too chicken to confront you, whoever I'm ready to jump all over. I don't care what Madison's gonna do for me if I can't somehow come feel better about letting things hang."

"I swear to God Chris; I don't know anybody who spends more time dwelling on your own little pity party."

"Right, and who do you talk to when everything falls apart?"

"You just don't know when to keep your mouth shut."

"Right, you're on your own."

"Yeah, and like you, I go home and spin in my head all these fears just rippin' me up, like the only thing in school that makes sense is to open up about it, so I don't keep trying to get caught in this same rut, like I see mom fight with her clubbed foot. Hers won't get any better. Mine? And, you know exactly what I'm talking about. We go out and have a good time, a burrito and a few laughs—these fears just tear me apart—no Hail Mary's gonna change it either. Everybody brushes me off, you included, when things get a little touchy. Tell you what."

"What? Like you're no different than me, Mr. Schwartzberg, or my little poodle Buffy."

"Whatever, could we drop this? This shit bores me to tears. God, could ya ease up on yaself, Chrissie, chill like? Can't we just have a little fun once in a while?"

"Sure, but could you turn on something other than Howard Stern?"

"Hey now, Howard's outlasted all of them. He da man."

"Right, talks to porn stars and acts like he's not trying to score, but yeah, he wants you to think he'll pull out all the stops if he has to: a real world beater."

"Who's done better with less than Howard?"

"He's just a guy who entertains you, tells you what you want to hear. He's like everyone else. Doesn't care about you, but that's OK, 'cause he makes you feel better about yourself up in that thick head of yours."

"That's your job. Nobody else can do it but you."

"What?"

"Figure yourself out. You see you can be pathetic. There are some things I don't talk to you or to anybody else: stays right here in Guilly's little heart. Take my lumps and, hell, it's a new day."

"Turn that shit off Guillermo! It's nasty."

"OK, so it is."

"Have you ever thought about doing something about it instead of going round and round in circles, like I could kill myself right now if I had a gun in my hand?"

"You can't lay this all on me. You're chicken; and you'd brush me off just to save your own hide."

"Maybe we should turn around right now."

"Who's stopping you? Could we drop this right now? See, I've come on some classic pop:"

It was the winter 1963

It felt like the world would freeze

With John F. Kennedy and the Beatles, yeah, yeah, Ah-heya ma ma ma, into the night-ahh.

"This is so-oh old. Yeah, you're right, Billie. Maybe I do take things too seriously. Mom must have liked this song."

"Eighties station: the power of Sirius XM Radio." *Life in a northern town.*

"Oh would you look at the corn fields. It's kinda nice to get out of the city for a while."

"That's why I dragged you out here. You think I like sweatin' my ass off moving cinder blocks around all day?"

Ah-hey ma ma ma, take it easy on yourself.

"See, babe, it's talking to you."

"Yes, but I still am tired of everyone just avoiding everything."

"What did we agree to?"

"Take it easy on myself."

"That's more like it."

"Here's County N, just up the street and we're there."

"Oh God. It's just all so green, ya know. Like, why are you bringing along a towel?"

"I'm gonna take a dip in the cool waters. There's a brick building back there. A hundred years ago, this was it man. People'd come out from Milwaukee, rich fucks, and spend the whole weekend here. Kinda like the Dells is for us. They'd come out here in horse carriages, husband and wife, their kids even, and spend a whole couple of days in these waters to restore their weakened spirits like you were talking about earlier."

"I just don't think physical problems are always affected by my personal problems."

"If you haven't noticed, I've left my dope at home."

"Well, there you go."

"Thank you. I'd have to get a bag of Doritos if I'd have to toke up."

"This is a long drive, Billy. There's no way I'd get into a car with you all lit up."

"Oh, come on. I'm not some kind of wuss."

"Right, one wrong move and both of us are in a world of shit. I don't want to get in a car accident, Willy. I've seen you doze off before while you were driving. We're going too fast for that shit."

"You didn't bring a towel. I told you to bring one."

"It's frigging hot out. Why would I bring a towel along?"

"You'll find out. Let's go."

"It's just a lot of calm water, like a little pool, so what?"

"We've gotta get there first. Hey, I didn't take you here to play with ya. C'mon man, gimme a break. So you're gonna have to walk a little. You've got your swimming suit beneath your sweats don't you?"

"Of course. You've told me to come prepared, and, hey I'm ready to go."

Lindens, maples, beech, and oaks hug its meandering banks, black-eyed Susan's and brittle thistles pop out from the shadows as they make their way down a well-groomed asphalt trail. "You see my dad says that none of these smooth black top trails were here a long time ago, just dirt trails from kids lookin' to have some fun. Too bad, I didn't bring along my cell phone. Would've been nice to get some pictures with you here going' into the clear waters."

"Where's that?"

"Oh, it'll be a while. First you've gotta see the old cement work that made this place what it was for the city folk."

"Dad's told me there are some poisonous plants around too. I forgot to ask him what they looked like, but they're out there."

"Look at all the rocks in there."

"Good-sized too: That's why I stay on the path. Don't want to slip on them and get hurt."

"Coming from a guy that works with bricks all day, you're not as tough as you think, Billy."

"I never seen anybody else try to go in there, especially when you get up to the marsh, fuck, no telling how deep you will sink in that muck."

The sound of the water running over the rocks, and its twirling, soft curlicues of water rolling off the mass of rocks, eases their minds as they continue. Long, narrow rows of worn cement rest within the algae-laden, still waters.

"Like, yeah, people way back when could actually put something beautifully together that could have meaning beyond all that commercial mother lode of watersheds, the Wisconsin Dells. My dad found this just driving around with his friends while they were camping near the Scuppernong just up the road. The DNR will take care of this for others to see. It's quite beautiful isn't it?"

Huge truck-sized oxidized circular metal contraptions rest quietly in the lush grass as they stop in front of a man-made eight-foot waterfall, and beyond it, the waters visibly deepen. "Oh, look there's a fish in there."

"Good sized too."

"Can you fish in there?"

"Sure, but you can't keep any. DNR's got some signs posted. So yeah, everything must go back. I gave up fishing when I was this high. Let 'm have his peace."

Beyond the aspects of humankind's alterations to the land, a huge marsh stretches out alongside the rusty metal as moss grabs hold of every surface stone, with the constant *buzzing* of a dragonfly to break the still afternoon's silence. Here croaking frogs, giant water bugs, and mud turtles are the homesteaders while Billy and Christine are welcomed in for a brief peak into their hidden existence.

Finally, they reach their destination, an old hexagonal cement stone & cement structure. And, outside the wall, sparkling water continues to flow out of it with a rippling effect.

"Alright, I'm goin' in."

"Wah-wah-wait, I'm comin' in too!" She quickly climbs through to open iron-blocked windows and follows him in.

"FUCK! You, you kiddin' ME! I'm F-reezing!"

"That's the big secret babe, thirty-seven-degree water fed by underwater cold springs. Cool, isn't it?" Christina sees that Guillermo wants something from her. Nah, that's never gonna happen.

"Banana yellow bikini, pretty hot."

"Now that I'm in, it's not that big o' deal."

"No? Spend another fifteen minutes in here. You'll be all black and blue and screamin' for mercy."

"Maybe so. But, for now, I'll back float."

"Yeah, but once the shade takes over, look out."

"Like I said, I'll come out when I'm good and ready." Both can no longer spend another second in the pristine waters, making a quick exodus.

"Come here and give me a kiss."

"No."

"Why not?"

"Ah-hah, because maybe I don't feel like it."

"Whatever: why'd did I bother taking out some stuck up wench who's always ordering everybody else around, and the minute you say something back, Wham/Bam! Like forget about it. Nobody's trying to get you Chrissie. You're doin' a good job of that all by yourself."

"Alright, so, tell me, Guillermo, when was the last time I've been digging in your backyard? Sure, there's been times when I'd call you out, but, it hasn't been in a real long time, like since I don't know when. But who's keeping score, right?"

"Ooh, Lassie, if I had the guts, I'd—a."

"Let's go. I've had enough of this?"

"We just got here. Besides, who's drivin'?"

"Nah, an hour's long enough. If you don't want a go, stay here. I'll find my own way home. This ain't Mount Rushmore or anything."

"Right, like Eagle's several miles back. If you get lost, well, good luck."

"We turned in right on County N by the big entrance sign. I turn left. Yeah it's a couple miles. I'll be just fine."

"Like who's gonna pick you up from Eagle?"

"You let me worry about that. Now, are we leaving now or do I have to find my own way out of this mess?"

"You're somethin' else."

After getting out of the spring water's edifice, Christina follows Guillermo several feet behind him, tired of spending another lost afternoon with someone fading ever so quickly into her rear view mirror. Guillermo mutters a slew of expletives and reaches for his car keys, beginning his trek back to his car.

"Why play favorites with anyone? She muses as she quickly dries off by rolling around in a nearby patch of grass. Like he's not in the same boat as she is. Who can make sense of this life? She grabs her attire and shoes, slips them on, walking as fast as she can to keep up with that speed demon, William. He's no more in the driver's seat than she is."

The ordinary ebb and ordered flow of her inner metronome ceases. She thinks that Willy maybe hurt by her frankness. Like his hubris really means anything, just something he picked up along the way. Life is personal, all of it. Friends will come without her doing; however, will she ever find an outstretched hand, with love wrapped within an enigma, to shelter this life of hers? Or will a moneyed career be her sole partner throughout her existence? Anxieties have dummied down, a serene calmness has filled her spirit that she cannot know as her trapeze act falls through the net of time and space. Stereotypes are but a hearty chuckle at another's expense as the chameleon's colors hide from her center, a center solely of her own design.

Cannot Guillermo sense this? Or is he like everybody else who's trying to get something out of the deal that she exposed? The pangs of life shutter at her better nature, his. There is no relationship, just an attempt to beat the odds. Whose odds? The water off a duck's back is purely delusional. She is no longer a pawn in a sorry game of chance. Everyone back home seems to have fallen desperately into his/her parts. What can she do about that?

She wipes away her smile and falls into her sullen presence. To have not even started life and yet to be so in tune with her very being mystifies her. Can life be anything more than an attempt to cover up her hidden failures? Maybe she needs to forget about all this and get on with her life, something her parents have pounded into her head ever since she can remember. Shallow is the confidant conversations she's had with her friends. They sheltered her from them, and, she reciprocated. Round and round it goes, and where it ends?

School will be a challenge; and Madison poses that for anyone with all its passionate ways to lose oneself with little or no effort. However, will it just extend beyond the closed doors of Milwaukee Washington, where point-of-view remains one's cover, one's solace? It's all about a job.

How can she chart her own life's course? To be able to love someone without worrying about how she stacks up against the competition? Yes, Christina is like everyone else, and, yet is she? The road to freedom is also the road to perdition. Pluses and minuses fill her chart, balancing out no matter how hard she tries to do the right thing. She can walk out from her home and see the world, that ever-changing truth. Nothing's static, only the movies stay rooted in an image. Reborn in the water's alms, she effortlessly walks along beyond her thoughts mired in life's *should's* and *shouldn'ts*, by feeling the soft clay grass shape beneath her every step.

Without looking at each other, they mosey into his Lancer. He tromps on the gas pedal, spinning the front tire as he drops it into reverse.

"Easy, are you trying to get us killed?" he glares into her frightened eyes, dropping two tight doughnuts, smoke rising from the oiled asphalt, throwing it into first gear and tearing out of the parking lot. Saying nothing, Christina looks out the window as he races southbound down County Trunk N, heading back to Sherman Park. The shame cannot erase her spirits. She no longer centers on her/his every move, backing off from his proud mien. Along the county trunk roads, the huge trees create a canopy over the telephone wires, the cicadas chime in on the sun's amber twilight, the surroundings rest in ominous silence.

Within minutes, she falls asleep and the entire day's tension wanders off into the clouds.

"Hey, we're home, Christina."

"Oh, my God, you've got to be kidding? We're already home?" She touches Guillermo softly on his left shoulder. "Guillermo, please don't take this badly. It's nobody's fault. But I can't do this anymore. It's not that you did anything wrong. Just ask first, OK?"

"Not this again?"

"Put it this way, I'm not your slave. Like you wanted to get something goin' on with me but you thought that I would just go along with all that. No big deal, right?"

"Look, let's drop it. I gotta get going anyway." Christina cranes her neck and gives him a warm kiss on his forehead.

"Adios."

"Yeah, hasta nunca." Her mother is standing on the front porch with her soft cafe eyes and advances toward Christina as the youth steps over the curb. Surprisingly, Guillermo eases away from the Guicciardini residence and disappears onto Capitol Drive.

"Mijita, ver la belleza en todas partes. Que su amigos están de acuerdo con usted cuando se encuentra juntos, pero una vez que paso, el veneno de. Algos de vengarse, siempre caen, nadie lo ha ganado el juego. De alga tan bonito, sí, usted es la primera universitario miembro de la familia. Recuerde que maravilloso campus, caminando a través de sus corredores, el lago, el capitolio del estado mirando sobre sus anchos ominosos, se encontrará con nuevos amigos, los enemigos que deben dejarlos. Caminar por sus pathless tierra. Brillará, no en su camino o mío, pero nuevamente, una mujer solitaria en un mundo—Una. Aqui. Ahorra…"

"Mama, la vida no sea conocida pero soy cansada de los juegos. No aparece que debemos desempeñar el papel que nos corresponde para que encaje en. Que quiere unirse a la los ideas antiguos que nadie, se lo puedo asegurar. La mayoría de nosotros queremos tirar el dado y pregunta nada. Quieron probar algo Nuevo solamente cuando es conveniente. Es muy obvio. Más vale muerta que para seguir adelante con esta vida. Los molinos de las llanuras de castilla giran en el agobiante calor sin intenciones.»

"Claro que si pero mija, you can't hide in your dorm room, conceal your feelings otherwise you will miss on that unknown bliss, like the winds of change that brought me Giancarlo Guicciardini. And, within the alms of that mystical, magical sea of green, you came into this world, a miracle unto the Gods. Come out unto the sun and moon to join us. Defend your prowess and you create an asylum all your own."

"That's easy for you to say. You have lived your life."

"Yes, but a flower in bloom loses its luster if it cannot reach out to the sun. Vente, your father's asleep. Let's slip for a while to catch something other than that dreaded cannoli and marinara sauce."

"Italian food's just as basic as Mexican food, mom."

"And just as spicy in different ways: my leg feels fresh today. Let's get out of here for a while. Dad's not gonna get up. He'll sleep right through after all that work he put in to prepare me homemade lasagna from scratch."

"But he likes doing that kinda stuff."

"Your father's just turned sixty. I think in the back of his mind he is looking forward to retirement, that is, after you graduate from college."

"Well, I haven't even started yet. Don't put all those expectations on my back until I get my feet wet."

"I know you'll do just fine."

"Well, some of my teachers told me that it will take a lot more effort at Madison then it did at Washington."

"People want to see you fail. You won't. Your ability to tackle things have always impressed me."

"Where are we going?"

"In 'Tosa there's a place called Rocket Baby Bakery that serves the best cringle I've ever had. Scrumptious is more like it. Magnific."

"If you want something else, we can quick pick up something along the way. Otherwise, you can eat there with yours truly. They have pork sandwiches with greens or you can even get a Milano, which is out of this world. They've an array of teas and gourmet popcorn. A little bit of everything to fill you up, honey. Ready? Let's go."

Mrs. Guicciardini locks up the house and they walk over to the driveway and pile into her Prius. "Your father has agreed to spend vacation next spring in Genoa and Bologna; and, later on we're going to head over to Venice and Lake Como."

"Right, right, right, right, Milan and Florence, Raphael."

"Right, all that art and futility, Machiavelli that you educated me on, Dario Fo. Really, a girl your age needs to loosen up and spread her wings first."

"Bonfire of the Vanities is my favorite. Siena's right there too mama. Bernini touches on love the way the Master Michelangelo couldn't even imagine."

"Right, Tuscany and Lombardy. I swear if we could spend a whole year taking in the whole scene, now that would be something, wouldn't it. Besides, Raphael ran into sexual proclivities that drove him out of this world. He never grew up, Christina. Still a young man; but, those paintings are perfection, timeless. The Siren sings."

"Ah-hah, I don't want to see you go overboard and get lost in the web of what you've learned about the country. It probably does not ring true to the real Italy that neither of us knows anything about."

"We've been to Mexico several times."

"Right, like the nice parts of Guanajuato and Cabo San Lucas: that is not where my grandparents came from. And. like this big bunch of people just completed walking with the fallen body of Christ, on their shoulders in quiet solitude—here comes my grandmother right behind them on her knees with hundreds of other devoted souls, their faces glued to the capilla, their hands held in prayerful meditation. I'll never forget that for as long as I live. You would not fit in with that crowd nor would I. My two boys from my first marriage don't even come around anymore, Diego and Jack. They just don't want anything to do with me because I can look them in the eyes and settle things with them the way their father never could."

"Oh, c'mon, mom, Joachim wasn't that bad, really he wasn't. But all that talk about our ancestors and how tough Mexicans really have it, feeding us, everyone for that matter; he couldn't let all that go and just tell me what bothered him about himself. Your father had no problems with that. His grandfather told me He's the most unblemished naked man of old Calabria he's ever known. He doesn't even want to be recognized as an Italian. He's completely totally himself even if he feels out of place. This is why we don't go to church or pray to Jesus. Life is a mystery. This stuff tries to explain it. You can't. It's that simple. So here we are."

"68th & North, wow, I don't think I've ever been here before. It's really nice."

"Well, we'd live down this way but your father is only thinking about putting money away at this point and paying for your education. You know how the construction place lays him off all the time."

"He's back on his feet putting in over 80 hours a week supervising a bunch of scruffy dry-waller's downtown. We've made it out of the dust."

"Good, there's a parking spot right across the street … Let's go."

Chapter Fourteen

Things Will Turn Around Sooner or Later

"Look, there's our slacker—finally made it in Tommy. What's taken you so long to get here? Well Jiminy Christmas, it's already 9:00 o'clock."

"Yeppers, my grandfather just wouldn't get off the phone. It looks like the family's a bit worried where I'm heading. Hey, it's Friday anyway. Let's get the weekend going."

"I'll be back in a bit. Gotta relieve myself."

"Oh man, Brad. The night's still young, and you're already heading out to the can?"

"Brad, I've already put down a couple of drafts."

"Seven's more like it," Garth cuts in, "We thought you'd be the first one in here to see if that little stone fox of yours, Connie what's-her name's jiggling her tight little ass around here somewhere."

"Awe, c'mon man, give me a break. I have been trying to forget her for a year now."

"You're right about one thing, she's a looker."

"Right, she herds you in then can't get rid of you fast enough."

"You didn't get down her pants, did you?"

"Sure did—once. Dude, she's an acid head. One minute she's staring at me then she's telling me about some of her dirt bag friends scraping the white shit off car battery posts to catch a buzz off it."

"No Way."

"Oh, yeah. Seriously. God, she's one intense bitch, someone you could forget about all your problems; and, ma-a-an, F the living hell out of her all day and all night."

"Sounds like crystal meth. First time you've got the best high of all time, nothin' compares; then after that everything's downhill from there, like you're locked in your own shell and you can't get out—hopeless. Speaking of the devil, there's our dear, sweet little princess, you know, maybe I should head over there and ask about your little so-called connection with her, every curly blonde inch of her body."

"You do that. I'm telling you the truth. She'll laugh you right out of this place, Garth. How old are you anyway?"

"What's that supposed to mean?"

"She'll feed me to the sharks like that stuffed hammerhead over at Headquarters."

"You have a cynical way of looking at things my man."

"How so?"

"You ask anyone around here that knows you—you'd be surprised how 'down-in-the-dumps' people see you as, like, like you're a seeping cancer that can't get out of his way for the life of him."

"Where did this come from?"

"Oh, just enjoy it. I got it for you."

"Oh, yeah, listen to that, Blue Collar Jane. And, your wet dream sporting her tight little caboose around the place like she owns it. Go for it, dude. Whatchya waitin' for? Four wheel drive, that's how she gets around. You're gonna sit there and let that beast of a dominatrix all to her lonesome? M-m-mn. Can you believe this guy? Just gonna sit there and not even have the balls to even talk to her."

"OK Brad, the man with the plan, you go over there and ring her little belle. Yeah, that's what I thought. Cat's got your tongue?"

"You know sometimes Tommy, you're really suck. I'm not tellin' you anything you don't know now, am I?"

"No less than you. The punching bag holds no prisoners."

"What you talkin' about? I swear man, sometimes you're—
nah forget it. I don't what to hear about it dude."

"Fuck You, Man, you piece o' shit, like you're the only person in the world with problems"

"Ha-ahh?"

"No, you listen. For once in your sick fuck little life, the mike's ripped from your hands. Poor little Tommy, Oxy Contin junkie fuck, who we had to pull out of the bar because, well, our big little man here got so pissed drunk/stoned that he wouldn't shut up because the bartender wouldn't play your request."

"Ah, that was a long time ago, Brad. The Districts play much better stuff than all that eighties shit they were playin'. Besides, that was when I was still in college. What does that music have to do with us anyway?"

"If you haven't noticed, most people at that bar are a lot older than us."

"That's true. But, as I recall, after I sobered up later that night, I had to drive your ass home because you blacked out. No, no, no, no. Now you let me finish. I even called the cops that night to leave your car there so it wouldn't get towed. Right?"

"Fuck you, Bierman."

"It's not like you're some hot shot sales exec like you always said was comin' your way."

"No, I'm at the same place I started at after I graduated from college; and, you and Garth here are both working over at Sendik's. Just admit it Bradley, you're pissed at the world and it doesn't give a fuck. Ain't that more like it?"

"Cut it out guys or I'll dump both your sorry asses in the garbage. None of us is world-beaters. But we don't have to pick at each other all night long, now do we? We've been doing the pub-crawl game for a while now. Nothing's changed in any of our lives. Seems like we're meant to do a lot at our stupid jobs for a little pay as long as we don't step on anyone's toes, like we all went along with the program. My cousin's still in Afghanistan, been there for almost a year—when he gets back, he'll be joining' us. Like the good jobs in Milwaukee are just waiting for a hero like Jake Neuendorf to come back home. Fuck, we all know what's up. None of us ain't gonna do shit about it. Same ole', same ole.'"

"Right, like my boss John Stumpf said, just go along with the bullshit. Otherwise, you can always go somewhere else."

"You're kidding?"

"No, I'm not. Pro Light Windows and Doors has a Will-Call area I take care of. Management can give you that look. And, you know, voila, everything falls in place. Well, at least it seems like that. It's just his way of saying to back off, ya know. He's not trying to one up me or anything. Most of the time I'm moving crap into place on my forklift. It's not rocket science guys, far from it. Sometimes you gotta move because some contractor demands his shit like yesterday and it's the middle of rush hour. Some people man just ain't too cool."

"Yeah, I know what you're saying. I mean, Sendik's seems a little uppity. But, once you've been there a while, everything's crystal clear even if I'm a little buzzed."

"You're not doin' any of chronic at work are you?"

"Hell no! That shit'll put you to sleep in a heartbeat."

"Now there's a job for you Brad. I mean you always wanted to move to Colorado to be a ski bum. Work in a dispensary during the week and hit the ski hills on the weekend."

"Yeah, right Tom. Why don't you take that college education of yours and put out some articles for web sites?"

"Oh, and blog about the merits of a good pungent buzz at 5:00 AM, why not sample one of those Reese's peanut butter cup-like THC bars?"

"Nah, I'm thinkin' about dumping all this party crap anyways. I mean, I'm spending all my checks on rent and car insurance, add that and all I do is run for the Credit Card in tight spots. And, that's about every week guys."

"You ain't gonna give up dope man. Remember, right after you graduated, we were so stoned. And, there was your grandfather looking straight at us right after we've been all toked up."

"Right, that hookah that you took from your old man's and those long thin silver pipes with that white resin just peeking out of that little bowl, kinda like opium madness, some Asian madam with a nice tight butt staring at you lost, so Lost yet so ready to join you. Man, you're parents Brad. One thing I gotta say is that they certainly didn't hide their little hobby, did they?"

"Yeah, well, what are you gonna do? Dad's a roofer; he's went through a lot of help over the years. Now he's got a couple Mexicans working for him. They're fuckin' awesome! Thank God for that because if I ever had any money problems, that type of work would be my way out of it."

"You could deal ganja man. Brad, you doper dandy, you. I can just see it now. Getting' the best scale around, weighing everything to precision. Oh, and don't quit your day job. That's your cover. Know what I'm sayin'?"

"Right and I'd get my scale from you because, hey, you dealt dope for years."

"Brad, you know I hardly smoke anymore. Even quit cigarettes. As you know, I came in seventh place last March at the Lucky Leprechaun 7K Race."

"I never would have guessed. It's like every time I see you in this bar you're wearing that green T-shirt. Well, I am at Leff's Lucky Town, right? So, I'll parade my prowess around my banshees all night long."

"Nah, we've spent enough time here. Let's head up to Headquarters. I know a couple of girls that are heading that way."

"What do you think, Tommy?"

"Nah, you guys go ahead. I'm just warming up. Besides, I don't want to drive all the way back from Brown Deere."

"Sure?"

"Yeah, if you want to join my grandfather sometime for a game of bocce ball, just give me a ring. He's pretty good but once I get the hang of it, I'll wax his ass all night long."

"Ah, that's all right. Some things are better kept in the family."

"You have no idea what you're missing until you give it a try.

I'm just sayin."

"Hey, Bierman, bet you wouldn't see me in these haunts anymore would you?"

"W-why did you hit me like that?"

"Looks like you could use a friend, seein' that all your friends flew away."

"Connie, if you weren't such a hottie, I'd have to belt you right back."

"Oh, you wouldn't hit a poor innocent girlie like me, now would you?"

"Try it again—we'd find out, right blondie?"

"Decadent recidivist such as yourself: I just thought you could use a little company is all."

"What could a young woman attired in a fuchsia t-shirt and covered with a see-through chartreuse top with meringue cut-offs leaning on lonesome Tommy, with her rash talk and rockin' good looks, be thinking?"

"Corona, huh? Yeah, you know it's my deal. Could you buy me one?"

"Nah, I'm thinkin' about checkin' out soon."

"Still can't handle the fact that this chick gets around?"

*("Who does she think she is? Margot Robbe? OK, OK, she's
fuckin' hot. God, what I'd do to get your pants just one more
time, Please?")*

"Got somethin' to say? Fine, you little twit, couldn't get it up if you
wanted to."

"Limp wrist, needle nose dick, yeah that's you, butt fuck. Ah, what
am I saying anyway? Your cock's so small you couldn't even get a flea
knocked up."

*("Say anything to you—you'll cut my nuts off and I'll enjoy
every last moment of it.")*

("Could I just die?")

"Piece of shit—always hiding from someone like little old me. Little
Tommy, man-boy who has no idea what to do with his shriveled up little
penis."

*(Visibly shaking, Tommy pumps down a huge gulp of his
prized Corona.)*

"Always wanting my ass but always havin' someone else approach
me … fuckin' winner you are."

"Can't even stand up for yourself: God, you wouldn't know what to do
with a prostitute makin' a move on you. What am I wastin' my precious
time with this jag off anyway? Good riddance you letch."

(He breaks into a cold sweat and heads toward the bar.)

*("Why don't you go back to your cheap thrills and get your
Madison High boys to get you some of that rank battery
acid? Don't see you hangin' around with anybody—so go get
yourself a nice piece of ass. That's what you're after isn't it?")*

"Hey, you mother fucker, I'm not done with you. Didn't think you
were gonna get off that easily, now, did you? Tommy Bierman's a pederast!

I think we should all kick his ass and finish him off before he slithers back into his sorry little black hole. He's a flat out menace to society. We'd be doing everybody including him a favor."

"A mercy killing," breaks in from the crowded bar as Tommy pays for his two beers. No time for tipping the bartender, he makes his way to the front door. Before he exits, Tommy turns around. A silent mob of midnight blue Milwaukee Brewer hats watches his every move.

"Hey! Where'd' you think you're going fuck wad. Come over here and suck my cock!"

"Why don't you go suck your own, little doggy boy," Tommy counters as the muscular miscreant thrusts his six packs against his backside.

"Think you're funny don't you dickless wonder? I oughtta pull out that little thang you call your love tool and shove right it in that baby face mouth of yours, make everyone wanna just get up and scream. God, you sure a worthless piece of shit, *mierda boy*." Actually, Tommy teetered between uncontrollable laughter and innate fear as he sped up his every step, leaving behind those callus, stoic marble white eyes of the crowd only some old curmudgeon could pull out of his bag of tricks, lunges toward the door.

Tommy dips right around the corner, his beat up Buick Regal just yards away, awaiting his weary being to show him some sign of promise. Not even the recollection of Turgenev's serendipitous skating around human suffering could soothe him. Tom, this victim of others' words, he could not control even if he wanted: has spun in a web around his pain and deceit, feeding his blasé outlook on everything, devouring his desire to do anything.

Escape? Run? Floor it? Fuck it. It is like embracing madness, and his sweet desire has once again failed him, ripped him to shreds, shreds that even his dead weight cannot save him. His retreat from those around him is a continual proposition, where nothing can save him, only his desire to escape, to fly away. Pin-cushioned into his lost play, he languidly pulls out an aluminum foil packet of Thai stick and listlessly stares at it.

"Head home, toke it up! Sit in a daze, never get up. Fuckin' swim in my shit, wander off to work with that fucked up game face on, marble eyes weighing every moment, doing favors for others just to get by: to be left alone. That's it, I'm done."

He's made his bed, *now sleep in it*. What has he done to himself? The million-dollar question. If he knows that, he could bottle it up and make billions. Nah, trillions!!! A real venture capitalist.

"Move on over lover boy Leonardo Di Caprio. "I'll be savin' your ass. You and your little years of excess bumpin' shoulders with prissy Dana Giacchetto in majestic New York, pumping up Cobaine's inherent millions, wow, what was your secret? Or was there just your IDEA, the ideas of the millennia's, chasing "The Dream," some opiate dressed up in a boa tied around the netherworld, so stylish like that sassy Anais Nin grasping her fool's gold, adorned in that soft sachet she has christened across the dance floor. Go back to your band, Eighty's excess done in style, *Daddy Mildew,* no, *social destruction*, yeah, that's right, I spin the records here; *I'm a Kilo, Second to none.* No, no, no, no, that's not it. *I'm genuine Gucci, raw like sushi.* Mommy dearest, Element 4, the water pours through my throbbing veins, I aim to please, retro 80's style, *something's wild*, Madame *Black Destruction*, chanteuse noire Nico crawling, summons her very chic banshee, Ms. Guinness, Daphne, *oh my mama, oh my, my,* (in those gray spiked heels and oh such decadent svelte-slit black tights, thighs exposed. Come), I order you to light up Century Hall with me, call it our last fling, this vernal thing coming to a close—takin' a dive for the last time. Daphne strutting her stuff upon stage in her black surroundings, those high cheekbones and vibrant eyes just grab hold of your squeamish psyche, and, bam! Wow, the whole world evaporates into a messianic mist."

Hah, ahhhhh, forget New York. One more journey cannot take hold of him. Tommy understands that willing himself to be tied up in some new discovery is all right until the anguish pours in, that the end game is his own device: a half ass junkie at that. His high school buddies could put down an OZ in a week where he'd take nearly a month. Couldn't handle his booze either, even his trusted Chesterfields rest on the dashboard for days on end.

A devoted follower of the fashionably unfashionable was relinquished. Daphne's pouting strings is a phantom he's stored for his most dire moments. So much time being withdrawn from the public, hidden in a shame he has created.

Like his mother always said, "Tommy, there are things we know about you that you Have No Idea."

"Well, that may be, but their perception can be no less muddled than his own. "Just stay in line. Hey, you think we like it. So, you think we're a mess. Boy, I've got some stories about the neighbors that'll make your skin crawl. You really wanna give us the kiss off. When the shit hits the fan, who's gonna be there to pick up the pieces young man? Yeah, that's what I thought. By the way, we're having our family picnic at the Zoo. Do you think you can make it? Sure, bring along a date. The more the merrier. See you then."

Well, maybe if he was headin' for the grave, he could set aside some quality time to chew the fat with his family and relatives. How about taking part in a bocce ball extravaganza? Perhaps he can just mail it in. "I can't make it man." He'd rather have a drink on them from a distance as he reminisces about a past he would rather forget.

"Dad would always say that everybody's a little off-balance. So don't throw rocks at glass houses. You might not like what comes your way. Poor dad, he thinks somehow all these mind-game shenanigans are gonna make it a little easier on him." He takes a long drag on his cigarette.

"Hello? Hey gramps, yeah, bocce ball, that was cool. Aunt Diane's gotten hold of you, hasn't she? Yeah, I lost it—blew chunks. Of course, I feel rotten about that gramps ... I know, I know, a guy my age pullin' off something stupid like that ... Yes, grampa, I said I'm sorry to her and her boyfriend—big dude man ... Kicked your ass at bocce bowl though didn't I? Yeah, I was king of the lakefront for a day... We gotta do that again I know, I know, I did that on the last ball, beginner's luck I guess ... Oh, I think I'm gonna head down to Hart Park, ball it a little ... I'll tell you what. Is next Saturday open for you? Great! Put it on your calendar. Pick you up at say, 10? Be ready. I'll take you out for breakfast ... Yeah, it's on me ... Nope, no more booze. Well every now and then ... Grampa, no I don't go to church anymore but St. Sava's alright. But yeah the fish was great but that naïve artwork ... Yes, and Jesus of course, our little son of a carpenter ... I'd love to go there someday... the Krka Falls ... I know. America's plenty beautiful too ... I know, I know, Mouthy Lake and Kettle Moraine ... yeah, right here in our own backyard ... Just like a picture postcard. Oh, you're going fishing there tomorrow, great... Be ready for our big game this Saturday ... Yeah, work's OK, but, grampa, I've got a college degree; and, look what I'm doing ... Nah, I've gotten help ... All that stuff… What color is your parachute, Meyers, Briggs … Nah, I don't really want to talk about it anymore … Love You, Bye."

"Knocked him out on ball four—didn't even cheat, took the Cup. Gramps plays at least once a week. Man, I gotta get out of here."

"Hey you what did you just throw out of your car there?"

"Wouldn't you like to know?" The twisted rapper rests beneath the vibrant auburn moon's reflection.

"Who does that guy think he is anyways? Probably one of those functioning drunks making their way to their next pitiful stop in a string of many more to follow."

Tommy slowly exhales as he makes his way past Washington Circle where his comfortably rich sisters and their cuddly children hail in old red brick two storied mini-mansions.

"No balling tonight," he heads up 68th Street to head home, taking another drag on his cig as Tommy turns west onto Watertown Plank Road.

"Oh, wow, hey? Those pics of Suzy "do me a" Favor Hamilton pops into his scattered thoughts—Big Ten Champ and Olympian in the mile— all decked out in hot black panties and stilettos exposing those long, taut legs of hers. High class escort no less. Suzy Favor who could be his mom strutting her stuff to all those secret wolf hearts who just want to get a taste: 'Like she married a lawyer for Christ's sake'. Yeah, she just had some issues to work out. Keep your skeletons in the closet; A little Dead Live. Everything's forgotten, man. Connie, Suzie, who cares?"

Tommy must shed all this romper room mindset and ease up on his need to find a woman. Easier said than done, right?

Not all the practice in the world can prepare him for that special moment. Philosophy almost ruined his need to become a natural thinking, acting person. But Master Pascal even said that no matter what you may think of a law or question the character and greatness of Jesus, should it help in keeping human beings from acting on our every thought that consumes the brain, then it would have served its purpose, kept order through its ordered rules. In other words, even if Jesus was a man, his doctrine can serve as a rulebook for how to act and treat others in both public and private. It is sort of a highfalutin revisionist sublime history of manners a la Confucius.

True, but Special K (Krishnamurti) went beyond this and clearly stated that all thoughts have antipodal effects, that none is full proof. Reasoning can only go so far. Come into the world anew, by realizing that one's thoughts are not empirical, and feel the power of everything without all that slavery clinging to the past (What's gonna happen to me if I don't go along with what they're telling me?).

He walks up to the flat's second floor entrance. "Home, sweet home. Time to crash—woe, woe, woe, what do we have here? A hit of sinsemilla ready to fire up in the ole' apogee. No lighter? Now, where the hell did I put it? Ah, don't tell me I already lost it. Fuck, I just had it after I left the bar. Yeah, here's my last book of matches from the Exotic last week. H-h-h-h-hahhh-ahhhh-shpfal-hmm-mmm: Hahh."

His supreme sacrifice mirrors Nietzsche's offering his foolhardy rants to the dogmatic public, walking into Churches, attacking Jesus and his followers to the very core. Poor guy just lost it. Nobody wanted anything to do with him. Yeah, the man might have buckled under his own construct. But, the dude was dangerous for everyone, he crumbled beneath his scars. Like I'm not headin' down that path. Fuck, my shit ain't any different. Yeah, I can see it all now, old Tommy getting' a rub down and cleaned up from some buxom blonde nurse somewhere on the East Side. Life is really a bowl of cherries, isn't it? Not a bad way to go out if I say so myself."

He knows tomorrow it will start all over again where he'll just accept the stupid rules like everyone else just to make it through another day. Yes, but here sits reclusive Tommy thinking, "Why didn't I rip off that Robin Yount poster over at the bar? Fuck it up? Who cares? At least he would have had that moment to laugh at all those cantankerous blue hats who would be out of luck," trying to hunt him down for some old poster. You know, get a piece of that soft-spoken California golden boy gold mine that almost single-handedly put the Brewers on the map. What would all those blue hats do without dear old Robin Yount bolted up on the bar wall?

"Hey, what's this?" Yes, a business card his grandfather had given him: how has he kept that in his wallet at all? Oh, yes *"What makes one's last love so terrible is that it is not love at all, but fear of loss."* Signed off by a poet named Yevtushenko, Yevgeny Yevtushenko.

"Wow, Good old grampa trying to pawn off his Russian poetry onto me," some misanthropic half-ass philosopher, not so much rationalistic, mind you, but not a lost soul looking for a handout from the bourgeoisie that surrounds his flat. Russia is that nation of failing philosophers and iconic writers that sucks you in whole with its tragic characters, both broken and choleric. But how would "The Birth of Tragedy" ever have fully developed had not Frederic Nietzsche ever come across Dostoevsky's "Crime and Punishment?"

Within his milk carton bookshelf, he spots Heidegger's *Being and Time*. Tommy has not read the book since college. However, the softness of the words move his emotions, not as some megalomania decadence that stormed early twentieth century rural Germany. Moreover, as something that asks "why am I not seeing myself as a separate thinking and feeling human being, and, not as some other poor sot who's plodding along, accepting everything that comes along even if I completely disagree with it?"

"I am not so obsessed with myself as to think that I am somehow better or worse than anyone else. But I am certainly not anyone's toy either. Ubermensch? How about taking a walk in the park with a stunning beauty like Ruvi Bazaz? "You go for the gold, I will take the low road to save the damsel in distress because she's such a knockout. Game over: You got that right."

"The linden leaf on the book's black landscape reminds him that there is a need to dig out of his own grave and get on with things. Exactly, but just what is that?"

Stretching his arms, Tommy holds the book in his hands, thinking back to the time he had first read it as an inwardly destructive student. It places his faith in relating anything to death. Whole truth is divine even when he first realized that his idea, once understood for its falseness, has fallen to the wayside. Thus, he understands that he is an innocent not trying to seek or refrain from anything. Wholeness of Truth, "Deadly stuff, isn't it? Courage? Nah. Time for bed." A long weekend ends.

Beneath a beautiful amber Saturday sunset, Ha Chen kisses his two daughters good-bye as they scamper about with their girlfriends from Watertown, Bao and Qi Hong. His wife, Biyu grabs his credit card as he heads to his car. A big day is in store for Mr. Ha. "See you not too late, OK—maybe before twelve. I hope plan works. We need more money to move to Oconomowoc. Bye everyone."

"Mr. Ha—we'll take you guys to the Octagon House tomorrow. You'll like it. The place is old, but it's right in town by other houses."

"Really nice, huh?"

"Ha, do you need anything before you go?"

"No, I got everything in this file here. You guys have fun with the girls, OK?"

Ha Chen steps into his Honda Odyssey in contemplative silence wondering if he should spend any time talking with co-workers he only knows by sitting in front of their cubicle computers as they relate to clients mostly from the U.S. regarding technical concerns of engineering plastics and bearings. Mr. Ha has just completed his 20[Th] year at ERIKS, a Dutch technical trading corporation with over 40 subsidiaries.

He could have performed the position's technical help back in his college days. Nevertheless, at 47 he has felt the age bug catching up with him. No longer can he scream foul play for being an Asian worker. Two fellow specialists are older, and have hinted that they are not going anywhere even though their qualifications have more than exceeded their responsibilities at ERIKS USA. The dreg's fight has caught up with even the silent majority.

A twenty-minute drive up I-94 to Wisconsin Highway 57 north will land him at Feng's, his favorite Chinese restaurant outside of metropolitan Milwaukee. Even though he has found few restaurants to match Mandarin Cuisine from back home, he must admit that their attempts have sometimes even surprised his native taste buds.

Today he is all business as he was able to get all five fellow engineering applications specialists to show up for a night away from their better halves. Pabst Farm Boulevard is in view as Feng's field of vision focuses right on its bend in the road. "8:30, great." He is a bit early, but that is fine. He is here for both himself and his former intern, Moshe Tambor to put forth an engineered part they tinkered with over the past six months.

To sell his peers on this brand new mystery part for monitoring the oil amounts to lubricate the air conditioner's compressor is nothing glamorous, but both have found it to be more effective than a similar part that has recently come off the patent list. Parking in the easternmost corner of the newly black topped parking lot, he takes a moment to gather himself, grasps the folder from the passenger seat, and slowly combs his hair, taking off his sunglasses.

The parking lot is almost devoid of cars, which is a good thing. Perhaps he can exchange ideas with them with more flair. Ha has not a clue as to what he is doing. However, he is going through with it anyway, at least for Moshe's sake.

"Ten to nine—another ten minutes they'll be here." He hopes so anyway. With the lazy days of summer ending perhaps, one or two will be no shows.

He takes a deep breath and heads into the restaurant. "Hi, have you a reservation?"

"Ah, yes, Chen for table of six at nine."

"Right this way or would you like to wait for your guests?"

"I would like to be seated to get ready what I need to do, OK? They know the reservation is in my name."

"Fine. Right this way."

The host leads Ha into the furthest corner of the dining area to allow the group some privacy. "Your guest here is Pat. Pat, this is Mr. Chen."

"Hello, Mr. Chen is there anything I can get to drink?"

"Yes, ice water please. I will get something when my people get here."

"Fine, six menus then?"

"Yes, six."

"Hey, the Ha man."

"Dick, glad you could come. Terry, I thought you wanted time away."

"Yeah, time away from my wife you mean. God, I swear the older I get the more I realize I'm on a ball and chain. You hinted at something that interested me, I think that is mechanically brilliant, but it has little to do with technical advice over the phone. Am I warm?"

"Possibly."

"Here's your water Mr. Chen."

"Yes, yes, here is Dick and Terry."

"Great, your menus I'll just put 'em over here; and, is there anything I can get you two to drink?"

"Yes, I'll have a dry Martini."

"Make it a Miller Lite for me, Terry adds."

"Could I have iced green tea?"

"Sure."

"Ah, our very own tee-totaler, Ha Chen: I knew I could count on you for your sound morals."

"Somebody has to make sure he gets home without problems. I not thrilled with taste of drink, you know."

"It kind of takes the edge off of all the day's pitfalls."

"You sure about that?"

"The only thing I am sure of is that I am here."

"Here, here," Terry cuts in, "Beer's a bit bitter but I've acquired a taste for it, sometimes I even crave it."

"Like squid for me—so hard to find fresh eels and pea pods—even at Farmer's Market."

"Well, Margaret's cooking is all I know since the kids have all grown up."

"Dick, Chinese cooking here is the only thing that still like Shanghai, closest, you know?"

"Hey, looks like Tony's dragged in the final tally."

"So-o, what's up everybody? Tell you what. I can't wait for school to start to get my kids out of the house."

"How old are you kids anyway?"

"Carmen's starting first grade—Joe's sixteen and Chrissie's just turned 13. God love 'em but there's a fine line between love and complete loathing of their kindred spirits. That's all I'm gonna say before my better half divorces me."

"Our young little Armando, our hearts bleed for you."

"No kiddin', just wait 'til they get out of the house and there's no buffer zone between you and your wife," Joe amiably states. "Your menus are right in front of you guys. The lady will be back in minute to get your orders."

"Great, some American food's listed. No offense Ha, but Chinese food's not high on my list."

"My wife changed your mind—remember?"

"She blew my mind," Armando interjects, "her veggie dumplings, out of this world: egg foo young, bro', there's no place in Town that touches her cooking, phenomenal guys. I'm not kiddin'.'"

"She says cooking is simple, the food is the champ."

"Yeah, the straw that stirs the drink."

"Go deep Reggie: those damn Yankees. They always get the right players at the right time—even that hot head Billy Martin could get his way, even goin' after King Reggie a couple of times."

"Hey Armando, I've got four tickets for the upcoming Cubs series next weekend. Get 'em dirt cheap."

"Nah, the Brew Crew shut things down a long time ago— The Cubs? Need I say more? Maybe next year."

"Wake me up when they get a pitching staff that's worth a damn. That's when I'll give 'em their due."

"Your dry Martini and Miller Lite—gentleman."

"Yes, Ms. That is Tony, Joe, and Armando."

"What would you like to drink Tony?"

"Mm, I'll have a Pina Colada, summery, yeah."

"Joe?"

"Ah, ha-aha-hmmn, how about a Plum Brandy and Cognac or do you have that?"

"I'm sure our bartender can come up with that—Armando?"

"How about a Molson Golden Ale."

"Anything else gentlemen, bread?"

"Nah, we're good."

"Be right back."

"Look at this place on a Saturday evening. Nobody's here."

"Just what I wanted," Chen smiles, "I know you may have other things you want to do on beautiful sunny weekend—like we do this when we want to."

"Why Oconomowoc?"

"You had us up in Cedarburg."

"Cedarburg's a ways, but Oconomowoc's a haul," Tony laughs. "Cause I want to move here soon, before Christmas. We visiting friends in Watertown, but like Oconomowoc more."

"That's a long ways from New Berlin my man."

"Over thirty miles, yes. But school has great teacher in high school, Chinese program. Ms. Xiaopeng Pang has one of top Mandarin Chinese programs in country."

"Really?"

"Yes, really—called the Confucius Classroom Network."

"Good guy but kind of a mannered go-between the rich and poor folks long time ago," Terry adds. "Who in this country do any better?"

"Nobody—we all sort of go along and hope for the best."

"Ever works?"

"M-no"

"Even Lao-tzu becomes no good after we get our acts together, right?"

"You're getting too deep for me, Sir Chen. I mean Confucius and Lao-Tzu. Seems to me one was a kiss ass and the other a great Hermit thinker whose ideas would fall off the planet if he tried to work with society."

"It's about threat of losing power—killing to keep things copasetic. Who wants that?"

"Not me," Dick muses, "maybe we can find a way to survive without sneaking around and ratting others out."

"Yeah, the old is the new," Joe smiles as he grabs his plum brandy & cognac from the waitress' tray.

"Ready to order?"

"Another green iced tea?"

"Make it another Miller Lite."

"Shag along another dry martini while you're at it and bring us some of your best bread if you could."

"Sure thing. Plates for everyone?"

"Great Ms.?"

"I'm sorry, haven't I introduced myself—well, I'm Pat. Take all the time you want. As you haven't already noticed the sticky heat's kept this place a ghost town."

"Cool, so how long have you been at ERIKS Ha?"

"Twenty years, why?"

"Oh, nothing really, twenty years? I don't think any of us have ten in there," Joe responds.

"I don't know what to do. Went to employment people who help Chinese engineers—got nowhere. That was long time ago. Now, with kids and wife that works part-time, need to find other ways to make money."

"Who doesn't," Armando cuts in, "mortgage payments, credit cards, and kids who don't know the answer to the word NO!"

"You two are about the only two who have kids here."

"Nah," Tony utters, "I've got a thirty-eight-year-old, my oldest still holding his spot on the couch at home."

"Sammy, right?"

"You got it."

"What does your wife think about it?"

"It's not so much what she thinks about it. It's just that we've tried everything, psychological help, even went in on family therapy sessions with him. Wrong move: I mean yeah everything he said about us was right on. But what about him? Like he doesn't have some deep dark rut to crawl out of all by his lonesome. I really don't want to talk about this. Yeah he has a job, but that's all he does. Takes the bus. That's cool but some people aren't meant to have soul mates or friends for that matter. Just doesn't trust anyone, including yours truly.

I'll tell you one thing. If this doesn't change soon, I'm gonna look on ways to get him into some living situation away from us. You couldn't cut that silence with an industrial black diamond."

"We're all powerless, Tony."

"Yeah, well saying it is one thing and living around it is another."

"Ms., Ms.?"

"Yes-sir."

"Could I have a Margarita, please?"

"Tony's movin' it around a bit."

"Yeah, I miss that rimmed salt. Too late for Bloody Mary."

"Packer season's right around the corner."

"Yeah, they need a running game though and their pass rush can be anemic at times."

"I know. The offense puts up points in bunches, and the defense provides the punch to finish the game off. You can't play Oakland every week."

"Sooner or later the Lions will get their act together."

"And the Vikings may have to find another coach—Frazier's days are numbered."

"Yeah, he's pretty good, you know. Go back to find a defensive coordinator position somewhere and keep his eyes opened for a new coaching gig somewhere down the road."

"Guys?"

"Yes, Ha."

"I have ideas about something, making a product, monitoring oil intake to lubricate air conditioning unit."

"What about it?"

"A patent has come to end and I developed materials and shaping that beats this accumulator oil filter" (Ho passes around two facsimiles of his engineered device as opposed to its aged competitor).

"Do you have the blueprint specs and materials used?"

"Yes. I pass 'round each one."

"Your iced tea, beer, and Margarita. Allow me to pass around the plates. Put the bread here? Wonderful. Anything else?"

"Another Martini and bring me a water if you could."

"A coke for me."

"Another Molson Golden, please?"

"Joe's gone on the wagon."

"No, I just want the taste of a cold Coke that's all. So hot, you know? My taste buds have changed for the evening. Get me at home and sipping a nice Montoya Zinfandel with my haunches plumped on the recliner hits the spot while taking in a movie. Yeah, that's what I call perfection. Away from the crowds, ya know?"

"Except Armando here, we've all become sedentary creatures of habit. By the way Ha, how does your device stand out from this patented one?"

"It is easier to put on because it's smaller." He reaches in his pants pocket and pulls out one of his own and its antediluvian counterpart.

"Wow Ha, I didn't know you had it in you."

"Moshe did metals and I the plastics. I know machinist who did work for us. In three months, we had this. What do you think?"

"Engineered well—the blueprints show you having an obvious edge, but they gotta work."

"Right, we made 50 pieces. They move in the oils with better precision, saving companies lots of money. No wasted oil and solid working heater/ air conditioner. Modine and Johnson Controls would love us, right? Beat the pants off the old patent in every way in over sixty tests over past three months."

"Great, so what do you want from us?"

"You guys worked at big plants, right?"

"Yes," Joe states, "so what? We've hung our hats up for a false economy that we all know will not come around for a long time."

"Like I don't know? I worked long hours in Shanghai and made nothing, no safety standards, worked on dirt floors for hours at a time, for pennies."

"And, we're the lazy Americans who've had everything handed to us, right? When right behind us with shrinking job opportunities for us old folks, boom, out come in an implosion of Asian engineers with great qualities mind you. But really, to tell you the truth, I don't see them any more advanced than any of us, Ha."

"We're all smart, Terry. We know the real stink is us believe me. We get paid less. Now just listen, yes, not in all cases. This gone on for long time in this country. Chinese are only people who could not come into this country after 1882 because you scared of us, too many of us might take your jobs."

"That was 1882, so what?"

"You kept it up to 1937. That is when Japan was murdering us, you know Shanghai, the Rape of Nanjing. All governments' ugly."

"Right, and we're ugly because we do nothing about any of it, waiting for someone to stick up for us. Never happens but at least we get left alone for the time being."

"Until they knock on your door and take you' house from you … then what?"

"Hasn't happened yet."

"We do what we do to eat, feed our kids. We know they're slobs but look like world beaters to each other, right?"

"What is this, some sort of Existentialist mumbo jumbo?"

"I got two young girls. Here, they can have chance to get good jobs, have children, in China, no chance. Pictures tell you nothing. You must live there."

"Right, brand new skyscrapers, luxury hotels, many inoperative."

"And pollution from fossil fuels, coal gas, pollution you can't understand. You live in it, then tell me. Like you, Armando, we are human beings, not Chinese or Americans."

"We're selfish, Ha, what can I tell you. You scratch my back and I'll scratch yours."

"Only if you really like product. What you think about mine?"

"I'm no genius—give me a couple of weeks to check out the specs and materials related to this industry, cost constraints, manufacturing possibilities and I'll let you know. Wait, you're not asking us to invest in your little concept here, are you?"

"Yes, I am. I have machinists who will work for me, but where I do this? Don't know."

"Plant, large or small, Ha. Big bucks: you're talking about needing start-up OEM loan money. You only need enough for one small-engineered product. But no matter how easy it seems to put together a quality finished product, it's gonna cost you a pretty penny. How will you market this? Efficiency means nothing if you don't have customers, Ha. Maybe not high-end OEM upstarts, but, OK, I'm no expert but, with the low-end maybe, you could find a place to rent out a tool & die machinist shop that can cater to your needs. You're going to have to figure out how you're going to develop your clientele base. That's really the bottom line."

"Ha, just speaking for myself, there's no way that I want to tie up a portion of my mortgage in a scheme that could go south in a heartbeat. My wife would throw me on the streets."

"You told me your house was paid for."

"Yes, it is but the wife just wants me to get through to retirement and head for Florida soon thereafter. I know that sounds base. But, that's the way it is. I'll tell you what, you bring me another part with you next Monday morning and I'll check things out with a few specialists I know that just might know someone who can push you in the right direction. Me? Nah, I just want to put in my time at ERIKS and eventually retire to tee time at 7 and find a way to swim a mile in the Gulf of Mexico to strengthen my heart."

"Anything you guys can do, I really appreciate. Help me present my product to these people Moshe has talked to. If he not there, maybe one of you can help me—we can talk about money then, right? I know engineering consulting fees. Your English much better."

"This looks good my man, but I've gotta see it work, comprendeme?"

"Sure Armando. I got cell phone number of two machinists who made my new accumulator oil filter. They even tested it against old product. I can even get them to do it in front of you."

"Again, give me a couple weeks to check things out on my own. I'm forty years old and am stuck in the mud, my wife puts in several hours a week to get her some spending money and a discount on those gnarly shoes she's got a full closet of. If she wasn't so God Damn beautiful, I'd have to kick her out of the nest and start all over. I'm serious guys. When it comes to money, she can spend it like a drunken sailor."

"We all do that in one way or another, Armando."

"I grant you that Terry, but when you're pulling in 50 grand a year, you don't need your wife to spend everything she makes then asks you for money she's run out of--which is all the time."

"Gotta get off the pot and tell her what's up, Armando. We've got all our roles to play, find ways to keep ourselves in line."

"I know. Believe me I know."

"What the hell does that mean?"

"Ah, it's a top/down game; and, the pressures from the top destroy you if you try to fight it."

"That's where my sloth gear sets in. Take it easy. Let her know where you stand."

"Rosy takes care of the money, puts it in our investments every month, pays on the car and our mortgage. We've got nothing left at the end of the month. My God, if I owed any tax money at the end of the year, I'd have to take out a small loan. Financially, I couldn't help you out, Ho, but maybe as a technical communicative assistant."

"You might have something here but money's not our strong suit. If you need a solid loan amount we're going to have to talk it over with our significant others. Believe me, Jeannette's the only person in this world that frightens me. This materialistic world drains me. The hell if I want anything to do with it, be-lieve me. She's the only person who's seen me for me."

"We have it posted on You Tube under Moshe's A/C accumulator oil filter."

"How many hits?"

"Seventeen, I think—probably a couple of his friends and my wife. But, guys, it works. I have apartment manager in Menomonee Falls using it right now. He has it couple of months already."

"So, what does he get in return?"

"I gave him couple of oil filters that I told him last longer than his patented oil filter. Does it save petro money for him or not? That's what I care 'bout."

"You have done your homework, Ha."

"Moshe Tambor, he helped a lot. We need more help. I hope you guys can help me."

"Not to get off the subject, but my wife and I are thinking about joining up on a group vacation to Hong Kong and Shanghai. What might I look for when I go to Shanghai?"

"They got great theater but you don't speak Mandarin Chinese. Americans they got the Shanghai refugee Museum, even shows an old 1930's paper article, the Jewish Chronicle of Jews coming to this area, being accepted by my ancestors. A beautiful menorah rests by entrance. I light it every time I visit. There's a temple on other side of the Huangpu River, the Longhua Temple. Sometimes you see old people do Tai Chi— silent meditation, right?"

"The old south of River, big new buildings on the north side where the Magler Train goes more than 200 miles an hour, in Pudong, that is modern Shanghai. Puxi is old Shanghai where rows of hanging clothes are everywhere near Fuxing Park where local hole-in-wall restaurants called *jishi,* sell crabs, green beans, and mushroom, even cucumbers aged in vinegar. Kinda like pickles, but different. North of River is Hyatt on the Bund. I sat in the whirlpool on the terrace for many hours. My younger sister like the Vue Bar in Hotel, lot of dancing and drinking, really fun for young people. Shanghai no mystery, many problems and stealing like New York, worse probably."

"Shanghai in a nutshell, cool. Don't drive. Many car accidents. Hey, we're just learning from you guys. You know that."

"China Airlines quite cheap. Yes, have some bad accidents, but we take it every time. Still alive, guys."

"Well, we'll take whatever our host decides is best for our group."

"When you going Tony?"

"Probably the fall of next year. My wife and I want to spend a month over there, maybe even head up to Beijing and the Great Wall. We don't take a lot of trips but this is the granddaddy of all trips. If Marco Polo could make the trip, we sure can too. We'll have a great time there."

"Yes, where we'll be fighting each other."

"Why are you so pessimistic about Sino-American relations?"

"Cause America talks and China walks: both garbage. When you see peasants in countryside, they are slaves to costs of farm vegetables set by local and central Party comrades. Hundreds of millions of people guys, caught in this mess. Many more people than in all the Americas, many more."

"Only thing workers look forward to celebrate is the Chinese New Year. We come home to eat with *fu* in our hearts, we dance and sing— on the 15th day of the year's first month of lunar new year, "the Lantern Festival" roars—we laugh and eat our many foods and are decorated with red paper, songs new words sung. Fu—yes we are happy again."

"That is China. What do you do for fun here?"

"I live here since I was twenty- one, still talk to ma and pa. Yes, but my life has problems like yours. I human being, not Chinese or American. We can tell lies of Washington. They are not best. Can see their game. You me, we go along. How can you make some difference in this game? I avoid what my people did every day as boy, they planting and picking bushels where that sun kills you. Year of the Snake I tell you."

"Sartre's not the only ruined person. We all are, Ha. It's like everything's entertainment, even school. Don't wanna step on anyone's toes. Live and let live, or somthin' like that. Really Ha, I thought you were such a child with all your meeting of management's numbers and exquisite telephone etiquette."

"No east or west—just us."

"I'll drink to that."

"Are you ready now my men or can I order another round of drinks?"

"Serpents rule, did you know that Pat?"

"Hm."

"Next is the horse's Year ma'am."

"Oh, really, well I'll just have to run home and tell my significant other all about that now, wouldn't I?"

"So, Ha, so you have decided haven't you, on your order?"

"Yes ma'am…"

Chapter Fifteen

Strangers in Paradise

"Now, Dad, promise not to fight with Eric, this evening."

"I can't guarantee you anything on that Missy. Your hair's awn fi-ah twenty-four seven."

"That's not it dad. You just go along wid everything and want me to follow. After all, father knows best."

"Where'd you pick up that pasty fifties show, bunch o' uppity white folk with manners eatin' that bland white food?"

"What you talkin' 'bout? The only shows I watch are with Chad: Curious George and Sesame Street is all we got goin' on."

"Chad's in the front seat and Jeremy's got his glove: remember yours?"

"Of course, he's fast and swingin' the bat real good at T-ball. I'll start pitching to him next spring. The little man's got it."

"Oh, I just got texted from Eric, he'll be here soon."

"Will you take a look at that big ole' wicker basket?"

"Gram's gave it to me a while back. The first time I'm gonna use it. We've got just snacks dad, pbj's, plates, plastic forks, and some potato salad. We'll pick up drinks when we get there."

"Where are we going anyway?"

"Peninsula Park."

"Peninsula Park? Never heard of it."

"I took a drive the other day with Eric and we ended up in Saukville, right on the Milwaukee River No baseball fields or swing sets but a flat grass area near a brook. You know we saw a Canadian Geese couple and their cute little babies, the morning sun reflecting off their cute little yellow bodies."

"Goslings, Aisha. Babies are people, not birds."

"Goslings, huh? Ryan Gosling, Canadian isn't he? There is that connection, isn't there?"

"If you say so. Ah, your prince charming has just pulled up behind my car. I got the basket, why don't you grab the beach blanket and towels. Why are you bringing them for?"

"Oh, dad, right there the brook just ripples over some fallen trees. Chad's gone swimming in city pools. I'd like to see him plop his feet in the muddy Milwaukee River, so natural, you know?"

"Where is this Saukville?"

"Saukville?"

"I took your mother there a long time ago to the Painted Lady Restaurant back in the eighties in Newberg? Yeah, that's it. Just outside of Saukville. Beautiful place, great food. Closed down a while later. Pricey but worth every cent. But honey, that ain't exactly where black folks hang out if you know what I'm getting at."

"Dah, like I don't have two eyes but I went with Eric's instincts, like hangin' out at 43rd and Lisbon's gonna keep me happy. I know when people are judging me dad, doesn't take a day of school to figure that one out. You need to understand that what you want or what I want has nothing to do with truth, has nothing to do with us. Most of the time we run from it: that's all I know."

"Right, now let's head downstairs and get a goin'."

"After you."

Eric Sorgen, impeccably dressed in his Sunday's best helps Aisha put the basket, blanket, and beach towels in as Darrin checks to make sure the baseball gloves and softened hardballs are also in the trunk. Two-year old Chad peers over the front passenger seat and smiles at his mother while Jeremy is fidgeting with his baseball cap.

"OK guys, hop to it or we'll never get there. And that'll make granddad a very unhappy man."

"My God, there is so-oh much room in this vehicle that it feels almost as if I was in a truck of sorts."

"Everybody buckled up? Let's get a going then."

"Hey Eric, I know how to get there. I'm Aisha's father, Darrin."

"Hi."

"Why are you so dressed to the nines today?"

"I just got off work and didn't have any time to change."

"We could swing by your place if you need to."

"Nah, I'm used to wearing these clothes. My job demands it."

"He's a 'Next Generation Associate Pastor dad, he helps out kids from all walks of life, right Eric?"

"Eric's really smart grampa, not just 'bout Jesus either."

"Well, that's wonderful, right Jeremy?"

"Yep."

"Kids have a difficult time with accepting Jesus as their Savior. I mean I'm twenty-nine and finally it sunk in that clothes are just clothes, cool crazy kind of stuff, but if I really mean it, that awe and love of Christ's Spirit transcends everything, like even the fact that I am me, and You Are You. Does that make sense?"

"I get ya, but as you know your significant other may lock horns with you every now and then on that one."

"But I've been through the battles and somehow I've never felt good about any of it. And, that's not even the half of it."

"I've never been a father Mr. Jackson, but to see these two precious boys and their mother go to the Park pool gives me an easy feeling that that part of my life has not completely passed me by."

"Want some chips, Chad?"

"Yeah."

"That's a good boy. Your grampa loves you. His hair's getting thicker sweetheart. He's gonna have a 'fro that whole world will take notice."

"He'll have all the girls eating out of his hands, won't you Chad?"

"Yea-aah, drink some juice."

"Not after you spilled those chips all over the place."

"Ah, look at you boy, already a mess and we barely got started."

Aisha takes some wipes from her purse and forcefully wipes off his face.

"NO juice Aisha. He'll just work all that crap onto the floor and there goes my day off."

"Chad's fine gramps," Jeremy chimes in, "he's always like that."

"You tell him, dear," Aisha purrs as she reaches for a childproof cup and pours some Tropicana and softly places it into her love's hands.

"Courting my spoiled daughter will lock you in her home Eric. The world outside will have to take a back seat while the next Barry Larkin here takes the baseball world by storm. Ever play any sports?"

"Tennis—intramurals in college, yeah, pretty consistent with my serve and volley. But team sports? Not so much."

"I played half back at Stout, not a football factory mind you. But it was nice to get away from the city for a while even if you're one of the few black folks in the area."

"I know; UW La Crosse was just like Mad Town U. The only brotha's I rubbed shoulders with were jocks. It's like you're on an island. You just keep your focus, and don't say too much."

"You got that right. Remember when we took you kids to the Dells sweetheart to all those indoor water parks in the middle of winter. Who stood out like a sore thumb?"

"Yeah, I was ten I think. Whites were everywhere, but nobody said anything nasty or pushed me around."

"Well, let me tell you Aisha, when I applied at Stout the staff treated me great—little did I know that my City Conference stats were all that they cared about when I got there. But when they could see that I could hit the books and conceive of the micro-being no different than the Macro-, well, that wasn't real pretty now, was it? Sounds good though, doesn't it? Your mother had to stand her ground at times because she was black. Jackie and Martin did their best. But if you ask me, we haven't really gone that far from Selma now have we?"

"I work with a lot of white folks every day. Just a few Blacks would ever be able to afford Elmbrook's {501 (C) 3} *rites of passage.* Now don't get me wrong they're a wonderful spiritual organization. Many struggling families attend our non-denominational church. If you want to donate what they ask for, there's no way you can do it unless you want to do without a badly needed new family car or a place to live."

"You're always so theatrical, overbearing is more like it. We ain't got the bank, that's it."

"Dearie, thirty to fifty per cent unemployment's in da hood. Tell me where that exists for our special white folks. Let's call it for what it is. They take care of themselves first and we get the leftovers if we're lucky. Otherwise our kids go to foster care and we brood, asking for food—anything to do. Anything'll do, even sweep the sidewalks if we have to. What's so complicated about that?"

"I don't really get into this with my children who have a hard enough time dealing with their own lives. Life is like a bad peyote trip. Over time, we become incoherent, lonely people trying to connect with other lonely souls we somehow run into, and failing miserably at everything we set out to accomplish. Hey, without any sense of direction, what are we to do?"

"Like an endless space that you cannot conquer, having wasted all that time. You cannot order your life, deary, Jesus takes away your worries."

"Grampa takes us to church every Sunday. Jesus has a white dove in his hand."

"And the sun shines through him unto all of us. Well put Jeremy."

"We all have our little delusions," Aisha mutters, our little nonsense. It's not like I'm trying to be right all the time although daddy cakes here would tell you what I was like forever. The truth is not forever, it's now. Later today? Who knows? It's right now. We're kinda like, "I'm afraid you'll all leave me because I'm this scared little girl who could care less about what you see as wrong or right with me as long as you leave me alone, keep your hands off."

"Honey, you know I'll leave you alone. You can bet on that sweetheart. Besides, I thought you just got done telling us to drop all this adult talk for the good of Jeremy and Chad?"

"Ya can't avoid things, dad. They just get worse. Like the minute you tell me for the zillionth time that everybody's got flaws, watch where you're goin' with that, you may not like what comes back."

"Yeah, *tit for tat*, couldn't have said it better myself. Watch where you throw stones: Aisha, sooner or later you're gonna have to come to terms with yourself regardless of what we said or did to you. Jesus may not be your passionate rebirth, but for people such as Eric and myself, that's the key."

"You mean to shut my mouth, there's a time and a place."

"Right on Aisha, that's it."

"It's crap."

"What?"

"Why say anything? Nothing's certain, dad. All that talk at home was so matter-of-factly, like we're all so playful and happy that how can I see anything less genuine than this, this game we play on each other?"

"Hey, we've been all over this stuff a million times babe. This crap's like pulling your teeth. Sooner or later you're gonna have to get off the pot."

"And, what medication has worked to turn things around for me, pops?"

"Honey, let's just drop this, this, crying game of yours. Lay off the 'woe is me' pity party. We're just going round and round. Life if difficult for everyone."

"Because we can't just shout out the truth. Just got to go along with everything because there's no way to challenge the nonsense: too powerful, right dad."

"And if you do, you Will Pay the Price. Yeah, that's right. The brain farts when you go to work; and, so you do the same thing over and over while the mind drifts into some new thoughts to take you away from this hell. Can't fight City Hall, babe"

"Like some new mini-hell that I can say to my kids, hey look at the rest of the world, ain't so bad here. And, look around you, what's changed?"

"Nothing."

"You got it. So you can talk about how my depression worsens, how I'm so passionately self-absorbed, pop a pill to numb my pain so that I can still function. Better off dead, for real."

"Maybe we oughtta head home."

"Do what you gotta do, dad. Like you said, "maybe I should just go off on my own and drop your money strings, and get on board with Head Start. Maybe even grab me some education money and get a whole new bedroom and living room furniture. So, what do you think about that?"

"Ah-h-mm-n."

"No, no, no, no. Let me answer that Eric. I'm gonna say this one more time. Aisha, there is no way to channel your mess. You've got to get in there with yourself, feel every aspect of it, YOU, and no one else. FEEL IT. Dig in, babe."

"Right, I am nobody. But dad, this is not a one-time deal and everything's peachy. When crap rolls downhill, I'm gonna have to take all the punches again and again. There are no answers. But counting on the way things went to get out of my funk last time, might as well jump off a cliff."

"If we weren't pulling into Pick 'n Save; we would be saying good-bye for a long time. But, for your children's sake, we're gonna make this work."

He stares into Aisha's eyes as Eric, withdrawn, peers down at the pristine black carpeting, quietly tapping his fingers on his slacks. "I'm going in and get me some Orange Crush. Y'all want somethin' else?"

"I'm comin' in with you."

"Dad, watch the kids. We'll be back in a minute. Hang tight."

"Don't you ever put me through with that childish harangue ever again or so help me God."

"Oh, so help me God. Pa-lease, go find some other sucka. Get me?"

"Don't you threaten me."

"OK, big boy, leave if you want. If Jesus works for you, then more power to you."

"Oh, my little Dark Genius, can't even do that, can ya?"

"All that stuff puts food on the table, supports life. Ain't life though. Nothin's really good about this. We're just doin' what we gotta do. That's it. Lie, lie, lie, right? Then we turn to God to ask for His forgiveness. Never changes Eric. All I know is I'll be a prayin' my entire life until I'm blue in the face, thinkin' just maybe this time, things will be alright. The hand of God will come down and finally hear my prayers. Ain't gonna happen, is it Eric?"

"That's your take on it. I swear girl, the devil's got hold of you. So cynical. Maybe you could see a therapist. We've got some specialists over at Elmbrook. Your insipid balderdash dooby- doo's gone on far too long. Grow the hell up or I will catch a cab."

"OK Grandstand Boy, check yourself before you put your foot in your mouth. Hold it all in. Yeah, see where it gets you Mr. Clean Cut Holy Roller. Oh, yeah, nothing to say, right? Life cannot make sense like a bunch of words written thousands of years ago or yesterday for that matter. Check yourself bro'—that's what I'm talkin' 'bout."

Quietly they grab a shopping cart and walk over to the beverages aisle as he picks up his Orange Crush in a two-liter bottle as Aisha moseys on over to the Cherry Coke and grabs three two liter bottles. She motions over to the Styrofoam cups and he snatches them. Strange thing is that her anger has withered and his furor has been eased as they wait in line with a calmness they share.

"Got some change?"

"You mean to tell me you don't have enough to pay for it?"

"Nah, I'll pay you back when we get home."

"Thank you Miss."

They push out the carted soda and walk toward the SUV as if nothing has happened.

"Could you open up the back door dad?"

"OK, everything's in?"

"Hurry up, the train's running."

They pass back under the I-43 overpass and drive beneath a statuesque rustic iron bridge.

"Look at that grampa."

"Yeah, an old, old bridge. Very strong like you, Jeremy."

"There it is dad. Peninsula Park, go left."

"Alright everyone, let's move out while the day's still young. Look at the sun, not a cloud in the sky. Jeremy, get our gloves and baseballs."

Eric peers over his left shoulder and sees some old gravel patches raked into the grass's overgrowth, perhaps an old business torn down decades ago. The sky, heavy with humidity, looks on with static silence as the browns of dog day August converge upon the sprawling flat fields of grass, as the robins frolic about within the day's ominous stillness.

"Dad, Chad and me are gonna take a little walk in the brook."

"Is our little pool champ ready for the wild?"

"We'll see. Eric. Just what are you doing?"

"*That's Batman & Robin. Miles on Smack playing faded PEACE OF… dese niggas is nice knees like.* Risqué, intelligent, the guy's a real Masta' P. Who is this anyway?"

"Lupe Fiasco. Where've you been boy? Lupe may not be Moss Def but he's been around. From Chicago no less"

"Yeah, livin' the dream. He was toastin' it back in my school days."

"Yea-ah, he tells a story. A little history, and, whew, comes through, you know? My little man here's getting a little antsy.

Yeah, his sugar juice has kicked in and my man's gotta go."

"He's not potty trained yet?"

"No, he's fine, just a safety precaution. If you haven't noticed, there are no public rest rooms around. I mean we could go back to Pick 'n' Save, ask for the restrooms and all that. But, hey, we're here, so let's have a good time, right?" She confidently places her large white sun hat on her head and grabs Chad's hand.

She motions to Eric to grab the beach towel bag as they briskly scamper over to the crick.

"It's gotta be all 'bout love babe. Too many people strugglin' and getting' nowhere. Don't wanna be dat statistic. Gotta have more of a life den just keepin' da kids outta da hood. Not some feminist bull-shit, real life, ya know?"

"You still have your windbreaker on. You've come prepared haven't you?"

As they stand before the slow moving waters, Aisha slowly works the navy garment off her soft ebony shoulders. And, beneath it appears a lovely meringue one-piece swimsuit.

"Ooh, ooh-wee, that wild white hat parading down your back like a proud peacock makes a man just wanna scream! And, those two tone burnt sienna and beige colored buttons really do a number on me: brings everything to life, like I got the whole world in the palm of my hands. Where'd you get this sculptured piece of art?"

"Oh, I got the picture and dimensions from Cynababy and my friend Esther tailored two for just over a couple hundred bucks. Regular retail for one suit is $189.00, with the same materials."

"Kept the middle man out of the deal."

"I guess. Pretty cool, ha? Wanna join us?"

"Nah, these dress pants won't dig the muddy water."

"Whatever, c'mon Chad,"

"No!"

"See the water's warm. Mama loves this—the water's so ni-ice." Aisha reaches for Chad and grabs him, softly pulling him toward his chest. His tearful anxiety-ridden cheeks calm as he looks back at Eric. The young man has taken over Aisha's cell phone tunes, delving deeper into Lupe's lyrics. "God, it's gotta be almost a hundred out here."

"More reason to undress yourself and make your way into these heavenly waters my man."

"Right, bouncing around in my under garments, cops would be here in a heartbeat. If you haven't noticed, this ain't exactly where black folk hang out."

"There's a Stop 'n' Go at the corner, probably the worker's car parked in front. It's the middle of the day, Eric. Ah, party pooper. Chad and I will just mosey on down the shoreline."

"Mom, look, duck."

"Very good, Chad. See his bright green head? That's a Mallard duck. Listen:" quack, quack, quack. Say, mal-lard."

"Mah-lahd."

"Mallard."

"I want to go."

"We just got here."

"Don't want ta stay?"

"OK, let us get Mr. antsy out of the waters."

Aisha locates a level shoreline to step onto and puts her son down on the grass.

"Could you get me a towel Eric? Great."

"Chad, look what mommy brought you."

"My train!"

"Yes, now could you please come over here and sit on the beach towel."

"You're so good with him."

"He's no different than any other child. He has his moments; and, believe me, when he does, heaven help me, he can be more than a handful."

"Aren't we all?"

"Yes, that's what I have been trying to get through with you from day one."

"Not again."

"What do you mean by that?"

"I don't want to fight anymore."

"I can't avoid things Eric. That crap between dad and me— that's all the closer we're ever gonna get."

"You mean you like to fight."

"No, dad wants to have his way. He knows all my blunders and I know nothing about his."

"What do you mean?"

"C-mon, Eric, he's been around the block longer than I have. That's not mind blowing, is it? He needs to be in control."

"You're thinking too much into things."

"Eric, he's got to be right. Otherwise his whole world falls apart."

"So he thinks."

"Exactly. I'm twenty-six going on ninety-six—so-oh old. Why do you think I take care of myself?"

"You're a beautiful woman."

"I hate to tell you but a lot of beautiful women have eighty-sixed themselves. Chad, look at how wonderful he is with that toy. He's so-oh connected. When you're not engaged like he is, forget it. I need you, Eric. I get knocked down every day. Perseverance without someone to talk things out is hopeless. Might as well put me in the ground. You think I'm kiddin' around? Hah!"

"Could it be that you take things to heart too much?"

"Right, like people always say life is unfair 'cause if I try to do anythin' about changin' things the whole deal'll fall on me 'cause everyone's just goin' along for the ride: you know, didn't mean anythin' by it but you gotta go along to get along. How boorish"

"Look we've only been dating for a short time. You know maybe we should just ease off the gas pedal a little bit, stop trying to figure everything out."

"You mean just leave things alone 'cause if you do, it'll make ya feel more comfortable. Enough of this, Eric. We only have right now. Tomorrow's not here. I, we only got NOW!"

She touches his wiry sienna right shoulder with her long, thin fingers as he looks over at the body of water.

"Not to get off the subject, but your father wants to double date, you and me joining your parents for a night at the Fox Theater in Madison to see Ship's *In Dahomey* later this fall."

"Oh, a musical comedy by black performers, the first ever by Negro Folk. You know that Dad's been tryin' to get me to go to that since I was a little girl. To tell you the truth, I could see something more like *A Raisin in the Sun*. It's real. Musicals are a hard thing for me to deal with, light and cheery without any lewd, bawdy, bawdy. OK, cheesy stuff: it's not for me. Dad and mom know this. I mean, this has nothing to do with you; but, wow, I'll get back to you on this one after I have little heart-to-heart with daddy-o."

"I'm not trying to force you into something you don't want to do."

"Oh, and you can bet that they already have a good idea of what they are going to do with the kids. Have you ever been to the Majestic Fox?"

"No, can't say that I have."

"Oh, my God, intense. It like a blast from the past. Crystal clear, huge chandeliers just overtake you. Now, seeing Chris Rock's a hell of a lot better than sitting through a whole show of song and dance from way back when that I don't wanna know anythin' about, ANY-THIN. Wouldn't mind goin' out to eat though. That would be right up my alley."

"Oh, Hi dad. What's up?"

"Jeremy and I have had our fill of catch and infield practice. The sun's pretty hard to avoid. And, without the bats, baseball's hard for our future short stop to get used to."

"It's too hot. Could we go to McDonald's? I don't want to get sunburnt."

"See those birch trees over toward the park's far side? Tell your mother I'll meet her at the end of the parking lot area where we'll grab the food and head for da shade."

"Come on Chad, let's go."

Aisha caresses her man's tightly cropped black hair as she nuzzles her coiffed caramel hair against his pulsing chest.

"You're the best thing that's ever happened to me Eric, you know that."

"I haven't done anything."

"You're still here aren't you?"

"So?"

"The others, they took off before I could even turn my head around."

"I'm a Christian. You're not gonna scare me away that easily. Mr. Briscoe's got faith in me to hold fast with truth even if no one else will even take the time to listen."

"This is me, not your reverend or whatever you call him."

"He's my mentor. Aisha, you need others that you can trust."

"Aside from Jeremy and Chad, I have you then. Jeremy, could you grab Chad's hand? Mommy has a surprise."

"C-mon, Chad."

She caresses Eric's back and softly kisses him. Confused, Eric jerks away, then stays with her and reciprocates.

"Come guys, we're ready to go. Not in front of the kids. Jeremy and Chad, let the old folks have their way. Peanut butter & jelly sandwiches and chips, soda too: oh, and your mother's very own potato salad. Grab the paper plates and plastic forks Jeremy. Later on, we'll throw down some watermelon. Your mother has no idea what she is missing. M-m-mm, M-mmm, yummy."

"Eric, thank you."

"Yeah, I'm crazy about you. Let's join the crew for lunch: after you my little prize fighter."

A haze falls over the skyline as a lone great blue heron wades in the river's mild waters; and from a distance, strangers laugh and frolic beneath the welcome shelter from the sun's ominous presence.

Back in their neighborhood, Tom Schadek pulls into Alice Padilla's driveway, shoving his keys recklessly into his pocket shuffling quickly toward her front door. He peers inside and she waves him in.

"I've tried to get hold of you but your line was busy."

She motions him to "Ssh" as she continues speaking with her ex-. "Manny, I've called the police as I told you a million times … They won't do anything for the first twenty-four hours … Haven't seen her since she went to bed last night … Snuck out?"

"Probably… I don't expect you to put down all your great plans and run down here … Do you even care? Even your daughter has reservations about you … Manny, I had to force Jazz to go up to your place in June … No, don't tell me how it went down. I know how it did … No, I'm not pulling your wig—sometimes Manny, you gotta pick yourself up by the bootstraps and get on with things … You're stuck in fetus mode, man … Limp wrist panderer who's always out to hold onto his satyr Puck-like beast of a carefree spirit whose only ambition in life is to get a laugh out of me … No, I don't want to talk to your girlfriend, Margot right? Either she's the laziest sleaze that's walked the face of the earth or she's the one pushing your buttons … How's that for a TMZ size up of that little game you're playing with Margot and me for that matter? Nah, I'll text you if I hear anything from the cops … Tom's just pulled in… Bye Manny … Right, if I find anything out about Jasmine I'll call you immediately … Manuel, one last thing, some of those pictures Jazz took of bears in the wild, precious … You've not quite drawn an anarchist's blood. But, yeah, you're on to something, I mean it … No. With you Money is Everything … Your quality coffee table book *Bears in the Great Northwoods,* that's on you … Manuel you only contribute just over two hundred a month for Jasmine's well-being … I don't need a psychoanalyst to tell me that you got the better deal on that one … Why should you get part of the house? You pay peanuts for her… You get a lawyer and we'll talk… I've paid on almost everything, including all the repairs… Yeah, yeah, yeah, you also contribute to her clothing; but I've put every last dime into this house, including a brand new patio and kitchen… Nah, you're the outdoorsman, what do you care what this house looks like… Sure, I'll e-mail you a few photos. Forget it. I don't want to waste my time. You are who your are sweetheart. Get a real job… Manny, Jazz had told me what your place looks like… No, that's not my idea of home life… Let's face it. You're a slob! Rust all over your kitchen sink and bath tub… Hey, if Margot's alright with it then who I am to crash your party? No, Benny Profane you ain't but neither are you a proper member of the bourgeoisie… Right, wander along on your own, take a purposeless jaunt into seeking that perfect picture of bears you could never conjure from any blueprint… Yes, yes, I know, but, but-but, can't you accept the fact that that's not me… Yes, I gotta go. Tell Margot I said 'hi'. Ciao."

"I see this must be about Jasmine."

"She hasn't been home since last night and I don't know where she's gone. I can't lose her Thomas, she's all I got left in this world."

"Alice, now don't take this the wrong way but I coulda told you so."

"What's that supposed to mean?"

"You're insuperable."

"Insuperable?"

"Yes. That girl of yours is more of an adult than most people my age. My God, Alice, she dissects and compartmentalizes everything. Of course she's going to fail somewhere along the line. And, then, who will she have to answer to?"

"Me?"

"Ah, pilgrim's progress? Yeah You."

"Why don't you just get out of here you ole' tub o' lard."

"That's right, kick me to the curb and tell me you don't need anyone. When Jasmine goes against you, what will you do then? Get a dog? Heaven help that poor creature. You'll throw it out and let it fend for itself. That is if you can get away with it."

"And, who is the pessimist here?"

"You've seen my two youngest many times, right?"

"Yeah, so?"

"They are nowhere near the achiever your daughter is. Have you taken the time to hear how that child can play the flute? Godlike, I mean really. Oh, and now you don't want her to play basketball because it might interfere with her schoolwork."

"So, what's your point?"

"Three point nine five: Is all this success your fear of having her fall back in your lap?"

"My daughter's missing and here I am listening to this little sermon from a balding grey man whose stomach covers up his petty manhood."

"Always pushing me out the door."

"OK, leave. I'm not stopping you."

"You're just falling apart in your own little mess."

"And, just what that might be?"

"Seeing yourself for who you are."

"Yeah, well money bags, you walk out that door, there is no turning back."

"Right, like if I pick myself up from my bootstraps maybe I can find a moment or two to morph into your crystalline world."

"Ah-hahh-hm-n-n. I don't have time for this, Tom. My daughter's been gone since, since who knows when. And, she was gone before six this morning. Do you know this was the first day I've ever missed from work?"

"I think you haven't followed your own way of sorts, but you make good money, can spit stats at the drop of a hat. But, h-ah-hahhhhh, I gotta tellya, there's that hardness staring me down again. I mean really,

Alice, what if all that stout business acumen comes to a screeching halt, then what?"

"Is this about the time last month I quit yoga and you were able to carry on without me?"

"Yoga's not about becoming over a period of time. Remember, that's what the instructor stressed. I mean is the lotus position about attaining form simply through meditation or meditation right now?"

"I know what you're getting at. I've chosen to be my own silent gargoyle and grab at whatever I need. It's fucked up. But to be a part of the team; to go along with it, how am I going to get along in this sordid house of cards?"

"Ooh-what's the point of living if this is what you accept?" Softly, Thomas reaches around her back with both hands and hugs her.

"You can't rationalize your game, love. There is no way I'm going to be your whipping boy. To tell you the truth, I didn't really like coming over here. Like, what's the point? But when I look into your eyes, it's like I see directly into your soul, like even the fog of my insipid life couldn't keep me from touching you."

He rocks her in his arms with complete understanding, transcending the logic of an entirely illogical life.

Quickly she pushes him away and looks outside.

"It's dark out, Tom. I'm really worried something bad's happened to her."

"It's only eight o'clock, hun. Have you spoken with her friends?"

"I talked to Danelle. She has no idea where Jasmine might be. You see, this isn't like her. She's never missed her flute lessons all summer long."

"Well then, maybe you could call the police again?"

"No, the police told me that they will not do anything with me until at the earliest of 6AM tomorrow morning."

"Well, I'm going to get a glass of water. Is there anything I can get for you?"

"Thank you, no."

"I'll tell you what."

"What?"

"How about if I make you a couple of loaves of bread? Corn bread That is, if you don't mind?"

"Really, Thomas, a man that bakes to soothe the heart of his lover. A strange twist of fate, don't you think?"

"Ah, it lessens my own stress levels because I really don't know what to do at this point."

"I could just scream! I gotta help you, or there's no telling what I might do."

"OK, just take it easy. Everything's put together."

"Hey, wait a minute, this isn't cornbread."

"No, it's sourdough bread."

"I left the artistic part for you to do. Get your cutting board with a little flour to spread out and knead that wonderful bread before we pop it into the oven. Yeah, there you go. Right, press down on the dough, work it. That's it, where's your bread pans? Down below? Yes, there they are. OK, in you go, and there's the last piece of dough. Go for it."

Alice meticulously works through the dough, pressing it, palming it, rolling it.

"What do you think?"

"I think it's as ready as it ever will be. We'll slide you atop your brother, and we'll have fresh bread in the wink of an eye. Nah, don't worry about the dishes, I'll take care of everything here."

"But I want to do something to take the edge off my daughter's disappearance."

Thomas rubs her shoulder and gives are an ice-cold glass of water.

"Here, might you want an Advil or Tylenol?"

"No, I just never felt this way before. Not like I could figure any of this out, but I didn't deserve this Tom."

Just then, a car pulls into the driveway and two youths walk toward the front door.

"Girl, where've you been? You've had your mother tied in knots not knowing where you've been. And, you, Damon, you're not going anywhere until I've had a talk with your mother about this maniacal nonsense. Like what did you two think you were doing staying out without letting me know where the hell you've been? She's my daughter, Damon, mine! Now whatever you and your family do over where you come from, that's your business. But you've put the ball in my court with your childish decisions. Heaven help you. Get your mother on the telephone right now. Right NOW! No more ifs ands or buts. DO IT RIGHT NOW. NOW!"

"Alright." Damon dials up his mother who is wrapping up at her position of delivering Pizza Hut pizzas. "Ma, yeah, I need you to come over to where I am at my girlfriend's house."

"AND HER MOTHER WANTS YOU IN ON THE LITTLE THOUGHTLESS CRAP YOUR SON PUT ME THROUGH … NO THIS ISN'T 'MERRY CHRISTMAS … WAR'S MORE LIKE IT.'"

"Look Ms. Whoever you are. I'll be off of work at ten. And, you can bet your sorry ass I'll be there. What's your address?"

"It's north of Burleigh Street on 57Th Street just south of Roosevelt at 3166 North 57Th Street, you'll see us in a white single story home on the East side of the Street … Yes, the Wanderer's Rest Cemetery runs on 60Th Street just three blocks west of us. Here's your son."

"Jasmine, get over here right now. Tom, make yourself comfortable. Jazz and I have a few things to straighten out."

"Fine. Want a cold drink of water?"

"Nah, I want to get out of here as soon as possible. You don't know my mom. She don't take things so lightly. Mrs. Padilla better be on her A Game 'cause when shit hits the fan, man that's when she just goes off. Ain't no turnin' back, know what I'm sayin'?"

"Damon, Jasmine's been gone all day long. She didn't know where Jasmine went. Now, you can understand where Mrs. Padilla is coming from."

"I was with her all day and she said nothin' 'bout any phone calls from her mother."

"I can tell you that she got hold of the police and her friends. Nobody was much help."

"Ma'll be there in twenty minutes—da Mrs. Better be on her best behavior that's all I'm gonna say about that one."

"But that's her child, Damon."

"Who cares about their kids, huh? Like everythin's 'bout getting your way. Don't matter who you are. So, man, don't think I'm scared o' you or anybody else. Da world's about getting its way as long as ya don't step on too many toes, dat's it. Like I'm supposed ta care 'bout that?"

"You have to grow out of your own ills too, Damon. I'm not your father but there's a lot of hooey about ourselves."

"And, once you try to make sense of yaself, you're done. Dat's it. Ain't you or anybody gonna set me straight on that one. You can bank it, Mrs. Padilla"

"Now, I didn't say you have to buy the farm to get along, that's hopeless. Nothing's set in stone. Like, is your tumor cancerous or benign—that's what you have to ask yourself. Nothing's owned in this world. That's solely our perception."

"I'm not tryin' to get in your cool aid, man. Just keep your hands off. I ain't your kid, know what I'm sayin'?"

"Alice, someone just pulled into the driveway."

"See if it's Damon's mother." Damon nods. "Yes, it is."

"O.K., let her in. we'll be out in a minute."

Mrs. Jameson, eyes focused squarely on the front door, rings the doorbell. Thomas introduces himself and lets her in. She veers toward her son and stands alongside the living room couch without sitting down.

"Mrs. Jameson, my name is Alice Padilla, Jasmine's mother."

"Mrs. Padilla you have no idea how pissed off I am at your insinuation that my boy, Damon had anything to do with your child's, what she do anyway, your child's own garbage?"

"Jasmine's got something to say."

"Now, just wait a minute.

Mrs. Jameson, I dragged your son into my decision to take off this morning. I just never got 'round to tellin' him everything about it. I know it was wrong. But you gotta believe me Mrs. Jameson, I like your son a real lot. Please don't punish him. He didn't do anything wrong."

"Ma, I've been goin' with Jazz for a couple months now. I like it. She's cool, you know? I don't have to be nothin' wid her."

The husky woman glares into Alice's eyes motioning her to speak with her on the porch. Hesitantly, Alice inches toward the door and looks at her recently purchased painting on the living room wall.

"Alice, right?" Alice nods. "Don't you ever think that you can push me around just because maybe or maybe not your daughter's in trouble. Now, I ain't gonna give ya da same old crap what goes around comes around. Dat's old as the hills. Instant karma ain't gonna cure us missy. You ever push dat cart my way, I'm gonna shove it back in you' face, understand?"

"Sounds like karma to me."

"Touché; guess I deserved that one. But dat's not what I'm sayin'. You ain't no mo' special than me or my kids. Did alright for yourself, sure you worked hard for all this. That ain't mean nothin' about bein' a human being though. Now, I didn't know nothin' 'bout my son and yours, but he's fine. Your daughter won't get played, and I mean that. Hell, I don't want to fight wid you or nobody. You give me a reason though, you got a War. No getting' around it. Now, whatever made your daughter do what she did, my son had no idea what she was plannin'. I'm not askin' him to dump her or nothin' but get your own house in order before you come tryin' to tear down mine."

Alice looks into Mrs. Jameson's eyes, saying "you're right. Damon had nothing to do with any of this. If there's anything I can do to make things more amicable between us, you let me know."

"Ah, dis is all chicken shit. Just don't let it happen again or we're gonna find out what kind of woman you are made o'. Come on Damon, I gotta get somethin' other than pizza to take care of my hunger."

"Bye, Mrs. Padilla, tell Jasmine I'll call her after work tomorrow, sometime around nine. Nice to see you again Tom."

"You too, Damon. Take care of your mother now."

"Oh, there's the timer, bread's ready."

"Tom pulls out the bread and sets the two loaves on top of the stove. Everything's cleaned up Alice."

He reaches over, caressing her soft arms, gently kissing her on the lips, "Tom, would you mind if you were to leave now. I mean if you could. Colleen and Tammy probably would like you to be at home with you rather than your mother."

"That ain't much of a stretch. Mom, she can be a handful. God love her, she didn't have to help me out at the last minute. Jasmine, I'll let you and your ex-iron things out. Alice, if you could call me when you'll have some time this weekend just to touch base?"

"I'll give you a call, promise. Thanks for stopping by. I mean that Tom. Love you."

"Alright Jazz, we've already talked about this for a while now; and, no, you're not going to get off that easy. Now, don't interrupt me. My God, I even brought in the police on your little charade. I gotta give it to you that you managed to make it back before the 24-hour timeline passed. I'll let you talk to your father later on your dime after we finish up here."

"I'll text him."

"No you won't. You went through with this, this crap now you'll have to take complete responsibility for it."

"Hah-ah-h-mmmmn, you don't have to worry about me giving up on the flute but I will play b-ball this fall."

"That's been put on hold hasn't it?"

"No."

"After what you just put me through, thinking you were just gonna show up whenever it felt it was convenient for you?"

"You just don't get it, do you?"

"Where are you coming from?"

"You're not gonna push me around even if I live under your roof."

"That's somethin' comin' from a child who hasn't spent one day at the office."

"You're the one who's decided what I need to do to make something of my life."

"You're like a broken record: over and over."

"Maybe I don't, tell me what I don't get?"

"When I was your age, there was no way that I'd even dream of saying things like that to gramma and grampa. I'd a been kicked out on the streets before the door even hit me on the ass. Girl, you have no idea how miserable I could make your life."

"Grounding?"

"Hell, put this way, you wouldn't have a life anymore. And, Damon, well you can just forget that one."

"Couldn't handle Damon's ma could you?"

"What are you talking about?"

"I saw the way she stood over you. One-step closer and she woulda laid you out UFC-style. Why bother trying to explain it away. You were dead meat if you would have opened your mouth. You're not as tough as you think, are you?"

"You keep it up and there's no telling what your mother might do. Hell, keep it up and you might end up in foster care."

"Ah-hhh, remember when you told me that I know more about what's right for me than you do?"

"Not really, like who's gonna bail you out of jail when you've decided to take off with your partner in crime?"

"Damon?"

"You said it."

"You have no idea what I've told my friends about trying to do anything in this world, like the only thing I do around here is clean the toilets and cut the grass. I don't learn anything from you, mom. The only thing I can make out is that I'm gonna play that flute in some symphony if not in America then Europe, highfalutin like. And, what if I can't cut it? It's not like there's a billion flutists in the world, now are there? I'm not that stupid. Really mom, Damon has a good time and does really well in school. God, every test I take feels like a cancer is just eating at me, like the whole world's gonna fall apart at any time. And, this school game is really that important to you, isn't it? I mean, Iggy Azalea probably didn't need it, but she sure can dance to her own tune."

"How slutty do you have to be to make a buck?"

"Successful though, isn't she?"

"That doesn't make it OK. But, hey; there's the door if you think you could make it happen for you. No, this is how it is. You gotta have thick skin to make it in this world. All the touchy, feely crap doesn't fly. Nobody's friends."

"You can say that again. After Mrs. Bartusek left, the only person that comes around here is your boyfriend. Don't lose him mom. And, you can tell me all that crap how great you are at State Farm, but without him, you might as take all your money and bury yourself in it. What good's it gonna do if he decides to leave? All I can say is to leave me out of your little hell. I mean, first you had me hating dad because he wasn't making it. You know, yeah, he's no homebody, but cool girlfriend, they laugh, hang out, like they don't have to hide anything. You and this house, might as well be your grave. Like your taking on the world shouting orders at the walls to get things done because, like nobody'll listen to you. Tires your out real quick, doesn't it"

"It's all about you, Jasmine. Don't even think of bringing me into your little comebacks. You've cut your throat a long time ago. Things are gonna change around here, and I'm gonna make the decision what goes down. Understand?"

"Oh. Like here's another life example that will help me make peace with a world that nobody cares about but everybody settles in with. Have a positive attitude about what? Nobody really cares, me, you, we all try to avoid all those dumb decisions my teacher made, you know, like Mrs. Webster. She held me back in kindergarten because, like you couldn't tell me until much later that I just wasn't getting along with my classmates."

"Why are you dragging that crap into this discussion? That was years ago. Besides, what the hell does that have to do with your bullshit?"

"Right, the Come to Jesus meeting you like to bring up when you just want to go off on me, right mom?"

"Ah, this punky crap you throw about. Haven't heard a word I've said, have you? Nothing's fair. You're a fool to think I'm gonna let you destroy everything I worked for because you think I'm the mother from hell."

"That's not what I'm saying. I don't want this. You can take that any way you want. If this is what life's about, better off dead."

"We're gonna get you some help. Before school starts, you're gonna see a therapist I know about one from the Upper East Side over on Downer, Mr. Woolfe, no ifs and or buts about it missy. If I have to sit in on a couple of sessions, then so be it."

"Straight A student, never come in too late, oh except for this morning when I snuck out at the break of dawn to spend the day with Damon. But, here's ma who'll play the silent treatment with me for days, weeks sometimes. And, my mother of the year was all frightened that she wasn't told about her daughter sneaking out the back door before she got up."

"Really, you throw that Iggy Azalea CD in your backpack and you can say good-bye to your so-called life. You'll wish to hell you've never left here. Keep on goin'. Who knows? Just maybe you'll find your Rainbow. I wouldn't count on it though. Mr. Right will be Mr. Wrong. You'll wish that shoveling gravel was your fate. Everything's wrong but how is Mrs. Right gonna change things for the better?"

"I never said I had any answers mom. But you can have this world. I'm not fightin' you for it. It's all yours."

"Hook, line, & sinker. I'll take the ball and run with it. Just think, when you've got your flute box opened up at Disneyland playing your sad parade of hits, you know maybe work in a little Ziggy; and, there you have it."

"I'm just tired about people telling me how great everything is. And, then always hearing the same old things that this is the greatest country, try living anywhere else."

"I think this discussion ends now."

"Oh, the Big Cheese decides when everything begins and ends. And, if I get in a few hits that she can't take, well then, Go to My Room!"

"Nah, not yet. You'll go to your room when I say so."

"Never heard that before."

"Listen you shit, if I have to come over there and slap your face, don't think I won't."

"If you want to keep your arm, I'd advise against it. Just because you're my mom doesn't mean you're exempt from my steady right."

"Grandstanding Hollywood little bitch. Get ready for next week. You'll need to free up the whole week. Don't worry. I'll let you know tomorrow after I get home from work. But, you're going to see a therapist, that I can assure you."

"You're embarrassing. The only thing you know is to keep me in line. I just want to have fun and all you want is to make sure I become an accomplished musician. Couldn't have done it without you, mom."

"All right, that's enough. Now, go to bed. Oh, and by the by, get the grass cut before I get home tomorrow. Remember to call your father. I'll be talkin' to him in the morning. So, let's hop to it."

("God Almighty, why the hell did I ever have kids?")

"Oh, and one more thing, how's that 'Planned Parenthood' thing going down with your boyfriend? No, no, no, no, no, no— don't wanna ruin your beauty sleep. He can wait until you change your tune."

"Who knows mom, maybe I'm already pregnant."

"You better hope not. There's no telling what I might do."

"Watch your step Jasmine, 'cause maybe I should take you down to a shelter to see how the other half lives? Yeah, that's right—open your eyes a little. Ain't no fairy tales out there, girl."

"Oh, just one more thing you and I will talk it over with you when I get home tomorrow night. You will be here when I get home or else. Sweet dreams Cinderella. You're gonna need it: That I can assure you."

She pours herself a Chianti and reminisces about all the talk regarding her aunt's empty pint bottles of gin and vodka laying hidden around the house. Lao-tzu stated that all living and apparently non-living things are treated with equanimity as her daughter had so eloquently stated earlier. Work was and is a pain. Her education was merely a tool used to earn more money. But, why did she need to earn her Masters of Business Degree to sell insurance? Perhaps the only thing she has learned by being around her mother lately was that the pangs of life do not go away. Her lingering new anxieties are directly tied to her past insecurities.

It really does not matter: Alice is a trooper. Whatever current adversities that have come to a head with Jasmine will ultimately Make Alice Stronger.

Chapter Sixteen

Some Time Away from Home

"Come in from the sun, that's more than enough rhubarb to put my rhubarb-meringue pie together."

"You need to taste my Pavlova with rhubarb and pistachio, munificent, m-mp-ah, mother would make that every summer when we had friends over for something or another—piece of heaven, Scout's Honor."

"Seems like you have a ton of that unsightly rhubarb and zucchini."

"I tell you what. If you can't grow any rhubarb or zucchini, you'd better rely on the grocery store 'cause both grow like the wind. I end up givin' as much away, the rest I end up throwin' out."

"Ah, poor baby, I was thinkin' maybe we could make a little rhubarb wine. But, with your checkered past, maybe that's not such a great idea."

"I still have a beer every now and then. Don't believe me? Take a look in the 'fridge bottom left. By the way, who were you talking with on the phone just a minute ago?"

"My friend asked me if I wanted to see a movie tomorrow evening. You know, it's a tradition that goes back years. Can't seem to break the habit. Not saying that it's necessarily a bad thing, mind you. Paul, really now, do you know many movies that you truly enjoy seeing? You know blips of Cary Grant and Myrna Loy pop into my day at random. Quite profound if I say so myself. It's not that I'm fanatical about this, but this thing, I can't explain how it all comes together, is unique though isn't it? I mean I can't take any credit for this. I mean, like clockwork these images of great movies just pop into my head from who knows where. I guess it's sort of like some mystical magical thing taking hold of me."

"Like you don't have to go to Church anymore?"

"Ah, I wouldn't go that far. The Catholic in me will never go away, Italian mother and Polish father, quite the combination. Besides, they didn't force it upon me. No guilt trips. I'm gonna have to drag you down to the south side to St. Josaphat's to show you what Jesus and the community are all about."

"Well, then I can take you to Saint Michael's on the south side. Show you a little Ukrainian gold, maybe listen to the language filter throughout the walls of the beautiful artwork. Closer to home, I can shuttle you over to Santa Sava's for a wonderful fish fry. And, while you're at it, just walk through the church and take a look at all the fantabulous Byzantine artwork."

"Oh, yes, Josaphat's is pristine in its own right. We'll make it a date sometime soon. Last time I checked, I just turned eighty. Can't sit around and talk all the time. You gotta get out there."

"Well, I got my grandson interested in bocce ball. You know he beat me his first time out?"

"Ah, that's wonderful, isn't it? At least he's there for you."

"Oh, I agree. Ya never know when you're going to see him again because I'm 83, and with the exception of my cats who I'm sure are tearing up the house right at this moment, I really don't have any friends until you of course, darling, somehow walked into my life."

"Since my husband died, God has been that long, yeah, over twenty years ago, I holed myself in my house and just went to work at Sisters of Divine Savior. Retirement without much to do, now that's a tough one. Bridge on Mondays, the library. TV, God, I mean that's all there was for me."

"Not much different than mine. Hey, the clouds are rolling over. Might you want to go inside?"

"Nah, it's still quite warm out. Besides you haven't touched your iced tea."

"I was thinking about goin' inside to grab a beer and listen to the maestro."

"Who's that?"

"Must you ask? Bob Uecker, who else? The Brewers. Yeah, they mailed it in again. What else is new? But who else is so funny yet so engaging that you can't help but be taken over by him?"

"What do you mean be that?"

"He's himself and he really likes what he does. I mean, how does a guy our age get along with twenty-year old ball players at the batting cage and end up laughing with a bunch of retirees meeting him after a game?"

"Well, I used to have heroes until Archbishop Rembert Weakland fell from grace."

"Weakland? Who's that?"

"He was very smart clergyman that held the archbishopric of Milwaukee for a long time. At 75, he was retired; you can't go beyond that age. Those are the rules, you know."

So?"

"That's not the point. The point is that he was dating a man on the side a long time ago, for something like twenty years. And, later on that man in turn blackmailed Rembert for $450,000.00 or else he vowed to leak it the Press and tell it everything about their indiscrete relationship. Where do you think he came up with the money?"

"Oh, I don't know—say, He dipped into the funds?"

"Sure did. That wasn't the worst of it. There was a case about a former Polish Priest in the midseventies who was allowed by Weakland to head a Catholic School for the Deaf in northern Wisconsin. Not a big deal, right? Well, it just so happened that this old priest had an enflamed history of pederasty. Weakland knew about it, so did the police. Everybody turned a blind eye to it, and the old bugger died a while back, so the lost soul didn't have to face any charges."

"You must understand, the Archbishop possesses a most remarkable mind, articulates everything, can sit with you while you listen to Messiaen in a charming cathedral setting, piano or organ doesn't matter. The Archbishop always has that calm demeanor about him. Heaven flows from Messiaen's symphonic composition, Oh the Ascension Suite, the Pentecost, to die for. You have no idea what you're missing until the masterpiece unfolds before you."

"About your friend passing the buck?"

"Well, the former Benedictine monk admitted his folly but added that the police knew about the Priest's past."

"What else is new? The more the merrier. It's like we make excuses for ourselves, and why should your friend be any different?"

"I haven't seen him since he stepped down on his 75[Th] birthday."

"Really, the man does have a point. Expose that Priest and he cuts his own throat."

"You're so cynical, Paul."

"No, I'm not. His situation called for keeping his mouth shut so he could ship the sick man away in the sticks to make sure he's out of sight, out of mind."

"Not for the 206 cherubic souls who have come forward since the investigation began. And, don't tell me about settlement. What does that mean to these adults who've got to live with the sexual abuse that didn't have to happen?"

"We're just a bunch of gerbils that can't get off the spinning wheel."

"Well, all we'd need is a few sunflower seeds and sweet corn, bring along a water bottle and you and me babe, we'd be lovers hidden in the haystack away from all that noise around us. No more boohoo for the frou-frou. I guess what I am trying to say is that I cannot listen to another person who is faking it just to keep me away from his own little problems. I just need people who want to talk about something more than what we heard in the news or how we're gonna turn around this little mess of what Milwaukee has become. Because I've had it up to here with all those clichés piled on top of each other. I love you. Now, drink your iced tea before it gets warm."

"Yes mom."

"By the way, have you heard from your friend?"

"Ah, who do you mean?"

"You know the one who I turned down and asked you out instead."

"Yeah, we've gone fishing since then. He claims he's all over it. But I think deep down he accepts it. I mean I didn't put my two cents in, kept out of it. But you brushed up against me, and the rest is history."

"You know. These are two really beautiful trees."

"Yes, I've spent hours beneath them, my children chased each other 'round them. Those dark red leaves somehow keep my mind at ease every time I look up at them."

"The shaded areas almost make them a deep blue. Fascinating."

"Yes, could I have a couple of your carrot sticks?"

"Sure, go ahead. I'm not much in the mood for eating anymore. That tuna salad sandwich hit the spot."

"You know that after years and years of doing mostly everything by myself, Phyllis. I must admit, my sexual libido has brushed off its cobwebs and was wondering if not tonight, then sometime soon, you may have a sleepover?"

"Oh, you men. Why is everything about sex?"

"Beats doin' push-ups."

He softly touches her left shoulder and kisses her on her cheek. "I mean it Phyllis. You have been a pleasant surprise in a life that I have found hard to bear."

"Well, you have two daughters and grandchildren, even great-grandchildren. Now, don't you tell me that you are lonely and misunderstood."

"I'm sure my relationship with them is not much different than it is between most folks."

"What's that?"

"I can put up with them at like Thanks-Giving and Christmas, throw in Easter Sunday and your set. I love playing with my great-grand kids, but, Phyllis I don't know them anymore than my neighbor's kids. We're all so distant in some way."

"Hiding, afraid you'll get hurt and won't be able to face yourself anymore?"

"Yeah, that's pretty much it."

"I mean I still get out, do my Meals-on-Wheels thing a couple times a week. My grandson Tommy, the new bocce ball Phenom that he is, is pretty down-to-earth. We actually have wonderful conversations. He's got to do something with that philosophy major of his. He only cares about the truth between us, but he's done some stupid things lately."

"Haven't we all? The important thing, Paul, is to understand what that is and get on with things."

"My youngest daughter has just told me that to really live, we must come out and confess our fears to those we want to connect with."

"Yes, like those old flapper movies I used to watch as a little girl where they all looked so sensual, so carefree, but as I got older in my late teens, I began to grasp that their shielded drama didn't really go anywhere. Everything just rots. Sooner or later you've got to share your life without all that pageantry and fluff. Just be real with someone. Let loose."

"M-m-m-mn: I wish everything was that simple."

"Oh, but it is. You're just afraid the other person's gonna make your life miserable."

"Most of the time it works out that way. But when that gift comes along."

"And, it has. Just don't blow it. Better yet, don't suck. C'mon, let's take a walk before it gets too hot."

"Paul, did you ever think about asking your children and grandchildren about what you wanted?"

"I have. Unfortunately, they tend to see me as the old fool who messed everything up with all the booze that I put down over the years, especially after my wife's death."

"You don't have any pictures of her in the house."

"When you've spent as much time as you have over at the house, I've decided to take the last couple I did have down."

"Not even one in your bedroom?"

"Not even in my bedroom. Phyllis Kossolowski, I need you."

"Wonderful. I can see that we have something in common. Are you sure you talked to your kids or are you just making that up?"

"Now why would I do that? I've nothing to prove to you.

Like your friend, my daughter takes me to a movie once a month. And, this has been going on for quite some time. We always hit the early matinee at the earliest time slot; and, guess what? She makes a beeline to get me home so she can tend to her precious husband. You know what? Next time I see her; I'm going to tell her that I have a date to take me to the movie of our choice."

"You mean to tell me that I'm going to have to see a couple movies every month?"

"That's up to you. Ms. Kossolowski, would you like to be my guest at the next movie we agree to see at the Downer Theatre?"

"Oh, so you're an art house fan?"

"You got it. Rather engage in life and see it through a director's eye, a guy who's trying to connect with us living souls than someone who's trying to get us in his next heroic message that has nothing to do with the world you and I tinker in."

"Hollywood can work some magic once in a while, especially around Oscar time."

"No, I've seen some great movies in the spring, even in the summer every now and then."

"One thing's for sure, without the senior discount, you couldn't catch me dead in the movie house."

"Spoken from a true outdated local yokel."

"You got that right. Have you thought about selling your house?"

"And moving in with you? Not so fast Mister."

"I was thinkin' about putting my house up for sale and we could move to Florida. I got a little piece of property near Fort Lauderdale and we could build a nice little something that would be to our liking. Just you and me; and, I could get some deep sea Ocean fishing in that I have always wanted to do in the past. Say what we want and rub our toes in the sand every now and then, under the umbrella of course, seeing that we're not spring chickens anymore. Not right now, but say before the year's up. Whatdya say?"

"I'll think about it. It's not like I'm leaving anything behind, but this has been my home for my whole life."

"You'll get over it once you see the temperature never dips below freezing."

"Hurricanes?"

"You can't have everything."

"That's for sure. Gotta take the good with the bad."

"I'm hearing a lot of good about the Naples area."

"There's a good old and young mix."

"That's a little island, isn't it?

"No, it's on the Gulf side, growing like crazy with the southwestern Florida hospitality flavor". "You surprise me so, Paul. Outta the blue like that?"

"We're not getting' any younger. A one-year commitment to anything is a big deal at this point in my life. Honey, this is our year. Believe me; this has been spinning around in my head for quite some time now. Whenever you want to discuss this in more detail, just let me know."

"Oh, God, it's starting to rain. Let's get back under those trees before it starts pouring."

"Run for it!"

"Whew! I didn't know I could still move my legs like that anymore."

"Paul."

"What dear?"

"Could we quick slip inside."

"You're gonna get a little wet."

"We stand here beneath your trees long enough we'll be drenched anyway."

"You're right about that."

"So, what's so important that it can't wait?"

"Let's talk about Florida. I mean, like you said, we're not getting any younger. And, I do not want to spend another winter in snow and sub-zero temperatures."

"You got that right, tarpon, here I come!"

"Could you just calm down or should I reach in your pocket and grab the keys."

"Ah, you caught me in one of my shaky moments. Alright, alright, here we go. You're not going to leave me are you?"

"Oh you incurable ole' coot."

"Maybe I should introduce you to my daughter, Diane. She's a free-lance writer for several magazines."

"Does she blog?"

"Maybe, I really don't know."

"You have no idea?"

"No, why?"

"If you had to ask, heaven help you."

"Well, I read the sports page and look over the weather if I'm going out. Phyllis, it's a job. Even if she's a master at it, she ain't no expert. For that matter, who is an expert? Even some of those gurus overseas needed some help to get out of the world because they couldn't really face death."

"I thought you said you weren't much of a reader."

"Not exactly. I do pour over the obituaries a little bit because I can read about people that I haven't heard about before. These religious figures pop in every now and then, Jainists and Buddhist monks even, people I've never heard of before: folks from all over the world that have worked their way in and out of my head over the years."

"Blue collar guys will shock you sometimes."

"I'm no different than anyone else. Sometimes curiosity piques my normal inclinations about life, and wherever those words take me, something new catches my eye."

"God, it's great to get inside. Keep those cats away from me!"

"I thought you'd love cats, bein' a woman and all."

"Give me some time to get used to them."

"Cute little critters, aren't they?"

"I'll grant you that."

"Ooh, I'm soaked. Care to share a cup of coffee?"

"I'm fine. Boy, it's really coming down."

"Phyllis could I ask you something?"

"What about?"

"You know that priest you were talking about?"

"Rembert Weakland?"

"Yeah. I can't recall that music you were talking about."

"Oh, the late composer Messiaen."

"Messiah?"

"No, Messiaen is so, how can I put this? He's like a drawn out note. Sort of distorted like Schumann on piano before him: pianist/ composers that found a different way to communicate with the crisp, clear composition. But, you can hear the soul arise in a completely new method. It's kind of like when you look at an impressionistic painting. The colors softly come at you to bring in more colors that work off the tapestry of a Degas or Renoir. Blurred is as best as I can describe it, tarnished. Does that make sense?"

"Maybe we should put that on the back burner and take in Tony Bennett next time he comes to Chicago."

"Great example, like the scenes he paints in the city traffic and majestic buildings, distorted reflections off the rain-soaked streets. The lights' reflections merge, bouncing off one another. Like everything's intertwined but not at first glance."

"I think we will have to operate more on a gut level, and then you will come down to my level."

"Keeping it simple."

"I guess so."

"Well, that's what Messiaen does. What you first come across is not really what you're seeing or feeling. Who's not hidden to begin with?"

"Not quite so open."

"Right! The other person is no longer hidden, nor are you. Voila, Christ pours into your soul."

"There are no authorities. We just put up with them forever, and look at what we ended up with?"

"A whole lot of damage."

Paul faces Phyllis and kisses her in studied silence. "Would you like to come to bed with me?"

"You're on your own."

"Ah, I thought we'd just shed our skin."

"Doesn't mean I'm going to have sex with you right now, does it?"

"You feminists always think the world owes you something."

"I'm not a piece of meat you can just waltz into. I'm Phyllis Wossolowski."

"Well, Phyllis, I'm Paul Bogdanov and my kind kicked yours around for centuries."

"Perhaps you can go catch your trophy fish all by your lonesome."

"If I keep this going, I might just fall asleep standing up. Look, I've gotta take my nap. If you want anything to eat, please help yourself. I've enjoyed today."

"Me too: everything's been quite lovely, really."

"There's split pea soup in the refrigerator. And, by all means, please don't let the cats out. Not just yet anyway."

"Oh look, you left the rhubarb outside."

"It'll be there after the rain stops. Who's gonna steal it from me?"

"Just a reminder."

"Phyllis, if you want to go home, please don't just hang around here on my account."

"Oh, you needn't worry about that. Old Phyllis here can take care of herself."

"My own little book of change?"

"So funny."

"Wow, you know I haven't heard that one in ions. I have some bluegills thawing. Perhaps you could join me for dinner?"

"Love to."

"If you would want, maybe you could put together a salad and broil the potatoes. You know where everything is, right?"

"Yes I do. We'll see you in a bit."

"Oh, wait a minute. I got this call from a De Marco Jefferson."

"Yea, Eddie's kid."

"He said to tell you that he was setting up another interview with Evinrude."

"Could I see that?"

"That's pretty much what it says. You know, I'm gonna call him to see how things are going."

"How'd you get hold of him?"

"Ah, his father asked me if I could do anything for De Marco, you know the Black Thing, give him a helping hand. He's right you know. Things haven't changed that much. But his kid's bright, really is trying. So, why not help him out?"

"That's good."

"I wish I would have come clean years ago. If you only knew my family."

"Florida sounds better every time I think about it. God, I never would have thought I would do something like this at my age."

"Oh, wow. I gotta catch some Z's like yesterday."

The rains beat down with merciless precision, and the following morning Gene Bartusek peeks out the upper flat window and witnesses the sun peeking over the taciturn clouds.

"Paulie, road trip. C-mon ma-an, you promised. What's with you? I'm not gonna spend another day in this musty old house of yours."

"So Christmassy, just chokes me up to no end. Alleluia, Noelle, be it heaven and hell and all that rot. Are you ready? We're headin' out to the Horicon Ledge: I'm sure you've never heard about it. You know, a County Park miles from here. If you've got a camera, I'd bring it along."

"I've got a cell phone."

"Good enough. I'm going to take a shower."

"Hurry it up. I've got to get out of this place, chop, chop."

"OK, why don't you quick get something to eat while I clean up?"

"Been there, done that."

"I get the point. You want to get a move on."

"The Horicon Ledge is a place close to Paul's heart. His parents would take him there at least once a summer to escape the city life. They would often have picnics. Alongside the county grounds was a large plot of farm land where popcorn was grown. He can still remember the time when he finagled his yearning body over the barbed wire and danced around like an Indian from a 1950's movie, yelping like someone has just scarred him for life. No one could see him, so he was able to carry on his antics to grasp his own idea of an Americana that has lost its very being to a calculating Wasp's ideal of a road to a better life."

As he has grown older, he has begun to understand that things really do not change. Human beings have chosen to avoid their inherent vices and to attempt to get on with the Capitalist malignancy while forming a smile to hide all of one's own inner turmoil that they cannot ever conceive of fully healing. The thoughts have riddled him his whole life: "How am I ever going to prevail in this edifice of falsehoods, being only average in the classroom, an underachiever in gym class, where as I have divined, no matter how high the eagle flies, everything falls apart in a restless and sullen heap. It never fails: fuck everyone who wants to get ahead to ease the pain. That's all death anyway. Why not come to terms with what has bothered me my entire life?"

It is not that the egoistical pangs enflame his psyche and destroy his way.

"Hey, Paul, I've already loaded up the car. So, get your shoes on, you know, one foot in front of the other. C'mon now."

"Would you just shut the hell up? It's six in the morning. Even the neighbors haven't awoken yet. See their car over there?"

"Yeah, so?"

"So-oh? They own this house, that's why we take it easy around here. Alright with that?"

"God, you're such a consummate low brow."

"Oh, and if I don't talk or walk a certain way, that somehow defines me. And, no, I'm driving. Give me the keys. Alright, let's go. Everything's packed right?"

"Like what are we gonna need other than sun block and some snacks?"

"You know, I like a woman who knows what she wants."

"You have no idea what I want."

"Let me rephrase that. Me lady knows how to take care of all the sundry items with the greatest of ease."

"Yeah, while that great insecurity in you just seeps out and oozes into the very being of everyone you come in contact with."

"Here we go again."

"That's right. Strap it on bright boy with all that crap you constantly spew about the Rise and Fall of Ziggy Stardust."

"Oh, I see you've been dipping into my eclectic collection of oldies."

"It's just about weirdos who can't get off the pot. And, all they have to do is shit on everything after they've taken their share. Real losers, Paulie."

"Yeah, but insipid losers with flair."

"Maybe it's about Ziggy spankin' too much Frank."

"Yeah, Frank's Wild Years."

"Bowie?"

"Nah, Tom Waits, crusty Minnesotan, Jew no less—ever hear of the *Cold, Cold Ground*?"

"Ancient, I'm sure."

"*Step right up*, I'm gonna sell you anything, and pull your strings. There's no way you're gonna walk away from this one without you struttin' out the door with one of my *ya gotta have its* tucked away in that vacuous mind of yours. So special"

"What is it with you?"

"What?"

"One minute I bring up Ziggy Stardust, the next you're talkin' about this Waits guy."

"Both were junkies at one time. Different drugs of choice mind you, but junkies all the same. Now they're family men. So there is some connection isn't there?"

"Not to get off the subject how far is the Ledge?"

"Another 40 minutes."

"Right, out in the middle of this bum fuck dairy state."

"OK, I'm gonna cut through all this crap and get to the nuts and bolts of our talk last night."

"I'm not gonna go into therapy with you, first because even though my company offers insurance for people getting psychiatric help, you must also realize that therapy points at the person getting help."

"You mean whatever I am hurt about you, there's something in me that I might have chosen to overlook?"

"We talked about this last night."

"Everything is purposeless. I minored in philosophy and did a thesis on Slavoj Zizek. Great mind, really. He's been a Princeton professor for years now, giving Harvard all it can handle for the Grande Dame of World Renown, the International devotee to Marxist Philosophy. He's even had the gall to cut down even the openness of a Spinoza."

"Yeah, even though he was extremely complicated in his phrasing of words and defining human beings as social animals. From what I gathered, he was pretty much a hermit."

"Right, right, right, right, never-mind that. But you got the inkling that freedom was within all of us, that intelligence flowed through us no matter what our lots in life were. Anyway, Zizek really enjoyed cutting into his Ethics. But after I left the school grounds, I got back into his work and found he's done philosophy slams, many in New York City, talking to college-aged kids whose intellectual acumen is working overtime."

"Hubris."

"Exactly, anyway some are even loaded onto You Tube and the guy even admits his thoughts, like everyone else's, crash into oblivion. The name of one of his seminal books end by him stating that it doesn't matter that everything we do to push progress, even if it fails, is alright to push forward because even if it all falls apart, new job pursuits will have been created to correct all those wrongs. And, you know, even if everything crashes, we are at least kept busy. Yeah, well after all the crap we dump in the oceans, that gives us the incentive to find ways to clean it up."

"The motivation? Now, c'mon, Genie, when has it been that it ever worked in this country?"

"Right, don't take the garbage problem too seriously."

"Cleanup involves money; and, how do you make a lot of money out of recycling?"

"Well, that's conventional wisdom."

"And, mine is, 'Genie, have you got any job leads yet?'"

"I'm looking."

"Like what, Seven Eleven, Piggly Wiggly? What?" Genie looks away out the window, turns back and says: "I don't know what I'm gonna do Paul."

"I'm, I can't believe what I'm hearing. I see that this is bothering you but basically the world is based on power, and if you don't get off your butt, the game will take it from you."

"Musical chairs."

"Exactly: Somebody's gonna be left behind, and we're either goin' to get on with things or we're gonna be the next to get walked over."

"Base senselessness. This is what philosophy has tried to rid us of."

"What's changed since Plato's and Socrates' days?"

"Not a whole lot."

"So, don't try to get me into some new age healing process. Who says the teachers are so honorable because they have spent years in spiritual cleansing with noted gurus from all over the place?"

"All of the past. We're defenseless, babe."

"Yes. The cons also reside in these spiritual groups. I sat through a discussion years ago about a daughter whose father was a Taoist who had an alcohol problem. In fact, his cardiac arrest was triggered by the alcohol. You know what her response was to this?"

"Might as well tell me. Nothing really shocks me anymore."

"Well, she felt that it made him more comfortable to go about his daily tasks, meeting people, and so on."

"He was making excuses for his inability to deal with his own petty emotions."

"Exactly. It ain't rocket science."

"Look, I know that everybody knows that it is about us. We lie to protect ourselves."

"Society tells us not to trust anyone. Not that I go along with that, but to make money whether it's a business or of a spiritual entity, you gotta build credibility by blowing your own horn."

"Some are a little fuller of themselves than others."

"Yeah, but a soft sell is no less a lie than a hard sell. I mean, just because someone talks to everyone in a soft, positively assured voice doesn't mean that the person is not deluding the public in some way. I love you, Genie, you know that."

"I know, but why does everything have to be so hard?"

"I don't know. It's really about us, not God. That's all I know. My dad always told me as teen-ager to tell the truth. Like, fuck, do that, and your pants start on fire, right? At least as a contributing liar, your pants stay dry."

"At least for the time being."

"Oh yeah. The lying game will become the killing fields sooner or later."

"I'm scared."

"Who isn't?"

"No, about my children. You know the slut story Norm and his attorneys are throwing at me."

"You didn't have sex with me until you were separated. You weren't sleeping around before, were you?"

"God no."

"Well, then stay with yourself and see what happens."

"I just don't know anymore. Letting everything fall—I just don't know if I want to even try picking up the pieces."

"You know Norm's gonna do whatever he can to keep the settlement money and your kids from you. I think you need to get a job just to let go of some of the anxieties you're faced with. And, don't give me that shit that your daily yoga sessions can clear up all that."

"Well, a little bit."

"A little means no dice."

"Stay in the moment."

"Cute."

Paul rests the palm of his hand on Genie's thigh as he turns off old County TW right onto Raasch Hill Road. A rich copse of oaks and maples come into view. The lush green grass awakens Genie's foreboding presence as Paul smiles effortlessly.

They drive around and park alongside the picnic area as Paul looks into Genie's eyes, "we're on."

"This is kind of a small area, don't you think."

"Oh, you'll see."

Paul leads her away from the car, smiling, looking onto the playground of his distant childhood. As they approach the wooded area, they spot small campers nestled beneath the trees.

"Hey, this is just a bunch of trees atop a farm hill."

Just a few steps ahead, Paul says, "look down to your left." Genie sees a drop-off some forty feet. He leads her to the left side of the dirt path into quaint cliffs of limestone.

"Pretty neat, huh?"

Softly Genie eases her long fingers across the layered green moss, running on the soft lime-stoned walls.

"Geology taught me about the Wisconsin Ice Age and how all this is its aftermath thousands of years later."

"Not millions?' Nope, even Indians traipsed through here scavenging for food. This is part of the Niagara Escarpment."

"Like Niagara Falls."

"One and the same."

They carefully weave their way through the rocks and narrow cliffs as they run into families taking their children on their nature walk:

"How far down are we from up there?"

"Oh, maybe forty feet."

"Wow, when you're down in here, it looks a lot higher than that."

"We've become small players in a world we have no comprehension of."

The moist green rock, water trapped beneath hidden crevices, wraps 'round like an old, old river bed.

"Honey, stand right over there by the opening Yeah, say cheese."

He carefully snaps off four pictures. They continue meandering around the snake formation of an array of cliffs as Genie contemplates a once flourishing riverbed.

"This used to be a river once, hasn't it?"

"You got it. Come on. Let's get back above the cliffs. I want to show you something."

They get back onto the main path and come upon a clearing amongst the underbrush.

"Oh, would you look at that view."

"Yeah, look at that. You can see for miles."

"Yeah, a couple hundred feet above the Rock River Valley. The river's a good several miles from here."

"Where is it?"

"Oh, we'll go by it when we head to Madison to indulge ourselves."

"Really Mr. tight wad."

"Genie, I don't even have a hundred thousand in investments and savings nor do I have a lot of cash on hand. Norm does though."

"It's done, Paul. I can't go back to him."

"Well, I can't make those decisions for you."

"I know that I must make my own decisions. It's my life; but, God, I can't even find a job pumping gas."

"Have you made an effort?"

"I'm more interested in having our child."

"And, Cutler Hammer's gonna give me a raise because we have a baby?"

"If you haven't noticed, I've worked myself into Aphrodite."

"Yes, your blossoming yoga at the Center and all that walking you do."

"The firmness of my arms."

"A heathy pair of lungs."

"My butt's my greatest asset, don't you think?"

"Do you think I should do something about my physique to please my dear Goddess of Mother Earth?"

"Temptress is more like it."

"Oh, my distant damsel in distress."

"You said it, I didn't. Could you stand by the top of the hill over there? I want to get your picture."

Genie snaps off a couple of pictures of smiling Paul. "You know when we were kids my dad said that the Woodland Indians used to do their smoke signals from right here to alert their peoples. Kinda cool, isn't it?"

"Makes sense. By the way, 5-8, 135 pounds."

"Cool: are you trying to hint at something?"

"Like what?"

"Like, maybe I'm not the Adonis you crave?"

"Adonis was taken out by a wild boar as a mere youth."

"I can rub up to you and you return the favor. Just don't push me away."

"Why would I aside of course from those porn references you put out there."

"What?"

"Oh, 5-8, 135, strutting your stuff. Van Nuys is never short of acquiring new talent with your sensuous raven hair and ruby lips." Paul softly massages her forehead and passionately kisses her. "Could we get a goin' now?"

"By the way down in front of the back road picnic area down there, my best friend and I found a low-lying limestone cave of rocks. We were like twelve, and anybody who tells you kids don't get frightened in tight areas, better think again. We'd go in, fumbling around in the darkness, dig out what rocks we could to make more space, then scoop out dirt. We got a long way in, even went back there sometime later on, and moved on from where we'd left off."

"No wonder why you guys get so horny. Like what would you have to do if you didn't have a ball to chase around?"

"I could say the same thing about women."

"How so?"

"Perfumed Goddess making sure that I see every step she takes, becoming her slave or is she out hustling something else behind my back?"

"We-ell, and what if that is the case?"

"Ba-ang in Da-Nang Madame Wu."

"You're my bitch, doesn't take much to see that you're linked to Sacher Masoch. Keep your focus on this woman's ass that's launched a thousand ships."

" Queen of cunts you mean?"

"Balls to the walls is more like it. You've always got to get the last word in. Touché."

"Let's go, I gotta go to the bathroom."

"You go ahead. I'll find my way back to the car."

"See you in a bit."

After walking back to the car from the rest room, Paul notices Genie tucked away neatly in his car.

"Where'd your jeans and tennis shoes go?"

"Yawn, how boring. Aphrodite has consumed this pragmatic Genie Bartusek."

"Yeah, black silk stockings and your favorite fuck-me boots that I've never seen leave the bedroom."

"Get ready for the brawl bro'. I'm gonna eat your cashew cock and fellate its very core unto the depths of despair."

"I guess you saw my virility check-up from doc?"

"You left it on the kitchen table, Paul. How could I miss it?"

"You know why I left it there."

"Madame Wu needs bang-bang in her way of course."

"You're not going to expose me to the public are you?"

"I'm not a black widow sweetie: Madame gives and takes all in due time of course. If you feel comfortable in Masoch's chains, why, what's stopping you?"

"I may not be fully equipped with my tools of intrigue but I'm ready to answer the bell."

"Ding, ding, ding, let's do it. How 'bout some music."

Paul turns on XM Radio 'Seventies' Music: *Don't let it bring you down, it's only Castles burning, find someone whose turning and you will come around…*

"Oh, Gawd, that voice, like his shrieking, squeaky voice is caught in puberty."

"Neil Young man, After the Gold Rush—the whole album's fantabulous. That's like a flashback to my college days."

"Oh no, here we go again, Paul embellishing his boring days of youth."

"We-ell, I'll have you know that there were these dudes I knew that lived above the bars downtown, went to their place to blow some dope and they had these fairly big square boxes. In one of 'em, they put their cat in there, closed it up and blew hits into it with a straw. The cat then ran out of the box and kept out of sight in a big room made up of a couple of beat up couches and a table to clean the weed of course."

"Right, probably had a black and white TV as well."

"How'd you know?"

"That's like solving the Simpson Murder Case. What does any of this have to do with Neil Young anyway?"

"On the outside of their huge bleak sienna- colored door was written in black magic marker, Everybody Knows that this is Nowhere. You know, I wonder if it's still there. It was Young's second album. Grunge owes him his distorted guitar slam due: an original guitar assassin from Winnipeg of all places."

"Grunge. Oh God, I was dancing my way every Thursday and Friday night doing my best to avoid all that shit. You know hippie wannabes."

"With a lot of talent Genie: theirs' was the most recent number one rock music revolution city this country's ever seen."

"Rock music, yeah. But dance house music and pop music has touched many more lives than grunge even back then."

"What's that beneath your blankie?"

"What?"

"Beneath your blankie?"

"You'll find out soon enough. Oh, what's this town?"

"Horicon."

"Horicon, huh?"

"Downtown Horicon. Not much to look at, is it? See that river over there? It's the Rock River."

"Oh, the Marsh."

"Yep. If you follow the river past John Deere, you'll be smack dab in the middle of the Marsh."

"This is the river that was once part of where we were?"

"That's it."

"Kinda cool."

"Yeah, not all neat things have to be Grand Canyonesque. Things are like that even in Iowa Genie."

"How did I ever end up with such an unassuming man that is so easily taken by such trite matters?"

"Even great people put on their pants just like us."

"They've cashed in on their fame."

"Yeah, so why do you look so much into their faces pasted over a bunch of magazines that have nothing to do with anything really?"

"They're hot. What can I say?"

"How far is Madison?"

"About fifty miles."

"Hmn, all farmland out here isn't there?"

"Genie, this is Dodge County. Watertown's its biggest community even though a portion of it resides in Jefferson County—maybe what, 20,000?"

"I have to go to the bathroom."

"Why didn't you go when we were back at the Ledge?"

"'Because I didn't have to go back then."

"That was fifteen minutes ago. OK, I'll tell you what. There's a wayside a couple miles down the road. No toilet though. You'll have to make do, leaves and things, to cover up your crime."

"I have to go."

"I know, but you don't want a deputy sheriff spotting your little whims."

"You let me worry about that. Otherwise, you can pull over at that house over there, and I'll find a way in."

"Hold on."

Paul steps on it and pulls into the agrarian wayside. He drives to the backside of the site's entrance as Genie sneaks out to relieve herself. As she was taking care of business, Paul strolls over to an old cast-iron swing-set that he had fond memories of playing on with his younger sister. Nothing's changed; time's stood still.

"Yoo-hoo, Paulie, over here."

"There stands his better half attired in his ancient black and white plaid flannel shirt that covers up her curvaceous presence."

"Come."

She takes him by the hand, holding her blanket in hand walking towards the wayside's barbed wire borders.

"Marshy land sprinkled with feed corn and soy beans. Do you really wanna do this here?"

Ever so tenderly she spreads out the large blanket and guides him onto it, motioning him to lay down on it. Pushing down on his eager legs, she slowly unzips his overalls.

"No underwear, you dirty, dirty little boy." She, too wears no undergarments.

"Mother's gonna do all the work here, no ifs-and's-or-but's." Genie massages her vagina with passion fruit and carefully places it back into her purse.

She teases him by rubbing her breasts on his tentative penis, awakening it with her intense confidence. Like a child that has finally accepted his fate, Paul allows her to have her way as she numbs him with her tongue, pulsating her lips upon his cock. She looks into his eyes and his fears fall behind his eminence. Finally, she takes hold of him and guides him into her. Savoir Faire a distant memory, Paul feels her shamelessly thrust into him. She opens up more and more with every pelvic movement. Killdeers scamper about in the fields beyond. Silently two animals become one.

Forcefully, Genie rubs her thighs into his being. Helplessly, Paul looks into her eyes heedless of thought. She forces herself into him and licks his clavicle without a sound. He comes like a river imploding into the ocean.

For minutes she coddles him, softly kissing him all over and he stares at her trying to make sense of it. Genie then rolls him up with her in the blanket; and, he picks her up, pushing his thighs into her.

"Did you rape me?"

"What do you think?"

"Man, I was schooled."

"So was I."

"You? How?"

"Oh, being on top is not much different than being on the bottom."

"Except for one thing."

"What's so bad about being on the bottom?"

"The control: and that thrusting. Swivel hips."

"Yes. A call to action. They got it wrong about Christmas."

"I don't follow."

"It's much better to receive than to give."

"OK Prince Charming, let's get a going. You owe me a party dress and shoes. Unless you wanna see me like this when we go out to eat."

"Alright, let's go."

"Forget these?"

"Oh, yes," she hands him his pants and he wiggles them on, "God, I feel so rancid like hair of the dog couldn't touch this."

"It's just a ride, enjoy the it while you can. Where's your adventurous spirit?"

"A shower would do wonders."

"With me joining you no less."

Paul fumbles about with his shoes and socks. "You know, I've never seen such blue skies and check out those clouds, man."

"You've left this world for a while you naïve little boy you. After I have this child, I'm going to teach your vaginal little ass a thing or two with my strap-on."

"Oh on, you ain't getting' anywhere near my hole dear."

"Oh, that's what you think. With a little persuasion, the Huntress can take a mile without you even knowing the world's being pulled from under your feet."

"If you only knew Madame Wu how childish you sound."

"Madame Wu? Who's that?"

"I don't know, some Chinese Empress perhaps. Ask Steely Dan. They'll fill you in on all that mystical, magical stuff."

"Enough of that 70's shit. I'm gonna let my fingers do the walking. Well, how about that? Old Daft Punk."

"Kinda mechanical."

"Yeah, but colorful without those burdensome highs and lows: besides, the rhythm gets me oh so horny no matter what."

"Bestial?"

"You could say that. Hot without all the fall out."

"Mayhem in line with Mars?"

"Such a funny little he-man. No, Revolution number 909. This came out right after I got married. Even Norm could sway with it. And, that takes some doing."

"You're so attractive."

"Not again? No, I'm not pulling over."

"Silly," she strokes his long graying hair, "I just want to thank you for letting me take care of you."

"Your beauty simply beguiles me."

"Always the proper English. So cognizant of my needs. Would you listen to that?"

"Yeah."

"It's about mundane everyday life, bringing a pulsating joy into the artless antics of our boorish existence."

"You should have been a philosopher."

"Nah."

"OK, spiritualist, move to California and become a yogi."

"Like you said, they have their own ways."

"Right, no different: This one guy from Chicago wanted me as his little boy toy but he couldn't ask for it, realizing I would cut ties with him. Instead he would talk softly with me about the precariousness of people and everyday life. The guy just didn't care. If I had walked into his arms, he would be triumphant. If not, well you know, there's more than one fish in the sea, right?"

"My Pablita, ah, so very sorry things didn't work out between you two."

"That's not what I was getting at. He's a psychiatrist, Jungian analyst, whatever that means, talking about nurturing the wounded child within and starting anew, but he couldn't do it for himself."

"Oh, Planet Love, another oldie."

"Techno pop."

"Yes, but with vigorous tight beats and lightness, so vibrant, so alive."

"Veruschka."

"Veruschka?"

"Yeah, Avedon's princess of the catwalk: most beautiful woman besides you of course."

"Of course. I detect a sliver of angst popping through your quivering pecs."

"Sometimes Genie, you seem to distance yourself from me as you zero in on yours truly."

"You're joking."

"Not really. Sometimes Genie, I can see where you're coming from. Other times, not so much."

"Because you're trying to protect yourself: you're no different than I am. We're just kindred spirits. If you would just let me in, let me soften your blows."

"I'm on the edge here, Paul. And, to tell you the truth I'm tired of being pushed aside."

"So Aphrodite shows her true colors."

"I let it all hang out."

"Let it rip. I love you Genie. If you don't want to work, don't. Have our child. But there's no way you want to work. Let's face it. Really, how many jobs have you applied for this summer?"

"I hate work, what it stands for. Bunch of lies."

"People lie to each other all the time. What makes work any different?"

"Norm's gonna fight me every inch of the way. He thinks I failed him in some way."

"There's no court in the world that's gonna keep you from seeing your children, Genie."

"I know, but he's gonna fork over some of that estate he's sitting on. And, don't you tell me it's no big deal. It is."

"All I'm gonna say is to not get too hooked on your mission. Vengeance will tie you up in knots. You know this. And, mediocrity breeds evil if there is such a thing."

"I just want what I'm entitled to."

"We've talked about this umpteen times."

"And, we'll mull over it a million more. You don't get off the hook that easily."

"Madison's just minutes away."

"West Towne Mall! Nothing's wrong with East Towne, but West Towne's got a more urbane edge to it."

"Newer."

"That too: Besides, it's got a lot of nice restaurants in the area."

"Yep."

"Get your credit card ready because the Princess needs her wares."

"Your allowance is 300 bucks, no more."

"I got you covered. My creative juices will come up with something frugal yet sexy chic."

"Here we are."

"Maybe you should get a shirt and slacks. Those jeans are utterly rancid."

"As long as you're comfortable within your own skin, right?"

"Ooh, men: couldn't see the light of day if it hit them in the mouth."

"Yeah, but we're a cheaper date."

"Need I say more?"

"Just be yourself Genie. Isn't that what it's all about?"

"Whatever that is?"

"Oh look. New York & Company. C'mon Paul. I'm sure I can find an outfit in here that will work."

"Remember, you've got less than 300 dollars to spend. Keep that in mind."

"I know, I know. Would you get a move on? We don't have all night."

"I'm thinkin' about catching the wild ones at the Madison Zoo, you know reptiles: alligators, iguanas and snakes, including a huge anaconda.

Spend a night at the Motel 6, catch a Mickey D's, and maybe mosey on over to the University Campus and have a beer looking out at Mendota."

"That'll be the last weekend you spend with yours truly."

"Otis Redding's plane went down there."

"Otis Redding? Who the hell is that?"

"C'mon, Sitting on the Dock of the Bay? You haven't heard about that?"

"When was this?"

"'68. R-E-SP-E-C-T. Now, where would Aretha Franklin be without his lyrics way back when?"

"'68? Fuck, I wasn't even born."

"Bascom Hill and '68. Even Cal-Berkley couldn't hold a candle to us. Mad-Town was on fire."

"Oh, would you look at that paisley t-dress. Exquisite."

"Speaking of the sixties."

"Gotta try that on. Miss, do you have that in a size six?"

"Let me see."

"Oh and those faux letter T-Strap Sandals, just 25 bucks. See smarmy Paul, even Madame Wu can be a bargain shopper."

"Right, so I can get my pair of black Dickies and a pair of Chuck Taylors."

"You could care less about fashion. You're lucky you have me to coordinate your ties with your rancid wardrobe of khaki and sand-colored slacks."

"That's why I have you, sweetheart."

"See miss, he's such a smarm. I recommend you don't get stuck with such a beached whale."

"Miss, we have it in your size but in lime rather than meringue."

"Even Better: I wanta try it on."

"Now, don't fall asleep on me Paulie."

"Oh, you can count on me."

Review Requested:

If you loved this book, would you please provide a review at Amazon.com?